RED RIVER REUNION

JOHN LAYNE

Labrador Publishing

ISBN Print: 978-0-9998796-7-2

ISBN Ebook: 978-0-9998796-6-5

This is a work of fiction. Names, characters, places, and incidents are the product of the author's imagination are used fictitiously. Any resemblances to actual persons, living or dead, business, events or locales is entirely coincidental.

Editor: Christine Baker

Cover Design: Christine Baker

Labrador Publishing

24 W. Main St. Suite 330

Clinton, CT 06413

www.labradorpublishing.com

Printed in the United States of America

First Edition - October 15, 2020

To my daughter, Rachel.

ACKNOWLEDGMENTS

The fact that Red River Reunion is my "second" effort in novel writing is mind-boggling to me. I was never completely certain that I would ever write one book, let alone a second. It is with these thoughts that I wish to thank the following people, businesses, and organizations that have led me to this wonderful place in the literary world.

I must certainly begin with my wife, Elizabeth, whose inspiration, encouragement, and support made my title of author possible, and to my daughter Rachel, who is my biggest fan.

To Christine Baker, my agent, editor, publicist, and friend, whose talent and guidance is second to none.

To everyone connected to Labrador Publishing, who made this book the best it could be.

To fellow author and mentor Brian W. Smith for teaching me the "Ten Things Every New Writer Should Know," then guiding me down the path to their uses.

To Trish Stevens, Kimberly McCall, and everyone at Ascot Media Group, Inc. for launching my name and works into the realm of public relations.

To my attorney and friend, Sam Johnson, whose firm Johnson & Sparks P.L.L.C. keeps me "mostly" worry-free.

To fellow author, Donigan Merritt, whose profession and skill as a writer was much more of an inspiration than he ever knew all those years ago.

To Janelle Twyford-Silvis and AlleeOopS Photography, who made me look far better than I really do.

To Joseph Durepos of Durepos Literary, whose suggestions and other words of wisdom were not lost in translation.

To William Clay Cox for his proofreading efforts and subsequent enthusiasm, which built confidence and momentum for this cowboy writer.

To Michelle Stellato and Jason Lee, who provide constant, and occasionally valuable, insight, even when it's not requested.

To my Family, Friends, and Supporters.

And, of course…the many members of the John Layne Posse.

AREA MAP

Click on image for a link to a full-screen view or visit
https://www.johnlaynefiction.com/rrr-map

PART I

CHAPTER 1

WES PAYNE – BUFFALO GAP

Horse and rider burst from the bosky, ducking beneath the drooping tentacles of a huge willow tree on the southern edge of Buffalo Gap. Racing toward the gunfire that had permeated the otherwise quiet, sun-drenched October afternoon, Texas Ranger Wes Payne, atop his trusted steed Ringo, charged head on into the bustling town that Ranger Payne now considered home.

Wes jumped off Ringo as he sped past the weathered wooden edifice passing for the county Sheriff's office. His spur-clad boots crashed onto the front steps of the one-time sawmill. As he rolled over onto the porch planks, he drew both pistols ready to return fire. At the age of twenty-eight, he possessed cat-like agility that defied his six foot five, two-hundred-pound frame. Bullets smashed into wood and glass raining shards of the shattered window down on Wes as he fired both Colts back across the street to no avail. Sheriff Dan Kirby, a short, thin man of forty, ripped the front door open only to be met with a hail of gunfire.

"Get back, Dan!" Wes hollered. "There's four of 'em over in the store!"

Wes dove headfirst through the blown-out window frame tumbling over a split-rail bench inside. Kirby pushed aside the wooden shutter opposite the door and emptied his Colt at the storefront, accomplishing nothing more than punching holes in the windows. Diving to the floor, he popped open his cylinder loading gate, and quickly loaded six fresh cartridges.

"I thought you said this was an easy job!" Kirby yelled to Wes. "You damn Rangers think every job is easy! I should've known better!" Kirby snapped his cylinder cover closed as outlaw bullets sailed in through the gaping window frame shredding the wanted posters hanging on the opposite wall. The hot lead singed the paper, burning holes into the old wood. The smell of gunpowder filled the small room.

"I heard he was a tame tack thief! Broke into tack buildings during the night and lifted saddles. Hated confrontation!" Wes tried to explain dumping empty cartridges onto the floor. "I reckon' he's with three others who'd rather shoot their way out of town!" Wes continued.

Kirby knelt on the floor and peeked over the splintered sill. Wes did the same. The shooting stopped. A strange moment of silence hung in the air.

"Can't see a damn thing inside the store. Is there a back door to that place?" Wes asked his fellow lawman.

"Yep. The door leads out into a hog pen and small corral that Ed uses to keep his wagon horses. I can see part of the corral on this side of the store. Looks like both his horses are back there. Where are their horses?" Kirby asked his gunslinging Ranger buddy.

"Tied up in front of the saloon. Where'd ya think?" Wes chuckled. "They all busted through the front swingers when I walked in the back door. Didn't take the time to get their horses. They ran down the street then ducked into the store. Your storekeeper was sweeping' the front when they all blew past him. He took off," Wes reported.

"At least Ed's not in there. Don't need any hostages," Kirby snapped rhetorically. "What did you say this jackass's name is?" Kirby asked.

"Pete Calhoun. Skinny little cowhand known to let others do the killin' for him. Don't know who his friends are," Wes added.

"Well, it seems they're willin' to stay in there for a while. Got any ideas, Ranger Payne?"

"Sure, circle around the store, charge in, and shoot 'em all," Wes answered flatly.

"That's right. One riot. One Ranger," Kirby laughed.

"You're coming with me, aren't ya?" Wes asked through a wide grin.

"Reckon I have to, being Sheriff and all," Kirby grinned back.

"Let's go out the back, I'll take the left side, you go right. Go down a couple of buildings. That way they won't see you coming. You'll be able to get to the back door easier than me. I have the coral in my way. Holler when you hit the back door, and I'll come in through the front. Just watch who the hell you're shootin'. I don't want one of your slugs ruining my day," Kirby barked.

They both crawled to the back door of the jail and quietly slipped out. Wes looped around the freight building while Kirby ran around the barbershop. Both sprinted across the empty street. The crisp, autumn air felt cold against Wes's sweat-soaked face.

Crack! Crack! Crack! Bullets kicked up dirt at Kirby's feet as he hustled across Main Street. He hadn't crossed down far enough to be hidden. He rolled under a buckboard and waited. The outlaws' gunfire ceased. Wes made it across undetected, then circled around to the back of the store. The back door was open and facing him. Wes could see silver spurred brown boots under the bottom of the door as he crept toward the opening.

Rear guard. Good, one less gun to fight inside, he thought.

Wes snuck up to the side of the hog pen wire where a half-dozen pigs obliviously munched in the slop trough at the back of the coop. Wes carefully stepped over the barrier. Kirby crawled out from under the wagon, taking cover behind three grain barrels perched on the edge of the store's front walk. The gunfight drew curiosity seekers to the area like flies to a dung heap. Several of the men in town darted in and out of building nooks and around corners to get a better look. Kirby waved his hand toward the crowd, begging them to stay back. He heard rustling inside the store. He waited for Wes's call.

Wes holstered his Colt, then rushed at the flat face of the door, hitting it with his shoulder at full-force. The door smashed into the tall, skinny, unsuspecting outlaw, knocking him into the muck with a splat. The scrawny brigand rolled over, drawing his gun from its mud-caked holster. Wes's draw was too quick. Crack! One dead, three to go. Hearing the collision and shot, Kirby thrust himself through the store's front door. Wes charged through the back. Crack! Crack! Two shots took down a second outlaw crouching near the counter. Kirby opened fire, sending tobacco, coffee, and molasses into the air. The third outlaw reared up and fired wildly at the Sheriff. Kirby's last shot blew out the bottom of the gunmen's throat, dropping him to the floor.

Kirby quickly looked around the store but saw nothing. Wes looked around the corner of the back wall leading to stairs up to the second floor.

"We know you're up there, Calhoun! Come down and live! No way out now!" Wes called up to the fugitive.

"Don't shoot! I'm coming down!" Calhoun's voice squeaked like a field mouse.

He staggered to the top of the stairway with his hands raised above his head. His shirt and trousers were two sizes too big, and his buck teeth protruded from blotchy patches of red whiskers, dotting a chin-less round face. Calhoun cautiously stepped down. As soon as he reached the bottom, his face met Wes's huge, scarred fist, knocking him out cold.

"I'll carry him over to the jail," Wes calmly advised.

"I'll take a look at these other three and see if I recognize 'em," Kirby offered.

Wes threw Calhoun over his shoulder, then walked out the front door, and across the street where a large group of onlooker's had gathered. Twenty or so men tried to speak over each other, claiming they'd had the best view of the shootout, while half that many women clutched their children, whispering to each other. Cowboys got back to business while wagon and carriage traffic started again on Main Street. Wes ignored them and marched into the Sheriff's office, threw

Calhoun onto a cot, where the man landed with a thud. After removing a derringer from the little outlaw's left boot, he closed and locked the cell door.

Kirby stood in front of his office, directing someone to fetch the town's undertaker. Ed and Rita Rogatzki, the owners of the now bullet-riddled Double R Mercantile, made their way through the titillated crowd.

"Can we go into our store, Sheriff?" The elderly, short, heavyset store owner asked.

"Sure can, Ed. You might want Rita to wait outside until we can get those other dead men out of there. There are three of 'em. Two inside the store, and one in your hog pen. I'm sorry for the mess. Let me know what those front windows cost, and I'll see if the county will pay for it," Kirby advised.

"Yes, sir. Go on over to the hotel and wait for me," Ed directed his diminutive wife, who didn't need further encouragement.

Kirby walked into his office, brushed splinters off the stack of wanted posters on his desk and began to thumb through the list of varmints. Wes took a look at the few bullet-ridden posters Kirby had tacked to the wall.

"Nothing here," Wes reported.

"No, no. No. Nope, hmm?" Kirby muttered after stopping to look closer at one of the fliers. He flipped the poster over and showed Wes.

"Looks like the one at the back door," Wes agreed.

Kirby read the notice aloud. "Martin Daley. Wanted for murder in Galveston. Dead or alive. That takes care of him. When your friend wakes up, I'll see who the others were. I didn't see them come into town. This place is growing so damn fast I can't keep up. Now that we've been named the county seat, they're coming in from all over. Fixin' to start building another hotel and boarding house," Kirby lamented.

"I remember when Buffalo Gap was just that. A wide open grass filled gap between buffalo herds stopping for water on Elm Creek," Wes reminisced.

"Yep. I need to go over to the lumber yard and fetch wood to board up my window. Gettin' cold at night around here. Watch the place for me," Kirby ordered Wes before leaving for his repair materials.

Wes followed Kirby out of the office in time to see four wagons coming into town. An old timer with a short, gray beard, drove the lead wagon. A younger man dressed in black handled the reins of the second. Wes watched the wagons pass until he saw the driver of the third, who happened to be a young woman wearing a peculiar hat. As the wagon came closer, Wes realized what the young woman was.

A nun. Definitely a nun, he thought.

A nun also drove the fourth wagon. Wes watched all four wagons stop in front of the boarding house down the street. Out of the wagons emerged several women dressed in black and white outfits. Wes strained to see. *Six, yep six nuns.*

Nuns in Buffalo Gap? This town is changing, he thought.

CHAPTER 2

RACHEL BRENNEN – CANYON CREEK

R achel had just finished cleaning newly vacated rooms at the Sundown Hotel in Canyon Creek when she heard the front door open, then close quickly. She hurried to the top of the staircase and felt a brisk gust of cold October air sweep up the stairway. Ding! The sound of the front desk bell confirmed the presence of a visitor.

"Coming!" she called down as her heels clapped on the polished surface of each wooden step.

Entering the lobby, she saw the back of a tall, lanky cowboy wrapped in a tan trail coat and wide brimmed brown hat. He examined the painting of a longhorn steer mounted high on the wall behind a large polished dark oak desk Rachel spent most of her days behind.

"Can I help you?" Rachel asked in a voice fit for a songbird.

The tall cowboy turned and removed his hat in one motion. Rachel stopped in her tracks and gasped, clutching the top of her white apron. Her throat tightened and her heart raced. For a moment she couldn't speak. Before her stood the ghost of a man she once loved. The young man stepped forward, brandishing a wide grin, and extended his right hand.

"Good afternoon, I'm Ben Chance. I'm looking for Mrs. Rachel Brennen. I believe she knew my father."

Rachel's head spun like a top. Her legs weakened and she felt as though she would faint at any moment. She clutched her forehead and took a deep breath.

"I'm Rachel Brennen," she managed to weakly say. "I'm sorry, I don't mean to be rude, I'm just a little in shock. I didn't know Ben had a son. Please come into the dining room and have a seat. Would you like coffee or something else?" Rachel asked, her voice shaking like the shiver of an earthquake.

"No, ma'am. Are you all right? I didn't mean to startle you," Chance stated, offering a steady hand to the hotel proprietor.

Rachel led young Chance into the dining room, where she directed him to a chair at the head of a long rectangular table covered in a crisp white cloth. She took Chance's duster and hung it up on a peg near the doorway then took a seat near the wraith cowboy.

"It's amazing how much you look like your father. You're just as tall, too," she added, blushing a bit.

Chance smiled. "I've never been told that. That's why I've come to see you. I believe my father gave you a letter to send to Judge Parker. Is that right?" Chance asked, setting his hat near the edge of the table.

"Yes, I didn't know it was a letter." Rachel leaned forward folding her hands on top of the table. "Your father gave it to me the night before he left and told me to send it to Judge Parker if he didn't come back." Rachel paused and took a deep breath. "When he didn't, I gave it to a U.S. Deputy Marshal named Luxton Danner, who was returning to Fort Smith," Rachel explained.

"Yes, Judge Parker sent Marshal Danner to Texarkana. He gave it to me there. It contained a letter and two thousand dollars," explained Chance leaning back in his chair.

"I see," Rachel acknowledged, dipping her emerald eyes toward the tablecloth.

"Marshal Danner told me what happened to my father, how he was killed, but he didn't know much more. The letter told me some, but my father wrote that if I wanted to know more about him, I should come to Canyon Creek and see you at the Sundown hotel. So, here I am." Chance shuffled his boots and sat straight up, looking directly at Rachel. "I hope you don't mind answering some questions?" He asked with a friendly smile.

"Not at all! I'll be happy to tell you all I know about your father! I only knew him for about a year, though, so I may not have all the answers you're looking for," said Rachel, with a warm smile of her own.

"I know, he said that in the letter," admitted Chance.

"Before we talk, do you plan on staying in Canyon Creek for a while? I have a room for you if you like," Rachel offered, pushing herself back from the table and standing.

"That would be fine. I'll probably stay a day or two before I head back to Texarkana," Chance said, quickly standing for his lovely hostess.

"Good. I'll get your room ready. Then we can talk after you put your things up," Rachel said, smoothing the wrinkles out of her apron.

Rachel hurried to her desk, where she removed the number three key from its box, then quickly went upstairs. Chance retrieved his gear from his horse, then slowly climbed the polished stairs, where he met Rachel coming out of room three.

"Here you are, Mr. Chance. If you need anything, please ask."

"Looks great, and please call me Ben."

Rachel proceeded down to the kitchen, where translucent rays of sunshine found their way through the back window, glistening off the steel pots and iron frying pans that would soon be used for the supper crowd's arrival later in the day. She placed several fresh sugar cookies and two cups of hot coffee on a tray before delivering it to the dining room. Rachel removed her apron, tossed it onto a chair, and glanced in the mirror next to the doorway. She ran her fingers through her long auburn hair, smoothing it as best she could. She moved into her chair when she heard Ben's boots hitting the top of the staircase. Chance reached the bottom of the stairway and looked to see Rachel seated behind two steaming cups of coffee and cookies that looked like the kind his aunt used to make on special occasions.

"Thank you," Chance offered as he took his seat. "The hot coffee is good on a cool day like this. These cookies look like the ones my aunt used to make," he added with a nod toward the silver tray.

"Did your mother bake pies and cookies?" Rachel asked hesitantly.

"My mother died when I was young, while my father was in the war. I was raised by my aunt and uncle in Texarkana," explained Chance.

"I'm sorry I wasn't sure. I knew Ben wasn't married. He didn't say much about his family. I shouldn't have asked," Rachel stated, her face turning a rose color with embarrassment.

"Not at all. It's okay. She got sick; we lived with my aunt. My mother died a short time later, and I thought my father was killed in the war, so I stayed at my aunt's farm. My uncle returned from the war and said my father must have been killed because he didn't come home. I didn't know my father was alive until a couple of years ago when he sent a letter and money to my aunt. He said once he found out my mother died, he knew it was best if my aunt and uncle raised me," Chance explained.

Rachel dabbed tears from her eyes with the corner of a napkin. "I'm afraid I didn't know your father as well as I thought. I didn't know any of this," she said.

"No reason to cry, ma'am, he was right. I grew up just fine on a good farm. Learned about crops, cattle, and other livestock. I learned to ride, shoot, and hunt. I also went to school. Learned to read, write and do numbers. I just wish I could have found him before he died," he admitted.

"Wait here. I have something of yours," Rachel said.

Rachel hurried to her room, then returned with an envelope of money. "There's a thousand dollars in there. Your father left it for me, but I haven't felt I should use it. Now I'm glad. It's rightfully yours. Please take it," she insisted, sliding the package across the table to Chance.

"I will not take this money, ma'am. He gave it to you, and you should keep it. He told me how important you were to him. I will not argue about it." Chance threw up both hands, shaking his head.

Chance slid the envelope back across the table to Rachel, who placed her hands on it.

"You're just as honorable as he was," she said, looking straight into Chance's honest brown eyes.

"Could you answer some questions now?" Chance asked leaning forward onto the table.

"Certainly," Rachel anxiously responded, then turned her body toward Chance ready to do her best in answering Chance's questions.

Rachel proceeded to tell Chance of his father's mannerisms, such as putting his hands on his hips when frustrated and scratching his jaw when perplexed. His card playing, sense of humor, hesitation at new friendships, intolerance of dishonesty, dislike of drunkards, loyalty to old friends, and respect for women regardless of who they were or what they did. They both laughed and silently paused at various examples Rachel shared with her dear friend's son. Rachel felt relieved after telling Chance as much as she remembered of his father.

After about an hour of reminiscing, Rachel's daughter Adeline rushed through the front door, her buckle shoes echoing through the hotel. "Mommy! Mommy! I'm home!" she announced, racing into the dining room.

"Young lady! What have I told you about running around here and screaming?"

"Sorry mommy. Hello, I'm Adeline, what's your name?" the little girl asked Chance.

"My name is Ben. Nice to meet you."

"You look like Mr. Chance, only younger," the astute eleven-year-old girl stated.

"Adeline, this is Mr. Chance's son, Ben," Rachel explained.

"Oh. You even have the same name?" she asked crossing her arms behind her back.

"Yes, I do. Benjamin Franklin Chance, at your service ma'am," Chance formally greeted the energized young lady by standing and taking a bow.

"Wow! Are those cookies just for you?" she asked grabbing a handful of her brown hair in each hand.

"Not at all. Allow me," Chance offered the tray of cookies to Adeline, who first looked at her mother for permission. When Rachel nodded in assent, the girl grabbed a cookie and took a bite.

"Now go upstairs and wash your face and hands," Rachel ordered.

"Yes, mommy! Bye, Mr. Chance!" she called, then ran up the stairs, stumbling halfway. "I'm okay!" she assured her flustered mother.

"Well, thank you for your time, ma'am."

"Call me Rachel, please!"

"Yes, ma'am, Rachel. I saw a livery stable near the end of town. I'll put up my horse and come back a little later if that's all right?"

"I serve supper at six if you'd like to join the rest of the hotel guests."

"I would like that. Thank you."

Rachel watched Chance as he lifted his duster off the hook, then strolled out the front door of the Sundown. *He even walks like Ben*, she thought. A chill ran down her spine. It was like Ben had returned from the dead.

———

Francisco Garcia saw the tall rider coming down the street toward the stable as he cut hay bales apart. Garcia stopped and watched as the rider stopped his horse in front of the wide open double barn doors. Leaving the hay, Garcia stepped out, and stopped in his tracks. The rider swung down off his horse, tying it to a nearby post.

"Good afternoon. I was wondering if I could put up my horse here for the night?" Chance asked.

Garcia looked Chance over carefully but said nothing. He stepped closer to get a better look.

"Do you speak English? My Spanish ain't too good," Chance advised.

"Yes, sir, I speak English. Sure, you can leave your horse here, mister. You're not from around here, are ya?" Garcia asked.

"Nope, Texarkana. Just passin' through. Be here a couple of days, I reckon."

"You look like a fella used to live here," Garcia finally said.

Chance nodded. "You're thinking I look like Ben Chance, huh?"

"Yes, sir. Younger, I think."

"You're right. I'm Ben Chance's son."

"Whoa! You don't say! Happy to know you!" Garcia shouted through a grin that stretched from ear to ear. "I'm Francisco Garcia. Your father saved my life once!" he shouted, grabbing Chance's hand and shaking it vigorously.

"I'm Ben Chance, same as my father. I'd like to hear about that."

"Oh my! Ben Chance! Sure, come inside!" Garcia waved Chance over to a stack of uncut bales and sat down.

"Just before your father left town, a couple of hombres came here to steal my money. They hit me on the head, and one choked me when your father showed up with Mr. Danner. Your father shoot one of 'em, but the other shoot your father in the leg, and he fell down. Mr. Danner killed the other one. I very sorry that yer father was killed. He was a very good man. We all miss him," Garcia said, his grin fading as he spoke.

"Thanks for the kind words. I'll leave my horse," Chance said.

"Yes, leave him right there. I will take care right away."

Chance decided to take a look around town before heading back to the Sundown. As he walked down the street, several people stopped to stare as he passed. At least he knew why they were all looking at him like he was a ghost. He figured he kind of was.

Chance made his way back toward the Sundown when a cluster of riders rode up to the Creekbed Saloon, rustling up a thick cloud of dust. Chance kept his eye on the group as they tethered their horses, then piled into the bar like a herd of buffalo.

"Riders from the KC," a voice sang out from a nearby doorway.

Chance stopped and found himself face to face with Andrew Carson.

"Figured you might be wondering where that bunch was from. I'm

Andrew Carson, the town's doctor. I patched your father up a couple of times while he was here."

"Ben Chance, doc. Glad to meet ya."

"Pleasure's mine, son. Rachel came down and said you were in town." Doc Carson leaned his right shoulder against the door frame and his eyes narrowed. "I must say, I was as surprised as she was when I heard Ben had a son. Guess we just never thought about it."

"Yeah, the fella down at the livery stable seemed surprised, too."

"I'm sure. Francisco was friends with Ben. He saved his life."

"Yeah, he told me all about it," Chance chuckled, rubbing his cheek.

"Well, I just wanted to say hello. Anything I can do, let me know," Carson offered before stepping inside his office then closing the door.

Chance stepped up onto the Sundown's wide porch and took a seat in one of the inviting rockers Rachel had set out. Despite the cool breeze, the late afternoon sun kept the temperature agreeable. Watching the town's activity, Chance understood why his father had written that he had decided to settle down here. The shop keepers busily tidied their respective stores, an abundance of carriages and buckboards made their way up and down the wide street, and everyone seemed to know one another. He also understood why his father felt the way he did about Rachel. She was beautiful and pleasant. Before he could think too much about Rachel, the sound of thundering horses and clattering harnesses turned Chance's attention to the approaching stagecoach. A few moments later, he was engulfed in another dense cloud of red dust as the coach drew to a stop in front of the hotel.

"Sundown Hotel! Next stop, stage office!" the driver called out as he jumped down to open the carriage door. Two well-dressed men wearing dark brown suits and gambler crown hats to match, along with a young woman clad in a white blouse, dark gray prairie skirt, and bonnet, emerged, walking past Chance into the hotel. Looked like Chance would have company at the dinner table tonight.

CHAPTER 3

WES PAYNE – BUFFALO GAP

Wes stepped over to his trusted white stallion, Ringo, who dutifully waited next to the jail while his partner finished his business with the fugitive. Wes pulled a handful of grain from one saddlebag and fed his mount, then snatched a handful of jerky from the other for himself before stepping back onto a poorly maintained jailhouse boardwalk that looked like a rabid coyote chewed it during a fit. The dark orange sun had begun to dip behind the jagged tips of the Guadalupe mountaintops, dropping the temperature from cool to cold. The Sisters' arrival caused a bustle of activity in front of the boarding house. Several men had gathered around the wagons to assist in putting them up for the night. A thin man dressed in black directed the men to and from each wagon. Every man unloaded a bag from the wagons, matching them to their owner.

"Son of a bitch! What the hell is this!" Calhoun yelled from his cell.

Reluctantly, Wes strolled into the jail and looked at his sozzled prisoner through black iron bars. Calhoun attempted to get up off the cot without much success. His bloodied nose and missing teeth were victims of Wes's knuckles. Aside from that, Calhoun appeared to be no worse for wear. Wes said nothing, just watched the show. After multiple failed attempts to sit up, Calhoun finally slid off the edge of the cot and crashed to the floor, sending an echo under its marred boards. He tried to stand only to tumble face-first onto the dusty floor. After listening to his prisoner mumble for a bit, Wes spoke up.

"You're in the Buffalo Gap jail, Calhoun!"

Calhoun rolled over and looked up at the sound of Wes's voice, attempting to focus through bloodshot, glassy eyes. "Who the hell are you?" Calhoun managed to ask, the words whistling through gaps where his teeth had been.

"Name is Wes Payne. I'm a Texas Ranger. You're under arrest for stealin' saddles and be'n party to a murder," Wes explained.

"I ain't stole no saddles," Calhoun slurred. "I ain't killed nobody, neither!"

"Well, there's a group of ranchers that beg to differ. And you sellin' those five stolen saddles down in San Angelo last month don't help your cause," Wes offered. "And then there's Joel Thornton and Ben Chance."

Calhoun paused at his attempt to stand and glared at Wes but said nothing.

"What were you doin' with those three idiots at the Split Rail Saloon this afternoon?" Wes demanded.

"Who?"

"Those three fellas who ended up shootin' it out with me and the Sheriff?"

"Go to hell," Calhoun snarled.

Wes stepped into the front office, as Kirby entered the bullet-riddled front door with an armful of lumber.

"Getting colder out there. Sooner I get this window boarded up, the better," Kirby said, closing the door behind him.

"Calhoun is awake back there but still too drunk or scared to tell me who those other three with him were," Wes told Kirby.

"I stopped by the Split Rail and talked to the bartender. Calhoun knew one of 'em and started talkin' about a job he had. The other two joined in. He didn't know anything else. Seems you came charging through the back door, and they all ran out together. On the way back, I saw that wagon train of nuns show up at the boarding house, so I went over to see what they were doing in town," Kirby said.

"What are they up to?" Wes asked.

"On their way up to a town on the Red River to start a church and school or something."

"Hope it's not too close to the river. Otherwise, those nuns will have to deal with raiders coming across the border and causing them trouble," Wes offered.

"I warned em about that, seems they've been told the U.S. Marshals are taking care of the outlaws. I ain't heard nothin' 'bout that," Kirby added.

"Me neither. Marshals got their hands' full chase'n outlaws in the territory, and up Missouri way," Wes stated.

"You headin' out tonight or in the morning?" Kirby asked.

"In the morning. I'll be over at the hotel if you need me tonight," Wes advised, then left Kirby to his carpentry.

Wes took Ringo to the livery stable, then walked over to the hotel where the owner, Amos Gentry, a short stocky man with a thick neck and perpetual frown, was ordering his wife to make coffee for the dining room.

"Evening, Mr. Payne. You stayin' with us tonight?" Amos asked.

"Yes, sir. I'll be heading out early in the morning," Wes advised.

"Fine. Just leave yer key in the room. We'll take care of it after you leave," Amos curtly instructed out the side of his mouth.

"Yes, sir." Wes said before leaving the room. *I really don't like that guy*, he thought as he started up the staircase when he heard yelling coming from the street. He turned just in time to see Kirby riding fast past the hotel.

"Mr. Payne looks like a ruckus over to the saloon," Amos hollered from the front door.

Wes hurried out to the street to see Kirby heading into the Split Rail Saloon. He noted the piano music had stopped. Never a good sign. He hustled over to the saloon and pushed through the swinging doors to see Kirby locked in a wrestling match with a tall, stocky cowboy in the back of the crowded barroom. The men had stepped back, forming a circle around the combatants, giving Kirby room to take care of business with the obviously drunk cowboy, who was incoherently hollering something about women. Wes slid through the patrons' ring.

"Need a hand, Sheriff?" Wes asked in between a chuckle.

"If...you...don't...mind," Kirby managed.

Wes approached the two men, slipped the cowboy's gun from its holster and tucked it inside his belt, then sent a scarred fist into the side of the ruffian's head, ending the battle.

Kirby let the cowboy fall to the floor in a heap. The delighted spectators then laughed and applauded the two lawmen.

"Thanks," Kirby stated, then turned to the crowd. "Where's Daisy?" he asked.

"Over here, Sheriff," she answered, then stepped forward in her bright green hoop dress with white feathers lining the top, and a wide black belt tightly wrapped around her narrow waist.

"What happened?" Kirby asked for clarification.

"I was walking past this fella, and he just grabbed ahold and reached down the front of my dress, taking liberties. I slapped him, and he started to get rough, so Dale there told him to let go. He punched Dale in the face," Daisy reported.

Kirby glanced over at the bartender, through the cloud of perpetual smoke that hung in the Split Rail Saloon. The bartender nodded in agreement. Kirby looked over at Dale, who was propped in a chair with another dance-hall girl, getting his bloodied face dabbed with a wet bar towel.

"That right, Dale?" Kirby asked the towns' bantam bald-headed telegraph operator. Dale nodded, checking his mouth and counting teeth.

"That's what happened, Dan," a smiling Dolly Flynn, assured in between wiping Dale's forehead with long narrow fingers.

"All right everyone, show's over. Wes, give me a hand with this fella," Kirby asked.

He and Wes each grabbed an arm then dragged their prisoner out of the Split Rail to the yips and hollers of the crowd. As the lawmen reached the doors, they were met by one of the nuns who had arrived a moment earlier closely watching the events.

"Excuse us, Sister," Kirby stated, wanting her to step out of the way.

She looked at Wes with a cool, emotionless expression. "Did you have to hit that man so hard, Mister?" she asked the big Ranger.

Startled, Wes paused. "Well, Sister, I didn't know there was any other way," he stated, while the crowd roared with more laughter. Wes tipped his hat, and he and Kirby continued on their way to the jail.

"Huh, oh. You're in trouble now, Ranger Payne," Kirby laughed as they marched down the street.

Wes said nothing, just chuckled.

After tossing their prisoner onto his cot, Kirby took the liberty of waking the man by dumping a bucket of cold water on his face.

"What the hell!" the stranger yelled, spitting a mouth full of water onto the floor. "Why am I in here?" he demanded.

"Being drunk and disorderly for the moment. I'll see if Daisy and Dale want to charge you with assault later," Kirby explained.

"I didn't assault her. Just took a handful, Sheriff, if ya know what I mean," the cowboy mumbled.

"Well, she didn't take too kindly to that, and you can't be punchin' fellas in the face when they offer help to a lady," Kirby added. "Who are ya anyway?"

"Name's Ty Derrick. I'm with the Overton outfit running a herd through. We're leavin' in the morning."

"You square with the bartender?"

"Nope. Didn't get the chance," Derrick admitted.

"Got two dollars on ya?" Kirby asked.

Derrick reached into his pocket and withdrew two silver dollars, handing them to Kirby, "Why'd ya hit me like that, Sheriff?"

"I actually didn't hit you," Kirby responded.

"Who the hell did?" Derrick asked.

Wes stepped around the corner and looked down on the cowhand.

"That'd be me," Wes advised.

Derrick looked up at Wes. "Who the hell are you?" he asked.

"Name's Payne. Texas Rangers."

"Son of a bitch, you're a big one, ain't ya?"

Wes said nothing, just glared through steel-gray eyes.

"Figures I'd get into it when there's a Ranger around. I reckon I had it comin'."

"You did," Wes stated then left the room.

"I'll go over, pay your tab, and explain you're headin' out in the morning. That should take care of it," Kirby stated.

"Can you stick around until I come back?" Kirby asked Wes.

"You really should hire a deputy or two, Sheriff," Wes pointed out.

"Why? When I have you around," Kirby said, chuckling.

Wes sat down in Kirby's chair and propped his size twelve boots up on the desk. After a moment, he realized Calhoun was snoring loud enough to be heard out on the street. He went back into the holding area and banged a tin cup on the bars, jolting Calhoun awake.

"Thanks," Derrick said as Wes walked by the cell, heading back to Kirby's desk.

Wes propped his feet up on the desk and got comfortable. He revisited the stack of wanted posters sitting on Kirby's desk. A half hour later, Kirby returned and informed his cowhand prisoner that all had been taken care of, and he would be released tomorrow, in time to leave with his outfit. A quick handshake later, Wes was on his way back to the hotel, listening to loud piano music coming from the saloon. *Always a good sign*, he thought.

CHAPTER 4

Wes spurred Ringo onward, moving sporadically back and forth between thin-leaf sage, desert willows, and mounds of brown bunch grass that had seen better days. Crack! The rifle shot broke his concentration. He looked over and saw Chance falling backward off his horse, causing Jake's horse to rear up. Jake lost his grip and fell to the ground with a wild scream. Wes quickly pushed Ringo into a gallop and saw the muzzle smoke from a second shot ooze out from behind a big sage. He saw Danner charging forward in an arc toward the shots. Wes drew his guns and fired into the sage, emptying both cylinders setting the water-starved cluster of twigs on fire. He heard Danner's Russians pounding away in the distance. Ringo kept charging toward the burning bush ignoring Wes's pull on the reins. He yelled for his stallion to stop, but it was too late. He flew off Ringo headfirst into the blazing inferno.

Wes grabbed his gun belt and sat straight up in bed. He gasped for air and was soaked in sweat. His eyes darted around the dim room. A bright beam of moonshine tunneled through the window, providing enough light for him to recognize his room at the Bison Hotel. He wiped the sweat from his eyes, caught his breath, and leaned back against the thick wooden headboard. *Damn, I wish these dreams would stop*, he thought.

He closed his eyes, took a deep breath, and set his gun belt back onto the gathered bed sheets next to him. After all these years and all he'd been through, watching Chance get shot still haunted him. He remembered the faces of the Mexican banditos that nailed him to the barn in Presidio years ago, scarring his hands, but even that didn't haunt him like this. He had seen men killed before, including earlier today. None of them haunted him.

Why Ben Chance? He wondered as he rose from bed and looked out onto the street. All looked quiet but for the faint sound of the fall breeze dancing through the buildings. It must be late. Even the Split Rail Saloon was dark. He didn't own a watch, and there was no clock in the room. He decided he didn't care enough to walk downstairs. Wes poured water into the washbasin and splashed it on his face, then took a drink from the brown adobe pitcher. He sat in a chair and leaned back. *Hopefully, the sun will be up soon,* he thought before drifting off into a fitful sleep.

A few hours later, Mrs. Gentry made coffee in the kitchen when Wes descended the stairs. The sun wasn't up yet, but he decided it was an excellent time to head back to Fort Griffin.

"Good morning, Mr. Payne," Mrs. Gentry greeted him. "I'm sorry, I haven't started breakfast yet," she advised.

"That's okay, Mrs. Gentry. I'm not hungry anyway. I could use a cup of coffee, if it's ready, though."

"Certainly. One moment." She hurried to the stove and poured the fresh brew into a large glass cup. She brought it back to Wes, who waited at the lobby desk. "Are you going to the jail?" she asked as she handed him a steaming cup of black coffee.

"Yes, ma'am," Wes answered as he took a sip.

The woman nodded. "Just leave the cup there. I'll fetch it later," Mrs. Gentry offered.

"Thank you, ma'am, see you next time," Wes said, nodding in approval toward the beautiful young wife of the cranky hotel owner. He flipped his saddlebags over his shoulder and let himself out the front door. Wes heard the click of the lock catch behind him then stepped out into the chilly October air. The horizon was nothing more than a black line at the bottom of an orange-tinted sky as he walked down the street, steaming cup in hand, to the jail. Wes paused on the front step. "It's me, Wes," he called out before proceeding.

He heard the big cross-board move and waited for the door to open. He was met by Kirby, standing in the dim glow of an oil lantern perched on his desk.

"Come on in," Kirby offered before closing and latching the door behind him.

"You're up early, Sheriff," Wes stated, setting the steaming cup on Kirby's desk.

"I let that cowhand go a bit ago so he could get back to camp before his trail boss fired him. Didn't want him left behind and hanging around town after last night."

"Calhoun make it through the night?" Wes asked.

"Damn drunk was see'n things most of the night. When he wasn't screaming out or mumbling, he was snoring like a hibernated bear. I don't know how such a loud noise can come from such a little dude," Kirby complained. "He finally quieted down a few hours ago." Kirby removed the keyring from its bent nail next to his desk and headed to the cell block with Wes close behind. Kirby unlocked the cell and swung the door open.

"Okay, Calhoun, time to go!" Kirby shouted.

Calhoun didn't move.

"Calhoun, let's go!" Kirby shouted again before entering the cell to shake the prisoner awake.

The former trail boss of the KC ranch still didn't move. Kirby rolled him over. Calhoun's face was a grayish-white, with both eyes wide open, and mouth packed with dried vomit. He was dead.

"Hell, looks like I'll be ride'n back to Griffin alone," Wes muttered.

"Damn. That it does. Stand by for a bit this morning so I can write a report for the Judge. I'll go wake up the undertaker and have him buried," Kirby advised the Ranger.

"In that case, I'll head back to the hotel and get some breakfast. I'll stop by later," Wes announced. He started back to the Bison, looking forward to Mrs. Gentry's cooking after all.

After breakfast, Wes made his way over to the livery stable where the stable boss, Dalton Jones, oversaw the horse hames being hooked up to the wagons that brought the nuns in the day before.

"Morning, Mr. Payne. Ringo is in the back ready to go," Jones advised.

"Thank you, Jonesy," Wes replied. He paused and looked over the wagons. They were old and in poor condition. The axles were bowed, and each wheel had nails and metal straps all along the edges where they had been repaired. In addition, the hub bands were plum worn out. "They came in these?" Wes asked, surprised the wagons had made it this far.

"I know. Haven't seen any like this in a long time. Those nuns said they were heading up to Red River country. I don't know if they'll make it that far in these," Jones said.

"They say where they're going?" Wes asked.

"Yep, a town called Range. Deacon said it's right on the riverbank. I don't know of it."

Wes nodded. "It's a growing town. Sits close to the Great Western Cattle Trail in Hardeman County. I was through it a couple years back. Not much there back then. It was settled by Confederate soldiers and their families after the war. Damn sure don't see why a bunch of nuns are headin' there, though," Wes added.

"I thought that Red River border was bustin' with outlaws raidin' the settlements," Jones said.

"Yep. I heard the same thing. Been talk of sending a company of Rangers up there. Problem is, we don't have a company of Rangers to send," Wes advised.

"Well, I warned 'em, but them nuns weren't interested in listening. They just told its God's will," Jones replied, as his hand reached out toward the sky.

"I don't think God will fight off bandits for 'em, though," Wes said before checking his billet strap, then stepping into a stirrup and swinging up on Ringo. Wes tapped his spurs and headed out of the stable past Jones.

"Take care, Mr. Payne!" Jones called as Wes passed through the big old barn doors.

Wes waved and started down the street when the group of nuns standing in front of the boarding house caught his eye. He slowed up and reined Ringo over to their location. He stopped and removed his hat.

"Good morning, Sisters," Wes greeted the nuns.

The nuns returned the greeting in unison, but for the Sister who'd scolded Wes at the saloon. The Deacon, still dressed all in black, stepped forward to offer a handshake that Wes accepted without dismounting.

"Good morning, sir," the Deacon offered. "Would you be traveling north toward the Red River?" the Deacon asked.

"No, sir, on my way to Fort Griffin. I understand ya'll are headin' up to Range. You folks have an escort?" Wes asked the little man.

"We have a gentleman, Mr. Nolen, who knows the way and is driving a wagon," the Deacon answered.

"That's not what I mean. Anyone riding guard?" Wes asked.

"Guard?" the Deacon asked, clutching his hands behind his back and leaning forward.

"Yes, sir. Anyone that can handle a gun?" Wes clarified.

The Deacon smiled and shook his head from side to side. "Oh no, we don't need guns, we are protected by our faith in God."

"As you wish. Just remember, out here, faith doesn't protect anyone," Wes advised his devout audience. "Good luck." Wes pulled Ringo around and galloped out of Buffalo Gap.

CHAPTER 5

RANGE

Dark, dense clouds cut a trail through the gray sky, ushering in a gloomy beginning to November in Range Texas. The town of Range began as a temporary settlement by a group of former Confederate soldiers and their families. Three years into reconstruction, a trio of men, led by one-time plantation owner Lawrence Benson, decided that life west of the Mississippi River had to be better than what they were experiencing in Georgia. Benson, together with businessmen Bradley Jamieson and Lee Conrad, persuaded another thirty men and their families to join them in seeking a better future in Texas.

After a month-long journey that saw their wagon train attacked by hostile Indians and renegade outlaws fleeing the Union army, the travelers from back east were exhausted from the trip and the oppressive summer heat. Pushing ahead, the throng came upon an open range along the south bank of the Red River. With ample grass for livestock, an abundance of pecan trees and water, the decision was made to stay until fall when the cooler weather arrived. Then, they'd forge on ahead.

When fall arrived three months later, only a handful of the settlement decided to move on. Now, nine years later in the fall of

1877, Lawrence Benson, Bradley Jamieson, Lee Conrad, and newcomer, Otto Wilhelm, gathered again for the good of the town.

The cold temperature kept many of the town's residents inside their stove-and-fireplace-heated shelters. The three businessmen braved the chill, making their way down Main Street to the end of town where Lawrence Benson waited to discuss the hiring of a town Marshal. The recent raids on the town and murder of a Texas Ranger by border outlaws fortified the men to take action. Their town had grown, and now had enough money to find a man or men who could protect their interests. Their frequent protection requests sent to the U.S. Marshal's office in Fort Smith had failed to generate a response. The constant trouble along the Red River border had led to periodic cavalry visits, but the troops didn't remain long enough to deter the bandits. A passing Texas Ranger opted to stay for a spell but was gunned down by bandits during a recent raid. Now, the town's leaders took action themselves.

Lawrence Benson, owner of the Red River Stagecoach line and now Range's mayor, began the meeting with a summary of the outlaw activity, the murder of the Texas Ranger, and what had been done thus far regarding the requests for assistance. Benson reiterated his insistence on hiring a man who could handle a gun, pin a star on his chest, and help the townsfolk to sleep easier. Waiting for outside assistance appeared futile.

Bradley Jamieson, the town's storekeeper, had made his skepticism in this plan known. He had previously told the men that while he was willing to pay for a lawman, he couldn't see one man making much of a difference. If one man had been the answer, the previous Texas Ranger would have been more than enough to deter outlaws from Range. Jamieson declared the town needed something more, but he offered no other options.

Lee Conrad, owner of the Purple Sage Hotel in town, had gone on record saying he was also unconvinced that a town Marshal would make much difference. He had written a letter to Mayor Benson that he feared hiring a lawman would simply be an invitation for another man to be murdered in Range. If that occurred, the word would spread that Range was too dangerous, and travelers and settlers alike would choose to settle elsewhere. All of this uncertainly even led to a few random suggestions that the town strike a deal with the outlaws.

Otto Wilhelm ran the livery stable and cattle pens on the edge of town. A German immigrant who spoke limited English, he arrived in America with money and a knowledge of livestock dating back two decades. His experience in his homeland had not prepared him for the lawlessness of the new country. Not that Germany was free from thieves, but the level of violence displayed by these raiders was new to him. He knew of the Polizei in Germany but had little contact with that political group back home. Here in Range, he decided to follow the wishes of the other men and do as they felt was necessary.

After the four men had each had an opportunity to speak, Lawrence Benson continued. "Gentlemen, I have sent word of Mr. Wallaby's death to the nearest Ranger station via Fort Phantom Hill. I have not received a response as our telegraph system is unreliable, at best. I'm certain the outlaws are responsible for the constant need for repairs of the wire. Nevertheless, I am uncertain of the reaction or response the Rangers may have. Therefore, I strongly believe we should establish our own law and order and hire a town Marshal. I'll open the floor for any additional questions and suggestions," Benson concluded.

"Men, as I've said, I'm in favor of a Marshal dedicated to keeping our town safe, but I'm not convinced that one man, regardless of his ability, will discourage the behavior of the outlaws running wild along the river, but I'll support the group's decision," Jamieson stated.

"I completely agree with Brad. If we hire a lawman and he's killed, the word will surely get out that Range is too dangerous to pass through or settle in. There are many other towns further south that are not being victimized by these bandits. Settlers will choose to go elsewhere, and our businesses will suffer mightily, but I also agree with Lawrence that we need a law enforcement presence here," Conrad added.

"Mr. Wilhelm, what are your thoughts?" Benson asked

"I do not know any answer. I tink it may be good to have Polizei here in Range. Thank you," Wilhelm stated in his best English.

"Very well. Mr. Donovan could not be here this morning, but he informed me that he was in favor of a town Marshal, as his saloon business would be better if the men knew there'd be trouble when they didn't pay," Benson added. "I will send word to Sheriff Evans in Margaret that we are hiring a Marshal, and any assistance he could provide would be welcome," Benson advised. "In the meantime, anyone with a suggestion about who would be a good Marshal should let me know. We will also immediately begin the building of a Marshal office and jail," Benson announced before adjourning the meeting.

Brad Jamieson left the freight office, heading directly to the Red Dirt Saloon where many of the townsfolk had gathered to hear about the meeting. Michael Donovan, a tall, thin Irishman with flaming red hair and a beard to match, had prepared pots of coffee for the occasion.

Mrs. Wilhelm, the town baker, had brought baskets of sugar biscuits and honey to the gathering. Jamieson heard the sound of loud chatter as he approached the saloon's big wooden swinging doors. As he pushed in the doors and entered, the chatter dissipated. All of the town's residents wanted the raiding to stop so they could live without the fear of more pillaging by the dregs of the border.

Jamieson stepped up to the bar where Donovan greeted him with a steaming cup of coffee. "Drop a little whiskey in there if ya don't mind, Mike," Jamieson ordered the lanky proprietor.

"Sure thing!" Donovan laughed as he reached under the bar to grab a bottle of his best whiskey.

"Okay everybody. Looks like we're going to hire a Marshal and build a jail as quickly as possible," Jamieson began. "I know we may be limited on materials with other building going on, but if we're gonna make a real town of this place, we'll need to stop these bandits from crossing the river and causing trouble any time they feel like it. Lawrence said he sent word to the nearest Ranger office about Mr. Wallaby being killed but hasn't gotten a response yet." Jamieson paused and took a long sip of his whiskey-spiked coffee then continued. "We still haven't heard anything from Fort Phantom Hill either. So if any of you know of a good man with a gun that would be interested, let us know," Jamieson announced as Lawrence Benson entered the saloon.

"Just letting everyone know what was said at our meeting Lawrence," Jamieson informed the Mayor before stepping down from the bar.

"Very good. We should have another cattle drive coming through in the next few days. We can get the word out to the hands on the drive and see if there is any interest. Sheriff Evans may also have a suggestion. I encourage all of you to be patient until we can settle this business," Benson requested.

"One man ain't gonna make no difference!" One man spoke up, with many of the other residents calling out in agreement. "We need more help from the surrounding ranchers!" another man shouted.

"Agreed, agreed," Benson calmly stated holding up his hands in a gesture to quiet the group. "I'm going to visit with all the nearby ranchers to ask for their support and assistance. Most have already said what's good for Range is good for them. They all put money into this town. We can count on their backing," Benson assured.

Benson's words had struck a nerve with most of the town's folks eliciting low chatter among themselves with an occasional abrasive word here and there as they filed out of the Red Dirt Saloon into the cold gray morning. Benson and Jamieson waited until everyone had left before discussing the matter further.

"I understand their frustrations," Jamieson opened the conversation.

"As do I, but we're behind the times on this one. We should've had this issue addressed a year ago," Benson added, nodding toward Donavon, who'd handed him a whiskey-spiked steaming cup of coffee.

"Town's grown quite a bit since that cattle trail was cut," Donovan acknowledged. "Some nights the hotel and boarding house are full-up turning folks away. That's why them outlaws from the territory come poking around," he said. "A bunch of 'em come in here, drink, don't pay, and harass the women. Next thing ya know, they're pullin' guns and fightin'," Donovan added.

"Well, we're doing the right thing. Now we just need the right man in charge," Benson stated.

"What we need is the right gunslinger in charge," Donovan corrected the mayor.

CHAPTER 6

LUXTON DANNER – FORT SMITH

U.S. Deputy Marshal Luxton Danner slammed the rusted iron cell door shut and rotated the grinding gear lock into place. Ignoring the shouts of insult from the three prisoners he had just spent the last six days with, he ascended the jail steps and emerged into the sun-drenched courtyard of the Western District Federal Court located in Fort Smith, Arkansas, near the Oklahoma border. The two-story red brick building housed the Federal court, Judge Isaac Parker's chambers, as well as U.S. Marshal Daniel Upham's office. Prisoner cells occupied the lower level beneath the first floor. The deputy Marshals' quarters were across the courtyard and the stables beyond that. Tall pine trees surrounded the structures, making for a majestic scene.

Danner glanced up at the familiar white-framed second floor window and saw it open despite the coolness of the day. The open window meant Judge Parker was in and conducting business as usual. He decided to get cleaned up before paying a visit to the vaunted Judge, then reporting to Marshal Upham. Danner had deemed the trip a success since he'd brought back three of the five fugitives, he had been given warrants for. Halfway across the square, he stopped to shake Deputy Bass Reeves' hand, then disappeared into the dingy washroom where he looked forward to eradicating six days of dirt from his hide.

"Good to see you back in one piece, Danner!" Deputy Zeke Proctor called out as he stepped past buckets of clear water lined along the wall of the musty facility.

"When you headin' back out?" Danner asked his fellow deputy.

"Two days. Goin' back into the territory with a fistful of paper," Proctor answered over his shoulder, not pausing to visit.

These were the times when Danner enjoyed his job the most. Being back in Fort Smith, seeing many of the deputies he had either heard about or worked with, brought a feeling of satisfaction to him. He was due for a two-week leave, but he wasn't sure he wanted that. Since Six Shot, Danner had hoped for as little downtime as possible. Down time meant time to think. Losing Chance was tough enough, but his thoughts kept drifting back to Elizabeth Thornton.

How was she coping? Did she decide to stay in Thornton and run the ranch or go back east? Did she think of him, or had young Jake Rawlings filled her thoughts? He mused. These were questions that kept banging around in his head, but he couldn't figure out why. She never said or did anything that led him to believe she was interested in him. Still, he'd felt terrible for her loss and wanted the best for her. The one letter he received from her shortly after leaving Canyon Creek didn't say much other than thanks and good wishes for his future.

He kept hoping for an assignment back to Texas so he could stop in on both Elizabeth and Rachel in order to satisfy his unexplained curiosity. On top of that, the nightmares were getting worse. His fear of his guns not firing caused him to start carrying a third gun just in case. He stopped and smiled at the thought of carrying the third gun. *Wes would appreciate that,* he mused.

"Danner, you in here?" Zeke Proctor's voice thundered inside the stone-walled room.

"Yep! I'm here." Danner replied.

"Marshal Upham wants to see you right away. He's in his office." Proctor advised.

Daniel Phillips Upham had been appointed the U.S. Marshal of the

Western District by President Grant a year ago. In his effort to impress the President, and distance himself from his controversial past, he was known to push his deputies hard.

Good, maybe I have another assignment I can get to right away. The Parker visit will have to wait, Danner thought as he quickly wiped his face, then changed into a clean shirt before heading to Upham's office. A few moments later, Danner paused and knocked on the heavy oak door sending an echo through the empty hallway.

"Enter!" Upham shouted from behind his equally impressive oak desk on the opposite side of the sprawling room.

Danner turned the brass handle and pushed the massive piece of wood inward, causing the brass hinges to squeal like a wounded possum. He turned and closed the door behind him and stepped to the front of his superior's desk. "Deputy Danner. You called for me, sir?"

Upham nodded, his eyes not wavering from his correspondence. "Have a seat Danner, I'll be with you in a moment."

Danner retrieved a stout wooden ladder-back chair from the adjacent wall and pulled it in front of the desk, then sat and waited. Even seated, the strapping deputy towered over his boss.

"I'm sorry, Danner. I don't mean to be rude, but I wanted to read this communication a second time before I made a decision on what our response should be," Upham explained as he handed the letter to Danner for his review. Danner was far more educated than most of his fellow deputies, having spent two years at Franklin and Marshal College before shedding his eastern upbringing and heading west. As such, he read through the text quickly then returned it to his boss.

"I have no doubt that many of these bandits raiding along the Red River are fugitives we already have warrants for. Since I don't know that for a fact, I'm not inclined to send several deputies on a mission that may or may not fulfill the objectives of this position. Yet, these settlers deserve our interest, if not our protection. I've decided to send a single deputy to check on the towns along the Texas side of the river. Gather some intelligence and report back here. Because of the nature of the mission, it'll be a volunteer assignment. I know you don't like too much downtime, and since you've got a little history in Texas, I thought I'd ask you first," Upham stated.

"When would you like me to leave, sir?" Danner quickly asked.

"Rest up for a day or two, then submit your request for provisions. I've already approved whatever you ask for."

"I'll only need two weeks rations, and extra ammunition," Danner advised.

"Done. Pick up what you need from the quartermaster tomorrow. Also, take double the standard travel money. I don't know for certain what you'll find out there, but I have a pretty good idea. These sons-a-bitches along the Red River have been thorns in the sides of many good people. Unfortunately, until a decision is made about the Indian Territory, they'll continue to run ram shod all along the border, knowing sanctuary is a river crossing away. If you can, find out who the leaders are, and determine how many of these outlaw bands we're dealing with," Upham ordered.

Danner stood and accepted Upham's firm handshake then turned to leave.

"Danner?" Upton added, a warning in his voice.

Danner turned back to face his boss. "Yes, sir."

"Remember, this is an information and assessment mission. Find out what you can, then report back here for reinforcements. Don't try and clean up the problem all by yourself. I need you back here. You're no good to me dead. Good luck," Upham offered, cracking a smile for the first time.

"Yes, sir. I'll take all the precautions I feel are necessary," Danner assured the Western District Marshal, returning the smile as he left the office, relieved he had an assignment. Especially one that would take him back to Texas.

CHAPTER 7

BEN CHANCE, JR. – CANYON CREEK

T he Stratford Stagecoach rumbled to a halt in front of the Sundown Hotel, bringing the customary cloud of red dust with it. Cletus Bradley, the driver, slid down from his perch, opened the door, then circled around back to unload the bags. From his front porch rocking chair, Chance heard muffled cursing coming from the driver as the man fought a losing battle with the luggage. Suddenly, several bags slid off the top rail, hitting the old timer square in the face, sending him onto his backside with a thump.

"Damn women! Always bringin' stuff they don't need, and I'm still the one that has to deal with it!" Cletus shouted while sitting in the cloud of red dust with various sized bags scattered all around. Two female passengers stopped at the hotel door and looked hard at Cletus. Their disapproving frowns and narrow eyes showed their obvious displeasure with his crassness.

Seeing the ladies' reaction, Chance chuckled, then vacated the comfort of his rocking chair, and walked over to the fallen driver.

"Give ya a hand there, old timer?" Chance asked, extending a hand to help the old man to his feet.

Cletus looked at the red dirt covering his already soiled overalls and held up a left hand without looking. Chance took a firm grip and pulled the old timer to his feet in one fluid motion. Cletus half-heartily brushed off some dust then looked at Chance. "Thanks, partner," he said as he leaned forward to stare at Chance.

Chance laughed and began to reach down to retrieve a bag when Cletus grabbed his arm and stopped him.

"Leapin' crickets! What'd ya say yer name was, stranger?" Cletus asked, sending a stream of tobacco juice into the parched street's dust.

Chance took a step back and put his hands on his hips. "First, I didn't say what my name was, and second, I know I look like Ben Chance. That'd be cuz I'm Ben's son," Chance offered.

"Well, I'll be a jackass's behind! 'Ole Ben had a son! Why don't no one ever tell me 'bout these things! I'm Cletus Bradley, young man! What 'ole Ben name ya?"

"Benjamin Franklin Chance. Good to know ya, Mr. Bradley."

Cletus's tobacco-stained smile faded, and he removed his hat before stepping forward and offering his hand. "Mighty fine to know ya, son. I'm rightful sorry about your father. He was the best thing that happened to this town in a long time."

"Thanks. That seems to be the general feeling around here."

Cletus nodded and returned his ragged old Calvary hat to the top of his head before sending another stream of tobacco juice into the street.

"Cletus Bradley! What have I told you about spittin' that nasty stuff in front of my hotel! And, where are my guests' bags! Laying all over the dirty street! Now you pick those bags up and get them in here at once!" Rachel finished her tirade, turned and stomped through the door.

"Yes, ma'am," Cletus offered in a weak response well after Rachel had disappeared into the hotel.

"That there's a fine lady, but when she gets mad, look out, partner!" Cletus said before busting out in loud laughter.

"I reckon we do as she says then, partner!" Chance managed in between chuckles.

The two men hurriedly moved the luggage from the street to the lobby in front of the big, shiny, oak desk that Rachel worked behind.

"I see you have my guests helping you these days?" Rachel snapped at the 'ole stage driver, before flashing one of the prettiest smiles in Canyon Creek. "Looks like you met Ben's son," she noted.

"Yes ma'am. He's the spittin' image of 'ole Ben, ain't he?" Cletus blurted, sending dots of tobacco juice atop the desk.

Chance chuckled and shook his head.

"You left your key on the desk," Rachel said nodding toward Chance. Rachel quickly handed him the key to his room while wiping the desktop with her apron. "Cletus Bradley! You always make such a mess!" Rachel added.

"Sorry ma'am," Cletus offered before he waved at Chance, then walked out the door.

Chance stepped into the lobby and took a seat in one of the big cowhide chairs near the window. He watched Rachel battle the tobacco juice on the desktop. Apparently dissatisfied with her apron's cleaning ability, Rachel removed a white rag from her apron and wiped her desk again before assigning rooms and passing out keys to the ladies who'd been perusing the dining room. She then headed to the kitchen to start dinner. Chance decided to head up to his room.

Rachel lit the oven and poured herself a glass of water. Peering out the window at nothing, she waited for the oven to heat up. That feeling of emptiness crept back inside her. Her face felt hot and she realized how tired she was. She'd not slept well since Ben's death, and her constant attempts at blocking thoughts of him had taken its toll. She dabbed a tear with her apron and took a deep breath. Before she could take a drink, Adeline burst into the kitchen with a shout. "Mommy!"

Rachel jumped, and dropped the glass, sending broken shards in every direction on the floor. "Adeline! How many times do I have to tell you not to run and yell like that?" she scolded her daughter. Rachel knelt, and began to pick up the glistening shards of glass when tears flooded her eyes. She sat on the floor and cried, to the surprise of her daughter, who stood frozen in the doorway. This time, Rachel couldn't hold it back like she had so many times before. The arrival of Ben's son had thrown her, and her sorrow over his loss was too great to bury this time. Just when she thought hope had found her again, Ben's death snuffed out any glimmer of happiness she desperately wanted.

"Oh my! Rachel, what's the matter? Are you hurt?" Mrs. Carson asked, as she entered the kitchen only to see her friend slumped on the wet floor amid broken glass. Mrs. Carson handed Adeline a cookie and shooed her from the room. "Go outside and play," she said gently to the little girl. Emily Carson, Doc Carson's wife, had been helping Rachel cook dinner on nights when the hotel was full of guests.

"I'm all right, Emily," Rachel assured her friend, as she stood and wiped the tears from her face.

Emily looked at Rachel then wrung her hands in worry. "I heard Ben's son came to town. Is that what this is about?" she asked.

Rachel nodded. "I'm sorry. It just hit me pretty hard today, I suppose."

"Nonsense. That's the last thing you need to do is apologize, Rachel Brennen. It's not every woman that loses two men in her life. Go get some fresh air. I'll get started here," Emily insisted.

After dinner, Emily ordered Rachel to spend the remainder of the evening resting while she cleaned up, with Adeline's help. Rachel didn't argue. In the quiet of the pending night, she lit the oil lamps in the lobby and sat in one of two matching overstuffed, cowhide chairs. It wasn't often she allowed herself the pleasure of enjoying one of the items usually reserved for guests. Two well-dressed men who had arrived on the stagecoach earlier in the day passed by, tipping their hats to her as they undoubtedly headed to the Creek Bed saloon for a night of cards. A few minutes later, Chance walked into the lobby.

"Good evening, may I join you?" Chance asked his hostess.

"Please do," Rachel said, afraid Chance caught her voice wavering.

Chance took the matching chair opposite Rachel and leaned back.

"Boy, I ain't never sat in anything like this before," he declared, leaning back into the supple leather.

"My late husband purchased these chairs in Dallas when we first opened this hotel. They're a little fancy for out here in Canyon Creek, but everybody likes them. Is your room okay?" she asked.

"Yes, ma'am. I wanted to let you know that I'll be leaving in the morning. I really appreciated our visit when I first arrived. Thank you for telling me about my father. I now know why he felt the way he did about you and this town."

"Will you take the stage, or head up to the rail station, and take the train back to Texarkana?"

"No, ma'am. I plan on riding back along the Red River trail. Take my time, you know, check out new towns, and such," Chance replied.

Rachel felt jubilant at the thought of helping Ben's son. "If you like, I can have a letter sent to your aunt and uncle if you want to let them know you're on your way back?" Rachel offered.

Chance paused. He looked at the stitching on the chair's arm. He realized he'd not told Rachel of his aunt and uncle's fate.

"I must have misled you. My aunt and uncle are dead. I stay at the farm alone now," Chance admitted.

"I'm so sorry. I thought–"

"They were killed about a year or so back by a gang of rustlers. We didn't even have a herd, just a handful of cows and a few horses. I was away at an auction buying hogs. When I returned, the Sheriff was waiting for me. Told me what happened, and said my uncle had left me the farm. Funny thing was, it was the first time my uncle had let me go to the auction house without him. He'd said I was ready to judge good stock. Had I been there, it would have been different."

"You don't know that for sure," Rachel offered with a sigh, pushing a lock of auburn hair off her face.

"No ma'am, that's true. I'm glad I was spared though. Now I can fulfill a promise I made to myself." Not wanting to discuss his intentions with Rachel, Chance stood and offered a smile. "I'll turn in now. Thank you again for everything," Chance stated as he stood to leave. "I'll be gone before you rise tomorrow," he advised walking away from his hostess.

Rachel remained seated and let Chance's words sink in. Chance's boots tapped half the oak steps when Rachel called after him.

"Ben. What do you mean fulfill a promise?" she asked, fearing the answer.

"There were five men that came to the farm that day. The Marshal got three. That leaves two. I'm searching for them."

"And when you find them?"

"You ever heard of Bert Cullen or Isaac Tucker, ma'am?"

"No, I don't know those names. I'm sorry," Rachel responded.

"Just as well, I guess. Mr. Danner told me that he tracked Cullen here."

"And, when you find this Cullen and Tucker. What then?"

Chance just smiled. "Good night, ma'am."

CHAPTER 8

RED RIVER COACH – BETWEEN RIVERBEND & RANGE

The sound of twenty-four hooves pounding the dormant, drab terrain in unison was music to Levi Jackson's ears. The cool rushing air felt good against his unshaven chin. He'd been driving the Red River stagecoach since boss Benson started it just after the war. Back then, there was no trail cut into the countryside between Range, Eagle Springs, and Riverbend, let alone Wichita Falls. These days, Levi and his shotgun rider, Montana Jones, could make these runs blindfolded.

Levi heard the railroad had made it to Sherman, but it was comforting to know that it'd be a good while longer before any locomotive would rumble down a rail in Range or the other towns the Red River stage line ran to. Full-up with four passengers, the evenings trip from Riverbend to Range wouldn't take long enough to see much darkness. The wheels spun through the sandy loam and red dirt trail smooth as floating on a calm pond when Montana broke Levi's bliss.

"Riders come'n!" Montana Jones called to his driver.

"How many?" Levi asked without turning to look.

"Three, coming fast on the left! Get down on the footboards and crack them reins!" Montana ordered before crawling up onto the top of the coach.

Levi slid down, ducked, and frantically whipped the reins. "Yah! Yah!" Levi called to the six-horse team, pulling his hat down tight on his head.

The passengers rocked back and forth, one woman falling to the floor of the coach. Ross Mabry, the only man inside the bedlam buggy, pulled himself to an open window to look out. All three riders charged hard toward the coach guns drawn with bandana's masking their faces. Mabry drew his Colt.

"Get down on the floor with her!" Mabry yelled to the other women who now hung on for dear life.

"What's happening!" One dazed woman asked.

Mabry took no time to answer. He just grabbed the woman's coat sleeve and pulled her to the floor with a thud. Crack! Crack! Crack! The chasing bandits opened fire. A bullet shattered the door post behind Mabry's head. Mabry leaned out the gaping window and fired. Crack! Crack! Boom! Montana let loose with both barrels from the top of the coach.

One bandit slumped, then fell, from his charging horse. Bullets hit all around Mabry, causing him to duck back into the carriage where the ladies cowered down on the floor. Mabry reloaded, then leaned hard against the door and fired again. Crack! Boom!

Montana dropped both hammers on his ten-gauge. One bandit pulled right, moving directly behind the coach, and continued to shoot. A bullet ripped through the back wall of the carriage, smashing into the front, sending an explosion of splinters onto the women. Mabry fired again. Crack! The buggy door's latch broke loose from its brass clasp. Mabry swung out away from the coach, nearly tumbling to his death under the spinning wheels. Thump! A bullet hit Mabry high on his right shoulder. His Colt flew from his hand, banging against the rear wheel before being catapulted into the brush. Mabry began to fall out the open door. One of the women grabbed his belt with both hands, Mabry's weight nearly pulled her out the door before the coach rocked back, tossing both onto the floor. Boom! Another blast from the ten-gauge sent another bandit sprawling into sage and cactus along the trail's edge. The last bandit pulled up on his reins and slowed as Levi snapped the team's reins, pushing the horses to their limit.

"Whoa! Levi! That got 'em! Only one left and he give up! Slow 'em down!" Montana shouted to his partner.

Levi pulled up, bringing the team back to a steady gallop. He stood and looked behind, needing to see for himself the attack was over. Mabry pulled himself and savior back into the carriage, drawing the door shut. A blotch on his tan coat grew red with blood.

"Everyone okay in there?" Levi shouted to the carriage's occupants.

"No! Mr. Mabry is hurt!" Betsy Phillips reported.

"Whoa!" Levi called to the team pulling back hard on the reins now. The coach came to a stop. Montana kept a close watch down the trail with two new shells locked and loaded in the ten-gauge. Levi jumped down from his driver's perch and checked his passengers. The women had reclaimed their seats, and Betsy used her scarf to bandage Mabry's wound.

"I'll be all right, driver," Mabry announced without taking his eyes off his pretty nurse.

Levi grinned, turned, and spit a stream of brown juice into a clump of bunch grass. "I reckon you will!" Levi agreed.

"What's goin' on down there?" Montana Jones shouted.

"This young feller took one in the shoulder, but he's in good hands!" Levi cackled back to his partner.

"Let's keep a move on, Levi. I don't like that there's one left back there," the stocky shotgun rider ordered.

"Yes, sir! I'll keep it slow and let the horses recover a bit," Levi stated.

Before jumping back into the driver's seat, Levi cut a length of rope and tied the door closed.

"Driver, I lost my gun back there," Mabry announced.

"Sorry 'bout that, fella, ain't goin' back to fetch it, though," Levi stated.

"Ain't no man puttin' his hands on me," one of the women said pulling a two-barrel Derringer from her carpet bag.

Everyone paused to look at the stoic woman seated straight and looking forward at no one in particular.

"Yes, ma'am," Levi said then headed back to the team.

After a quick check of the hames and harnesses, the Red River coach was back en route to Range.

"Thank you, kindly, ma'am," Mabry offered to Betsy, who smiled and nodded in return. "What's taking you to Range?" Mabry asked.

"My uncle Redmond is the doctor there. I'm going to help him," Betsy advised. "What about you?" Betsy asked.

"I'm on my way to Wichita Falls. I plan on opening a hardware store there," Mabry stated.

"Oh," Betsy answered in a low voice, turning her gaze to the floor of the rolling coach.

"I wonder if Range could use a hardware store," Mabry said aloud, looking out the window.

"My uncle says the town is growing faster than it can keep up," Betsy offered with a bright red-lipped smile.

The other two women said nothing, one casting her own bright smile at the banter between the two young people, the other keeping a dark frown clutching her Derringer.

Montana joined Levi back on the top bench watching the trail disappear behind them. The team had recovered, their hooves churning up the trail leaving a red, dusty cloud behind the coach long after it had moved down the path.

"I don't like it, Levi. Damn unfriendlies gettin' mighty brave along the trail," Montana said.

"Yep. Too darn close to that blasted river!" Levi answered.

"Best see what Mr. Benson gonna do about it," Montana added.

"What we need in these parts is the army," Levi suggested.

"I'll take a couple a good gunslingers on the right side of the law," Montana mumbled under a bushy mustache.

"That'd be good too. Ain't many of them around, though!" Levi shouted snapping the reins. Just as the team picked up the pace, the coach started yawing to the left. Two of the horses stumbled, sparking Levi to rip back on the reins. "Whoa! Whoa!"

"What is it?" Montana asked, his eyes darting in all four directions.

Levi jumped down from his teamster perch and let out a sigh. "Damn. Front wheel's busted," Levi announced.

"What is it?" Betsy Phillips asked, leaning half out the coach's window.

"Well, ma'am, we've got us a pack a trouble. The felloes split, hub band cut, and two spokes are snapped. Looks like we took a bullet or two in the wheel," Levi reported.

"Ya reckon we can make it to Range?" Montana asked, joining Levi at the damaged wheel.

Levi peered at the go around and stroked his wiry beard for a good while before speaking. "Can't risk it with three women on board. Better turn back for Riverbend. We can return before dark, get repairs in the morning, then head for Range," Levi suggested.

"We'll lose a day," Montana stated the obvious.

"Yeppers but look at the bright side. We might find that young feller's pistol along the way!" Levi cackled before slapping his shotgun rider on the back, sending a puff of dust into the air. Levi slowly turned the coach around and headed back to where they started, nursing the battered wheel along the way.

CHAPTER 9

WES PAYNE – FORT GRIFFIN

The clear night sky hosted an endless splash of stars that glowed like sparks from a blacksmith's hammer. A cold wind swept at the back of Wes as he walked Ringo toward Fort Griffin. A giant tumbleweed raced past on its way into oblivion when Wes stopped to gaze upon the Flat. The makeshift settlement of shacks, wood-frame huts and tents, had grown since his last visit to the Fort. Lantern light shone brightly from a smattering of structures, while smoke billowed up from countless chimneys. Not an official settlement or town, the Flat grew from settlers, nomads, and weary homeless voyagers that stopped at the Fort, then realized they had nowhere else to go. The soldiers assigned to Fort Griffin found many of its inhabitants to be unruly, and at times a nuisance, as they traveled to and from the Fort. That didn't stop curious soldiers from frequenting a few of the establishments during off-duty hours. It also served as a stopping-point for cattle drives making their way north from the southern ranches. This clientele promoted the development of saloons and bawdy houses, along with the lurid activity that was often associated with them.

On this night, the activity appeared to be minimal as the frigid temperature kept the locals inside. Wes reined Ringo to the right, giving a wide berth around the area. He had no use for anything the Flat had to offer tonight. A short time later, Wes paused at the front gate of the Fort and checked in with the guard post. Satisfied there was no news, he headed over to the Ranger station doorway where Dan Wheeler sat with his battered boots propped up on a water barrel and his head tucked low inside the collar of his weathered wool coat. Ranger Wheeler's stealth position was only given away by the small dot of fire at the end of his cigarette. At the order of the post commander, the front entrance of the Ranger station was always kept dark.

"That you, Payne?" Wheeler asked, not moving a muscle.

"It is," Wes answered as he swung down from Ringo.

"Wasn't sure until I seen that white horse a 'yers," Wheeler admitted as he dropped his boots from the barrel, then stood to shake Wes's hand. "Good to have ya back. We're runnin a little short these days."

"Where is everybody?" Wes asked.

"Captain Tobias let out a few days back for San Antonio with four Rangers. Guessin' they havin' a little trouble with some Mexican banditos. A couple others headed out west lookin' fer a killer."

"Who's running the post?" Wes asked.

"Charlie Franklin's in charge for now. Heard we got another assignment from the Governor, just don't know what."

"Franklin awake?" Wes asked, not pausing for an answer.

Wes entered the moderate Ranger post where Captain Charlie Franklin read at his desk. Franklin looked up and smiled as Wes approached.

"Good to see you, Payne. Got the telegraph about Calhoun," Franklin advised.

"Yeah, sorry about that, sir. Never thought somethin' like that would happen," said Wes.

Franklin waved his hand. "Don't matter. I got more urgent things to deal with. One of which involves you."

"Oh?" Wes asked, surprised.

"I know it's late but might as well tell you now than wait until morning."

"Sure enough," Wes agreed pulling up a chair to the rickety table passing for a desk.

Franklin shuffled several stacks of paper, then pushed each to the side before he settled on one letter in particular. "This-here is right from Governor Hubbard," Franklin advised. "I got word two days ago that Bill Wallaby was killed in a town up on the Red River border. He was heading back from Texarkana and decided to follow the river for a bit since he knew of the border raids. He stopped in a town called Range for a couple of days, tangled with a raiding party, and got killed. The people sent a telegram to our headquarters. About the same time, Hubbard's office got a letter signed by every business owner in the town asking for help with the raids. Seems they're getting worse. There's talk of women being kidnapped and killed. The order came down earlier today to send a couple of Rangers up that way. Problem is, I don't have a couple. I just have you, and if you hadn't come back to us when ya did, I wouldn't have you. So, here it is. I need you to go up there and meet up with a U.S. Deputy Marshal who's been dispatched from Fort Smith. It's not enough, but at least there will be two of ya."

Wes sat quietly and listened carefully to Franklin. After Franklin paused, Wes didn't immediately respond. His mind raced to formulate a plan of action and route to the border.

Franklin remained silent as Wes decided on a plan.

"Do we know who the Marshal is?" Wes asked, finally breaking the silence.

"Nope, Marshal Upham didn't give a name, just that he was sending one deputy due to a shortage of men. Looks like they're in the same situation we are. Not enough men to go around. I'd like you to leave in the morning. That okay? You deserve a couple days off, but I'm in a fix right now with this letter from the Governor and all," Franklin explained.

"Yes, sir. No problem. I'll leave first thing after sunup." Wes stood, and turned to leave.

"Wes, stop over to the Fort for provisions. I've already cleared it with Colonel Dunley," Franklin ordered his lone Ranger.

"Yes, sir. I'll only need some hard tack and extra ammunition," Wes advised before heading out into the cold night. *Weren't the nuns heading to a town called Range? I wonder if there's any chance the Marshal's office sent Danner? Could I be that lucky,* Wes thought with a grin. As he walked, he clenched his hands into fists, then repeated the process several times to keep his hands loose. He didn't want them seizing up now. He looked down at Wheeler watching him.

"What'd Captain Franklin want, Wes?" Wheeler asked from his seat on the porch.

"Sending me up to the border to check on a town."

"The same town Wallaby got killed in?"

"Yep, that's the one. Range. What are you up to these days, Wheeler?"

"They got me sittin' on the Flat. Damn place needs a Marshal or Sheriff or somethin'. Too many problems down there, so I ain't gettin' no assignment until further notice," Wheeler grunted slamming his cigarette into the wooden planks.

"Enjoy it while you can," Wes offered the disgruntled Ranger.

"Buffalo chips! I ought to be goin' with you!" Wheeler shouted before heading to the bunkhouse for the night.

Wes untied Ringo, swung up into the saddle, and sat for a moment gazing up at the star-filled sky. A cold breeze swept by causing him to shiver. Just as he pulled on the rein, a sharp pain fired through his right hand. He quickly let go, grabbing at the rein with his other hand, but it was too late. The fingers on his right hand curled into a grotesque-looking claw. He couldn't move his fingers, and the pain in the back of his hand crept down each finger like a coyote stalking its prey. Wes looked over at the post door and made sure Franklin hadn't come out and seen him in distress. He closed his eyes, grit his teeth, and waited for the episode to subside. Ever since the banditos had nailed him to the barn down in Presidio, his damaged hands had caused him grief. The excruciating pain and spasm had started months ago, and with each attack, it took a little longer to pass.

Come on! Open! Damn it open! He thought. He tried to pull back on his curved fingers to no avail. The pain moved up into his wrist and to his fingertips. He took deep breaths, rubbing his hand, trying anything to relieve the pain. Nothing worked. Nothing but time. After several minutes, the pain began to drift away, and his fingers unfurled to their normal position. He flexed his fingers back and forth many times until he convinced himself that the episode had passed. He realized he was breathing hard and sweating profusely. He sighed and leaned back in the saddle.

"Damn, Ringo, that was a bad one, partner." He tapped his spurs and started out to a group of cypress trees not far from the post. He preferred to sleep out under the stars rather than in the bunkhouse, even on a cold night like this one.

A short ride later, he and Ringo were set for the night. He'd started a small fire and put his bedroll close to the flames to combat the cold. Leaning back against his saddle, he thought about Six Shot, the Thornton ranch, and Canyon Creek. With any luck at all, he'd meet Danner in Range.

CHAPTER 10

RACHEL BRENNEN – CANYON CREEK

Rachel stepped out of the hot kitchen and walked out to the sitting area in the front of the Sundown. She tied her long, auburn hair back, then settled back into one of the cowhide chairs, and closed her eyes to rest. She allowed images of Chance's father to float through her mind. She replayed the few times he allowed himself to be gentle, as well as the times he put up his gruff façade as a form of self-protection. She chose to embrace whichever personality traits he displayed, because all of them endeared him to her more.

Back when she had first met him, she'd decided then and there to ignore the vast difference in their ages, although she was often not-so-subtly reminded of his advanced years by the ladies in town, and by Ben himself. "If I were only younger," he used to say when tender moments between them moved toward intimacy. Her thoughts drifted to Danner and the tenderness he displayed when breaking the news of Ben's death to her. Danner possessed many of the same qualities as Ben, she mused.

"Someone's thinking pleasant thoughts," Emily Carson noticed as she fell back into the matching chair opposite Rachel, attempting to tuck her steam-soaked hair behind her ears.

Rachel opened her eyes, pulled from her reverie.

"I thought I'd find you out here," Emily said through a wide smile.

"Just taking a few minutes before we cleanup for the night," Rachel answered.

"How was your visit with Ben's son earlier?" Emily asked.

"Very pleasant. He's very much like his father. He turned in rather early, though," Rachel offered with a frown.

"Turned in early? It's a little strange for such a young man to call it an early night, isn't it?" Emily asked.

"Well, I guess he's not the type to spend all night gambling and drinking in a saloon," Rachel answered.

"He's not like his father in that regard," Emily casually noted.

Rachel said nothing; she simply smiled at the offhanded remark and looked at her friend, whom she knew meant well.

"The girls are finishing up in the kitchen. A bunch of ruffians from that new Knox Ranch came in this evening. They all finally left," Emily reported, her voice tired.

"Knox Ranch? Isn't that the new name of Mr. Coleman's place?" Rachel asked.

"That's what Stewart told me. He said some wealthy fellow named Gilford Knox bought it, and a lot of land around it. Says Mr. Knox wants to buy up everything he can. You know, he's the one building that new hotel on the other end of town," Emily advised.

"I wasn't sure it was him. Has anyone met Mr. Knox?" Rachel asked, filing away the information about a potential competitor.

"I don't know, but if his men are an example of how he is, I have no interest in meeting the man," Emily proclaimed.

"What do you mean?" Rachel asked.

"His men come into town, get drunk, and pick fights all the time. They don't want to pay for their food and drink. Two of them broke dishes tonight," Emily explained as she shook her head.

"Why didn't you come and get me? I would've helped you with them. Sounds like they were a handful," Rachel said.

"Honey, all you've been doing these last few months is working yourself to death. You needed the break."

"It was lovely having some time to myself, to think," Rachel mused almost to herself.

"Anyone with eyes can see how worn out you are. Why don't you use some of that money Ben left you and hire a full-time helper for around here?" Emily suggested, perking up at her own idea.

"We've had this talk before, Emily."

"Please. That money is yours to do with what you will without feeling guilty about it!" Emily stated firmly, her dark hair falling back onto her face.

Rachel thought it over more than she'd allowed herself in a long while. *It would be good use of the money, and I sure could use the help*, Rachel thought to herself. After a few moments, Rachel stood and straightened her dress.

"What are you going to do?" Emily asked.

"It's settled. I'm going to ask Ben if he'd mind if I use the money," Rachel said putting her hands on her hips and tilting her head.

"I thought you said he turned in for the night?" Emily grinned wickedly.

"I'm sure such a young man wouldn't be asleep yet," Rachel said, allowing herself a giggle.

"Now, that's my girl!" Emily boasted.

As Rachel slowly walked up the staircase, she used the extra time to build up her confidence. *What was she thinking going to a man's room alone at night?* She paused at Chance's door and took a deep breath. Her knock was nothing more than a nervous tap.

"Who's there?"

"It's Rachel. I'm very sorry to bother you, but I–"

"Just a moment!" Chance called out from behind the door.

Rachel nervously looked up and down the hall, praying no one would look out and see her. The door swung open, with Chance standing in the threshold clutching an open book to his chest.

"Yes, ma'am? Is there something wrong?" Chance asked, peeking cautiously up and down the hallway.

Rachel's confidence wavered. "I'm terribly sorry to disrupt your reading," she said, looking down at the book in Chance's hand.

"Not at all. Have you read *The Adventures of Tom Sawyer*?" Chance asked, holding up the book for closer inspection.

"No, I haven't read a book since my husband passed. I've not had the time trying to keep the hotel and all," Rachel admitted.

"I'm almost finished. I have to admit, I don't know all the words, but the things Tom and his friend Huckleberry Finn get into are pretty interesting," Chance said with a grin. "If I can finish it tonight, I'll be glad to leave it for you if you like?" Chance added.

"That would be wonderful. It will force me to take the time to start reading again," Rachel gushed.

"What was it you wanted?" Chance asked.

"Oh, my! I almost forgot!" Rachel exclaimed, cupping her hand over her mouth to muffle her shout. She exhaled, and took a step back, trying to calm her sudden nerves.

"I was wondering if you'd mind if I used some of the money your father left me to hire a helper for the hotel?" Rachel blurted out, her voice wavering.

Chance didn't hesitate. "I think that's a fine idea. I bet my father would feel the same. That would give you more time to read," He replied with a faint smile.

Rachel looked into Chance's kind eyes and thought for a moment that Ben, senior stood in front of her once more. It unsettled her, as if his ghost was somehow present, offering his assent.

"Thank you," Rachel said as she pulled herself together. "I'll leave you to finish that book." She smiled awkwardly to Chance and hurried toward the staircase. Before descending, Rachel paused at the top of the staircase and looked back down the hallway. She heard Chance's door click closed. A feeling of contentment cascaded over her. Her skin tingled and she suddenly felt weightless. She paused to examine her emotions. Was Ben fueling her feelings or his young son? For a moment, her thoughts collided. She wasn't sure. Of course, it was Ben. His son was nearly half her age. Still? She smiled and floated down the staircase. *Ben would be proud of how thoughtful his son turned out to be*, she thought.

CHAPTER 11

HARRY NOLEN – EN ROUTE TO RANGE

Deacon David had no idea how fortunate he was to have found Harry Nolen to guide he and the nuns to Range. The Deacon learned that Nolen had been one of the former Confederate soldiers who decided to avoid Reconstruction and move west after the war. Supposedly, Nolen had packed up his family and joined a wagon train headed for California from the wreckage of Atlanta with dreams of a new life. Those dreams ended in Texas on the banks of the Red River when his wife and daughter fell ill and ultimately died, leaving him alone at the stopping-point that would become the town of Range. Now, years later, Nolen had returned, now assisting the Deacon and Sisters back to the banks of the Red River.

The Deacon and nuns had been directed by the Bishop in Galveston to expand the Catholic faith into the west, with plans to build a church, school, and convent while spreading the word of the Good Book. Nolen admitted to the Deacon that he had lost faith after the deaths of his wife and daughter, and he didn't share their dream. Nolen made it clear he was only interested in getting paid for services rendered, which included his knowledge of Range and the trail that led to it.

Nolen's skepticism of their religious plans for Range, and his belief they wouldn't last very long before giving up, was no secret to his paying clients. The Deacon snapped the old leather reins, keeping the team moving with Nolen's lead wagon. Nolen pushed on in the lead wagon, rolling and rocking back and forth, as its wobbly wheels passed over uneven ground and rock. The two nuns riding with Nolen kept quiet, never complaining or commenting on the journey. Nolen didn't attempt to engage in conversation, probably not knowing what to say to nuns, anyway. After a couple of hours in silence, Nolen finally spoke up. "So Sister, why ya'll goin' all the way up to Range again?" Nolen politely asked.

"As we've said, Mr. Nolen, we're on a mission to spread the Good Word all over Texas. Our Bishop gave the order for us to bring the Catholic Church to the settlements. We've already been quite successful, you know," Sister Teresa advised her driver. Sister Teresa was a diminutive older woman approaching sixty, with serious gray eyes framed by deep lines making it appear that she was always deep in thought.

"Well, I'm just sayin' they're lots of heathens in these parts, and they don't take kindly to any Bible-thumpers," Nolen offered in between spits of tobacco juice.

"They're all God's children," Sister Teresa advised her doubting cowboy as dusk began to creep onto the trail, pulling the bright light of day with it.

Nolen kept his wagon centered in the ruts of the track, trying his best to keep the wheels from breaking down again. He had already repaired two of them and didn't want a third. As he reined his team to the left moving around a bend in the trail, he brought the carriage to an abrupt halt. "Whoa!" he called to out pulling hard on the reins. Nolen peered down the trail to a band of Indians mounted on horseback blocking the path.

"What is it, Mr. Nolen?" Sister Teresa asked poking her head out from under the canvass bonnet.

"Get back inside Sister and keep quiet. Got Injuns down the trail,"

Nolen reported, his voice tense. He pulled back on the brake handle then slowly slid down from his bench and stopped the second wagon keeping a keen eye on Indians. "Sister, pull this wagon up next to mine and stop. Then get inside and don't you come out." He ordered the same from the next two wagon drivers.

The fourth, and final wagon's driver, Jason Dean, a well-traveled young man with a boyish face, didn't need direction. "I see 'em, Nolen," Dean called down from his perch. He pulled his wagon up next to the third and stopped. Dean slowly stepped down waving at the two nuns inside his wagon to stay inside. "What'd ya think?" Dean asked.

Nolen scratched his beard. "I don't rightly know. Haven't had much Injun trouble lately. Heard about a few small raids though. Randall stage was hit a couple times a few months back, but I ain't heard nuthin' since. They ain't move in, just sittin' there," Nolen observed.

"Can't outrun 'em. Best we stay put and see if they move on," Dean offered.

"Sure enough," Nolen agreed skeptically.

Just as Nolen stepped up onto the Deacon's wagon, he noticed the Indians had begun to approach their caravan.

"Everybody stay inside your wagons!" Nolen ordered reaching under the wagon's jockey box for his double-barreled shotgun. Dean pulled his Winchester out at the same time.

Nolen walked to the front of the wagons and waited in the middle of the trail. Nolen counted nine Indians armed with both bows and rifles. They slowly walked their horses up to Nolen and stopped. Nolen swallowed hard. He felt his face begin to sweat. Dean carefully wiped his brow with a shaking wrist. Deacon David stayed quiet. He'd never met Indians outside the reservations. He closed his eyes, his mouth silently moving in prayer.

"Hello," Nolen offered, waving his hand in a wide arc.

None of the Indians responded. The brave at the front, a young muscular man with bronze skin and long coal black hair, remained mounted on his pony, and moved forward. He slowly walked his horse around the wagons, looking inside each opening. No one made a sound. The sister's heads were bowed in prayer. The Indian's horses hoof clapped against the tough ground.

After circling around the wagons, the Indian returned to Nolen and looked down on the wagon boss. His chiseled face and dark eyes showed no expression. He carried a lance adorned in feathers of the eagle and hawk. Two of the accompanying Indian's restless horses snorted and tamped their hooves. No words were spoken. Nolen and Dean kept their hands away from their guns and stood still, knowing the Indian leader was deciding their fate. Without a sound, the leader raised his lance, pointed it away from the trail and began to ride off. His band of warriors silently followed. Nolen and Dean waited until the last brave disappeared into the brush before they chose to move back to the wagons.

"Whew!" Nolen exclaimed, releasing all air from his lungs.

Dean let out an equally large sigh. "We're lucky today," he added.

"Let's get goin'" Nolen called back to the wagon drivers, eager to get back on the move. Moments later, the caravan was back in motion, wheels clanging against the rock and dried bunch grass that littered the trail.

"What did those Indians want?" Sister Teresa finally asked Nolen as she peered out suspiciously from the canvas.

"I'm not sure Sister. I ain't never seen Injuns act like that before. I reckon they decided we weren't worth the trouble."

"I thought the Indians were all on the reservations now," Sister Teresa mused.

"No, ma'am. Most have, but some refused to go, and they been cause'n some trouble here and there. Maybe that chief never seen no nuns before!" Nolen hooted and laughed. Just to be sure, he looked behind him as he snapped the reins to pick up the pace, unwilling to try his luck any further.

Seemingly satisfied with the answer, Sister Teresa nodded. "How long before we reach Range?" She asked.

"Should be there in less than an hour, Sister. Long as we don't git any more visits like that one!"

The four wagons made their way down the winding path toward Range. Unbeknownst to the travelers, a raiding party of a different kind had just crossed the Red River on its own mission.

CHAPTER 12

CRAZY BILL JORDAN – RANGE

Translucent clouds veiled the evening sun as it continued its western decent when the first of the outlaws' horses' hooves splashed into the Red River's murky crimson water. Crazy Bill Jordan, a young outlaw whose reckless actions were evidenced by the scars on his face, led five other brigands into the river in a single file. They moved deliberately so as not to find a drop-off that would cause a ruckus and alert anyone to their presence. Jordan cut a path to the far bank, then waited for his fellow outlaws to join him. One by one, each found dry land on the river's southern boundary.

Having ridden through Range the night before, Crazy Bill knew precisely how to enter and what buildings to attack first. He'd briefed his gang with the plan of hitting Range from the west, through the holding pens onto the main street, where each man would take a building, and relieve its proprietor of his cash. As the first man, Crazy Bill would ride completely through town and take the livery stable, which sat on the far east end of town. The next man would take the telegraph office, then next the store, next the stage office, feed store, and finally, the last man would hit the boarding house. The plan was for all of them to escape through the east end into the valley, and return to the river, where they would cross safely into the Indian

Territory. The six bandits gathered near the holding pens, then at Crazy Bill's order, they'd make their charge. They patiently waited for the crow's wings of darkness to ascend upon Range.

Several hours later, Crazy Bill carefully watched his prey from the edge of town like a hawk circling overhead. He had no idea Mrs. Mary Fields had received a telegram from the Ursuline Sisters of the Incarnate Word four days prior and had just finished preparing six rooms for the pending arrival. She swept the front porch of her beloved boarding house, apparently wanting to make a good impression on the new visitors. Harold Baker, the Red River Stage office operator, prepared departure of the evening coach right on schedule. The general store, telegraph office, and livery stable were all bustling with activity, as was the Red Dirt Saloon.

Waiting no longer, Crazy Bill drew his gun and spurred his horse, shattering the peaceful scene in front of him. "Let's Go!" He yelled. The six bandits brought their horses to a full run behind him. Crazy Bill cleared the pens and sped past Mrs. Fields, who dropped her broom and ran into the boarding house. Two men sitting outside the barbershop turned and ran down the wooden walkway, then darted into the ally next to the store. Brody Brown ran out of his feed store when he heard the commotion. The fifth outlaw swung down from his horse and fired one shot hitting Brown, sending him onto the red dirt street. The bandit rushed past Brown's body into the store. The last bandit jumped down and hurried into the boarding house where Mrs. Fields cowered in the corner of the front room.

"Where's the cash box?" the bandit yelled at the frightened woman. She said nothing.

"Where the hell is the cash box?"

Crack! Crack! Two bullets shattered a mirror on the wall over the terrified woman's head. Fragments rained down on her as she covered her head with her hands and began to cry. Mrs. Fields managed enough strength to point toward the drawer behind a small desk. The bandit ripped the drawer from its rails, then snatched the small wooden box, and ran toward the front door firing two shots over her head.

The same scene played out in the general store where customers stood against the wall with their arms raised, watching the bandits clean out the cash from the register. Gunshots echoed up and down the street as the telegraph office and livery stable were relieved of their cash boxes. Glass shattered in front of the hotel as well as from Doc Phillips' office.

The blacksmith, Belton Tanner, grabbed his Winchester and fired at Crazy Bill as he ran from the livery stable to his horse. Crazy Bill leapt onto his horse, firing back at the big blacksmith, hitting slabs of iron hanging from the roof beams. Tanner fired again, this time putting a bullet through Crazy Bill's leg, and another into his horse. Bill and the horse both fell, but a second bandit raced past, having shot up the telegraph office. Bill swung up onto his outlaw partner's horse and fled past the livery stable out of Tanner's sight. The four remaining outlaws kicked their horses with everything they had, charging down Main Street randomly firing at running people and buildings. Tanner shouldered his rifle and carefully took aim at the last bandit. Crack! The bullet hit its mark sending the last outlaw into the street.

A moment later the raiders were gone. Redmond Philips, Range's doctor, rushed into the street, medical bag in hand. Quickly he ran to Brody Brown where he found the feed store owner dead. Hearing Mrs. Fields had been wounded, he hurried to the boarding house to attend to her. Tanner stood over the bandit he'd killed and watched the other five race through the valley then cross the river east of town.

CHAPTER 13

LUXTON DANNER – EN ROUTE TO RANGE

A rooster crowed in the distance announcing dawn's arrival. The light of day had ushered in cold air confirmed by the sight of trumpet-shaped mist exhaling through the horses' nostrils and the men's breath. Anxious to leave, Danner had already washed, shaved, and eaten. Several deputies loitered about in the courtyard, most waiting for their guards and jail wagons to be assigned. He wouldn't need those accessories on this trip. He had packed the night before and already secured a second horse last night before turning in. Thankfully, his night was free of the nightmares that regularly interrupted his sleep. He felt good for a change. Deputy Bass Reeves sat on a bench eating a large piece of cornbread.

"You're one lucky man, Bass! Mrs. Reeves always takes care of you!" Danner called to the lawman.

Unable to speak with his mouth full of cornbread, Reeves smiled and nodded at Danner as he walked past.

"Hear you got a special assignment, Danner!" Another deputy yelled from across the yard.

Danner said nothing, just waved and made his way to the barn, where his sixteen-hand tall bay horse Bullet was already saddled and waiting. He checked the saddle and pack carefully. Once satisfied, he stepped up into the stirrup hanging off Bullet, and settled into the saddle. He'd never named his horse before but got the idea from Wes Payne while in Six Shot. If Wes had Ringo, then he could have Bullet. Danner tapped his spurs on Bullet's sides and rode out of the barn, pack horse in tow. As he cleared Fort Smith's stable doors into the crisp morning air, he was greeted with shouts of encouragement. "I'm not sure when I'll be back, so use my stall if you need to," Danner instructed the stable keeper. Weather permitting, Danner calculated he could cover about 30 to 40 miles a day, despite the second horse, extra provisions, and ammunition, snaking his way along the river's edge. That would mean he'd reach Range in about ten days barring any unforeseen difficulties.

After a few hours, he came to a wide valley covered in a thick layer of dense fog. The sky darkened with heavy clouds, and the air became colder than it had been the past week. The low-lying valley along with the lack of sun had made the perfect recipe of dense fog. Danner paused at the valley's edge. The fog began at ground level and stretched to the top of the tree line. It swirled and moved as if mixing in a butter churn. The fog didn't bother Danner, but the possibilities of uninvited guests did. He remembered the Indian attack on him, Wes, and Coleman while returning to the Thornton ranch, and he didn't rule out the possibility of another. Along with the raiding parties working the river's banks, he figured he would be a prime target if detected.

"Well, Bullet, we best not be detected then," he said aloud before spurring his equine partner onward into the condensed mist. Once inside the grounded clouds, he found he could still see the trail for about two to three horse-lengths ahead. He kept Bullet at a careful walk, doing his best to sense any lurking danger. He also knew that if his senses failed, Bullet's would certainly not. As he made his way across the belly of the valley, water droplets fell freely from the brim of his hat and rolled down the surface of his oilskin coat.

After a while, the mist became so dense, he and Bullet glistened with moisture. Finally, after a solid-hour ride, the mist faded away and his visibility improved. He saw the edge of the valley ahead. The terrain rose, and with each step, the gray blanket lifted its cover until he was into clear space, splitting the tree line on the beaten path. Danner recalled this stretch of the trail appeared more like a road with high trees on each side, forming forest walls.

Now in the clear, Danner picked up the pace and moved briskly, when he heard what sounded like the clangs of a buckboard up ahead. After a moment of nothing but the chirping of birds, he heard the sound of a wheel bottom out in a dip.

"No doubt about it now, Bullet. We have company," Danner whispered aloud, patting his partner's neck. He kept Bullet at a vigorous pace, knowing he'd catch the slower moving buckboard quickly enough. Soon, the wooden vehicle was in plain sight. Danner strained to see a wagon, driven by a man with a woman beside him. The heads of two children bobbed in the back, in between an array of items tied down, with what looked like a spider's web of rope.

The man and woman looked back, speaking rapidly to one another. The young boy in the rear yelled to his father, announcing Danner's presence. The man pulled his two-horse wagon over to the side of the trail, waiting for Danner's arrival. The man remained in his seat, but moved around, looking back several times, obviously nervous of meeting a stranger in such a desolate place. Recognizing their discomfort with his visit, Danner called out in an attempt to put the couple at ease.

"Hello!" Danner called as he approached the wagon on the left. Both children answered, before their mother could order them to stay silent. The man stood on the footrest and turned to greet Danner.

"Good afternoon, sir," the gentleman offered removing his hat.

"Good afternoon. My name's Luxton Danner. I'm a United States Deputy Marshal on my way to Texas. Who might you be?"

The man leaned over and shook Danner's hand. "I'm Zale Everett, this is my wife Mary, and my children, Debra and Daniel. I'm mighty glad to meet a deputy Marshal out here. I was afraid you might not be friendly," Everett admitted.

Danner took a moment to examine his new-found family of four. Zale was a thin man with deep lines traversing across his forehead and a short, well-groomed beard. His wife had big round eyes and a pale face to match, with her hair tucked up underneath a bonnet that had many years wear on it. The wagon was older but appeared to be in good repair.

"What ya'll doing out this way?" Danner asked.

"We're headed to Oneida, Texas. My brother lives there and offered me a job. Any chance you're going that far?"

"No sir, sorry. I'm working my way to a town on the Red River called Range. You folks plan on following the river?"

"Yes, sir, I reckon that'd be the easiest way. Something wrong?"

Danner looked at the man's wife and children. "Can I get you to join me up in front of your wagon for a spell?" Danner asked.

Everett jumped down from his perch and walked far enough away from his family in order to have a private talk.

Danner followed, and slid off Bullet. "I don't want to alarm your family, but there's been a lot of outlaw activity along the river. That's why I'm headin' this way. It's mighty dangerous for a single family out here," Danner advised.

"Yes, sir, I heard about that back in Jonesboro. We talked about it, but there ain't nothing back there for us. Our house burned down in the court building fire last year, and I ain't had no luck there. We finally decided to give Texas a try," Everett explained.

Danner looked back at the man's wife and children shaking his head. "I'd like to ride with you, but I'm expected in Range in ten or so days. I'm moving too fast for you to keep up in a loaded-down wagon. There's a few small towns along the way. I'd recommend you stay in them at night and only travel during the day. If you find anyone else heading west, join up with them. Range will be the first big town you'll come to. I'm sure you'll find other folks heading toward Oneida from there. Are you armed?"

"Yes, sir, I've a shotgun and Winchester under the bench. If need be, Mary can handle a pistol."

"All right. I'll ride along for a bit then I'll need to move on ahead. That okay with you?"

"Yes, sir, much obliged!" Everett exclaimed, obviously relieved.

Danner shook Everett's hand then jumped back up on Bullet. "I'll ride a little ahead. I'll stay with you until we reach Acworth," Danner advised, then started down the trail.

Everett snapped the reins and continued on telling his wife they had an escort to the next town. Danner remained with his buckboard family the rest of the day hoping not to see anyone else friend or foe. He didn't particularly like being responsible for a family. The good news was he figured they'd be in Acworth by sundown. Then he could move on with a clear conscience.

CHAPTER 14

WES PAYNE – BUFFALO GAP

Wes rode up to the Sheriff's office and tied Ringo to a post around on the side. He opened the new front door, and found his buddy Dan Kirby stacking firewood in the back room. "Hello Dan," Wes greeted the Sheriff of Buffalo Gap.

"Well, Ranger Payne, you're back here awfully fast. What do I owe the honor?" Kirby asked, shaking Wes's hand.

"On my way to the border along the river. Final stop is that town called Range. I needed to come back and see the gunsmith before I left," Wes answered, taking a seat next to Kirby's desk.

Kirby walked around and took his seat behind the desk.

"Range, huh. Ain't that the town those nuns were headin' to?" Kirby asked.

"That's the one. All kinds of problems up there, I guess. Hubbard got a letter or two, so I'm on the way to meet up with a U.S. Marshal sent from Fort Smith."

"U.S. Marshal, eh? Hmmm, must be big trouble, I reckon, sending both a Ranger and Marshal. Those nuns have anything to do with it?" Kirby asked with a grin.

"I don't know if they even made it or not. No, those damn bandits are running ram shod along the river. Once we heard Wallaby was killed, we didn't need an order from the Governor," Wes explained.

"How long you stayin'," Kirby asked.

"Just tonight. I got to hightail it double-quick. Thought I'd grab some grub over at the hotel and sleep in a bed for a change," Wes answered.

Kirby leaned his head back and laughed. "That's right, you do have a thing for Mrs. Gentry!"

"The woman can cook like no other," Wes quipped, cracking a facetious smile.

"I know, I know, but it helps that she's easy on the eyes, too," Kirby goaded his friend.

"Well, that don't matter none. 'Ole Amos scares me!" Wes waggishly declared, then stood to leave. "And don't be cause'n no trouble just because I'm in town," Wes instructed Kirby.

"As I recall, you're the one who brought trouble the last time you were here, Ranger Payne," Kirby chuckled. "Have a good dinner. Maybe I'll stop by later tonight. Just to make sure Mrs. Gentry is okay," Kirby laughed again, slapping Wes on the back, half pushing him out the door.

Wes paused, looking at the bullet-riddled building. Kirby was right. He'd brought plenty of trouble with him on his last visit. The windows were still boarded up, and the front door was a patchwork of mismatched lumber. He walked Ringo over to the stable, then headed for the Bison Hotel for a steak and potato dinner. Halfway to his destination, he heard footsteps quickly clicking along the boardwalk behind him.

"Good evening, Mr. Payne," a female admirer called out amongst giggles from two other ladies, all of whom were smartly dressed in white, lace-lined, dark-colored satin dresses for the evening.

Wes stopped and removed his hat. "Good evening, ladies," he sung in a drawn-out greeting.

"You going to come see us tonight?" A lady asked with an an exaggerated curtsey.

"I don't know if I'll have the time," Wes answered.

"Oh, you'll have the time, Mr. Payne, but will you have the energy?" The lady asked, brushing Wes's face with a feather as she and her companions hurried past him on their way to the Split Rail Saloon.

Wes laughed loudly, then redirected his focus on dinner. He strolled into the bustling hotel, immediately engulfed with the aroma of baked goods, fried steak, and other delectable smells he couldn't quite identify, but made his stomach grumble nonetheless. The dining room appeared to be full, with Annette Gentry hurrying from table to table. Wes paused under the big archway and removed his hat. Annette stopped when she saw him. She quickly wiped her hands on her draggled apron and rushed over pushing long locks of light brown hair back behind her ears.

"Good evening, Wes. How nice to see you back here so soon," she offered.

"Nice to see you, ma'am. Any chance I can get a table?" he asked.

"Of course, you can. Follow me," she ordered. Annette turned and made her way through the gauntlet of tables and customers back into the kitchen entrance. Wes couldn't help but watch his hostess as she seemed to move in one fluid motion as the bottom of her brown print dress swayed back and forth. Along the wall was a narrow table for two.

"Right here, Wes," she waved her hand over the empty table. "Coffee, steak, and potato?" she asked, then hurried on into the kitchen without waiting for the answer she already knew.

Wes leaned back against the wall and looked out over the dining room. Everyone seemed content and happy. He couldn't imagine doing something where everyone around him was happy. He had never experienced that. As a kid he joined cattle drives where men were always tired and miserable. He started riding guard when his skill with a gun was discovered, then became a Ranger.

Must be nice, he thought as Annette set a cup of coffee in front of him. He looked up at his hostess, who was caught in the soft glow of the kitchen lamp. He saw a mark on the left side of her face near her eye. No, a bruise worn through a hasty attempt to hide its presence with makeup that had worn thin after a long day of work. Annette caught Wes's concerned look, and quickly pushed hair over her eye, hurrying away to the dining room. Wes's chest felt heavy. Heat rushed into his face. His skin tingled. He rubbed the back of his neck and waited for Annette to pass by when he stood and stopped her. He turned her toward the light of a large oil lamp.

"Please, Wes, it's nothing. I hit my face on the kitchen door," she said in a veiled attempt at a false explanation.

Wes had been a lawman for too many years to accept her feeble attempt to hide a beating. "Amos do this?" He asked, holding her gently by the arm.

"It's nothing, Wes. Please, let me go," she pleaded.

Wes reluctantly released his grip and sat back down, his appetite gone, as Annette disappeared again. One of the women waiting on tables exited the kitchen. Wes stopped her. "I'm sorry to delay you ma'am, but do you know anything about Mrs. Gentry's face?" He clumsily asked.

The startled woman didn't make eye contact with Wes. "I really don't know what you're talking about, mister," she answered, then forced her way on to the dining room.

Annette saw Wes's quick interrogation and hurried back over to him. "Wes, please don't interfere. I told you, I'm fine," she insisted, forcing a smile.

"I'm sorry. You know I worry about you. Where is Amos anyway?" Wes asked.

"He went over to the rail station to pick up a new stove for the kitchen. Should be back later tonight. You still want your dinner?" she asked.

Wes paused. "Wouldn't miss it."

A few minutes later, he was glad he had decided to stay, and his appetite returned with a vengeance the moment he smelled the fried steak. As he ate, he thought about Amos Gentry. He'd only been to Buffalo Gap a few times, but Amos always seemed to be angry or dissatisfied about things. His reputation at being unfriendly was odd, given his profession as an innkeeper. Although the Bison Hotel was known as one of the better hotels in the region, Amos Gentry was uninviting as hell. His wife, Annette was the polar opposite. Warm, friendly, attractive, and many years younger than her cantankerous husband, she was the sole reason why the hotel flourished, or so Wes believed.

Wes finished his dinner, left four dollars on the table for a two-dollar meal, and headed for his room. He wasn't in the mood for the talk and jocularity he'd find at the Split Rail Saloon. He locked the door, and propped a chair up under the handle to secure the door. He looked out the window onto main street. People seemed to be everywhere. On horses, foot, in the street and on the boardwalks. *Looks like damn Fort Worth out there*, he thought.

He hung his gun belt on the bedpost then washed his hands and face. He looked closely at the gruesome scars on the back and palms of his hands. Each movement of a finger brought with it a corresponding dull pain. He clenched both hands into fists then released them flat open. They were getting worse. The doctor back at Fort Griffin said something about scarring inside the skin along with damaged muscles and such. All he knew was they were becoming more difficult to use, especially in this cold weather. The colder it was, the less flexibility he had in both hands.

Knock! Knock! The sound interrupted his thoughts. "Who is it?" he asked.

"Annette Gentry," came the reply.

Wes quickly moved the chair and opened the door. He immediately noticed she had freshened her face and brushed her hair, although the stained white apron still hid most of her dress.

"Yes, Mrs. Gentry?" he asked failing to hold back a wide smile.

"I noticed that shirt of yours could use a washing, so I thought I'd take care of that," she stated demurely.

"Oh? Do you provide laundry service for all your guests?" he asked looking down at his admittedly soiled tan cavalry bib shirt.

"No!" was the singular response.

"I'd be mighty grateful for sure," Wes admitted while releasing the buttons and removing the shirt exposing a muscle bound, albeit scarred, chest.

"Thank you again for your concern, Wes," she said, "I do appreciate it," then she spun on her heels and hurried back down the hall.

Wes watched as she swayed all the way to the staircase, where she turned and disappeared. *She's a married woman, Wes, and you're just a broken-down gunslinger with crippled hands!* He thought as he closed the door for the night.

CHAPTER 15

RANGE

Strong November winds charged down Range's main street, ushering in a bounty of frigid air. Dust devils spun red dirt onto porches and up against building windows, sounding like a wave of buzzing mosquitoes. The street was empty, but for a few cowboys making their way into the saloon. The chatter of the crowd inside the Red Dirt Saloon centered on the day's raid, and the arrival of the Ursuline Sisters. The loss of Brody Brown, and the treatment of Mrs. Fields, were fresh on everyone's lips, and eroded the usually festive mood into something more somber. The cards remained locked away, the piano remained silent.

Mick Donovan sat at one of his large round tables with Lawrence Benson and Jacob Turner, discussing the need for law and order.

"Gentlemen, today's events just strengthen our resolve," Benson bellowed. "Brody Brown's murder is the final straw. We are in desperate need of protection, and I have been assured that help is on the way. I received a telegram from Fort Griffin today stating that a U.S. Deputy Marshal has been dispatched to our town and will be here sometime next week. He's coming from Fort Smith, which for a deputy Marshal should only take ten days or so. I have yet to hear from Governor Hubbard regarding our request for Texas Rangers. I know we have a couple of cattle drives heading our way. That will be a good time to find a town Marshal. I've also sent word to Sheriff Evans about today's attack. I believe we are in for worse trouble. The outlaws have increased their activity and have become more brazen than ever. I'm no expert in these matters, but it appears we are in danger of a major attack. If anyone has any suggestions, I'm open to ideas."

"Lawrence, we need more than one lawman in this town. We're going to need to fight back when these bastards come to town. They need to know they're in for a fight if they come back," Turner offered.

"Agreed! Agreed, Mr. Turner. Mr. Tanner showed them that today," the short burly Mayor exhorted, stroking his clean-shaven chin. "His actions not only sent a message but will help fund our new Marshal and his office. That ruffian he shot had a one-thousand-dollar reward. Mr. Tanner has agreed to share the proceeds with the town."

The side door slammed, cutting Benson's speech short, and silencing the crowd. Deacon David stepped into the sound of silence. Seemingly embarrassed, the Deacon smiled and waved. "Good evening, everyone. I didn't mean to interrupt," the tiny man said. At five-foot-four inches and 135 pounds, the Deacon was less than intimidating, except for his all black attire.

"Nonsense! Sir, come right in have a seat over here at this table," Benson insisted.

The Deacon followed instructions and made his way through the crowd, pausing to shake several hands, and accept a hug from one of the ladies, turning his pasty, white pallor to a blushing crimson.

"I normally don't make a habit of visiting saloons, gentlemen, but it seemed that most everyone was here this evening, so I thought I would join you," the Deacon explained.

"As you learned earlier, you arrived at a somewhat unfortunate time, Deacon," Jacob Turner stated.

"Yes, I understand there was quite a scene just prior to our arrival. Mrs. Fields was terribly upset. The Sisters did provide some needed

RED RIVER REUNION | 79

guidance, though. I also heard of someone being killed. I'm sorry for that," the Deacon offered.

The men sat quiet peering into their glasses for a long moment before Benson spoke up. "Gentlemen, as you know, Deacon David and the Sisters have come to build a church and school in our town. We are honored to have been chosen for such a noble purpose. Deacon, I will show you the land that you may use for the church and school tomorrow if that's acceptable," Benson asked.

"Certainly. I believe we may use the meeting house for service in the interim?"

"Yes, that will be fine. I'll meet you tomorrow morning, say ten o'clock?" Benson offered.

"That will be good. I'll turn in for the night. Thank you." The clergyman then made his way back to the side door, delayed by offers of dinner, coffee, and handshakes. Once the door closed, the noise level elevated, and a call for a deck of cards was answered by Donovan who retrieved a deck from behind the bar.

"I'm still not sure why we have a Deacon and nuns moving into town," Brad Jamieson stated, stepping out from a group near the meeting table.

"Hello Brad, have a seat. What'll ya have?" Benson asked.

"I'll have a beer," Jamieson advised taking a seat next to the Mayor.

Donovan quickly headed to the bar to help his assistant bartender, who had begun to fall behind on orders.

"Well, you may remember about six months ago, Mrs. LeGary sent a letter to San Antonio asking if the Catholic Church would like to come to Range. I had the opportunity to see the letter, and it was signed by just about every lady, and a few men in town. I signed it myself. I'd heard the Church was moving to all parts of Texas trying to spread the Good Word. And, we had that open land behind the meeting house and store, so I offered that up. Next thing you know, we have a Deacon and nuns in our midst. This makes it more important to do what we can to prevent today's events from happening again."

"Mr. Benson! Riders coming into town down by the livery stable. Looks like quite a few!" Several men called over to the mayor. People hurried to the front windows to get a look.

"Any idea who it is?" Benson asked aloud pushing his way through the crowd to the front door.

"Looks like Mr. Henry from the Double O Ranch."

A towering man with broad shoulders and a commanding presence, Oliver Otis "Butch" Henry owned the largest cattle ranch near Range. Over six thousand acres, it covered most of the land east of town. Lawrence Benson may have been the mayor of Range, but Butch Henry's ranch fueled the town's prosperity. His ranch employed many of the men and supplied the town with beef and flour from his fields. He was one of the few men who didn't find themselves bankrupt after the war. He and his ten riders stopped outside the saloon and tied their horses.

Butch Henry was first to the door. "Good evening Lawrence," Butch offered with a firm handshake. "I got word of Brown being killed today. Damn shame. He was a good man."

"Yes, sir, he sure was Butch," Benson answered. "I have a table in the back. Join us?" Benson asked.

"Don't mind if I do." Butch waved to one of his men to join him.

Butch and his foreman of ten years took a seat at the table. Butch's foreman was a big man with a booming voice, and quick draw. He was a top-hand, and well-respected by all. Donovan quickly poured Henry and his foreman a glass of premium whisky then set the bottle in front of the big rancher.

"Thank you, Mick! You're a good man!" Butch tipped his hat to the barkeeper.

"Fellas, I know ya'll been wanting a town Marshal for a while now. I blame myself for not supporting this venture earlier. I've been down in Austin the last couple of weeks and have been out of touch. It so happens that I believe I have the right man for the job, if ya'll are in agreement that is."

"Please speak up, Butch," Benson suggested.

"You all know one of my guards, Lane Dodson. He's also a former

Arizona lawman. After today's news, Dodson came to see me and offered his services. Now, I'm getting ready to send a herd up to Dodge in another week or so, but I believe he'll do more good here in town than with us on the drive. I'll also cover his first month's wages."

"That sounds like a fine offer, Butch. I'll get with the town's leaders and run it past them, if that's okay with you," Benson asked.

"Of course. Decide what ya'll want to do and let me know. I'll wait to hear before I send him in," the rancher advised. Butch then drank his whiskey in one gulp. "Good evening gentlemen," he said, pausing at the bar. Butch reached into his vest pocket and withdrew a fifty-dollar gold piece and smacked it on the slick bar surface, grabbing Mick Donavon's attention at the beer barrel.

"Put all this on my tab, Mick," Butch instructed Donovan, who grinned from ear to ear, and nodded in agreement. The big rancher glanced around the smokey bar, and quickly counted his men. His commanding presence seemed to get the attention of all ten men without him uttering a single word. Butch then pointed to the door and headed out with his men following closely behind. The door closed, and a moment later, eleven horses could be heard thundering out of town.

Brad Jamieson exhaled a deep breath and looked around the table at a smiling Benson and Turner who held a blank look on his face. "Well, I didn't expect that," Jamieson stated.

"Nope, me neither," added Turner.

"You all know of Dodson?" Benson asked.

"Sure," was the collective response.

"Are we in agreement that he's our man?" Benson asked.

All three men nodded in agreement.

Benson stood and placed money on the table, then adjusted his pants over his large, round belly. "Okay. I'll check with a few others in the morning. If they're good with it, I'll send a rider out to the ranch tomorrow," Benson advised.

With that, the informal town meeting was over with Benson and

Jamieson calling it a night. Donovan waved as the men passed the crowded bar top. He stepped up onto a stool near the beer barrel.

"Attention everyone! Attention! It looks like we have our Marshal! The next drink is on the house!" Donovan declared to a resounding cheer.

CHAPTER 16

LUXTON DANNER – EN ROUTE TO RANGE

The sun had surrendered, settling darkness over the bristly trail. The high-reaching trees lining each side had a thick fall-colored canopy, obstructing the remaining daylight. The Everett's wagon rolled on. A brightly lit lantern hanging from a tall pole attached to the bench provided just enough light to see the trail's path and foliage walls. Everett's wife, Mary, gazed at the vibrant reds, oranges, and yellows of the leaves along the path's edge and tried to explain, to no avail, its wonders to their children Debra and Daniel. Debra played with her burlap sewn rag doll, and Daniel, floppy hat pulled down to his eyes, watched the trail disappear behind them in between complaints of hunger. The wagon's dilatory pace was not to Everett's liking, and his anxiety had risen with Danner's disappearance further ahead.

"Father?" Daniel spoke up.

"Yes, son."

"There's men riding behind us a little way back. I can hear 'em," his son reported.

Both he and Mary glanced over their shoulders and saw the movement of shadows approaching at a gallop. Everett said nothing, but his haste with the reins told his wife all she needed to know.

Everett snapped leather quickly on the horses' backs trying to get more speed, but the rutted trail and worn wheels would not permit much more. Quickly, the three riders overtook the buckboard with one grabbing the left horse's harness bringing the wagon to a stop.

"Whoa," the lead rider called to the buckboard team. Another man stopped on the right next to Mary. "Well, what do we have here?" the man asked through a matted, black beard that seemed to go halfway up his face. His black hat was pulled down low on his face covering his eyes.

Mary slid toward Everett. "What can I do for you fellas?" Everett asked in a quivering voice that failed to mask his veneration.

The man in front of the wagon turned around to face Everett and his family. He was a large, heavy man, with matted hair protruding from under a torn, brown, wide brim open-crown hat. His unshaven face showed specks of gray, and bits of dried tobacco juice. Saying nothing, he glared over Mary and the children, then back to Everett before speaking. "Well, partner, I'd say you have a bit to lose."

"We need to be on our way, and catch up to our U.S. Marshal escort," Everett advised the unwelcome visitors.

"Hear that, Buck? These folks have a U.S. Marshal escort!" the man in front shouted to his two partners, who both laughed.

"Well, before that Marshal returns, I think me and the lady here will take a walk into the woods!" The man called Buck boomed as he reached for Mary with a dirty hand.

Everett grabbed his wife by the shoulder, but the outlaw on his side drew his gun, smashing it against Everett's head, ripping open the timid man's head, knocking him unconscious. Everett fell to the footboard. Debra screamed, then began to cry. Mary turned to her daughter, but Buck slid off his horse and grabbed her by the neck of her blouse, violently ripping the front down to her waist. Daniel jumped up and began to yell at his mother's assailant, but the third outlaw stopped him. The outlaw behind the wagon threw Daniel to the floorboard of the wagon, and held him face down, with an iron fist pressed into his back. Daniel squirmed in an attempt to escape, but the man picked him up and slammed him back onto the wagon's deck.

Buck pulled Mary down from the bench, blocking her wild swings without much difficultly. She landed a solid slap to his ruddy face, which did little to dissuade him. His calloused hand landed against Mary's head, knocking her off her feet. Her bonnet flew off her head, sending long hair down onto her shoulders. She fell to her knees but kept swinging her arms wildly at his boot tops.

The same outlaw who pistol-whipped Everett rummaged through the containers and bags looking for anything of value. "Ask her where the money is!" He hollered at Buck, who had picked Mary up by her shredded blouse.

"You heard him! Where's your money?" Buck shook her back and forth, then pulled her chemise down to her waist. "I said where's the money?" he growled, eying her chest.

Crack! The bullet hit the right side of Buck's head sending the left half over the wagon into the tree line. His body fell into a limp mass.

The outlaw tearing up the family's bags jumped back. "What the hell?"

Crack! Thud! The second bullet hit the thief, blowing up his chest, knocking his dead body back into a rut.

The third bandit behind the wagon spun his horse around and buried his spurs into the horse's hinds sending the steed into a full run. Mary gathered her blouse in an attempt to cover her bare body when Danner charged past her on Bullet in pursuit of bandit number three. She managed to stand and leaned on the wagon looking at her husband who bled profusely from a wide gash on his face. Debra cried softly from inside the wagon.

The fleeing outlaw turned in the saddle and fired a wild shot at Danner as he closed the gap between them. He fired another shot that clipped a branch as Danner flew past.

Danner's anger had narrowed his vision to see only the shadow of his prey. Bullet moved at lightning speed when Danner balanced himself in the stirrups, calmly lowered his Winchester to fire. The bullet hit its mark, first pushing the rider forward, then the lifeless outlaw flipped backward off the fleeing horse that kept up its thundering pace without its rider.

Danner brought Bullet to a halt and dismounted next to the third man's body. He rolled him over and peered into his face in an effort to see if he recognized him but he did not. Danner checked pockets for clues to the man's identity in case he was wanted but found nothing. He dragged the outlaw out of the trail into the woods then returned to Bullet. He quickly rode back to the wagon where Mary had covered herself with a shawl, tending to her husband's wound.

"You all right, Mrs. Everett?" he asked.

Mary nodded and continued to wrap a bandage around her husband's head.

"Mary told me what you did, Marshal. Thank you for saving us," Everett offered, his speech slurred from his head wound.

"I'm sorry I was late, I thought I heard a scream, but wasn't certain. I guess I got too far ahead of you. I won't let that happen again. Can you drive that wagon in the dark?" Danner asked Mary.

"Yes, I believe I can. At least a short distance," she answered.

"Okay, we're less than an hour from Acworth."

"I can make it," Mary assured Danner as much as herself.

Danner dismounted, then pulled the other two outlaws off the trail. He searched each's pockets but found nothing. "Did you hear any names of these three?" Danner asked.

"One was called Buck, I believe," Mary answered, checking on her distressed children.

Danner thought for a moment. *No one named Buck that I can think of.* He jumped up on Bullet and started down the dark path. The same tall canopy that had impeded the sun was doing the same to any potential moonlight. Fortunately, the trail didn't hold many curves in this stretch.

Forty-five minutes later, Danner saw lanterns ahead in a clearing. He turned and rode back to the wagon where Mrs. Everett hung onto the reins with all her strength. Everett laid across the bench with his head on her lap.

"We're coming into Acworth, Mrs. Everett. Just follow me. I'll see where you can stay tonight. Can you make it?"

"Yes, Marshal. He's hurt bad. Do you think they'll be a doctor here?"

"I don't know, ma'am. I wouldn't think so, but I'll check around."

Danner rode into the middle of the cluster of small sheds and tents looking for a sign of life. One of the larger buildings, no more than a good-sized tack building, had smoke billowing from its stove pipe. He stopped there and knocked on the door.

The door swung open with an old woman holding a shotgun at Danner's belly. Danner threw up his hands. "Ma'am, I'm a U.S. Deputy Marshal and I have an injured man with me. Is there someone here in town that could provide medical assistance?"

"You have a badge, Marshal?" the woman scowled.

Danner slowly pulled his vest back to reveal his badge. The woman lowered the shotgun. "Sorry Marshal, but things been pretty bad 'round here. I'm Catherine Davis. We don't have a doctor here, but I may be able to help," she offered.

"Mrs. Everett, can he walk?" Danner called to the wagon.

"With some help. Kids, you stay in the wagon."

Danner helped Everett down from the wagon, and with Mary's assistance, got him to Davis' shack.

"Bring him over here by the stove," Catherine instructed. She gathered a towel and bowl of water, then unwrapped Everett's head. "Oh my," she exclaimed looking at the deep laceration going from his check to the top of his ear. "How did this happen?"

"He was beaten with a butt-end of a gun," Mary Everett explained.

"Who did it?" Catherine asked, gently dabbing the wound with a wet cloth.

"We don't know for sure ma'am. One was named Buck," Danner advised.

"Dirty ugly man with a nasty black beard?" Catherine asked.

"That'd be the one," Danner confirmed.

"We know him. He's been a thorn around here for a while now. Anybody with him?"

"Two others. Both good size with long hair. One had a black vest, and the other a dirty buckskin coat," Danner stated.

"Don't know those two," she said while working on Everett's wound.

"I'll need to check on the children," Mary told Danner as she opened the door.

"Bring those children inside!" Catherine ordered. "I'm guessin' ya'll haven't eaten either. I'll fix that," she added.

Mary hurried out, then returned with Debra and Daniel. "This is Miss Davis," Mary introduced her to the children.

Catherine moved with efficiency. Once she finished bandaging Everett, she turned to face the wide-eyed children. "I have soup and sugar bread. How's that sound?" she asked.

Both children nodded with wide smiles.

"Good. I'll have it ready in a moment. You people had quite a fright."

"Ma'am, would there be a place for these folks to stay the night?" Danner asked.

"No, sir, we haven't made it that far here, and probably never will. Most folks who stay here have no means to move on west. I can keep the woman and daughter here, and Mrs. Dugan can probably help with the menfolks."

"Fine. Can you direct me to Mrs. Dugan's," Danner asked.

"I'll take them over once the children have eaten. Mrs. Dugan's husband died about a month ago, so she'll like to have visitors. Her cabin is just across the way."

"Thank you very much, Miss Davis," Mary stated.

"I'll be moving on then. Mrs. Everett, when you get back on the trail, try to join up with others, and only travel during the day," Danner advised.

"May I speak with you outside, Mr. Danner?" Mary asked.

Danner held the door open and Mary stepped outside. Danner tipped his hat to Catherine Davis, then followed Mary, who stood next to the buckboard, wiping tears with the corner of her shawl. Danner's six-foot-six-inch frame towered over the diminutive mother of two. She looked up, then stepped into Danner wrapping her arms around the tall Marshal. Danner reluctantly returned the gesture.

"If it weren't for you I would have been raped and left for dead. I'm sure I owe my life to you," she added.

"I'm sorry you had to experience what you did. I arrived a little late. One of your horses is about to give out. I'll leave you my second horse," Danner advised.

"I knew our traveling alone was a bad idea, but my husband insisted we'd be fine. Now, I don't know. We'll follow your advice as best we can." Mary released her grip. "Thank you again, Mr. Danner," she said clutching her torn dress, then hurried back to her family.

Danner watched as she disappeared into the shack. Bullet stomped his hoof and snorted. "I know, I know, pal, time to move on," Danner agreed with his partner before stepping into a stirrup and swinging up into the saddle. He removed the extra ammunition from the pack horse but left the rest of his provisions. He figured the Everett's needed them more than him.

The moon was full-up now providing just enough light to track the path. *If this is how this assignment is going to go, things are gonna get ugly*, he thought, as he and Bullet disappeared into the trail.

CHAPTER 17

BEN CHANCE, JR. – EN ROUTE TO TEXARKANA

C hance added wood to his fire, careful to keep it just strong enough to provide a little heat on such a cold night. He didn't want large flames that could be seen from far away. The sky was clear, and the full moon shed ample light over his campsite. He used the glow of the fire to examine his railroad map of the area near the Red River. His best guess was that he'd be in the Childress settlement tomorrow late in the morning. From there, he planned to travel east, following the river all the way back to Texarkana. He leaned against his saddle and propped his Henry rifle up next to him. Although he hadn't seen anyone all day, he knew that could change quickly. As Chance folded the map and tucked it inside the saddlebag, a visiting stranger startled him, interrupting his quiet night.

"Hello in camp. I'm alone, and mean no harm," the voice called out.

Chance rolled over behind his saddle, cocking his Henry. He looked hard into the surrounding scrub but saw nothing. "Who are you?" Chance called out to the darkness.

"I mean no harm. I'm friend of cavalry soldiers. Indian scout."

"Step into the light. Let me see you!" Chance directed suspiciously.

"Put rifle down, I'll come into the light," the Indian responded.

Chance noticed immediately that each time the Indian spoke, the voice came from a different place in the brush. *Was he really an Indian? The man spoke good English. Were there more than one? Was this a trick to get him to lower his rifle?* He had no answers and knew he wouldn't get any. *Okay Ben, what do you do now?* he asked himself. Chance's horse pulled at his rein, restless at the commotion.

"Okay, I'll put down my rifle and step out. Come into the light of the fire," Chance ordered, laying his Henry against the saddle. He rose to a standing position, hoping he'd made the right decision. Across the fire, the visitor stepped through the sage and juniper concealment revealing himself to be a large man with long black hair wearing a buckskin coat and U.S. Cavalry trousers. The Indian held no weapons that Chance could see. The flames flickered in the visitor's black eyes as the two men looked at each other.

After a long pause, Chance broke the silence. "I'm Ben Chance from Texarkana," he announced stepping around his saddle.

"Leon Red Cloud Anderson," the stranger responded.

Chance cocked his head and frowned. "Leon Red Cloud Anderson, did you say?" Chance asked turning his frown to a faint smile.

Leon met Chance's smile with one of his own. "White father, Kiowa mother. She insisted I call myself Red Cloud."

"That explains your English," Chance offered.

"Yes, I speak English good. My father, Leon Anderson teach me and my mother. I learn more riding with Cavalry soldiers."

"You ride with cavalry as an Indian scout?" Chance asked, impressed.

"Yes, Indian scout for Colonel McClelland and the six cavalry."

Chance moved around the fire and extended his hand. Leon accepted and shook hands. Chance pointed to the ground next to the fire. Leon nodded, crossed his legs, and sat down. Chance took a seat on his bedroll. "Would you like coffee?" Chance asked.

Leon raised his hand. "No thanks, I don't drink coffee."

"Are you alone out here? Where are you headin'?" Chance asked.

"Alone, yes. Like the wind. Move free across the land. Indian Chiefs in reservations won't let me in. Say I'm white. White settlements not very friendly, say I'm Indian. I don't like the reservations anyway, so I move around. I have paper from Colonel McClelland says I'm good man. Ride with Cavalry soldiers."

Leon removed a folded piece of paper from his pocket and handed it to Chance. Chance opened the paper. It was a letter from Lieutenant Colonel Curwen B. McClelland, commander of the Sixth U.S. Cavalry.

"How did you become an Indian scout for the cavalry?"

"Many years, the Kiowa battle horse soldiers at Wichita River. Kiowa fight bravely. Horse soldiers find out I have white father, so they not kill me. I grateful. Chief Kicking Bird say Red Cloud a disgrace. After horse soldiers run away, Chief leave me behind to stay with white man. Horse soldiers' find me next day. I tell Colonel McClelland my story. I was young, but he asked me to be an Indian scout. I say I not fight Kiowa. We agree. I scout for many years. Fight Apache, Comanche, and Creek. I learn more English, get soldier pants, and become friend to white man. The Kiowa angry that I ride with soldiers. Disown me."

Chance stoked the fire with a stick. "Do you have a horse now or are you on foot?"

"I have big soldier horse."

Chance removed a bag of jerky from his saddle bag and offered it to Leon.

"Bring your horse into camp. You can stay here tonight if you like," Chance offered.

"Your father still alive?" Chance asked.

"No, Comanche kill him. He was good man. Friend to many Indians. Not Comanche though."

"Your mother?"

"She died a little while after my father. Kiowa take her back in death. You have same name as your father, yes?"

Chance paused and looked hard at Leon, suddenly suspicious at how the Indian would know that information. "Yes," he said carefully. He had not decided yet whether or not he would trust the stranger.

Leon smiled. "I know your father. Many years ago, I scout for him in Territory chasing bad men. You tall like him, but he much bigger," Leon spread his hands wide and high above his head.

"Yep, that'd be him, I reckon," Chance said with a laugh, relaxing his tensed muscles.

"What happened to big Chance?" Leon asked.

"Rustlers killed him about three months ago," Chance replied, then settled into his bedroll. "I'm heading for Clarendon tomorrow, then following the river back to Texarkana," Chance announced as he slipped his pistol under his blanket.

Leon watched Chance's actions and laughed.

"Don't worry, I'll not harm little Chance," Leon declared.

"What'd ya mean, little Chance?" he asked with a chuckle then rolled over to sleep.

The cooing of mourning doves broke Chance from his slumber. The smell of hot food brought a smile to his face. He rolled over to see Leon cooking a rabbit over the fire.

"Good morning, little Chance," Leon greeted his host. "Thought you might like some real food this morning."

"Well, that smells awfully good," Chance acknowledged as his stomach growled in agreement. He slid out of his bedroll and reached for the coffee pot. A short time later, the rabbit and coffee were both a fond memory. Chance strapped down his gear and saddle then looked over at Leon.

"I'm headin' east along the river. I figure on stopping in Clarendon this afternoon to get some supplies. Care to ride along?" Chance asked.

Leon paused and looked east into the rising sun.

"I'll ride along for a while. I don't know about going into town. Maybe."

"Good. Ready?" Chance asked.

"When you are," the Indian responded.

The two started out across a wide opening flushing a large flock of quail that darted through the air like a spiraling arrow. The light frost that had covered the ground had just about departed for the day when Leon slowed his horse. "Hold on, little Chance," he ordered. "Looks like movement far ahead along the ridge," Leon pointed to the left.

Chance looked but saw nothing. "You see what it is?" Chance asked.

"No, maybe just animals. Can't tell. We keep watch," Leon stated then spurred his horse onward. They rode in silence for about an hour, with nothing other than an occasional red tail hawk soaring above. Chance watched Leon pay close attention to the top of the ridge that jutted up on their left. He still wasn't certain of the movement Leon mentioned earlier. As they traveled, they closed the gap between them and the base of the hill, keeping themselves out of sight from anyone peering down from the ridge top. With the river on the other side of the elevation, Chance knew the untamed territory beyond would be filled with many unknown dangers.

"I reckon we're about an hour or so from Clarendon," Chance stated as he checked his map. "At least, that's what my map shows."

"Why didn't you take a train back to Texarkana?" Leon asked.

"I thought about it, but figured my father traveled this land by horse, so I decided I would, too. At least once, anyway. Besides, there's no railroad near here," Chance explained.

"Much trouble along the river these days. Safer to take the train," Leon declared.

"I know. I heard all about it. The Marshal who told me about my father warned me against taking this path alone. I figured I needed to prove something to myself, and maybe to him. I didn't have any trouble on the way to Oneida. Hopefully, it'll be the same on the way back."

Leon grunted and shook his head. "The graveyards are full of men who needed to prove something, my friend. And, it looks like you'll get your chance to prove yourself," he added.

"What is it?" Chance whispered, suddenly suspicious.

"We're being followed. Four, maybe five riders. They came down behind us from the ridge a while back. I wasn't sure at first, but no doubt now. We're still too far from town to make a run for it," Leon surmised.

Chance looked over his shoulder, seeing nothing but valley floor.

"Best we find a spot inside the wall of this rock. If we get a good spot, they'd be fools to charge us," Leon said glancing back and forth along the lower rim.

"Here they come! Let's go!" Leon shouted then kicked his horse into a full run. Chance followed checking over his shoulder again, this time seeing five riders busting fast after them.

Crack! Crack! Crack! The outlaws' bullets zinged past Chance and Leon.

Crack! Crack! Another two bullets came their way, the second hitting Leon's back-left shoulder. He twisted forward but recovered enough to maintain his speed.

"Here! Cut in here! Leon yelled, reining his horse left into a narrow gorge. The ground rose up slightly and turned to the right. Leon and Chance brought their horses to a halt and jumped off their saddles, pulling their horses with them. Both ducked behind a large jutting sharp ledge, Leon pulling his pistol, Chance reaching for his Henry. Chance knew he was an okay shot okay with a pistol, but damn deadly with his Henry rifle. He leveled off the Henry and waited for the first target to come into view. On cue, the first outlaw turned toward the opening. Chance didn't hesitate.

Boom! The bullet knocked the outlaw ten feet backward into a cloud of dust. The second outlaw couldn't stop in time before exposing himself to another Henry bullet. Boom! The second outlaw met the same fate as the first. Chance cocked his rifle and waited, taking a deep breath.

"Nice shooting, hombre," Leon said looking at his young sharpshooter. Chance said nothing, didn't move a muscle. He just kept his eyes focused. No sound. No movement. A hawk screeched overhead.

Crack! A wild shot hit dirt above Leon's head. Neither man returned fire.

"You can't stay in there forever! Just toss out your saddle bags, and we'll ride on!" A voice careened off the rocks.

Crack! Another wild shot pitted the rock wall behind Chance. Chance slowly adjusted himself, moving his aim to the right edge of the opening. He waited. Took another deep breath. Boom! He fired hitting the edge of the opening just as the outlaw leaned around to fire another shot. No shot came as the bandit spun wildly around and fell to the ground.

"Okay! Okay! You win this time! We go!" The sound of a horse galloping away floated into the ravine.

Leon clutched Chance's shoulder. "That was only one-horse, partner. Don't move." Leon looked up and around behind their backs to the wide open area that wouldn't offer much cover if another outlaw moved on top of the ridge. "I know this from my Kiowa days. One stays while the other moves behind," he whispered to Chance.

Chance looked behind him. "If we stay here, they'll pick us off from up there," Chance whispered.

Leon nodded. "Yes, but they have us trapped."

"Let me look at that shoulder real quick," Chance stated.

Leon said nothing. Just shook his head no and continued to stare up at the edge of the ravine.

"Our best chance is your sharp-shooting with that rifle. As soon as you see movement up there, you can't miss. I'll keep watch for the other at the opening," Leon advised.

Chance nodded, then turned and leaned back against a rock to watch the ridge line. He didn't have anything to rest the barrel on. It would be a far more difficult shot staring up into the cloudless sky. Despite the cool air, sweat trickled down Chance's face into his eyes, further complicating matters.

Crack! A bullet hit the rock at the back of the gap about ten feet away.

Crack! Leon fired toward the sound of the gunfire.

Chance thought he saw a shadow. He was ready. Crack! Crack!

Crack! Crack! Bullets rained down, blowing up dirt, and ricocheting off rock. Chance fired, boom! A miss! He cocked his Henry and waited. Boom! Cocked again.

Leon fired toward the front. Bullets hit the back wall. A shadow? No! Boom! This time Chance's aim was true, as his shot blew a hole through the bandit's gut. The bandit dropped his rifle and fell straight into the floor of the ravine. Chance spun to the opening and fired again, missing. The bandit exposed himself one more time, leaving Chance enough time to cock the Henry and squeeze the trigger. He missed, and realized the Henry was empty. He tossed it aside as the bandit charged forward, firing again in their direction. Chance drew his Colt and fired point blank, hitting the attacker square in the chest knocking him sideways on his saddle. He dropped his pistol and fell face-first into a prickly pear cactus, ending his raiding days.

"That's it! Five! That's all of 'em, Leon!" Chance yelled, turning to Leon. He saw Leon lying on his back, two bullet holes punched through the chest of his buckskin coat. "No! No! No!" Chance yelled, grabbing the former Indian scout and shaking him.

Chance rocked back and leaned against the wall of their rock tomb. He looked at the dead outlaws that surrounded him. *What the hell just happened*? He thought, in shock. He looked back at the Indian he'd known for less than a day. Leon would never worry again about what the white man or Kiowa thought of him. He had chosen to ride along with Chance. Now, he was dead because of that decision. Chance pulled himself together. Anger flooded his consciousness. *Is this how it is out here? This is how my father lived every day? Damn it! I never realized,* he thought.

CHAPTER 18

WES PAYNE – BUFFALO GAP

Wes pulled himself together, dressed, and slipped out of the Bison before the Gentrys' awakened. He'd decided to spend the early morning hours over at the jail instead of facing Amos. The thought of Amos striking Annette still angered him, and he wasn't sure how he'd react when he saw Amos. So, he decided to keep some distance, choosing instead to join Kirby for a quick patrol around town, then hung back at the Sheriff's office for coffee. "You know, this coffee isn't very good," he remarked.

"Maybe you should head over to the Bison for Mrs. Gentry's fresh brew," Kirby sarcastically suggested.

"You ever noticed bruises or wounds on Annette?" Wes asked.

Kirby set his cup down and leaned toward Wes. "No, can't say I have. But then again, I never looked too closely. Why?"

"I saw she had a black eye last night. Looked like she'd been hit on the left side of her face. She tried to cover it up, but the bruise was too big."

"What'd she say happened?" Kirby asked, a concerned tone in his normally rough voice.

"Said she hit the kitchen door. Said she was fine." Wes said, sipping his coffee.

"What makes you think Amos did it?"

"He pretty much always seems angry or in a foul mood over somethin' or other whenever I'm in town. He seems like the type to hit a woman, don't he?"

"Well, I can't argue about his disposition, but I been here a couple years now, ain't never seen any reason to think he'd hurt Annette," Kirby reported.

"You get a chance, take a look. She didn't hit no damn door. I know better."

"Okay, I'll ask her about it. Don't need any of that in town," Kirby said.

"Thanks. Well, sun's up. I'll be getting along. Thanks for the coffee." Wes rose.

"Wes," Kirby said, a warning in his voice.

Wes turned to Kirby. "Ya."

"You watch yourself up there on the border. Them fellas ain't playin' around," Kirby cautioned.

"Sure will. See ya on the way back."

Wes walked back to the Bison, remembering to retrieve the shirt Annette offered to clean. He stepped through the front door to find Amos talking to two men in the back of the dining room. Amos stopped his conversation and approached Wes. "Mr. Payne. You forget something in your room?"

"Not exactly," Wes responded cautiously.

"Good morning, Mr. Payne!" Annette announced in a nervous tone, hurrying out from the kitchen with his folded shirt in hand.

Wes removed his hat and accepted the shirt. "Thank you, ma'am. I appreciate this very much," Wes said politely.

"What's all this? You doing laundry for the guests now?" Amos snapped at his wife.

"No, Amos, Ranger Payne is on a long journey. I was just trying to be of assistance, that's all," she explained, virtually cowering near the doorway.

Wes reached into his pocket and removed two silver dollars that he handed to Annette. "You're right about that long journey, ma'am.

Thank you, kindly," he said. Turning his attention to Amos, he said firmly, "Mr. Gentry, can I speak to you outside for a moment?"

Amos followed Wes, glaring at his wife. Wes paused on the wide front porch.

"What do you want?" Amos said harshly.

Wes reached around Amos's boney shoulders and grasped a handful of shirt collar in his scarred fist. "If I ever find out you hit Mrs. Gentry again, I'll kill you. Understand?" Wes whispered to the innkeeper, whose eyes had widened in surprise and fear. Wes tightened his grip and leaned down closer to the little man's pale face and bulging eyes.

"I didn't hear your response, Mr. Gentry," Wes stated between gritted teeth.

"Yes, sir, Mr. Payne. I heard you fine," Amos stuttered.

Wes released his grip, and headed for the stable, satisfied he'd not punched the little bastard. He strolled over to the livery stable where the stable boss, Dalton Jones, waited with Ringo.

"Ready to go Mr. Payne!" Jones announced.

"Thanks Jones. You got a bag of oats I can take with me?" Wes asked.

"Sure. Won't be a minute." Jones returned a moment later, helping Wes secure the bag on Ringo.

Wes paid the stable boss, happy to be heading out of Buffalo Gap. He patted Ringo on the neck. "With any luck, we'll be back through here in about a month, pal."

Wes started into a gallop when he heard two gunshots back in town. He swung Ringo around to see Kirby heading his way at full speed.

"What the hell?" He said aloud.

Wes rode back toward the middle of town where he met Kirby.

"What's goin' on? That Amos Gentry start something?"

"Forget about Amos Gentry for God's sake!" Kirby yelled. "I just came from the telegraph office. We got a message from the Fort. Looks like hostiles hit a farm up on the border between Riverbend and

Range then raided Range. Killed a man. Thought you should know what you're heading into," Kirby explained.

Wes looked up at the passing clouds and took a deep breath. "Army didn't get all the Comanche at Palo Duro last year. A mess of 'em escaped. Looks like they're waging their own last-ditch war," Wes stated.

"Maybe, but killing innocent farmers and children ain't gonna change nothing," Kirby offered.

"Nope. I guess some of 'em just ain't ready to give up yet. Thanks for the information. See ya." Wes turned Ringo and started back on his quest with a new-found sense of urgency. He still wasn't certain what all he could do, but somebody had to do something, and he figured he was as good as any option there was. *Damn, I hope Upham sent Danner*, he thought.

F our hours into his ride, Wes came upon a cattle drive heading north. He'd been watching the dust trail for the last hour. A big herd moved slowly across an open range in a perpetual dust cloud that hung overhead as if it was attached with a rope. Twenty or more cowboys shouted cattle calls and snapped ropes above the constant snorting, grunting, and bellows from the cows. Four more cowboys remained off to the side, herding strays back into the group. Wes decided to catch the lead riders to find out what outfit they were from. He pushed Ringo into a full run, following along the west side of the herd, waving at the cowboys charged with the responsibility of containing the left edge. The smell of cowhide and manure filled the range. He pulled up next to a young rider, slapping his rope, and calling out orders to chugging steers.

"Howdy stranger!" the young cowboy greeted Wes.

"Howdy! Name's Wes Payne, I'm a Texas Ranger headin' north! What outfit ya'll with?"

"Overton Ranch, sir!"

"Overton? Weren't ya'll camped out near Buffalo Gap a few days ago?" Wes asked, remembering the cowboy from the Overton outfit whom he'd knocked out in the Split Rail Saloon.

"Yes, sir! We lost a day watering the herd. We're pushin' 'em hard, but the herd is so damn big, it's moving pretty slow!"

"Your trail boss or foremen up in front?"

"Yes, sir! Trail boss is Randall McClain! Tall fella wearin' a long brown oilskin! Can't miss 'em!"

"Thanks!" Wes spurred Ringo on galloping around the herd to the point where three men rode side by side.

The men saw Wes approach, and pulled off the point to the side where the herd could pass.

"Good afternoon, name's Wes Payne, Texas Rangers," Wes announced.

"Good afternoon, sir. I'm Randall McClain, trail boss, this is Denton Young, our foreman, and our lead guard, Clint Wade," McClain finished the introductions.

"Hello there, Wade!" Wes shouted over the cattle noise, moving Ringo up to shake hands with his fellow gunslinger.

"Hello, Payne. So, ya decided to join back up with the Rangers, huh?" Wade asked with a grin.

"Sure did. Didn't know what else to do," Wes answered with a chuckle.

"See you fellas know each other, then," Denton Young remarked.

"Yes, sir. Me and Ranger Payne rode together for a short stint a few months back when I was workin' for Sam Coleman. What brings you up this way, Payne?" Wade asked.

"Headin' up to the river. Town called Range. Been some trouble up that way. We lost a Ranger there. Any chance ya'll be goin' through Range?" Wes asked.

"Naw, we'll cross into the territory further west. You goin' up alone?" Wade asked.

"Sort of. There's a U.S. Marshal supposed to meet me there," Wes answered.

"Know which one?" Wade asked.

"Nope. I'm hope'n it's Danner, but figure I couldn't be that lucky," Wes said with a grin.

Wade nodded. "If it is, you'll do just fine, I reckon," Wade remarked with a smirk.

"Ya'll had any trouble on the drive?" Wes asked.

"Naw, too many guns on this one," Wade said.

"Good enough. Take care," Wes called then spurred Ringo on.

"You do the same!" Wade called to Wes as he rode away.

CHAPTER 19

BEN CHANCE, JR. – CLARENDON

Chance slowly made his way toward Clarendon, casualties from his gunfight in tow. As he approached the end of town, he noticed a young boy run into what looked like the stables. Caleb Johnston spread hay in his livery stable when his son ran in.

"Paw! Paw! There's a man coming into town!" Thirteen-year-old Junior announced.

"Take it easy, son. I'm sure he'll find his way here if he needs a place for his horse," Caleb flatly stated.

"No Paw, he's got lots of horses and dead men!"

"What? Dead men?" A moment later, Caleb stepped out of the barn to watch as Chance rode by, a single rider with one, two, three, five horses in tow, each with a man tied across the saddle.

Framed in a wide open space and big sky behind him, Chance knew his cargo was a startling sight. Chance watched as the man ran across the street to a shed and disappeared for a moment. *Probably telling the Sheriff or Marshal*, Chance thought.

"Jeb! Rider headin' in with dead men in tow!" Caleb informed the lawman.

Jeb Clancy, the settlement of Childress's closest endorsement of a Marshal, calmly strapped on his gun belt, then stepped out onto the porch, his boot heels tapping the planks in perfect rhythm. He narrowed his eyes to see the rider walking his horse slowly down the middle of the beaten path that passed for main street.

Chance saw Clancy exit the shed to take a close look at him. Clancy then stepped into the street, waiting for Chance to ride up. Anticipating being stopped, Chance slowed, and brought his horse to a stop a short distance from the man. Chance looked around as people stepped out of buildings and tents, crowding along the edges of the street to get a look at him and his caravan. Clancy walked toward Chance, looking hard at him. Chance met the man's eyes but said nothing at first.

"Afternoon stranger. Name's Jeb Clancy. I'm sort of the law in this settlement. Looks like you had some trouble?" Clancy asked.

"No trouble. Just five dead outlaws," Chance explained flatly.

"Outlaws?"

"That's right. They jumped me and another fella about a mile west of here. Trapped us against the ridge. We fought 'em off. The fella with me was killed. I decided to bring these in and see if ya'll know any of 'em. You get any flyers around here, Marshal?" Chance asked.

"The army drops some off now and then. So do passing Rangers. I'm not really the Marshal, though," Clancy clarified.

"You keep the flyers?" Chance asked.

"Yep," Clancy responded.

"Let's go have a look then." Chance didn't wait for an answer, just spurred his horse and continued down the street toward the shed he saw Clancy walk out of.

Clancy walked alongside, unsuccessfully shooing the growing crowd of onlookers back to their business. "It's this building right here," Clancy directed Chance to the front of his shed. "I didn't catch your name, sir," Clancy asked.

"Ben Chance."

"You a bounty hunter, Mr. Chance?"

"Nope. At least not 'til today." Chance swung down, his boots pounding the red dirt, sending up clouds of dust.

"Wait here. I'll get the flyers." Clancy snatched the thick pile of wanted posters from a shelf above his cot, then returned to Chance who loosened the ropes, holding the dead bodies on their respective horses.

"These two are Mexican," Chance reported motioning toward the two just behind his horse.

"I don't have any Mexicans here," Clancy definitively stated, looking down at the posters.

"What about these three?" Chance asked, lifting each of the other's heads up so Clancy could see their faces.

Clancy thumbed through the stack of paper, carefully examining each poster. As he passed through the stack, he pulled three posters which he handed to Chance. "Looks like you hit the jackpot, Mr. Chance. Those three are all wanted. Those two are the Blandon brothers. Both wanted for murder over in Wichita. This one looks to be Jack Strickling. Train robber further south. Railroad has a thousand-dollar reward on him. Two hundred for each of the Blandon's also. You'll have to collect over in Hardeman County though. Childress County here is pretty new. Ain't got a Sheriff yet. I'll sign the papers here and get a couple more witnesses for ya, if you like?" Clancy asked.

"That'd be fine Mr. Clancy, thank you. I'm not surprised they're wanted, but I didn't expect that kind of money," Chance admitted.

"The railroad's put big rewards out for train robbers. Ain't many trains yet. I reckon they don't want robbing 'em to become a habit. We don't have a caretaker here, you'll have to bury them yourself, or hire it done," Clancy added.

Chance looked around town. "I won't be staying long enough to bury 'em. I'll offer ten dollars per grave. Will that be enough?"

"Yes, sir, that'll be plenty. I'll ask around while I get you witness signatures. Do you plan on taking the horses?"

"No, I'll be leaving them," Chance responded.

"Our livery stable is right across the street."

"Thank you." Chance grasped his reins and walked over to the livery stable where Caleb and his son watched from the big open door.

"Good afternoon, sir. Can I help you?" Caleb asked, hiding his shaking hands behind his back.

"I'll be leaving those five horses, and I need some grain for mine. Mr. Clancy says you have some to sell?"

"Yes, sir, will one sack do?"

"That'll do fine," Chance said as he looked around. He knew he'd quickly become the talk of the town and was eager to leave as quickly as he'd come.

At the same time, Clancy pushed through the saloon doors, mobbed by fifteen chattering men wanting to know all the details of the stranger and the dead men. Clancy quickly spewed the story as he knew it, then asked for two witnesses who could sign their names. Once the signatures were secured, Clancy announced the job of burying the dead. For ten dollars a piece there was no shortage of takers. Money was hard to come by in Clarendon, which wasn't even considered an official town yet. The county had just been established a year earlier, and the proximity to the river had spawned this small settlement of dreamers and nomads. The barn Caleb built when he arrived six months ago was the only real building. There was so little of value in the settlement that the bandits didn't bother Clarendon, sans an occasional visit to the saloon.

Clancy found five men looking to earn ten dollars. Chance walked back from his grain purchase and handed Clancy sixty dollars. Clancy counted the money and looked at Chance, surprised.

"The other ten is for you, Marshal," Chance said with a glint of a smile.

"Much obliged," Clancy responded, then handed Chance the signed flyers.

Chance mounted his horse, then paused to look at the five men armed with shovels and pickaxes. "You fellas should make this man your official Marshal," Chance said then spun his horse around, and headed east out of town.

"Awful young to be a bounty hunter," one of the new gravediggers stated.

"I'm not sure what he is. Not sure he knows yet, either," Clancy said as all six men watched Chance fade into the horizon.

CHAPTER 20

RANGE

M ary Fields rocked on the front porch of her boarding house, enjoying the crisp sun-drenched air. She wasn't used to having time in the late afternoon to rest, but boarding six nuns, all insisting on taking care of themselves, and each other, had given her a chance to breathe. She might even have time to darn the hole she just had discovered in her favorite blue shawl. She looked over to the holding pens, watching the few horses galloping about in each. She always enjoyed the time when the pens were void of cattle. She knew cattle were the lifeblood of the town, but the smell of manure often bothered her and her guests.

I knew they put those pens too close to town. One of these days, I'll have to see if I can move to the other side of town, she mused. Beyond the holding pens, she noticed what appeared to be a wagon coming into town. Not an uncommon sight, as there were several farms filled with families west of town. She watched for a bit as the wagon slowly made its way in. *That's a little odd. Moving awfully slow,* she thought.

As the wagon neared, she noticed it also looked odd. She stood and shaded her eyes to get a better look. "Oh my God!" she screamed. She ran next door to the stage office where Harold Baker wrote in a ledger book. "Mr. Baker! There's a wagon coming and something's wrong!

There's no driver, and it looks like arrows are sticking out all over!" Mary began to cry. "Please come look!" she added.

Baker set down his book and removed his spectacles. "What is it, Mrs. Fields, what are you saying?" Baker asked his hysterical neighbor.

"Come look!" Mrs. Fields grabbed Baker's arm and pulled him out the front door. The wagon, a single mule buckboard, passed between the holding pens now in clear view. There looked to be dozens of arrows protruding from all four corners of the wagon, which resembled a porcupine. A slumped boy lay across the footboard, arrows protruding from his back.

"Oh no, that's Vincent Lewis's wagon, and his son!" Baker called out then ran to the wagon. "Get some help!" he called back to Mrs. Fields.

Baker stopped the wagon, immediately checking on twelve-year-old Jordan Lewis whose skin appeared gray and cold; his lifeless eyes turned downward. Baker looked in the back to see Susan Lewis lying unconscious on the floorboard. Her right hand was a bloody mess, but she looked to be alive. Baker jumped up and checked to be certain. Yes, the little girl was breathing. She was still alive! Baker looked back and saw a dozen townsfolk running his way. Doc Phillips hurried along with his signature black medical bag.

James Logan was the first to arrive. "What happened?" Logan yelled, jumping up onto the buckboard bench seat.

"Young Jordan is dead. Susan is back here still alive," Baker reported.

Other men arrived, each asking a barrage of questions, each woman screamed, then began to cry. Deacon David and the nuns tried to get through the crowd along with Doc Phillips.

"What is it?" Doc Phillips asked, still unable to reach the wagon.

"Get the hell out of the way! Let Doc through!" bellowed Logan from atop the wagon.

"It's the Lewis kids, Doc. Jordan is dead, but Susan is still alive," Logan reported while helping Phillips up onto the wagon.

Phillips quickly checked the boy, then attended to Susan. Her right hand appeared to have a bullet hole through it, and the bump on her head indicated a hard fall. "Bring her to my office at once," Phillips ordered, then scurried down and headed back to his office.

"I'll carry her to Doc's. You drive the wagon down to the livery stable," Baker told Logan.

"Sure will," Logan answered, then moved Jordan Lewis to the back before grabbing the reins.

The crowd, which had grown to include half the town, parted as Logan moved the wagon down the street to the livery stable.

"We'll follow the wagon," Deacon David directed the Ursuline Sisters, who were already in group prayer.

The entourage continued down Main Street looking more like a Fourth of July parade instead of folks shocked at the sight of a dead boy. Baker disappeared inside Doc's office. Logan brought the wagon to a stop outside Wilhelm's stables where Lawrence Benson led a group of men in examining the wagon.

"Deacon David, would you make arrangements to have young Jordan moved over to the meeting house. There's a room in the back you can use," Benson asked the clergyman. Without a word, two men assisted the Deacon with his task.

"We'll need a group of men to ride out to the Lewis farm and see what has happened," Benson began.

"I'll go, Lawrence," Jacob Turner volunteered.

"No, Jake, I'll need you to send a wire to Sheriff Evans in Margaret. Let him know what we have. Ask him to come right away. We'll also need someone to ride out to the Double O, inform Mr. Henry, and fetch Mr. Dodson. No time like the present to bring him in if he's still willing," Benson added.

"Lawrence, there must be forty arrows in this as well as a mess a bullet holes," Belton Tanner stated, pulling an arrow from the clutching wood. Tanner looked over the arrow carefully. As a former blacksmith for the army, he had the most experience with Indians of anyone in town.

"Any ideas Mr. Tanner?" Benson asked.

"No question. Comanche," Tanner stated matter-of-factly.

"I thought we were finished with all this," Benson said softly rubbing his head. "I haven't seen anything like this in five or six years since most of the Indians surrendered to the reservations."

"There's a rumor that Comanche warriors who survived the Palo Duro Canyon battles have joined with some outlaws along the river. I've heard some of the soldiers speak of it," Tanner continued.

"Well, if that's true, we should see a lot more army activity in the area. We need to telegraph Forts Sill and Phantom Hill immediately," Benson declared.

"Mr. Benson, the stage still hasn't arrived, and messages to Riverbend have not been answered," Baker informed his stagecoach owner.

Benson stopped and checked the time on his pocket watch. "Give Levi a couple more hours. If they still haven't arrived, hire two men to ride over to Riverbend and see what happened. Prepare the second carriage in case we need it for tomorrow's run to Wichita."

Baker turned and left for his duties. Benson entered the back-meeting room to find Deacon David and two Sisters kneeling beside the Lewis boy.

Benson paused, then stepped out the side door to the telegraph office.

"I sent word to both Fort Sill and Fort Phantom Hill. I got a response from Phantom Hill a few minutes ago. They'll try and send soldiers as soon as they can. Could be here in two to three days. I haven't received a response from Sheriff Evans yet. Could be the line's down," Turner reported.

"Very good. Thank you, Jacob. If the army sends soldiers, that could help us quite a bit. Tom should be back soon with word from the Lewis farm. I fear they'll find the Lewis's dead. That little girl's whole family murdered," Benson shook his head sadly.

"Don't the Lewis's have an older daughter?" Turner asked.

Benson's face flushed red and he closed his eyes tight. "Yes, I forgot about Molly," he answered. "She'd be about sixteen or so, I believe," Benson added.

The two men sat in silence for several minutes before they noticed Wagner coming into town with a wagon. The men jumped to their feet and headed out to meet Wagner. Despite the closing darkness of dusk, they saw the riders navigating the holding pens. Benson lit the lanterns on the meeting house front porch, waving for the procession to come there.

"Hello, Tom. Our fears were confirmed?" Benson asked.

"Yes, sir. We have Vincent and Mary Lewis here with us. We couldn't find Molly. It looks like she was taken," Wagner surmised.

"Taken?" Benson asked.

"Yes, sir. We looked all around before it got too dark. No sign of her, I'm afraid."

"Jacob, let Phantom Hill know we have a kidnapping," Benson ordered. "Gentlemen, can you take the wagon around to the back of the meeting house here. The Deacon and Sisters are inside with the Lewis boy. We'll make arrangements to bury them tomorrow. I'll get Doc to have a look at them," Benson added, then headed across the street to the doctor's office. Once inside, he found Doc reading over a book about the human hands and Sisters Phoebe, Sarah, and Mary sitting with Susan Lewis.

"Hello, Lawrence," Phillips greeted Benson with a pale and grim look.

"Tom Wager and the fellas just returned from the Lewis farm. They have Mr. and Mrs. Lewis with them. They're both dead. Could you go over and take a look. I had them put in the back room of the meeting house," Benson advised.

"Certainly. I'll go immediately." Phillips retrieved his bag and followed Benson out of the office to perform the unpleasant duties. While attending to the Lewis family in the back room, the front door opened and closed. Benson hurried to find Brad Jamieson removing his hat.

"I just left the Double O. Butch says he'll send Dodson over as soon as he can. Says he's out fetchin' strays. Says he'll cover the pay for a deputy also," Jamieson advised.

"Okay, thanks, Brad."

"I heard Tom brought the Lewis's back. They're dead, and Molly's missing?" Jamieson asked.

"Yes. It appears Molly is missing," Benson confirmed.

"Anyone volunteered to look for her?" Jamieson asked.

Benson hadn't even thought of that. He was so consumed with the death of the family he hadn't considered a search party.

"I don't know. I've not heard of anyone forming a search party. We haven't heard from Sheriff Evans, and the soldiers won't be here for a couple of days," Benson reported.

"I'll ask around. We can't wait for Evans or soldiers," Jamieson suggested.

"We'll talk to Mr. Dodson as soon as he gets here. I don't think it's wise to have men ride out tonight, do you?" Benson asked his impatient store owner.

"No, you're right. Tough to track in the dark," Jamieson admitted.

"We'll take action, don't worry," Benson assured.

As Jamieson left, Baker arrived with news the bullet-riddled stage had just arrived with a damaged wheel, having returned to Riverbend for repairs. The report included the outlaw attack and one of the four passengers wounded. Baker also announced that Doc Phillips's niece had arrived and proceeded over to his office.

"Thank you, Harry. Good news," Benson exhaled in relief.

Benson retired to his office and sat quietly at his desk. *Killing and taking children? Raiding Indians and outlaws. I haven't seen lawlessness like this in years. This will need a savage response. But who? Is Lane Dodson the right man?* he thought.

CHAPTER 21

LUXTON DANNER – RED RIVER CITY

D anner pulled his Winchester from its scabbard and cocked his Russian 45. Quietly, he slung his long leg over Bullet's mane and slid to the ground. He heard several horses nicker along the quiet riverbank. Slowly, he crept between the brush and scrub separating sparse leafed branches with the end of his rifle barrel. There, along the water's edge were three, no four horses bobbing their heads and tamping their hooves. None had a saddle which was the first clue. Second were the red and yellow feathers tied to the mane of a tall appaloosa stallion. Indians. At least four, maybe more.

Danner inched forward, slow and cautious, careful not to announce his presence. He leaned out around a small big-tooth maple, whose leaves appeared to be engulfed in red and orange flames. *Only four. Good.* These days, renegade Indians weren't in the habit of walking. *Okay. Four to one.* He liked those odds. He carefully stepped back and thought of his approach.

The trail opens into a savannah just ahead. No cover there. Stay along the edge of the brush. Be ready to fire both guns, he thought. He crouched down in a futile attempt to shrink his towering frame and skulked forward, trigger fingers ready. Three steps and he stopped. Three more steps and he stopped again. He did not hear anything, no voices, twigs breaking, brush moving. He took another step, then stopped.

Danner looked down straight into the eyes of a dead Indian warrior. He froze. Leaves and debris nearly covered the brave. Danner pushed the barrel of his Winchester into the Indian's cheek just to be sure. Danner made his way around the body, and quickly saw a second in a similar position on the ground. This one wasn't covered in leaves but had a chest wound covered in dried blood.

Suddenly, the brush to Danner's right shuffled with movement. On guard, Danner spun to face the threat, and was met instead by a huge black vulture's flapping wings. The scrounger erupted into flight, knocking yellow and brown leaves in all directions. Danner leaned through the brush and saw the reason for the big buzzard's presence. There, in the brush, another Indian lay dead, gruesomely missing both eyes and part of a nose, thanks to the scavenger.

Okay, four horses, three dead. Where's the fourth? He thought. Danner didn't have to look far. Another twenty feet up the trail lay the fourth dead Indian. The wounds were a few days old, and none had a weapon.

Bandits. They must have taken their weapons. Bows, arrows, any guns they might've had. Following the trail or across the river? Had to be a bunch of 'em to defeat four Comanche, he thought. Danner whistled for Bullet, who trotted forward and arrived promptly. Grabbing the rein, he moved the big bay through a narrow opening in the brush then swung up into the saddle. He rode up and down the riverbank looking for tracks. Finally, about a hundred feet up-river, there they were. Swirling half-round overlapping cuts into the red silt. Ten, twelve horses easy, he figured.

Good. Crossed back into the territory. I shouldn't need to worry about catching up with 'em on the trail, he thought. Danner swung Bullet around and pushed through another opening into the clearing. A couple more days and he'd be in Eagle Springs. For now, he'd do well to reach Red River City before sundown.

Like many of the settlements along the Red River, Red River City had sprung up seemingly overnight. With plenty of lumber nearby, the town began as a lumber mill then branched off into cattle ranching.

Surrounded by numerous small ranches, the town's settlers wanted it to be known as a city, thus its self-assured name. Despite it being susceptible to border raiders and the money that flowed from both lumber and beef, it seemed to avoid unwanted visitors from the north. Unlike other towns along the river, Red River City employed hired gunmen to ward off any ambitious bandits.

A while later, the evening's festivities in Red River City had just begun for the night. Piano music burst from the saloon, along with girls laughing, and men cussing the cards they'd been dealt. As the saloon showed signs of life, the mill slowed as the massive, whirring saws shut down. Kyle Britt lit the rusty lantern hanging from a bent nail in front of the guard's bunkhouse and took a seat next to fellow gunman Jonny Gallup. The other two hired gunmen remained inside catching some shuteye ahead of the night watch. The four men had been employed by the City going on six months now. They were paid well and earned it early on with five deadly gunfights to their credit. Britt made certain to keep track of fights and men killed in defense of the town. None wore a badge, and none cared to. Britt and company liked their arrangement just fine. Good money, free shelter, and plenty of women and whiskey whenever they found the time. Many feared Britt and his boys, despite their penchant for eliminating outlaw intervention.

"You need to fight lawlessness with lawlessness," Jared Barry, the owner of the lumber mill told his neighbors. "As long as we're left alone, I don't rightfully care how Mr. Britt and his men handle their business," Barry often boasted to anyone who would listen.

"Lone rider come'n in," Gallup announced, before sending a stream of tobacco juice into the spittoon at the edge of his boots.

Britt looked down the street to see one rider and a pack.

"Looks like he's on a long ride," Britt answered.

"Big fella," Gallup added.

"Let's see what the gentleman's intentions are," Britt stated standing up and stretching his arms out to each side. Gallup followed the action, and the two men stepped into the middle of the street to greet the visitor.

Danner saw the men on the bunkhouse porch and watched as they took positions in the street. Danner's senses peaked as he approached but did not see visible badges. He stopped Bullet well short of the men, forcing them to walk toward him. Any advantage he could create was beneficial. He took hold of his vest and pulled it to the side revealing his U.S. Deputy Marshal badge.

"Good evening, gentlemen. Name's Luxton Danner, U.S. Marshal."

Both men paused and smiled.

"Good evening Marshal, welcome to Red River City," Britt greeted the lawman. "We weren't sure what to make of you. Just earning our pay is all. No hard feelings," Britt continued with a cracked voice, a bit nervous himself now.

"No hard feelings. You fellas the law here?" Danner asked.

"Well, no, not officially. The town pays us to keep the border raiders out is all," Britt explained.

"And I looked like a raider, did I?" Danner asked without a smile, irritated by the gunfighter greeting.

"No, sir, just checkin' things out is all. Have a good evening, sir," Britt cut the conversation short, turned, and headed back toward the bunkhouse.

Danner let the silence send his message, then he looked around for a livery stable and hotel. Halfway down the street was one of the bigger hotels he'd seen this far out in the territory. Must be a result of the lumber mill he passed. Swinging down from Bullet, he tied him to a large trough in front of the River City Hotel and stepped into a wide room lit with more candles than he'd seen since his days back in Charleston. A beautiful young woman scurried from a room behind the desk, smoothing out her long gray dress, and raven black hair at the same time. Deep green eyes and bright red lips greeted Danner.

"Good evening, sir, may I get you a room?" She asked parting her red lips into a gaping smile.

"Yes, ma'am, you certainly can."

"Do you have a preference to the size of room?" She asked.

"No, not in size, but I would like one at the end of the hall, if one's available?" Danner asked, carefully looking around the wood paneled hotel lobby, still feeling uncomfortable with the welcome committee he had on the street. Large, used saw blades decorated the walls along with other tools Danner assumed had once been used at the lumber mill.

"I can do that. Room ten, and it has its own washbasin in it," the young lady reported.

"Fine. It'll only be for tonight," Danner advised, bringing his attention back to the young lady.

"That will be three dollars," she said.

Danner reached into his vest pocket and removed four dollars, then handed them to his hostess.

"A room with a wash basin in it is worth at least four dollars," Danner said with a smile.

"Thank you very much Mr.?"

"Luxton Danner, ma'am. From Fort Smith."

"Thank you, Mr. Danner. I'm Rebecca. My father owns this hotel," she announced.

Connecting the size of the hotel, the lumber needed to build such a large structure, and the mill decor, Danner figured the hotel owner also owned the mill.

"Miss Rebecca, is there a Marshal or Sheriff in town?" Danner asked.

Rebecca's grin disappeared and her bright face turned dark as if the sun had fallen off the horizon.

"No, sir. We only have Mr. Britt and his men. They just scare everyone," she replied with a frown.

Danner sensed discomfort and possibly fear in Rebecca. She stared at the desk counter and became quiet. "Why are they here?" Danner asked taking greater interest now.

"Mr. Barry hired them. He owns the lumber mill and pays those men to keep outlaws away. At least that's what he says."

"How many did he hire?" Asked Danner.

"There's four, I think."

"They ever do anyone harm here?" Danner pressed.

"No, not really, I guess. They're just not very nice is all."

"How long have they been here?" Danner knew he was pushing the young lady, but he had a bad feeling about those two in the street.

"About five or six months now. I think it was around the beginning of the summer when Mr. Barry built that bunkhouse and hired them. It was right after outlaws came into town and caused a lot of trouble. They tried to burn the mill, but Mr. Barry and some men fought them off." Rebecca explained, her discomfort easing as she spoke.

"Do you know where I could find Mr. Barry this evening?" Danner asked.

"He's usually at the mill until late at night. He built a house right behind it, so if he's not there he'll probably be at home." Rebecca advised.

"Has there been a Ranger or Marshal through here since Mr. Barry hired those men?" Danner asked taking another look around the hotel and out front through the big front window.

"I don't really know. My father doesn't like me talking to a lot of people in town," she stated.

"Are you a lawman or something?" Rebecca finally asked.

Danner took the key from Rebecca and smiled. He decided to keep his profession to himself for now. "Or something," he answered, then made his way up the wide staircase and down the equally spacious hall to room ten. After a quick scan of the room, he ducked under the frame and hung his saddle bags on the bedpost. He locked the door and propped a chair up under the door handle for added security.

Something's not right here, he thought. *Do I confront this Barry and find out what he's up to? That would fit into my assignment. This reeks of outlaws being paid to fight outlaws.* Danner looked out the window onto main street. Nothing really looked out of place. People going about their business. Music in the saloon; always a good sign. *There must be plenty of ranchers around that wouldn't put up with hired guns watching the town. Or would they? Had the raids along the river led to this?* Danner made use of the wash basin and cleaned up. After another quick look out the window, he laid across the bed, folded his long arms across his chest, and closed his eyes.

Suddenly, the door appeared to crash inward sending splinters from the chair flying on top of him. Danner rolled off the bed and drew both Russians. Bullets shattered the glass in the window and the mirror above the bed. Two men fired in all directions. Danner fired both Russians, his shots hitting their mark on the second man through the door. The first fired under the bed hitting him in the leg. Danner leapt away from the bed and got behind a big leather wingback chair set in the corner of the room. He couldn't see the other gunman but heard his hard breathing on the far side of the massive four-post bed. Swiftly, a gun appeared over the edge of the quilt, and fired. Crack! The bullet blew up a white pitcher sitting on a table next to him. Glass shards hit Danner, shredding the flesh on the right side of his face. The assailant fired again, this time hitting the back of the chair. Danner opened fire with both pistols emptying all cylinders where the gunman lay, shredding the bedding with an onslaught of lead. Feathers and fabric flew in all directions. He heard a gun fall to the floor, then silence. He carefully stood, wiping away glass fragments from his tattered face. He moved around the bed fighting the pain in his leg. There on the floor lay the two men that met him in the street. Both were dead.

A voice at his door broke the silence. Danner swung his left hand, smashing into the oak bedpost. Danner rolled over on the bed and looked toward the door. It was intact, with the chair still safely propped up under the door handle. No gunmen lay dead on the floor. He felt his face for the shards of glass or blood but felt nothing. His face was fine, but his left hand throbbed as a result of his wild swings at ghosts.

Damn it, Danner! Danner's thoughts banged around inside his head like a corralled bucking horse. He looked down at the bed. He must've removed both Russians from their leather holsters because they were strewn about on the quilt. He quickly checked to make sure neither gun had been fired. *Whew. That never happened before,* he thought, relieved he hadn't actually fired shots.

He made his way back to the wash basin, splashing water onto his burning face. He was sweating and his muscles were tense. He tried to get his bearings, to know for certain what was real and what was imaginary. He took several deep breaths, then put on a clean shirt just before someone knocked on his door. This was no ghost.

CHAPTER 22

Danner pushed the chair aside and opened the door to see a short, heavyset man with a round face, wearing a dark gray vest that looked like it was about to burst. The man removed his black bowler hat and swallowed hard. Danner said nothing but looked down on the stumpy fella.

"Pardon me sir, I'm Jared Barry. I own the mill, store, and this hotel. My daughter tells me you were making inquiries about where to find me. I thought I would simplify matters and call on you. May I come in?"

Danner stepped aside and waved Barry inside. Barry stepped inside, taking a seat on one of the wingback chairs opposite a small table.

"I don't mean to impose upon my guests, mind you, but most people that pass though don't ask for me," Barry explained.

Danner checked the hallway, then closed the door and took the leather wingback opposite Barry. "You say you own this hotel?" Danner asked.

"Yes, sir, that's right."

"Then the young lady that greeted me downstairs is your daughter?"

"Yes, she is."

Damn it, Lux. You should've made that connection. You figured the owner of the mill also owned the hotel. She said her father owned the hotel, he thought. "I see. She didn't indicate that when I asked about you," Danner offered.

"Is there something I can do for you?" Barry asked wiping sweat from his brow with a stained handkerchief that he quickly tucked back into his vest pocket.

"I was curious about the greeting on the street I received from two men before I could even get to the hotel," Danner chose his words carefully.

"Do you know who they were?" Barry asked his thick sausage-like fingers fumbling with his bowler hat.

"Said they were just earning their pay," Danner stated.

"I see. They'd be the town's lawmen, I reckon," Barry suggested.

"Oh? When I asked, they said they weren't the law, and your daughter told me there was no Sheriff or Marshal in town," Danner stated in a raised voice not caring to hide his annoyance with the little fat man.

Barry squirmed in his chair. "Well, what's it matter to you, may I ask?" Barry concluded, his voice wavering now.

Danner pulled his vest back allowing Barry full view of his badge. "I'm sure you know my name, but I declined to tell your daughter I am a Deputy U.S. Marshal on assignment."

Barry's eyes widened, and he coughed nervously. He wiped his face again then cleared his throat. "Glad to have a U.S. Marshal in our town sir. Very glad, indeed. Did you identify yourself to our peacekeepers then?" Barry asked, his voice fluttering like a bird's wings.

"Yep, and they acted the same as you."

"What do you mean?" Barry asked.

"Nervous. Now why would peacekeepers and the town boss be nervous about a visit from a U.S. Marshal? And, why would a young lady intentionally hide her identity as it related to you when I asked?" Danner asked rhetorically. Danner didn't wait for a reply. He stood and opened the door. "I believe our meeting has concluded, Mr. Barry," he announced.

Barry quickly stepped out of the room and paused in the hallway. "Don't misunderstand, Marshal. I'm, I mean we here in Red River City are just trying to keep our people and assets safe from thievery. Good evening." Barry scurried down the hall and disappeared.

Danner thought for a moment. *Okay, I get the protection. Gunmen? Fine. Why does he have his daughter acting as a spy on travelers. She clearly called him Mr. Barry and obviously didn't like the gunfighters in town. I didn't recognize those two from the street, but I only brought a handful of warrants and flyers. No time to find the nearest Sheriff and look further into it. Maybe on the way back?* Danner thought. Danner decided to head out and find the livery stable for Bullet.

He made his way down the stairs, careful not to move too quickly. He was on full alert now.

As he passed the front desk, Rebecca came running around, stopping in front of him. "Mr. Danner, I'm very sorry for speaking to you the way I did, but my father is a curious man, and he makes me be that way," she declared.

Danner looked at the young woman and could tell she was in complete discomfort over the meeting with him, both earlier and now. Her green eyes explored the floor and her bright red top lip quivered slightly. Danner looked around. The hotel was uncharacteristically quiet. No card game at the tables, no one in the dining room, despite the dinnertime hour. "Are there any other guests in the hotel tonight?" he asked.

"Yes, sir, only two others, and they asked for dinner in their rooms," she reported.

"Seems awfully quiet for a big hotel," Danner stated, then walked around the young woman and headed out to the street.

He noticed only a few people out, but the saloon sounded busy enough. Danner saw the stable down at the end of the street and started that way. Rather than ride, he decided to walk with Bullet between him and the gunslingers watching from the front of their boarding house.

"Good evening, sir. Need a stall tonight?" came a voice from inside the darkened barn. A tall slender man stepped out, wearing a wide brimmed cowboy hat and a knife Jim Bowie, famous defender of the Alamo, would have been proud of.

"I'll need a stall if you have one?" Danner asked.

"Yes, sir, Marshal, bring him right on in," the man stated.

Danner walked Bullet to the barn door, then removed his saddle bags and Winchester. "I'd like a small bag of oats early in the morning. Can you take care of that?" Danner asked.

"Sure, can. I'll have 'em ready at sunup," he answered.

"Thank you, but one thing: I don't recall telling you I was a Marshal," Danner added, then turned and walked away before any response could be offered. *Let's see what's happening at the saloon*, he thought, allowing a slight grin of amusement, figuring everyone at the saloon would have also been warned of his presence by Barry and his gunmen.

Danner stopped at the Red Water Saloon's swinging doors and looked inside. Like the hotel, it was big, with two bars and a second floor. Several girls made their rounds, looking for a drink or a customer. Danner pushed through and made his way to the bar on the back wall. He felt like Moses at the Red Sea as people parted, allowing him to pass. Some smiled, some didn't, but they all moved aside. Danner reached the bar, and was met by another short, fat fella wearing an apron and a gap-toothed smile.

"What'll ya have, stranger?" He asked cheerfully enough.

Danner hadn't had a drink in a long while, but figured he'd play the part.

"Beer," he announced.

The bartender made his way over to a large barrel mounted on a counter behind the end of the bar and poured a full mug, bringing it back promptly.

"Thanks."

"Yes, sir. Gonna stay a while or just passin' through?" the burly bartender asked.

"Just passin' through," Danner kept his answer short.

"Got a couple of good games goin' if yer interested," he added.

Danner looked over toward the front of the room and saw three tables full-up with cowboys flipping cards.

"No thanks. Haven't played cards in months," He answered.

"Suit yerself. Holler if ya need somethin'," he stated then headed down to the other end of the bar where a cowboy waved an empty glass.

Danner positioned himself around to the end of the bar, keeping his back to the nearby wall. He scanned the crowd. He noticed a piano and banjo player in the opposite corner to where he stood. *Nothing out of place. Awful lot of action out here in the middle of nowhere though*, he thought, then took a sip of beer.

After a few minutes, he noticed the town boss, Jared Barry, making his way through the crowd toward him. *This should be interesting*, he thought.

"Good evening, Marshal. Nice to see you again," Barry offered, seemingly attempting to begin this meeting better than the last one ended.

"Good evening. Looks like business is pretty good," Danner offered.

"Yes, sir. We do very well at the mill, and there are several small successful ranches no too far out of town. The saloon here does a good business," Barry nodded toward the portly bartender.

"The bartender owns this place?' Danner asked.

"Yes, sir. I know what you're thinking. I don't own everything in town. Just the mill, store, and hotel. That's enough for one man and his eighteen-year-old daughter."

"So, how'd you end up here, Mr. Barry?" Danner relaxed his approach.

"Well, like a lot of settlers along the river, I started west after the war and ended up down in New Orleans, or at least what was left of it. Hung around long enough to make a little money on the riverboats, then headed north. Ran into a group of folks making their way from Atlanta and such, so my wife and I decided to join them going west," Barry began, obviously feeling a little more comfortable with Danner's relaxed approach as Barry took a seat at his table.

Barry sat up in his chair and allowed a faint smile as he continued. "Made it all the way to Colorado, where my wife fell ill in the cold, and passed. I remembered the tall timber back this way and decided to come back. It took a few years, but I settled in here with a few others and built a small mill."

Barry looked around the big saloon and waved his hand at the wood paneled walls and larger than usual bar. "Another wagon train heading west stopped off and I convinced most of the folks to settle here. I told 'em we could make a good town if we had enough folks."

Barry paused and took a long drink from the mug of beer the bartender had set in front of him when he sat down. "We had a little Indian trouble initially, but the bigger the town got, the less Indian trouble we had. The soldiers from Fort Sill were regular visitors back then also. That didn't hurt. Anyway, most of what you see today has only sprouted up in the last couple of years. The only thing we're missing is our own stage line and telegraph office. I'm working on those now," Barry boasted nodding toward the front window out toward the street.

Danner nodded and took another sip of beer. "No wonder nobody knows much about your town, with no stage or telegraph," Danner stated.

"True enough. Lawrence Benson's stage stops off now and then, but we're too far from any of the bigger towns and these bandits running along the river scared off a lot of folks." Barry explained.

"You sure your gunfighters hanging around aren't scaring off more?" Danner asked, reverting to a serious tone.

"Look, Marshal, you know better than anyone that there's damn little protection up here on the border. You're the first U.S. Marshal I've seen here in a couple years, and the Rangers don't give a damn either." Barry's tone was strong now and he leaned in toward Danner with resolve in his voice. "Some of the neighboring towns tried to do it nice. Hired good men to be town Marshals and such. All they did was get killed. I decided to do it another way, and it works. That's all that matters right now," Barry concluded, leaning back in his chair with a huff.

Danner put money down on the bar. "Be careful Mr. Barry. These types of situations have a tendency to go bad before you know it. Good night," Danner stated then headed out of the saloon.

Moments after Danner departed, Jonny Gallup got up from a nearby table and walked over to Barry.

"How'd it go, boss?" Gallup asked.

"I don't know. I figure he hasn't got the time to hang around here."

"Some of the boys are gettin' restless. They wanna know when the next job will be."

"You leave the thinking to me! Wouldn't be too smart to pull something with a U.S. Marshal around! Tell them to sit and wait! That business of killing those Comanche and using their weapons was bad enough! Anyone connects that to us, and we'll have both the Comanche and the Calvary all over us! We wait until he's gone. Then I'll meet with the boys. I got something big planned. We can't have any mistakes though. Now go do what I'm payin' ya for!" Barry snarled.

"Careful, Mr. Barry, careful," Gallup drew his gun and rolled the cylinder along his sleeve, then holstered and left the bar.

CHAPTER 23

Danner closed the door to his room and made his way downstairs. The sun hadn't made an appearance yet, an eerie silence engulfed the hotel. Once in the foyer, he looked around the front desk to the office, but found it vacant. There was no movement in the kitchen, either. *Damn, I could have used a coffee,* he thought.

Danner opened the front door, closed it as quietly as it's grinding hinges would permit, then made his way toward the stable. It was downright cold. He had left his trail duster with Bullet, and now regretted that decision. In the pre-dawn light, he saw the big barn doors open with movement inside. The tall fella wearing the big knife walked Bullet to the front of the barn.

"Good morning, sir. I have your horse here with the bag of oats you asked for."

"Thank you," Danner replied, as he paid the man and quickly mounted Bullet to get out of town.

Rebecca Barry sat astride her horse in the shadows next to the hotel. She had packed a small bag which she looped over the saddle horn. She watched Danner make his way to the stable and collect his horse and ride west out of town. She reined her horse around to the back of the emporium that sat next to the hotel and rode to the edge of town, where she stopped and waited.

She had waited for the time when she could leave Red River City and get away from her controlling father. She didn't like his friends or employees, and certainly didn't like spying on everyone that came into the hotel.

She knew asking Danner to take her would be fruitless and her father would have to think hard to follow her now. Or so she thought. After a twenty-minute start, under the cloak of darkness, Rebecca Barry started off after Marshal Luxton Danner, wanting Red River City to be nothing more than a bad memory.

An hour later, Danner moved across an open sawgrass range at a crisp pace, the sunrise took the sting out of the cold morning air. The heavy frost made the path ahead look like a snowy scene he'd witnessed up in the higher elevations. Thick streams of misty air shot from Bullet's nostrils as he loped along, making the big stallion look more like a machine than an animal.

Danner slowed the pace, providing his companion a well-deserved rest. Taking it a step further, he dismounted and decided to walk a bit. He could see what looked like a creek up ahead which meant clean water and a long overdue cup of coffee. Sure enough, he came upon a moving creek cutting its way through the plain and into the Red River. It was a good spot for morning camp.

A few minutes later, Danner poured hot coffee into his tin cup and wrapped his hands around it. The warmth permeated his frigid skin, melting the stiffness away. While indulging in a long drink of hot brew, the nicker of a horse off in the distance confirmed his feeling of being followed. He carefully scanned full-circle around his small fire. In the distance, back on the trail he had just traversed, he saw the outline of a single rider. Bullet answered the nicker with a snort and bob of his head.

"I see 'em buddy. Lone rider coming slow." He pulled his Winchester and waited in between Bullet and a small clump of brush.

As the rider came into clearer view, he saw the long dark hair flowing from under a small-brimmed hat. The coat covered much of what he could see, but it appeared to be a woman. A shiver shot down his back when he realized the rider was Rebecca Barry. He returned his rifle to its scabbard and stepped out to great his unwanted guest.

———————

B ritt stepped into Jared Barry's office and waited.

"What is it?" Barry asked.

"It's your daughter, sir. We can't find her anywhere. People got up this morning at the hotel, and she wasn't around. I also saw her horse missing from the corral," Britt reported.

"What?" Barry slammed his fist on his desk, knocking a cup of coffee all over the papers he'd been reading. "Damn it!" he shouted grabbing the cup and nearly falling out of his chair. "What the hell?"

"That Marshal also left early this morning," Britt added.

"Damn it! He either took her with him or she decided he was her way out of here!" Barry roared. "You and Gallup get her now! I don't care what you have to do! You hear me?" Barry bellowed, his face red.

"That's a U.S. Marshal you're talking about, boss!" Britt reminded the little man.

"I don't give a damn who he is! I'll give you both five hundred dollars extra for her return! You got that?" Barry stumbled as he attempted to get around his desk. His rage had blinded him. "Get her back if you want to keep your job!" Barry finally yelled opening the office door. "Now!"

"Yes, sir. We'll head out right away," Britt answered as he hurried out of the mill.

———————

Rebecca stopped her horse. "I'm sorry, Marshal. I'm sure you're angry with me following you without asking if I could come with you. I've wanted to leave that town for a long time, and I just didn't see a chance until you arrived. I knew I couldn't do it alone, so I waited for the right person to come along. I don't like my father or his men. They are bad men. Everyone is afraid," she gushed, her eyes welling up with tears.

Danner said nothing. He just listened and tried to think how this would interfere with his assignment. His mind raced like barn swallows chasing each other in the loft. "I have a little coffee left. Would you like some?" he asked, not knowing what else to do at the moment.

"I would love some," Rebecca answered with a huge smile.

Danner walked over and helped her off her horse. She hung onto him longer than necessary, prompting Danner to clarify some things.

"Look Miss Barry–"

"Please. Call me Rebecca."

"I'm not the fella to be rescuing you from your family trouble. I've got an assignment and I'm not in the habit of bringing a woman along with me."

"I promise, I won't be a problem or get in your way," she began.

"You're already a problem, and in the way. You think your father doesn't know what you did and where you're heading? By now he's probably sent those gunfighters of his after you, which means me. Here's what's going to happen. With any luck, we'll reach the next settlement before they catch up to us. You'll stay at the settlement, and I'll move on as fast as I can. I don't want to tangle with hired guns if I don't have to. Understand?"

Rebecca looked into her coffee but said nothing. Danner saw her fighting back tears that finally broke through. She looked up. "I understand."

Danner put out the fire and stowed his gear. "Let's go," he ordered, helping Rebecca onto the saddle.

"How far to the next settlement?" She asked.

"I don't know for certain. Not even sure what settlement is next."

Danner tapped his spurs. He knew there'd be no negotiating with Barry's men. They'd only being interested in earning their pay but tangling with a U.S. Marshal wasn't the best plan, and he knew it. It'd all depend on how committed they were to Barry. One thing was for sure: if they challenged him to a fight, there was more going on in Red River City than met the eye. Barry was involved in a lot more than sawing logs. That gnawed at Danner.

CHAPTER 24

WES PAYNE – THROCKMORTON

The dawn of a new day brought with it a steady rain, making for miserable travel. Wes had felt lucky with the past four quiet days and nights of good weather. The flat terrain and clear weather kept him ahead of schedule so that he arrived in Throckmorton a few days earlier than expected.

Throckmorton was not exactly a booming metropolis. He passed by a shingle with the town's name scratched into it unceremoniously nailed to a crooked wooden post. Although one barn, six shacks, and a couple of adobe huts equaled more of a camp than a town, or even a settlement, the few people squatting there had ample water and fertile land to work with.

Wes hoped to seek shelter from the driving rain inside the barn, as his hands were freezing, despite the pair of deer hide gloves he'd purchased back in Buffalo Gap. His hat and oilskin kept most of the rain off him, but Ringo took a beating from the stinging rain. He stopped at the old barn door and knocked as hard as he could. The feeble door shook on its hinges. With no response, he walked around the side, and found a small entry door reinforced with rusty metal slats. His pounding there caused a rapid response. The door swung open, and two gaping barrels of a shotgun greeted Wes. Wes threw up his hands.

"Hold on, Mister! Name's Wes Payne, Texas Rangers!" He called out in between the clatter of driving water pellets.

"Sorry, Ranger! Come on in!" the old man called as he lowered the scattergun and stepped back.

"Didn't reckon anyone would be out in this! Name's Chet Unger, sir," the old man said through a long, gray, tobacco-stained beard. "You have a horse?" Unger asked.

"Yes, sir. Any chance we could bring him inside."

"By golly, yes! I'll get the front door open in a jiffy!" The old man responded

Wes quickly brought Ringo inside, and ushered him to a stall filled with hay that the old man pointed to.

"Wait right here, I'll grab a couple of blankets to dry him off." Unger hurried to the back of the barn.

Wes scanned the barn and noted four horses and two mules boarded. Unger returned with two multicolored, heavy Indian blankets. Wes accepted the blankets, wrapping one around himself, then wiping down Ringo with the other. After attending to Ringo, Wes spread the piebald blanket over the split rail to dry.

"Much obliged, Mr. Unger."

"No thanks needed, sir. What'd ya say yer name was again?"

Wes extended his hand. "Wes Payne, F Company, Texas Rangers." Wes reached inside his coat and removed his badge showing it to his host.

"By golly! A real Texas Ranger! I ain't never met a Ranger before! What's ya doin' here in Throckmorton?"

Just passin' through on my way up to the river. Got some trouble up there in a town called Range. Ever heard of it?" Wes asked.

"No, sir, can't say I have. I'm from El Paso. Spent some time in New Mexico before headin' over this way. Stopped here about a year or so back to water my mules and ended up stayin'. Got me a little garden out back of the barn here. There were a few people here, said I could have the barn if I wanted it. Couldn't turn that down!" Unger laughed. "How 'bout some coffee?" The old man asked.

"Sure would appreciate that, Mr. Unger."

"Call me Chet. I got a pot heatin' up now. Come on in," Chet said waving his hand toward a tiny room in the front of the barn. A small wood stove in the corner warmed the room to a comfortable temperature with the tin coffee pot sitting on top. Wes noted a window in the corner with a cot underneath it that had thick Indian blankets neatly spread across it.

Chet wiped the inside of a tin cup with dirty fingers then poured coffee into it, handing it over to Wes, who was more interested in thawing out his hands than drinking the muddy brew.

"Looks like you have the market on Indian blankets, Chet," Wes stated nodding toward the cot.

"Oh ya, like I said, I spent some time over in New Mexico. The Indians like to trade and I only could use so many pipes, so I took me several blankets. Come in handy on days like these. Have a chair, Ranger, and tell me all about what yer up to," Chet begged clearly eager for some fresh stories as he leaned forward on a rickety old stool. Wes assumed the old man saw few out of town visitors.

Thunder boomed overhead, shaking everything inside the barn that wasn't nailed down. Thankful to be safe from the worsening weather, Wes sat down and tasted the coffee. He winced at the harsh taste and set it down on the table.

"That was a good 'en!" Chet cackled. The rain pounded the roof's wooden planks sounding more like lead bullets than water.

"Going to see if I can help out some folks having outlaw trouble." Wes explained.

Chet leaned toward Wes as if trying to keep a secret. "You followin' them nuns?" he whispered as if someone else was in the room.

"You know of the nuns?" Wes asked, surprised.

"Yesiree, they come through here a few days back. A preacher and bunch a nuns. "Don't know where they's goin' but I guessin' you headin' to the same place," he added.

Wes nodded. Thunder rattled the barns walls and roof. Wes looked up and around. "Not sure this old barn will handle this storm," Wes stated, watching several leaks along the roofs seems.

Chet laughed. "She'll probably fall right down on me one day!" he exclaimed.

"Would you mind if I catch some shut-eye? I rode half the night trying to beat the storm," Wes asked, yawning.

"Not at all. Use my cot if ya like," Chet offered.

"No, thanks, as long as I have this blanket, I'll find a spot in the hay."

"Ok then, I'll leave ya be."

CHAPTER 25

RANGE

The Lewis funeral ended with a melancholy Bible reading by Deacon David. Three quiet days had passed since the gruesome discovery of the murdered family. The townsfolk, as well as Deacon David, pushed for a delay in the burials just in case they found Molly Lewis, the eldest daughter who had disappeared after the attack. Search parties had scoured the countryside with no sign of her.

The somber gathering made its way back from the cemetery when the rumble of horse's hooves thundering down the street near the east side of town caught everyone's attention. Butch Henry led Lane Dodson and several other riders from the Double O into Range. The well-dressed Henry relished grand entrances and always had eight to ten riders with him. A big man in his early fifties, Henry had a commanding presence about him that never waned. Over six-feet tall with broad shoulders, a touch of gray at the temples of his brown mane and a square jaw, he looked like every cowboy depicted in the dime novels back east. His hand selected Marshal, Lane Dodson, was no different. Slightly taller than his boss, with shoulders to match, Dodson wore a white Stetson, and carried guns on both hips.

Rumored to have been an Arizona Ranger at one time, he'd been hired away for the right price by Henry and his big cattle money.

"Damn sorry to hear about the Lewis family," Henry offered as Lawrence Benson approached with an outstretched hand. "Also sorry it took two days to get back here. I had Lane down along Jagged Rock Creek picking up strays with some of the boys when Jamieson came out and told me what happened," Henry explained.

"That's fine, we gathered several men, and sent out search parties for Molly, but found nothing," Benson reported as the residents of Range gathered around the men.

"That probably means she's still alive," Dodson said, sliding off his saddle.

"Maybe. I'm not sure that's the best thing though," Benson stated removing his brown bowler hat and rubbing his bald head.

"Mr. Benson, did any of the men cross the river and search over there?" Dodson asked.

"No, sir. We thought that to be too dangerous," Benson advised.

"If it's all right with you and the folks here, I'll take a few of our ranch hands and cross over into the territory and have a look," Dodson stated, seeing Butch Henry energetically nodding in approval.

"Of course, that would be supported, I believe," Benson said, facing the crowd, which responded in applause and loud cheer.

"Dodson, take four men with you. They can stay as long as you need them," Henry ordered.

"Yes, sir. I'll take Clark, Mack, Bo, and Cody. They've already volunteered," Dodson informed the big rancher.

"Very well, thanks men. Ya'll stay on the payroll," Henry ensured his cowboys.

"Before we go any further, I'd like to make an official appointment, if you're still willing, Mr. Dodson," Benson asked.

"Yes, sir," Dodson affirmed removing his hat.

Never wasting an opportunity for theatrics, Benson stepped up on the porch of the Meeting house with most of the town's people now gathered in front of him.

"Ladies and gentlemen, I have the honor of standing before you today with the task of appointing the town of Range's new Marshal. Mr. Dodson, would you please step up here."

Benson removed a hand full of metal pieces from his coat pocket. "I've been carrying these around since Mr. Tanner finished them," Benson announced to numerous turning heads and questions of what he held.

"Mr. Dodson, it is our understanding that you have agreed to become the Marshal of Range. Is that correct?"

"Yes, sir, it is," Dodson responded.

"As the mayor of Range, I ask aloud to all here. All in favor of naming Lane Dodson Marshal, say Aye!"

The crowd roared with the aye of approval.

"All against, say nay!"

There was complete silence except for the cry of the Jamieson baby held in Mrs. Jamieson's arms.

"Well, I'm not certain that is a disapproval or not," Benson stated flatly to the loud rumble of laughter from the crowd.

"By the power given me by the citizens of Range, I appoint Mr. Lane Dodson Marshal for the town of Range, county of Hardeman and state of Texas!" Benson shouted holding up his hands as if preaching the Sunday morning sermon. Benson pinned a new shiny Marshal's badge onto Dodson's vest. He then handed his new lawman five deputy Marshal badges all carefully crafted by the town blacksmith. "Please deputize your men with these. Our Marshal's office isn't much more than a bulky shed, but we'll get to work on it right away, Marshal," Benson assured.

"Let's take a look at it," Dodson suggested. The new Marshal stepped over to the shed, and opened the door. It was bigger and sturdier than Benson had indicated. It had a good-sized window in the front, and a solid wood back door that would require reinforcement around the frame. Dodson stood and envisioned a desk and a couple of chairs near the front. That would leave enough room for a cot and wash basin in the back of the building.

"This will be just fine, Mr. Benson. I'll need the back door strengthened and heavy locking bars put on both doors. The only thing missing is a wood stove for heat."

"Very well, I'll have Mr. Tanner get right on those metal latches and see what I can do about a stove," Benson advised.

"We can look to add a cell later," Dodson stated. "Right now, I'd like to get ready to leave for the Lewis farm. We'll look for a trail from there and see what we can find," Dodson stated.

Twenty minutes later, Dodson and his new deputies thundered out of Range heading for what was left of the Lewis farm.

On their way out, they passed four loaded-down Studebaker freight wagons heading into town. Two drivers and a guard manned each, which had supplies and dry goods for Range's merchants.

Tom Wagner saw the wagons coming and slid open the gaping freight yard doors along Main Street. The lead wagon, driven by freight boss Cole Shilling rumbled along turning into the yard with the other three in tow. As soon as the last wagon cleared the gate, Wagner slid it shut and engaged the metal locking arm as though the contents of the wagons were a deep secret. All this was a precaution in case there were bandits following the teams.

The freight wagon's arrival was always a time for excitement in town. Medical supplies, whiskey and beer and dry goods comprised the bulk of the load. Grain and hay came from local farms and lumber from the mill in Red River City and down south along the railroad line.

"How was the trip, Cole?" Wagner asked.

"Surprisingly quiet. We were ready for a fight, but none came. We passed a troop out of Fort Sill a couple of days ago. Captain said they were make'n patrols along the upper Red River. That might have been why we were left alone," Shilling speculated. "What's happened around here while we've been gone?" Shilling asked.

"Sad news. Vincent and Mary Lewis were killed along with their son out at their farm three days ago. The older girl Molly is missing, and their young daughter is over at Doc's with some serious wounds. A group of bastards that rode through also killed Brody Brown," Wagner reported.

"Oh no," Shilling mumbled removing his hat.

"Yep, it was a bad scene. The Lewis boy slumped in the bench of their buckboard with two arrows in his back. The little girl lying in the back. The damn wagon had a mess of arrows all over it, along with plenty of bullet holes."

Shilling shook his head slowly. "I don't know what to think of it," he stated. "Who was that bustin' out of here when we were coming in?" Shilling asked.

"That was our new Marshal and deputies. Lane Dodson, one of Butch Henry's gunmen, was appointed Marshal. The riders with him are also Henry's men. They're headin' out looking for Molly Lewis. Said they were gonna cross the river and look around the territory," Wagner advised.

"Well, if anybody was gonna cross the river, it'd be Dodson. I wouldn't want to tangle with him," Shilling stated.

"Agreed. If he's as good as his reputation, we should do well with him in charge," Wagner agreed.

A while later, Dodson and his deputies slowed their horses and spread out as they approached the remains of the Lewis farm. The main house and the barn were mostly burned out but a couple of other sheds, and the chicken coop, were still intact, providing possible hiding places for unfriendly foes.

"Let's check these buildings first!" Dodson called out to his men as he dismounted and approached one of the large sheds. Each of his men did the same, taking a structure to search. Dodson made his way around the shed, then in one motion, kicked in the door, and entered, guns drawn, but saw nothing.

Each of his men performed the same actions, all finding nothing. The five men regrouped and headed for the main house which had been built with field stone and log timbers. The logs were charred black and scorched while the stone stood strong. The men rummaged through the debris but found nothing to indicate the Lewis girl had returned.

"Mack, look and see if you can pick up a trail," Dodson ordered the former cavalry scout.

"Yes, sir," Mack McKinnon answered then began a circular search of the ground immediately around the house.

Dodson watched Cody Roberts closely examine the structures, then look around the immediate buildings and surrounding area.

"What is it Cody?" Dodson asked.

"The wagon was full of arrows," Cody mused.

"Yep. That's what I heard. Why?" Dodson asked tipping his hat back, his curiosity piqued.

"Well, there ain't a one arrow, arrowhead, or arrow marking on any of these buildings. Why would the wagon be covered in arrows, and there be no sign of an arrow attack here?" Cody asked out loud.

"You reckon somebody wanted it to look like an Indian attack when it wasn't?" Dodson asked his cowboy detective.

"That's exactly what I'm thinkin'," Cody replied.

Another deputy laughed. "Everyone knows Cody is one quarter Blackfoot Indian!"

"Yes, I know!" Dodson chuckled.

"Hey, don't ya'll pick on my gram maw. She was a fine woman!" Cody stated in between his own chuckles. "And she was full-blood Southern Arkansas Blackfoot!" Cody clarified.

A deputy rode up. "Got the trail. Looks like eight, maybe ten horses, all shod, headed north from here," the tracker reported.

"That settles it then, ain't no Indians riding shoed horses," Dodson concluded. "Okay, lead the way! Let's see if we can find these sons-a-bitches," Dodson added.

CHAPTER 26

LUXTON DANNER & REBECCA BARRY – NEAR EAGLE SPRINGS

Rebecca stopped along the trail and filled her hat with wild pecans that dangled from the crown of a bowed tree. Sensing his unwanted companion had stopped, Danner brought Bullet to rest, and looked back. Danner waited patiently while Rebecca collected her prize. Two days had passed since Barry's disgruntled daughter had fled his grasp on the heels of the big Marshal, and yet, no contact had been made with her certain pursuers. Danner was convinced the old man had dispatched his possé as soon as he discovered her absence.

Why hadn't he been confronted? Catching he and the girl would have been easy enough. They should have engaged him in less than two hours, yet two days later there was no sign of anyone following. It made no sense. Unless they decided to wait until he stopped and left the girl behind. Far safer to fetch her back after the Marshal was long gone, he thought.

"Let's go!" Danner called out after he could see her hat overflowing.

She kicked her horse and caught up with him. Danner removed a small burlap sack filled with jerky. He opened it so that Rebecca could pour the pecans in.

"We'll be in Eagle Springs this evening. It's a good-sized town. You can decide your future there. I'll be moving on," Danner advised the frowning girl.

"Is there a train or stagecoach there?" she asked.

"Stagecoach, I believe. The railroad doesn't come up this far. You'll be able to take a stage south to the railhead and go from there."

Rebecca said nothing, just nodded and fell in behind Danner as they continued down the trail. Danner checked the darkening sky to the west. Looked like a bad fall storm was headin' their way. The black and gray clouds were mixing and moving fast. They reminded him of the wet clay ground he'd traversed further north during the war. The wind had also picked up and was delivering a sharp chill through Danner's vest. He looked back and saw Rebecca hunched down in the saddle arms tucked in close and hat pulled down over her green eyes.

"Let's pick up the pace!" he called back.

Rebecca heard and spurred her horse into a gallop.

The girl can ride, Danner thought realizing he was grinning. *Oh no Danner, don't go getting any fool ideas!* He thought. *She's too young and a family fugitive.*

Danner kept Bullet in a gallop when the sound of gunfire cracked through the wind. He pulled hard on the rein bringing his big bay to a halt. Rebecca, not paying close attention nearly ran into the back of Bullet, pulling her horse to the left avoiding a last-second collision.

"Stop," Danner ordered. Gunshots rang out. Rebecca's wide-eyed glance at Danner spoke louder than words. Danner waved his left hand toward the ground ordering her to dismount. Both riders slipped off their horses and moved further into the dormant dense brush along the trail's edge seeking concealment.

"You stay here with the horses. I'll move up and have a look," Danner stated.

Rebecca grabbed Bullet's reins and nodded. To her credit, if she was frightened, she didn't show it.

Danner crept slowly along the edge of the trail which had narrowed considerably. The gunfire was sporadic now with just an occasional shot fired. Danner moved down the path that had become more of a tunnel than trail. He noticed several branches along the trail's edge appeared to have been freshly broken as though a wagon may have forced its way through.

About two hundred feet down the path, Danner saw an opening. It looked like a cave entrance. He lowered himself to the ground and crawled to the rim of the open field. Four covered wagons circled in the middle of the field. Several men crouched down near the wheels, rifles in hand. Deadening silence had replaced the sound of rifle fire. Danner heard the men talking but couldn't decipher their exact words. He didn't have to. He'd already figured it out.

The Wagon train, probably on its way to Eagle Springs, Range, or beyond, had entered the opening where bandits waited. An ambush likely ensued, and this was the end of the fight. *Were the outlaws re-grouping for another assault? Should I join the fight? That would put Rebecca in harm's way though. Damn it!* Danner mused. *I don't have a choice*, he decided, hurrying back to Rebecca without breaking cover.

"What is it?" she asked.

"Four covered wagons, probably filled with families. I figure they were jumped by bandits in a clearing up ahead. Look, I need to help them if I can. You're old enough to decide on your own what you want to do, but I'd rather you wait behind until this is over," Danner reluctantly advised.

"I'm not waiting!" Rebecca stated in an exaggerated whisper, her green eyes wide and clear. "What can I do?" She demanded.

"All right, since there's no time to argue, I want you to ride next to me with your hat off and sitting straight. I need them to see you're a woman. Maybe they won't start shooting at us if they realize that. It should be obvious that we're not outlaws, but they've just been through a gunfight. You'll have to ride behind me until we reach the clearing. The trail is narrow."

"Then what?" Rebecca asked with a grin.

"Then, Miss Barry, if we don't get shot, hopefully, they'll let us inside their wagons," Danner retorted with a grin of his own.

"Well, let's hope we don't get shot, then!" Rebecca giggled, obviously exhilarated by the danger.

"Yes, let's," Danner nodded.

When they reached the clearing, Danner swung Bullet to the right, allowing Rebecca and her dark flowing hair to take a position next to him to be clearly seen. As expected, the men behind the wagons turned their attention and rifles toward the two approaching riders. Danner held both hands up waving his arms across one another, scanning the brush line all around. Rebecca practically stood in the stirrups, her back razor straight, wanting anyone looking to see she was a woman.

"Stop right there!" One of the men ordered.

Danner and Rebecca stopped.

"I'm a U.S. Deputy Marshal! I'm here to help!" Danner identified himself continuing to scan the field's rim.

"What's a U.S. Marshal riding with a woman?"

"I'll explain if you let us in!"

Danner heard a woman call out from one of the wagons.

"Let them in Horace! He's with a woman!" she yelled.

"All right, come ahead. Keep yer hands away from those guns, mister!"

Danner and Rebecca moved toward the portable fort. One of the men moved a wagon, creating an opening in which Danner and Rebecca quickly rode through. Once they passed, the gap between the wagons was closed like a door. Four men held rifles on Danner.

"Say yer a Marshal, huh? Got a badge or somethin'?" one of the men asked.

"Yes, sir. Inside my vest." Danner slowly reached into his vest and removed his badge showing it to all four men. They lowered their guns.

"Best get down off those horses, Marshal. You're a sittin' duck up there. Can't believe them bastards didn't shoot you both."

Two women from one of the wagons hurried toward Rebecca the moment they dismounted. "Are you okay young lady?" one of the women asked.

"Yes, ma'am. Deputy Danner is escorting me to Eagle Springs is all," Rebecca stated.

"Marshal, I'm Horace Stone. I'm sort of leadin' this group west.

We're on our way to Eagle Springs ourselves. We came into this clearing and got jumped. One of the men was hit. He's hurt pretty bad. We used this old cavalry trick with the wagons, and it worked for now anyway," Stone explained.

"I've been sent out here because of all the outlaw activity along the river. How many of 'em were there?" Danner asked.

"About six or so, but we got a couple of 'em. They're over there along that tree line with the dead sage," Stone advised pointing toward the river's edge.

"I reckon you have children with you?" Danner asked.

"Yes, sir. We have four families. Six women, five children, and one baby," Stone advised.

Thunder rolled in the distance turning the group's attention toward the western sky.

"We got us a bad storm coming. My guess is this gang is re-grouping and will charge these wagons again about the time the storm hits. They may or may not came back with more guns," Danner advised, all the while keeping an eye on the tree line near the river.

"Well, we're badly exposed out here, but we can't outrun 'em. I don't know what is best," Stone admitted.

"It doesn't look like you'll have to decide. Here they come again," Danner announced reaching for his Winchester.

"Come with us!" One of the women ordered Rebecca grabbing her hand in the process.

The men returned to their defense positions. Danner leaned up against one of the wagon's sideboards. The five bandits spread out and began to circle around the wagons, resembling an Indian attack.

Crack! Crack! Crack! The bandits opened fire sending wood splintering in every direction. Danner leaned in and fired, knocking an outlaw from his saddle. The men opened fire as the assault commenced from all directions. Danner leaned in again and Crack! Another outlaw hit the ground with a thud. Bullets tore up ground all around the wagons. The horses snorted and stomped their hooves wanting to flee the commotion. One of the men inside the wagons screamed out.

"I'm hit!" he yelled then rolled to the ground.

A woman screamed then crawled out of her wagon toward the fallen defender. Bullets ripped through the canvass bonnets of the wagons.

"Get back inside!" Danner yelled, pushing the woman inside her wagon. Danner spun around as an outlaw charged a gap in the wagons. Crack! A bullet from Danner's Winchester hit the bandit in the face blowing the back of his head onto the side of a wagon's canvass top. The women screamed holding crying children in their arms. Thunder boomed overhead and lightning fractured the sky.

Danner leaned into another fearless outlaw charging the wagons, firing his pistol. A bullet sliced the outside of Danner's left shoulder. Crack! Another bullet from Danner's Winchester sent an outlaw plummeting to the ground. The last of the renegades charged toward the river's edge, wildly firing over his shoulder. Danner leaned into his rifle and fired. Crack! The last bandit spiraled off his horse!

The rider-less horses ran in the river beyond the tree line as the echo of gunfire faded into the distance. The women rushed from their hiding places to see if their men had survived. Rebecca ran across the inside opening of the wagons to embrace Danner. He winced at the sharp pain in his shoulder and looked down at his companion, surprised at her sudden display of affection. "You okay?" he asked.

"Yes, I'm fine, but I don't think that man is!" she said looking towards one of the men who had been shot.

Danner walked over but didn't need to ask. The crying woman kneeling next to the man reported his condition. He was dead. "I told him I didn't want to come out here! I told him!" she said through hysterical tears.

The other women did their best to console her, but she was out of control, shaking and flailing her arms. Danner stood silent; his thumbs hooked behind his gun belt buckle, his eyes staring at the ground.

"You're hurt," Rebecca said, moving Danner's shirt sleeve and seeing the tear and trickle of blood.

"I'm fine, it just clipped me. Never mind. We need to get them out of here right away," Danner said, his jaw clenched.

"Marshal, if it weren't for you, we'd all be dead like Martin there. You took them all on yerself, while the rest of us just fired and missed. We're just farmers, not gunfighters. I'm sorry." Stone stood shoulders slumped and head hung low.

"Mr. Stone, pick your head up. You're all brave men and women to come out here and make a life for yourselves. You did a fine job, placing the wagons and defending yourselves. I'm glad I came along when I did. We need to get moving though, that storm's not going to wait and those aren't the only bandits running up and down the river."

"Yes, sir. Give us a couple of minutes. We'll be ready."

"Don't you wish you had stayed in Red River City?" Danner asked Rebecca.

She climbed back up onto her horse. "I'm never going back," she said firmly.

CHAPTER 27

BEN CHANCE, JR. – EN ROUTE TO RIVERBEND

The driving rain pelted the back of Chance's oil skin duster as he guided his horse along the valley floor. With every muddy hoof print left behind, he questioned his decision to ride back to Texarkana instead of heading to the railhead. The idea of testing himself didn't seem as smart as when he started this adventure.

He knew he was a good farmhand, but since Marshal Danner had delivered his father's letter and told him of his father's death, he felt that he'd needed to prove something to himself. He'd already found more than he bargained for on this trip. He was proud of the way he defended himself but had seen a man he barely knew die at his side.

According to his map, which hadn't steered him wrong yet, he would arrive in Riverbend in less than a day's ride. But first, Chance decided to seek shelter for both he and his horse from the coldest rain he could ever remember under an enormous willow tree and its massive canopy.

Chance swung down from his waterlogged saddle and took refuge on the back side of the willow's broad trunk. Most of the rain barely penetrated the tree's broad canopy, creating a welcome resting place. Chance pulled the last of his beef jerky from his saddle bag and settled in to wait out the storm. Thunder rolled across the sky, shaking the ground he sat on while white lightning split the heavens. He thought back to his talk with Rachel in Canyon Creek, and about her memories of his father, and how honorable he had been.

He closed his eyes and clenched both hands into rock-hard fists. *I wish I had known him. Why didn't he come back after the war! Why? Is that honorable? Leaving your son? He tried to explain it in his letter, but why?* His heart pounded. He took a deep breath, then another. He'd spent many a night awake in his bed wondering about his father and what had happened to him. He remembered shedding tears at his father's expense. Chance cleared his mind as best he could. *It doesn't matter. He had his reasons. Best just to forget about it,* he tried to tell himself.

The rain's intensity diminished, and the thunder pushed on further east. Chance finished his sparse meal, gave his horse a handful of grain, then prepared to continue on to Riverbend. He didn't know anything about Riverbend, other than it was a town on the latest railroad map he could get his hands on. He hoped it had a hotel or boarding house as he needed to clean up and get some real sleep. His wet boot slipped into the stirrup, and with an exaggerated heave, he swung up onto the cantle of his saddle, then slid on its slick surface down into the seat. *Nothing like riding on a waterlogged saddle,* he thought as he tapped his spurs and headed east.

Not surprising, Riverbend garnered its name from its location on the river. It sat on the west side of a southern bend of the Red River. Despite the recent attack on a nearby farm, it was an emerging town with new settlers arriving each month, thanks to the Red River stage line and a new telegraph office that connected it to its bigger neighboring town of Range. The telegraph connection to the county seat of Margaret was still in the planning stages, but its prospects motivated the town's business owners to keep expanding when the opportunity presented itself. Although the hotel, cantina, and store were small, the constant passing cattle drives created a constant influx of prosperity.

The heavy rains left behind rut-laden muddy streets as Chance slowly made his way into town. Much to his delight, Chance saw a hotel and livery stable at the entrance. He stopped off at the stable, picketed his horse, threw his saddlebags over his shoulder, then navigated across the muddy crimson street to the hotel.

Stepping through the front door, he did his best to rid his boots of the excess red mud. He tapped a small bell that brought a short Mexican man wearing gray-stripped riding pants, a white shirt, and black vest dashing from a back room. Chance removed his hat and pulled off his soaked duster, assuming the man to be the hotel's owner.

"Hola, I am Bartolo Rivera; may I help you, sir?" he asked.

"Yes, please. Do you have a room?" Chance asked.

"Sí, señor. I have a nice room for you."

Bartolo turned the register book around on the desk and selected a key from one of the many hooks on the adjacent wall. Chance signed the register and accepted the key to room number two.

"Is there a good place to eat in town?" Chance asked.

"Sí, the cantina down the street is very good, señor."

Chance nodded, then made his way up the narrow staircase to the second floor that displayed three doors on each side of a narrow hallway. He let himself in number two and immediately noted the wash basin in the far corner. The black iron wood stove filled the small room with heat from the burning orange embers, relaxing Chance immediately. He peeled off his wet clothes, hanging each on a bedpost or over a chair to dry. His second set of clothes were surprisingly dry considering the saturated condition of his saddle bag. He quickly washed and welcomed his clean set of clothes, then decided to give the cantina a try. Hot food of any kind would be welcome at this juncture. Returning to the lobby, he noticed a single rider tying his horse in front of the hotel.

"You go have good dinner now, señor?" Bartolo asked, as Chance opened the front door.

"Yes, sir. Thought I would."

"You will like it, señor, Marilita is a fine cook," Rivera said through what seemed like a permanent grin.

Chance held the door for the man who had just arrived.

"Thank you, sir," the man stated, passing through the doorway as Chance stepped outside and closed the door. He paused, looking through the window back into the lobby figuring the man would be inquiring as to who Chance was. Chance watched the conversation unfold.

"Hello, Mr. Tolliver, how are you?" Bartolo asked.

"Just fine, Bart. Any idea who that fella is?" Tolliver asked.

"No, sir. He write his name here in the book. He looked like he has been on the trail for a long time. He was very wet and dirty when he come in. He just asked about food in town. He is going to the cantina. Is there trouble señor?"

"No, I don't think so, I just thought I'd come over and see if everything was okay is all."

Chance smiled to himself. He was becoming more familiar with how the town Marshals and Sheriffs handled new men in town. He didn't need to hear what they were saying. His suspicion was confirmed when the man looked at the register.

"Let me have a look at your register. Ben Chance!"

"Is that bad, señor?"

"Well, I don't know. I heard Ben Chance was killed a few months back. I'll be on my way then. Have a good evening, Bart."

Frank Tolliver had been Riverbend's Marshal less than a year. He had been Sheriff Zach Evans's deputy before that, and had known of Ben Chance, Sr., both as a U.S. Deputy Marshal, and town Marshal in Canyon Creek. News of Ben Chance being killed near Six Shot had traveled quickly, likely causing Tolliver some uncertainty as to who Chance was and what his connection to the old Marshal had been. Tolliver moved his badge from his shirt to the outside of his vest and headed to the Matador Cantina.

A few minutes later, Chance sat at a table away from the front door sipping coffee when Tolliver pushed through the solid wood door of the Matador. The Marshal's badge explained his presence to Chance. *He's checking on me. I'm sure I looked like an outlaw when I arrived*, Chance thought.

Tolliver made his way around the few occupied tables and

approached Chance. Chance stood and smiled at the Marshal. "Good evening, Marshal, Ben Chance," he stated extending his right hand, which Tolliver accepted for a shake.

"Frank Tolliver. Sorry to bother you Mr. Chance, but–"

"Let me stop you right there, sir. I'm Ben Chance's son," Chance interrupted.

Tolliver's shoulders sunk low and he exhaled loudly. "I'm sorry. When I saw that name, I had to check. It never occurred to me that you'd be Ben's boy. I was sorry to hear of your father's death. I didn't know him very well, but I knew of him plenty," Tolliver explained.

"Yes, sir, I've heard that a lot lately," Chance advised. "Care to join me?" Chance asked waving toward a chair.

"I'm sorry to have bothered you, but maybe for a spell." Both men sat at the table. A woman poured Tolliver a cup of coffee. He nodded thanks. "Plan on staying in Riverbend for a while?"

"No, I'm making my way back to Texarkana from Canyon Creek. I'll probably head out tomorrow. Maybe you can help me, though. I've got three signed flyers of wanted men I was a party to killing. Know where I can cash these rewards in?" Chance asked.

"Good for you, takin' after your father. About a two-hour ride from here is the town of Margaret. Ask to see Sheriff Evans. Mind if I take a look at the posters?" Tolliver asked.

Chance pulled the damp documents from his vest pocket. Tolliver looked over the names and shook his head, handing them back to Chance. Don't recognize any of them," Tolliver stated.

"Thanks. I'll see if I can get down to Margaret and collect before I make my way back home," Chance said.

"Be careful along the river. We have some bandits and possible Indian trouble around here," Tolliver warned.

"Yes, sir. I've heard."

"Have a good evening." Tolliver downed the remainder of his coffee and stood. "I can't get over how much you look like your father," he said as he walked off.

Is there anyone who hadn't heard of Ben Chance? The infamous Marshal's son wondered as his hot meal arrived.

CHAPTER 28

LUXTON DANNER & REBECCA BARRY – EAGLE SPRINGS

Water glistened off the jagged face of the elevated escarpment along the riverbank, highlighting the earth's layered red, brown and black soil. Danner led the wagon train alongside, into the headwind and rain that grew more intense by the minute. Thunder pounded the landscape while the piercing flashes of lightning blinded the weary travelers. Danner looked back to see Rebecca slumped forward in the saddle barely keeping pace without a hint of complaint.

That's one determined woman, Danner thought as he steered on.

The ominous black clouds sprinted across the sky as if in a race against time. Danner knew the squall wouldn't last long at the speed the clouds moved. Good thing, since the rain had begun to seep through his oilskin duster. *This nasty weather will keep the bandits' heads down,* he thought.

Bullet's hooves splashed in the muddy water, the rain pouring down in torrents faster than the ground could absorb it. With the ground swelling under the deluge, Danner feared the wagons may get stuck, or worse, break down. He had taken a closer look at them while the families recovered from the attack, and noted they were all in poor condition, and in need of new wheels.

Two hours into the storm, Danner heard Rebecca yell out behind him. He stopped and turned Bullet as quickly as possible to see the reason for Rebecca's alert. The second wagon in the caravan had broken a front wheel and was wedged in the muck. Horace Stone had joined several other men in an attempt to make a quick repair. Danner rode back to see the dilapidated wheel had broken in half and would not be repairable.

"Sorry, Marshal, we'll be delayed a bit. We have a spare wheel in the last wagon. We'll get this replaced right away!" Stone assured him.

Danner waved and rode back to Rebecca. "Looks like we'll be a while. Why don't you see if there's any room in one of the wagons and get out of this rain for a bit. It shouldn't last much longer. I can see the back end of the clearing further west."

Rebecca looked west and saw what Danner had described. Just above the horizon was a thin bright space under the black line of the storm. Rebecca nodded and spurred her horse back to the rear wagons where she dismounted and disappeared underneath the canvas of the third wagon.

An hour later, the men had the wagon ready to go with a different rickety wheel in place. Danner had used the opportunity to ride ahead a bit on a scouting mission, before turning back to find the wagon train already in motion. Rebecca had tied her horse to the last wagon, and was now perched up on the front bench, obviously resolved to making the remainder of the trip to Eagle Springs in relative comfort.

Danner and Bullet took point and resumed leading the downtrodden travelers on their western journey. The rain lessened considerably, and the wind diminished to a wisp of its prior ferocity. Danner leaned back in the saddle and settled in for the extended ride.

***

Two uneventful hours later, Danner caught a glimpse of Eagle Springs. Its dwellings dotted the landscape at the base of an elevated rise to the west with the crimson river's waters cascading down past its northern border. The promise of shelter and hot food spurred Danner onward as he waved his hat back toward the wagons.

As the caravan entered Main Street from the east, Danner noticed boarding houses on both sides followed by a cantina and a general store. He noted another large building under construction further down on the right that Danner guessed would be a hotel when completed.

"Mr. Stone, looks like these boarding houses are the best bet for shelter in town. There doesn't seem to be a hotel yet. Might want to check and see if there are rooms available, if that's what you're looking for," Danner suggested.

"Yes, sir, rooms for the families would be welcome, I'm sure. Thank you."

Rebecca climbed down from her wagon and untied her horse, then walked it up to Danner who remained atop Bullet.

"I'm sure you'll be interested in getting a room here, if you can," Danner stated.

Rebecca looked blankly at the houses, then back to Danner. "Are you staying here tonight?" She asked pulling the wet brim of her hat away from a tired face.

Danner quickly ran through his options. He welcomed a clean room and a hot meal, but he'd thought better of it. Distancing himself from boss Barry's daughter seemed like a more prudent decision. "I don't believe I will. I'll get something to eat, then move on," he answered.

Rebecca frowned, and watched her right boot push some Main Street mud around. After a loud sigh, she looked up at her savior and forced a thin smile below dark, sleep-deprived eyes before gazing down the street. "I suppose that's best for you," she wearily admitted. "Did you see a stage office?" she asked.

"No, I didn't. If there is one, I assume it's farther down the street. I'll go take a look and let you know." Danner spun Bullet around and headed down the mudded path without waiting for a response from Rebecca. He didn't want to wait for her to change her mind on their plan.

A short ride through town proved him correct. On the left, he found a small, wooden building with a big sign reading "Red River Stage Line" in tall white letters affixed to the roof. Danner swung off the horse and entered the office where a frail man reading a book by oil lamp sat behind an equally diminutive desk. Danner pushed the door closed, stomping his muddy boots on a rug strategically placed for such a moment.

"May I help you, sir?" the man asked as he gently closed his book and stood.

"Yes, can you tell me when you expect the next stage, and where would it be heading?"

"Certainly. I expect the stage to arrive any time now, as it's late due to the storm. It won't leave for Range and Riverbend until morning though. We usually don't run at night."

"Very well. Thank you." Danner turned and disappeared as quickly as he arrived. He rode back to the east side of town where he found the four empty wagons next to Chester's Boarding House on the south side of the street. After tying Bullet to the hitching post in front, Danner stepped into Chester's where he was met with the bustle of a dozen people scurrying about while a woman dressed in a gray Victorian dress attempted to match guests to their respective rooms. Danner looked about the lobby but did not see Rebecca.

He stepped out and strolled across the street to the Stanley Boarding House where he found a similar, yet not quite as chaotic scene as he'd just left. A tall thin man strode around the long desk and greeted Danner.

"I'm sorry, sir, but we've just rented out our last room," the man announced.

"That's fine, I'm not looking for a room. I'm looking for a young woman by the name of Rebecca Barry. Did she happen to come in?" Danner asked as he looked about with no sight of the object of his search.

"Let me check with my wife." The tall man disappeared down a narrow hall, then promptly returned. "I'm sorry sir, but we did not check in a Rebecca Barry," he confirmed.

Danner nodded then walked out into the street where the rain had stopped prompting the town's folks to scurry about the waterlogged boardwalks. Danner looked around but saw no sign of Rebecca or her horse. He stood on the walkway in front of Stanley's scratching the side of his unshaven face. *What the hell has she done now?* He thought.

Danner untied Bullet and slid his rain-soaked boot into the stirrup. Once in the saddle, he slowly walked his bay stallion down the street looking side to side for Rebecca. After a couple of puzzling minutes, he found himself back in front of the stage office where Rebecca's horse was now tied next to the livery stable. Danner leaned down and looked through the window. Rebecca seemed to be in discussion with the man he'd just met. *Good. That's exactly what she needs to be doing. The quicker I get out of town the better*, Danner thought.

He reined Bullet around, and headed to the cantina for a quick meal, then thought better of it. Instead, he stopped at the Littleton Mercantile. He tethered Bullet, then stood on the top step of the store, and took a look around the town. He looked across the street at the cantina. Leaning against the front of the saloon were the two gunmen that had stopped him in Red River City. *Barry's men.* Danner rubbed his eyes and took a second look. No doubt about it. It was them.

CHAPTER 29

Danner rushed into the store, hoping Barry's men hadn't seen him. He closed the door, then sunk behind a barrel, and peered out of the front window. A short, heavyset woman wearing a gray apron with white hair piled up on top of her head entered from the back room to see Danner crouching behind the barrel.

"Hello?" She asked as more a question than a welcoming statement.

Danner jumped up and spun around. His hat dipped low over his eyes, and his whisker-covered jaw, squared further by his clenched teeth, and dirty clothes caused the woman to scream. Before Danner could utter a single word, an equally squat, fat, bald man with a full beard stepped out of the back room with a shotgun leveled at Danner's mid-section.

"We don't want no trouble here, mister! Josephine, get in the back!" the man shouted keeping both barrels on Danner.

Danner slowly raised his left hand, calloused palm forward. "Pardon me folks, my name is Luxton Danner and I'm a U.S. Deputy Marshal. I mean no harm."

The man's eyes narrowed as he raised his gun. "Got a badge?" he asked, unwavering.

"Yes, sir, inside my coat."

"Let's see it, real slow," the shopkeeper ordered.

Danner slowly moved his right hand inside his oilskin and reached into his shirt pocket. He slowly withdrew the badge, keeping his eyes laser-focused on the shotgun. He extended his right hand toward the man showing the badge, then stood completely still.

"Here you go, sir," he added.

The man took two steps forward and squinted at the badge. Satisfied, he smiled and lowered the shotgun. "My apologies, Marshal, there's so much riff-raff in and out of here these days, we can't tell whose friend or foe," the man explained. "I'm Buck Littleton and this is my wife, Josephine," he added as his wife re-entered the room, this time much more friendly. "We own this-here store."

"Good to know you both. Turns out your problem is the reason I'm here. I've been sent to check on the outlaw activity along the river. Here, in Range, and at a town further west called Riverbend. I was watching a couple of men across the street. I believe their intentions are not good," Danner explained as he peered once again out the window. "Excuse me a moment."

But the men had gone. Danner did not see horses either. He peered up and down the street as best he could through the dirty window but saw no sign of Barry's men. *How the hell did they get here before him? Or did they just arrive? I'm certain they weren't following us,* Danner thought. Danner stood straight with hands on his hips and shook his head.

Sensing he had lost sight of his quarry, Buck spoke up. "The men gone, Marshal?" He asked.

"Yes, not sure where they went, and I'd rather they not see me just yet."

"I'm sorry, it's my fault you lost them," Buck apologized.

"Nonsense, Mr. Littleton. I'm a sight right now. I certainly don't look like a U.S. Marshal. I've got four days of trail grime on me."

"Anything I can do?" Buck asked.

Danner thought for a moment. "Well, if you're willing, you could go over to the cantina and see if there are a couple of strangers in there. One had a dark brown trail duster on with a black hat, and the other a brown leather vest with a brown hat. Both wearing guns and looking like me. They've been on the trail for days."

"Sure thing, Marshal. I'll go have a look," Buck agreed.

"Don't say anything to anyone about me being here," Danner advised his scout.

"Yes, sir. I'll be right back." Buck leaned his shotgun against the wall then waddled across the street and disappeared into the Silver Star Cantina. Danner watched and waited. After a couple of minutes, the rotund storekeeper pushed through the winged doors of the cantina and scurried back to the store.

"No sir, no one there looking like that, Marshal," Buck reported.

"Okay, thank you. I'll have a look around town before I leave."

"You're leaving right away?" Josephine asked through a frown.

"Yes, ma'am, I believe I am, but I'll be back. Do you have any canned beans or jerky?" Danner asked.

"Yes sir, we've got plenty of both," Josephine answered.

"Good. While I have a look around, could you put together a few cans and some jerky? I'll pick it up a little later."

"Yes, sir, I'll have it ready for you," Josephine assured him.

Danner nodded then walked out into the street to look around. No sign of Barry's men or Rebecca. Danner rode down to the boarding houses but found nothing. He then rode up the street to the end of town where the livery stable and freight yard sat near holding pens further west.

Danner jumped off Bullet and entered the livery stable, where he found what he was looking for. Rebecca stood just inside her horse's stall where she was telling Barry's men that she wasn't going with them. As Danner approached the trio, Kyle Britt stepped back and turned, reaching for his gun. Both of Danner's Russian 45's cleared leather before either man could draw. Danner stood silent glaring at the unwelcome posse.

"Good evening, Marshal. Mr. Barry sent us to fetch his daughter back to Red River City. She was just telling us she didn't want to go.

We were having a talk about how that wasn't possible," Britt explained.

"Marshal, I'm eighteen and I can decide where I want to go and I'm not going back there!" Rebecca shouted.

"Where's the stable owner?" Danner asked, looking around.

"He's in the office! They hurt him!" Rebecca exclaimed.

"Rebecca, see if he's all right," Danner ordered. "You two don't move or I'll send you both back to Barry in boxes."

Rebecca ran to the office and disappeared inside.

"Look Marshal, we don't want any trouble with you. That's why we didn't follow you on the trail," Jonny Gallup explained.

"How'd you get here ahead of us?" Danner asked with a raised eyebrow.

"We got here just before you. We saw you come in with those settlers. We rode past ya'll on the first night. Kept a wide berth. Like we said, we don't want no trouble. We're just following orders is all," Britt repeated.

Rebecca returned from the office followed by a man rubbing his jaw. "He's okay," she declared.

Danner kept his eye on Barry's boys.

"You okay, mister?" Danner asked the stable keeper.

"Yes, sir, I reckon I'll be all right," he answered, unwilling to make eye contact with any of the men who'd just roughed him up.

"Name's Luxton Danner, United States Marshal. Who hit you?" Danner asked.

"The fella in the duster cold-cocked me."

Danner eyes narrowed and his square jaw pushed forward. "That right, Britt?" Danner asked.

Britt said nothing, just glared back at Danner.

"Rebecca, get your horse and ride over to the store. Wait for me there," Danner ordered.

Rebecca obliged, quickly leaving the barn.

"Now, you two. Slowly unbuckle your gun belts and let 'em drop to the ground. Now," Danner ordered more forcefully.

Both men let their gun belts fall from their hips.

"Now, step back." Danner looked at the stable keeper. "What's your name?" Danner asked.

"Richard Burke, sir."

"Richard, grab those gun belts and take them outside to my horse. He's the big bay stallion out front."

"Yes, sir."

Burke snatched the gun belts and hurried out of the barn. Danner didn't move. "Now you two can pick up your guns next door at the stage office after me and the girl are gone. You will not follow us. Return to Barry and tell him what happened. Understand?" Danner asked.

"Mr. Barry's not gonna like that Marshal. He's a man who gets what he wants, and he wants his daughter back," Britt stated matter-of-factly.

"You tell Mr. Barry that I'll stop in Red River City on my way back to Fort Smith and he can tell me all about it himself. Both of you go over to the cantina and stay there until we're gone. Move!" Danner ordered.

Danner watched as Britt and Gallup slowly walked over to the Silver Star Cantina, pausing at the swinging doors before pushing through. He retrieved the gun belts from Burke, dropped them inside the door of the stage office. Next, he headed back to the Littleton Mercantile to collect his rations and inform Rebecca that her wish had been granted: she would be joining him on his journey to Range, after all.

Danner kept an eye on the cantina's doors as he climbed the steps of the store. As promised, Josephine had everything ready inside a burlap sack. Rebecca's horse was tied out front, but she wasn't present inside the store. "Did a young woman come in here?" Danner asked.

"She's in the back washing up. She'll be right out, I'm sure," Josephine said, her eyes twinkling.

Danner chuckled and removed his hat. "It's not what you think, Mrs. Littleton," he stated with a smirk.

"Well, maybe it should be? She's a very beautiful young lady," Josephine offered before stepping through the doorway.

"Don't pay no mind to Josephine, Marshal. She's always playing matchmaker," Buck groaned shaking his head.

Rebecca appeared with a fresh dark blue blouse, brown riding pants, and lips ablaze with red lipstick, no doubt provided by Josephine Littleton. Danner paused to take in his passenger's appearance, silently reminded himself of his duty, then paid for the food.

"Well, looks like you've managed to accompany me to Range, after all. That is, if you're still interested in doing so?"

"That'll be fine, Marshal. Thank you," she replied, shaking Mrs. Littleton's hands who winked at Rebecca conspiratorially before releasing her grip.

"I'll try and get back in a few days," Danner announced to the Littleton's before heading out to his stoic stallion.

Rebecca followed and swung up onto her horse. "Did you buy stage fair when you were in the office earlier?" Danner asked.

"No, Marshal. I was told I'd have to wait until morning."

"Very well. You can cut the Marshal stuff," Danner stated then tapped his spurs, heading west out of Eagle Springs without looking over to Rebecca, who had begun to laugh.

CHAPTER 30

WES PAYNE – THROCKMORTON TO RIVERBEND

The old barn's timber creaked and snapped with the sway of the wind. The storm had passed, leaving behind the thundering sound of silence. A horse's whinny brought Wes out of his peaceful sleep. He opened his eyes, took a moment to focus his eyes, and scanned the barn.

Other than the trivial movements of the horses and mules, nothing stirred. After a moment, he heard 'ole Chet snoring away in the other room. He couldn't be certain, since the window was covered with a thick layer of soot, but it looked like evening had arrived. The creaking aged wood seemed to speak in an ancient worrisome tongue, trying desperately to tell its story.

Wes rolled out of his nap cocoon and stretched. He had nearly dried out and felt alive again. He rolled his new Indian blanket and tied it to the back of his saddle, then pulled the cinch tight around Ringo's gullet. He strode over to the window leading into Chet's room and caught a glimpse of the old man in a deep sleep. He slowly slid open the tall entry door to the squeal of rusted hinges and rollers crying for oil. He closed the door behind him and swung up into the saddle. Nothing moved in the camp.

For a moment, he thought the camp seemed vacant except for his elder host. It wouldn't surprise Wes one bit if Chet had imagined Throckmorton to be more than a single shack outpost amid the vast wilderness. Wes tapped his spurs and headed for Riverbend.

With good moon light, I should reach Riverbend around midnight or so, he thought. And, just like that, his wish for good moon light was met. The three-quarter moon lit up the terrain like a hundred oil lamps. The stars glittered across the clear dark sky and the air was brisk, but not too cold, making for an exhilarating journey. Wes always loved traveling on nights like these. He kept Ringo at a steady pace, creating one fluid being of horse and rider.

After a long while, Wes pulled back on the reins to give his mount a rest. The familiar piercing pain shot through his left hand, coiling his fingers into its grotesque claw. The pain knifed down each finger, feeling like lightning shooting from their tips. "Damn! Hold on, buddy!" Wes said through clenched teeth.

He tried desperately to rub the pain from the hand and work the fingers open to no avail. His heart pounded and sweat poured from his body. He leaned back in the saddle hoping for a deep breath that would not come. Short, saccadic gasps were all he could muster. He looked up to the heavens, begging for relief. He wasn't much of a religious man, but he believed in a higher being, and needed assistance now more than ever. He stared straight up into the star-studded sky and the Big Dipper before everything went black.

Wes came to and found himself flat on his back atop a prickly pear cactus. The pain in his hand had dissipated, but it had been replaced by an aching left shoulder, and a hundred needle points in his back. He looked up and saw Ringo standing guard next to him. His hat was gone and his guns were laying several feet away on each side. He gingerly rolled off the cactus, sat up, and looked around. He opened and closed his left hand several times to ensure its use. Satisfied, Wes stood, retrieved his guns, and then searched for his hat, which he found snared by a half-dead juniper a few feet from the crushed cactus.

He drew his gun multiple times to make sure he could handle the pain in his shoulder. Not fun, but no problem. He reached around and pulled several thorns from his back, then pulled himself up into the saddle. He patted Ringo's neck. "Sorry about that, Buddy. Thanks for keeping a lookout," he said to his trusted horse. He had no idea how long he'd lain unconscious.

———

After a few hours of gentle riding, he saw the dim lights of Riverbend ahead. Riding into town, he heard music still coming from the cantina, a good sign that it wasn't too late. Stopping in front of the Ola Hotel, he tethered Ringo to the hitching post, and entered the lobby, finding Bartolo busy under an oil lamp at the front desk.

"Ola, señor, I am Bartolo Rivera, owner of this hotel. May I help you?"

"Name's Wes Payne. Sorry for the late arrival, Bartolo. Would you have a room?"

"Sí señor, I have one left." Bartolo pulled the last key off the wall and offered the register to his new guest. Wes signed the book and accepted the key.

"Do you have a coral? The livery stable was dark when I rode past.

"Sí, behind the hotel. You can leave your horse there."

"Thanks."

Wes put Ringo in the coral and entered the hotel through the back door. A back staircase led him to room three, where he let himself in, and then closed, locked and hooked a chair under the door handle. He wasn't tired, but his shoulder ached, and he was fatigued from being on the trail. A comfortable bed should be just the answer.

A short time later after he'd just fallen to sleep, Wes heard a commotion in the hallway outside his room. He rolled out of bed, grabbed a gun, and carefully opened his room door to a narrow crack. He looked out and saw Ben Chance struggling with a big man dressed all in black at the end of the hall near the staircase. Wes started toward the men when the stranger drew his gun and fired pointblank into Chance's chest, knocking him backward down the stairs. Wes fired point-blank at the shrouded stranger, who didn't flinch, but who just ran down the stairs after Chance. Wes had just reached the top of the stairs when he bolted awake in his bed.

He looked around the dark room but heard nothing. His door had remained locked and the chair hadn't budged. He took a deep breath and laid back down. Another dying Ben Chance nightmare to add to his growing list. He gazed up at the ceiling and rubbed his eyes. *What the hell is happening to me? My hands? Chance? How can I make this stop?* He thought.

Wes took a deep breath and sunk deeper into the bed's mattress. He closed his eyes and tried to re-focus his mind away from Ben Chance and back to the task at hand. Range was still a day's ride east. He looked forward to arriving at his destination and meeting the U.S. Marshal. It hadn't been a pleasant journey, and he was ready to get down to business. Now, if he could only get back to sleep before sunrise.

CHAPTER 31

WES PAYNE & BEN CHANCE, JR. – RIVERBEND

The sun crept skyward, its translucent yellow beams bursting above distant rolling hills. Dawn arrived with the combination of cool ground air tamped down by the warmth of the sun. The residents of Riverbend started another busy day. Doors opened, livestock rumbled about, and the occasional wagon plowed down Main Street. The fast-drying mud in the streets from all the recent rain had thickened considerably, making it difficult for wagons and carriages to navigate. Roosters crowed, and the sound of cattle calls could be heard deep in the distance.

Wes rose early and was already seated at a table sipping hot coffee in the dining room of the Ola hotel. The smell of bacon, coffee, and fresh-baked bread filled the quaint room with the promise of a fine breakfast. The small square tables filled up fast with local patrons.

Bartolo's wife, Isadora, a small attractive Mexican woman with long dark, black hair pulled back away from her face, scurried from table to table greeting guests and pouring steaming coffee and taking orders. Wes looked around, relaxed and relatively well-rested after his nightmares during the night, when a young, Ben Chance junior appeared in the archway. Wes, in the middle of a gulp of coffee, choked. A chill slithered down his spine. The spitting image of his nightmares, albeit thirty years younger, stood in the doorway. Isadora waved Chance over to Wes's table where three empty chairs awaited.

"It's okay, señor?" she asked Wes with a smile that sparked an image of Annette Gentry. "It's a busy morning and I no have no more tables," she said.

"Sí," Wes answered, a weak smile on his face.

Chance grasped the chair opposite Wes. "Mind some company, sir?" Chance politely asked before pulling the chair and taking a seat.

"Please do, I'm Wes Payne," Wes introduced himself extending a right hand that Chance accepted for a cordial shake.

"Ben Chance," he replied.

Wes took in a breath at the sound of that name and sat back in his chair, taking a long look at his table guest. Chance noticed Wes's actions and smiled.

"Let me guess. You knew my father, too?" Chance asked with a smile.

"Your father?" Wes asked, still trying to collect himself.

"Yes, sir. I'm told I look just like him."

Wes stared into his coffee as if it would offer up some missing answers. "I'm sorry. I'm just surprised is all, I guess," Wes mumbled.

Isadora returned to the table with two dishes of bacon, eggs, and toast, which she placed in front of both men.

Wes looked deep into his black coffee and contemplated his next words. Images of Chance, Danner, and Elizabeth shot through his mind like a Winchester bullet. Chance fighting death as he rode on to avenge his partner, his fatherly protection of Jake Rawlings, and the sight of Chance rocking back off his horse as the sound of the shot that felled him rang in Wes's ears. Then, watching this young man's father take his last breath in the middle of nowhere on what that man knew was a one-way journey. Finally, he looked Chance, Jr. square in the eye and forced his words. "I was with your father when he died," Wes plainly announced.

Chance's eyes narrowed and his face grew dark. His smile eroded to a frown. You were in Six Shot?" Chance asked.

"Yes, but your father didn't make it to Six Shot. We were ambushed before we made it to that hell hole."

"My father wrote me a letter before he left for Six Shot. He didn't mention you. Only a gunfighter named Luxton Danner, and his old partner's daughter, Elizabeth Thornton. I learned later when Mr. Danner brought my father's letter that he was a U.S. Marshal. He told me there were other men there, but I don't remember him giving me any names. All I know is he was after some rustlers that stole Mr. Thornton's herd."

Wes explained, "I joined your father and Danner later after Canyon Creek. Joel Thornton died after we got to his ranch. He believed the leader of the gang was an old fugitive that he and your father hunted down when they were Marshals. There were other gunfighters in the gang that Thornton knew. A kid named Jake Rawlings joined us at the Thornton ranch. The Rawlings kid fell off his horse and broke his arm when your father was shot. He's the one that took your father back to the Thornton ranch. Me and Danner rode on to Six Shot where we got the sons a bitch there."

Chance leaned forward and rubbed his leg, deep in thought.

"I didn't know about any letter, or about Chance having a son," Wes added.

"Seems that's been a big surprise to everyone I talk to," Chance mumbled.

"I didn't really know your father, but I could tell he was a good man," Wes said, feeling like he had to say something.

Chance nodded but didn't respond directly. "I reckon your breakfast is getting cold, Mr. Payne," Chance stated before digging into his meal.

Both men quietly ate their breakfast, equally lost in their own thoughts, when four men burst into the room. All four wore guns, one carried a rusty double barrel shotgun, and had a mangled face. A thick purple scar started above his left eye and ended near his chin. Everyone stopped their conversations, and nobody moved, including Wes and Chance.

Boom! The man with the shotgun fired a blast into the ceiling raining bits of debris down onto several folks.

"Nobody moves!" the man growled leveling the shotgun and fanning the people in the room.

Another outlaw wearing a tall, black hat and dirty, red bandana stepped forward, and drew a gun. His spurs pinged with every step against the wood floor. He walked toward the kitchen where Bartolo stood shaking in the doorway.

"You the owner?" the second outlaw bellowed at the little Mexican.

"Sí, señor," he answered, his voice quivering with fear. He wiped sweat from his face with a bare hand as the outlaw grabbed his shoulder and spun him around.

"Take me to the money box and nobody gets hurt. Understand, muchacho?"

"Sí," Bartolo nodded then entered the kitchen with the outlaw's gun at his back.

Chance reached down to his right side and palmed his gun. He looked at Wes who shook his head slightly and pushed up the fingers on his left hand being sure to keep his palm on the table. Wes scanned the room and noted the positions of the four gunmen. Two near the door, shotgun in the middle of the tables, and the fourth back in the kitchen. Not including him and young Chance, there were twenty or so people seated around the room.

Shotgun first, kitchen man second, then the two near the door. I'll need both guns at the same time, he thought.

"No! Stop!" Isadora screamed from the kitchen.

Wes flinched, and the fella with the mangled face leveled the shotgun off on him. "Don't even think about it, mister," the outlaw roared.

The ragged thief stepped through the kitchen door, bag in hand. Crack! He fired a shot across the dining room through the front window. "Nobody move!" He hollered over the cowering patrons.

Wes waited, counting the pings of spurs across the floor. *Wait till he gets near the shotgun*, Wes told himself. *Wait...wait... now!*

Wes sprung from his chair drawing both guns. Crack! Crack! Crack! Shotgun down! Kitchen thief down! One door guard down! Crack! A bullet zipped past Wes's head smashing into the wall behind him.

Crack! Crack! Crack! Chance fired three times sending the last outlaw backward through the front window out onto the boardwalk with a stream of broken glass. Women screamed and men dove to the floor. Amidst the chaos, Wes moved swiftly through the gun smoke, checking each outlaw to ensure his aim had been true. One, two, three, and four, dead.

Wes waved Chance toward the kitchen to check on Bartolo and his family. Isadora and a young girl knelt beside the little Mexican slumped on the floor, barely conscious, and bleeding badly, no doubt from a pistol blow to the top of his head. After a moment, Wes saw Chance return back to the dining room. Wes stood by the door watching folks hurry out of the hotel. "Marshal should be here right quick," Wes informed Chance, who seemed to be admiring Wes's gun work.

"Mr. Payne, I ain't never seen nothing like that," Chance exhaled.

"You did good kid. As long as you're up here along the river, always have your gun ready," Wes added.

Frank Tolliver stepped up onto the front porch and took a quick look at the dead man splayed across the planks. His glance was met by Wes, Ranger badge in hand.

"Marshal, Wes Payne, Texas Rangers," Wes offered quickly.

Tolliver leaned in and took a good look at the circled star, then smiled and shook Wes's hand. "Glad to have you in town, Ranger Payne. Hello again, Mr. Chance. What the hell happened?" Tolliver asked, peering into the hotel to see three more dead men scattered about.

"These four bastards busted in, ordered the owner to empty his money box. Me and young Chance here stopped 'em before they could get out," Wes reported.

"Bart and his family okay?" Tolliver asked.

"He's alive. Got a nasty cut on his head from a pistol whipping. The lady and little girl are all right," Chance added.

"Good enough. I'll send for the doctor. He's new in town. Just been here a couple a weeks. Let me take a look at these hombres," Tolliver said moving past Wes and Chance. Tolliver rolled two outlaws over to see their faces. "Nope, nope," Tolliver said aloud, looking at the one on the boardwalk, and near the front door.

The Marshal made his way to the center of the room and rolled the money box thief over.

"Well, what a ya know? Lucky McCann and Joey Blue. You did us a fine service, Ranger Payne. These two have been up and down the river for a while now. They hit Range a week or so back with Crazy Bill, and Lucky here was seen in Eagle Springs. They're both wanted men and have rewards issued by the state. I'll get you the flyers. You'll need to take 'em to Sheriff Evans down in Margaret to collect, though," Tolliver advised.

Wes stepped over to Tolliver and looked at the two dead bandits. "Which one is Lucky?" he asked.

"Fella here with the mangled face. Story goes he was attacked by a mountain lion a few years back and lived. Started calling himself Lucky. Looks like that ran out today, though," Tolliver observed, picking up the burlap sack still clutched in Joey Blue's fist.

Isadora helped Bartolo into the dining room and sat down holding a bloody towel on top of his head.

Both Wes and Chance made their way up to their rooms where they gathered their gear and returned to the lobby.

"Señor! Señor!" Bartolo called to Wes. "Thank you, señor! Thank you for this!" Bartolo stated holding up the burlap sack.

Wes smiled, then walked out into the street to see a young man carrying a black bag navigating the muddy street as quickly as he could toward the hotel. Wes saddled Ringo, then rode over to the Marshal's office where Chance joined him.

"I should've known you were a Ranger or Marshal," Chance chuckled.

"Why?" Wes asked.

"There can't be too many men can handle guns like you," Chance stated.

Wes gazed down the street. "There's more than you might think, kid. And, they damn sure ain't all lawmen," he added. "That wasn't an easy shot you took, either. Fella was across the room. Where'd ya learn to shoot like that?" Wes asked.

"My uncle, the man that raised me, taught me to shoot. He wasn't much of a gun handler, preferred a Henry rifle, but he encouraged me to practice. Even bought me my gun. My aunt wasn't too happy, but he didn't trust many men, and said I needed to be better than most. I haven't had the need to prove it until this trip back home," Chance explained.

"Back home?" Wes asked.

"Texarkana. After Marshal Danner brought me my father's letter, and told me what happened to him, I headed to Canyon Creek to see Rachel Brennen. My father said in the letter if I wanted to know more about him, I should talk to her. I've been riding back along the river the last week."

Wes smiled as Chance spoke. "I never met Mrs. Brennen, but I heard all about her from your father and Danner. I know your father thought a great deal of her and I'm pretty sure Danner was also a little sweet on her," Wes stated.

Chance matched Wes's grin and nodded. "You were right about my father, and I can see why Marshal Danner would've been interested. She's a beautiful woman."

"Here comes our town Marshal. I guess I'll get those flyers just in case I get down to Margaret," Wes stated.

"I have a couple of others to take there," Chance announced.

"You do?" Wes asked.

"I'll tell ya about it later," Chance offered.

Wes followed Tolliver into his office. Chance leaned against the hitching post and watched the activity over at the hotel. Some of the men carried out the bodies, while others stood around and spun yarns about what they'd witnessed. After a few minutes, Wes exited the office and swung up onto Ringo.

"Where ya headin', Ranger Payne?" Chance asked.

"Moving on to Range."

"Mind if I pass on Margaret and ride along?"

"Nope. Always good to have a fella that saved my skin along for the ride. One condition, though."

"What's that?" Chance asked.

"Stop with the Ranger Payne. Name's Wes."

Chance hopped up onto his horse. "Yes, sir, Ranger Wes," Chance laughed.

Wes shook his head and tapped his spurs.

CHAPTER 32

LUXTON DANNER & REBECCA BARRY – RANGE

The warmth of the afternoon sun cascaded down, cleansing the night's chill as Danner and Rebecca traversed a wide grassy plain east of Range. After a quiet breakfast of cold biscuits and tepid coffee, neither Rebecca nor Danner had said much on the trail. Danner was deep in thought, juggling the actions of Jared Barry back in Red River City, and his obstinate but capable daughter who'd been tagging along with him. He wondered if Barry's men would ignore his demand and continue to follow them, or if they would think the better of it and return to their boss with Danner's message.

Then, there was the matter of his budding feelings toward Rebecca. He liked her spirit and determination. Her green eyes were a striking equal to Rachel Brennen's, and she looked incredible in those riding pants. *I can't get involved. She's too young and running away from her father. What am I supposed to do with that?*

"Marshal Danner," Rebecca broke Danner's thoughts.

"It's Lux or Danner, remember? What is it?" Danner replied more gruffly than he intended.

"Do you think those men are following us?" she asked.

Danner turned around in his saddle to check the landscape. "I really don't know. If they know what's good for 'em, they won't."

"My father is a very persuasive man. I'm sure he offered a lot of money to bring me back," she added.

"Where's he getting all that money?" Danner asked.

Rebecca stayed silent for a long time before she spoke. "I know he gets a lot of money from the lumber mill, but I think there's something else. He can't be making all that money from the hotel and mill alone. I've suspected that he's been involved with some bad men and strange dealings for a while, but he kept me away from people in town – most likely to keep me from finding out much," she explained.

Danner paused and looked hard at Rebecca. He believed she admitted all she knew. If Barry was smart, and he believed he was, he'd make damn sure his daughter knew nothing of his illicit activity.

"Do those men he hires to protect the town ever leave for a while, other than to chase after you?" Danner asked with a smirk.

"Yes. Not all at the same time though. There's always one left in town."

Danner remembered Barry's claim that he hadn't seen a Marshal or Ranger in town for years but didn't believe him. There must have been a U.S. Marshal, Ranger or Sheriff stop off in town. "Do you know if there have been any lawmen come to town looking for them?"

"None that I've ever talked to, but my father doesn't like me talking to very many people, even at the hotel, " she reminded him.

Sounds like Barry's running bandits along the river all right, Danner thought. "Lux?"

Danner looked over his shoulder at Rebecca.

"Thank you for not letting those men take me back."

Danner turned and looked back ahead. "That was never an option. We should be in Range in about an hour or so." Danner snapped his reins telling Bullet to pick up the pace.

R ebecca followed Danner's lead and did the same with her horse.

Danner's hour estimate to Range proved accurate. He stopped Bullet on top of a small hill and looked down at the target of his assignment. He could see why the riparian town was susceptible to raids from the territory. It sat right next to a narrow stretch of the river and was far enough away from any fort for military assistance. He was surprised at the size of the town. It was bigger than he expected, and there were new buildings going up on the south side. On the far side was a cattle outfit herding livestock into holding pens. The trail segued into a dirt road leading into town. Danner tapped his spurs and headed for the road with Rebecca on Bullet's tail.

Entering town, Danner noted a Marshal's shack to the left and the livery stable to the right. The town seemed busy with people, carriages, and wagons moving up and down the street. Danner saw a big sign for the Purple Sage Hotel further up on the right. Fearing all the rooms would be snatched up by cowboys driving the cattle herds, he hurried to the front, tying Bullet to the trough where the big stallion plunged his muzzle into the cold water.

The hotel was also bigger than he'd expected. It's wide front porch and double entry doors were made of dark weathered wood, with a large window on each side. It had a second story balcony that stretched all the way across its façade. Danner opened the door and stepped aside, allowing Rebecca to enter. Several families, cowboys, and newly arriving guests filled the lobby as they checked in. An older woman, sharply dressed in a red blouse and gray gingham prairie skirt, did her best to answer questions and hand out room keys. Rebecca approached the big desk and caught the attention of the busy lady.

"Oh my dear! Looks like you've had a long journey!" The older woman exclaimed. "I'm Mrs. Conrad, and this is my husband, Lee Conrad," she waved toward a gentleman picking up two heavy-looking suitcases in front of the desk. "Welcome to the Purple Sage. I'll get a room for you right away!"

"Thank you very much. Would you have another for, um, Mr. Danner?" Rebecca asked looking at the big Marshal.

Mrs. Conrad stopped and looked up at the towering Marshal.

"Yes, sir. It's a smaller room with just a wash basin. Would that be all right, Mr. Danner?" Mrs. Conrad asked.

"That would be fine, ma'am," Danner answered, his relief of securing a room evident.

Mrs. Conrad turned her attention back to Rebecca. "Now, my dear, I haven't offered this to anyone yet, but we have a nice bath that you can use when you are ready," Mrs. Conrad offered.

"That would be wonderful! Thank you," Rebecca answered, accepting the key to room eight.

"Would you please sign the register?" Mrs. Conrad asked turning the book toward Rebecca.

Rebecca quickly signed, then stepped aside for Danner to do the same. Danner took the pen and noted Rebecca had signed the last name Smith. He flashed a quick grin, then signed. Mrs. Conrad handed him the key to room twelve.

"Mr. Danner, your room is at the end of the hall. We don't have a coral behind the hotel since our restaurant is back there, so you'll want to take your horses to the livery stable at the end of town. I'm sorry it's such a long way off," Mrs. Conrad explained.

Danner and Rebecca left the lobby and stepped out to the street.

"I'll take the horses, Miss Smith, if you'd like to get to that bath right away," Danner stated unable to hold back a wide grin.

Rebecca laughed tossing her head to the side. "I thought it best if Rebecca Barry wasn't in town," she said shrugging her shoulders. Rebecca began to untie her pack when Danner's massive hand and long fingers wrapped completely around her arm. He felt Rebecca shiver as he moved her arm down to her side, then removed her pack, placing it on the hotel porch for her.

She's only eighteen, Danner, he reminded himself. *Only eighteen and a runaway. Still, she was beautiful, brave and–* "Do you need anything else?" he asked, gently, cutting off his own internal dialogue before it got the best of him.

Rebecca tried to speak but no words came from her mouth. Danner matched her silence. He took her horse's reins, then hopped up on Bullet before riding off toward the stable. He quickly stopped and looked back at his traveling companion. Rebecca stood still watching him. She clutched her hands into fists. Danner fought back a smile.

No need to lead her on. She's already interested, and I don't need to force the issue. Darn girl may have never even kissed a man for all I know, he thought. Bullet snorted and clapped his front hooves. He turned back, tapped his spurs, and proceeded to the stable where a tall, skinny, young man wearing a white cowboy hat a size too big greeted him.

"Good afternoon, sir. Two horses?" the young man asked.

"Yep. They'll need grain and hay. How much for a good brushing?" Danner asked.

"That'll be three dollars for each mount, plus a dollar each for the brushing" the boy said.

Danner reached into his saddle bag and counted out nine silver dollars placing the stack into the boy's hand. He tossed his saddle bags over his shoulder and headed across the street to the Marshal's office, which now had two horses tied in front. He opened the door and ducked his head under the frame stepping through.

The man seated behind a small desk stood and introduced himself. "Good afternoon, sir, I'm Lane Dodson, Marshal of Range. This is my deputy Mack McKinnon."

Danner pulled his vest back revealing his badge. "Name's Luxton Danner, U.S. Deputy Marshal."

"Very good to see you, Marshal!" Dodson said shaking Danner's hand vigorously.

"We've been waiting for you. I understand Mr. Benson sent a letter or two a few weeks back. I've only been Marshal here for a few days. I'm just now catching up on what's been happening here. Mac and I have been over in the territory searching for a kidnapped girl."

"Kidnapped girl?" Danner asked in a low tone.

"Yes, sir. Please take a seat."

Danner obliged.

Dodson continued. "About a week ago, a family was attacked out on their farm west of here. The man and woman were killed, along with their young son. Their ten-year-old daughter came into town on a wagon with her dead brother. She was wounded but is all right. The boy had two arrows in his back. The townfolks remembered a sixteen-year-old daughter. Some of the men took a good look around their burned out farm but didn't find her. When I was appointed Marshal, me, Mack, and a couple of other fellas went out to the farm, then followed a track into the territory. The trail led us to a campsite, but it had been abandoned a few days earlier. We haven't been able to find anything since," Dodson reported.

Danner sat quiet for a moment, running his fingers over barbed-wire whiskers.

"You said arrows killed the boy?" Danner asked.

"Yes, sir. Doc Phillips said he didn't find any other wounds. The wagon they came in was also covered with arrows. We didn't find any arrows or markings out at the farm though. The house was burned, but the out-buildings were left alone, including the chicken coop." Dodson reported, carefully watching for the Marshal's response.

"Chickens still in the coop?" Danner asked.

Dodson smiled and nodded his head. "Yep. All there."

"It wasn't Indians," Danner announced.

"No, sir. We didn't think so either," Dodson agreed.

"Gentlemen, do I have time to get a haircut and shave? I'd be mighty grateful if I could get cleaned up before I continue with this. It's been a long trip."

"Absolutely," Dodson said.

"Is there a barber in town?" Danner asked.

"Right down the street on the left in between the store and stage office. Mr. Wilson will get ya fixed up in no time, Marshal," McKinnon advised.

"I'd like to come back in an hour or so and learn more," Danner suggested, not wanting to seem too abrupt.

"Yes, sir, that'd be fine. We'll head over to the meeting house and talk to Mr. Benson. He'll know more than I do," Dodson suggested.

Danner headed for the barber shop, finding the barber finishing up a customer.

"Be right with ya, sir!" the barber called out.

Danner leaned against the door frame and watched the activity on the street. Most of the women were well-dressed. Many of the men weren't carrying guns. Two big Conestoga wagons loaded with lumber made their way down the street toward the new building site. People came and went from both the store and the saloon.

"Ready when you are, mister!" The barber called.

Danner took a seat and loosened his collar. "Shave and haircut," he announced.

"Very good! Name's Charlie Wilson. I'll have ya cleaned up rightly. New in town? Plan on stayin'?" The barber asked in rapid succession.

"I'll be here for a bit," Danner stated.

"Towns fillin' up faster than a rooster can run!" Charlie exclaimed.

"I see that. What are they building down the street?" Danner asked.

"Oh, well." Charlie stopped and walked around to face Danner in the chair holding his silver straight razor out to his side. "That there is gonna be a church, school, and a house for them Sisters," Charlie stated in a muffled whisper as if he shared an important secret.

"Sisters?"

"Yep, ya know, nuns, religious ladies. Don't know what nuns be doin' round here, but they're a stayin', I reckon."

"What you know about the raiders around here?" Danner asked.

Charlie got quiet and stepped back again from the chair. "What you know about that mister?" He asked with a quiver in his voice.

"I know I don't look it right now, but I'm a U.S. Marshal, Charlie. Been sent here by the government to look into it."

"Well, jumpin' crickets! I didn't know! Glad to know ya, Marshal!" The barber said, suddenly much more relaxed.

"Keep the Marshal stuff under your hat for right now okay?"

"Oh, sure. You can count on me. Them bandits across the river. There's a few come and go, like that Crazy Bill fella, but the real leader is a bad 'un calls himself Tuff Jenkins. He's got a big gang. They come in town about once a month or so. Shootin' the place up. Drinkin' and such. There's been some stealin' and killin, also."

"You ever seen this Jenkins?" Danner asked his willing informant.

"Just once a few months back. He was here with ten or so men. They robbed the store, livery stable, hotel, and Mrs. Fields's boarding house. A couple a fellas tried to stop 'em but they were killed."

"There a bank in town?" Danner asked.

"No, sir. Mr. Benson said havin' a bank in town would invite bank robbers. Now he thinks we need one. He takes care of money and such over at the meeting house."

Danner closed his eyes and let Charlie finish his job, knowing if they didn't stop talking, he'd never get his shave and haircut. Charlie took the hint and got to work. Feeling better with a fresh cut and shave, Danner headed over to the hotel to wash up. He looked forward to learning more about the town.

CHAPTER 33

The whisks of a corn broom scratched across the wooden planks of the Purple Sage Hotel's front porch as Lee Conrad did his best to keep the ever-present red dirt and mud clumps off the hotel's entrance. Danner stepped out the door, donning a fresh set of clothes to go with his smooth chin and sharply-trimmed hair. He hadn't felt this good since he left Fort Smith eleven days ago.

"Good afternoon sir," Conrad said looking up at his formidable looking guest. "Turnin' out to be a mighty fine afternoon!" Conrad added taking a break from his sweeping duties.

"Yes, sir. Could you direct me to Mr. Benson's office?" Danner asked.

"Yes, sir, it's in the big white Meeting House across from the saloon."

"Thank you," Danner tipped his hat and started toward the saloon. After a few steps, he paused and looked up and down the street. He overheard Lee Conrad ask the stagecoach driver about his identity and the fact that the barber had violated his request and told who he was.

Danner smiled and continued catching the driver's explanation of a broken wheel, causing a delay in leaving for Eagle Springs before he noticed the town Marshal up ahead.

Lane Dodson waited on the steps of the meeting house as Danner strode across Range's main street. "You look different, Marshal!" Dodson remarked.

"Feel different, too," Danner answered, climbing the three steps to the front door.

The two lawmen entered to find Lawrence Benson filling up the doorway of his office. "Gentlemen, good afternoon!" Benson bellowed stepping toward Danner with his outstretched hand.

Danner shook the portly mayor's hand. "Luxton Danner, U.S. Deputy Marshal. Glad to meet you," Danner stated.

"Lawrence Benson, I'm the mayor of this fine town, Marshal. I can't tell you how pleased I, and the whole town are, that you're here."

"Thanks Mr. Benson. I'll do the best I can, but I understand we have a serious problem here along the river."

"We certainly do. Come in and sit down." Benson ushered the two men into his office and closed the door. Taking a seat behind a large oak desk, Benson looked at his town's new lawmen.

"Gentlemen, just a week ago, we had no law in this town. Now we have our own Marshal, thanks to Butch Henry and Mr. Dodson, and you, sir, thanks to Governor Hubbard. We're also supposed to have a Ranger arrive soon," Benson added.

"Any idea who the Ranger is, Mr. Benson?" Danner asked.

"Please, call me Lawrence, and no sir, I wasn't given a name. I had hoped for several Rangers but was informed that there weren't enough to go around. I expect him any day now. Has Mr. Dodson filled you in on what we've been dealing with?"

"He told me about the raids along the river, and about a family that was killed along with the search for their missing daughter."

"Yes, their ten-year-old daughter survived, but hasn't been able to tell us anything of value," Benson reported.

"I understand there were arrows on the wagon the boy and girl came in on. Anyone look at them?" Danner asked.

"Yes, sir. Our blacksmith was in the army for ten years. He said they were Comanche," Benson explained.

Danner paused, mulling over the details. He remembered the four dead Comanche he found along the trail. He also knew there were bands of Comanche hiding in Palo Duro country out west. *Comanche would've taken the chickens and livestock for food, and not waste arrows on a wagon*, he thought.

"I came across four dead Comanche about thirty miles east of here. Right along the riverbank. Tracks along the bank led across the river. I've heard there are Kiowa and Comanche hiding out in the Palo Duro canyon area, but that's a long way from here. I doubt the family was attacked by Comanche," Danner declared.

"Nor do I," Dodson chimed in. "I think we're dealing with a serious outlaw gang that's making their way up and down the river making it look like Indian raids," Dodson added.

"Who's this Tuff Jenkins?" Danner asked.

"He's been through here a couple of times. The one time was real bad. He and his men robbed several businesses and killed two men. That was a few months ago, and just a week ago a varmint named Crazy Bill rode through and robbed some of our people, killing our man at the feed store," Benson explained.

"I've heard of them both, but never seen either one," Dodson advised.

"I hadn't heard those names back in Fort Smith," Danner added.

The men were interrupted by rapid knocking on the door. Benson opened the door to find Deacon David shuffling back and forth and rubbing his hands frantically. "Hello Deacon, what's the matter?" Benson asked.

"It's Sister Sarah. She's missing," the Deacon reported.

"Missing?" Benson asked, incredulous.

"We all thought she went back to Mrs. Fields's boarding house, but when I got there this afternoon, Mrs. Fields said she hadn't seen her all day. The other Sisters and I have been working at the church since early this morning," the Deacon explained.

"Let's go have a talk with the others and find out who saw her last," Dodson stated before heading toward the street with Danner close behind.

Work on the church and the school had progressed rapidly. The school building floor and walls were erected, with the roof nearly framed out. Several strong men hoisted a thick oak support beam into place as Dodson and Danner arrived.

Sister Mary, a thin older woman with a narrow face and protruding nose, saw the lawmen and immediately hurried over to them. "Good afternoon, gentlemen, I'm Sister Mary. I'm sure you're here about Sister Sarah, correct?" she asked.

"Yes ma'am, I'm Lane Dodson, town Marshal, and this is Luxton Danner, U.S. Deputy Marshal. Your Deacon told us one of you were missing."

"We can't seem to find Sister Sarah anywhere in town. We all thought she was at the boarding house, but we discovered she was not," Sister Mary reported.

"Do you know who saw her last?" Dodson asked.

"I saw her last night at bedtime. We share a room. She likes to go for a walk early in the morning, so when she wasn't in the room this morning, I didn't think anything of it. When she didn't join us here this morning, we all thought she might not be feeling well, with the rain and all. Now, I just don't know what to think," Sister Mary explained, tearing up.

"Where does she walk?" Danner asked.

"She likes to walk along the riverbank. We told her not to, but she still did it anyway. Said it was peaceful there," Sister Mary said looking off toward the river.

"What does she look like?" Danner asked.

"Well, she's very young, and a bit taller than me, with a smooth round face and blonde hair," Sister Mary said.

"I'll get my horse and meet you in front of your office right away," Danner told Dodson.

"Sure enough," Dodson replied, heading over to his office.

Danner stopped by the stable to pick up Bullet, then met Dodson, who was already mounted and ready to go. He didn't have time to look for Rebecca to tell her what he was up to.

"Let's get to the river down by the dock near the freight yard.

That's the easiest entry point, and it's across from the boarding house," Dodson advised.

"Lead the way," Danner replied.

The two men galloped to the dock, riding down to the river's edge, checking for any sign of footprints or horse tracks. They saw nothing unusual.

"Let's work our way down river first," Dodson suggested, before snapping his reins and heading down the south bank. Danner crossed the river and started down the north bank, alternately looking from the red dirt water's edge to the high brush bending along the river. Both men rode in silence for several minutes before Dodson called out to Danner.

"Over here, Marshal!" Dodson called waving his hat over his head.

Danner tapped his spurs and crossed back over to the south bank where Dodson had dismounted, inspecting some type of clothing. As Danner arrived, Dodson held up the cloth.

"Any idea what this is?" Dodson asked.

"Looks like some kind of collar," Danner offered as he examined the ground near them. He walked several feet further down river and knelt for a closer look at what could have been hoof marks in the dirt. He followed the line across the water to the opposite bank. No doubt about it. Two horses came out of the water and rode north on the other side. "Looks like we have our answer," Danner said pointing to the markings on the north bank.

"Let's take this cloth back to the nuns and see if they know what it is," Dodson suggested.

A few minutes later, Dodson swung down from his horse to meet Sister Mary and the Deacon at the church. Dodson removed the cloth from his vest and handed it to Sister Mary. The nun said nothing, but she knelt and began to pray. The other nuns joined in the gesture. Danner looked at Deacon David who made the sign of the cross and looked skyward.

"Deacon?" Danner asked.

"The cloth is called a wimple. It is the white collar that covers the

Sister's neck. I fear it is Sister Sarah's," the Deacon remarked sadly before joining the nuns in prayer.

Danner looked back toward the river. He hadn't planned on this. Kidnapping nuns. Murdering kids. This was a whole new level of evil that would need to be answered with a savage response. "Damn," he muttered.

CHAPTER 34

WES PAYNE & BEN CHANCE, JR. – RANGE

Riding side by side, Wes and Chance stopped in front of the livery stable, scanning the street ahead. Range was much larger than both men had envisioned. People, wagons, and buggies filled the street, along with a few cowboys on horseback. At the far end of town, men herded cows into holding pens. A big Studebaker wagon loaded with fresh cut lumber chugged past them.

"Not what I expected," Wes admitted.

"Nope. Didn't know there was a town this big out here," Chance chimed in.

Wes heard a door slam shut to his left, and saw a tall man wearing a badge walking their way. He and Chance swung down from their horses to greet the lawman.

"Good afternoon, gentlemen. I'm Lane Dodson, town Marshal. Can I help you?"

"Just the man I need to see. I'm Wes Payne, Texas Rangers. This is Ben Chance," Wes announced.

"Glad to know you Ranger Payne and Mr. Chance," Dodson said, shaking each man's hand. "We've been expecting you, Ranger Payne. Glad they sent two of you," Dodson added.

"Please, call me Wes. Ben here isn't a Ranger. He's tagging along is all," Wes explained.

"I see. Would you like to put your horses up? I believe they're saving a room for you over at the hotel," Dodson advised.

"That'd be fine, Marshal. Ben, you stickin' around?" Wes asked his young coattail, anxiously awaiting his answer. He'd become fond of having Chance around.

"I believe I will," said Chance.

"My office is right here. When you've finished with your horses, come over and I'll take ya'll over to the hotel," Dodson offered.

"Oh, Marshal?" Wes began to ask.

"Please, just call me Dodson."

"Thanks. Has the U.S. Marshal arrived yet?" Wes asked.

"Sure has. He's across the river looking for a missing nun right now, though."

"Missing nun?" Chance beat Wes to the question.

"She turned up missing this morning. We found part of her clothing down by the river. It looked like two horses made their way back across to the territory. I wanted to go, but Marshal Danner thought it best if I stayed in town."

"Marshal Danner? As in Luxton Danner?" Wes asked with a raised brow.

"Yes, sir. You know him?" Dodson asked.

"Yes, indeed. We've worked together before," Wes answered unable to keep from cracking a smile into his chiseled jaw. He couldn't believe his luck. This was no easy assignment to start with. Hell, he wasn't even sure he knew what the assignment really was. He and one U.S. Marshal against an unknown number of ruthless bandits. The one riot, one Ranger thing was–but now with Danner here, and Chance with them, the odds had begun to turn.

"Very good! I hope to see him back before dark," Dodson added before heading to Mrs. Fields's boarding house for a visit.

Dodson hustled down to the boarding house and found the tenants in the midst of a disagreement. The continuous chatter surrounded Sister Sarah and what had happened to her. The Deacon did his best to calm his flock of nuns to no avail. Dodson located Mrs. Fields in the kitchen, who burned nervous energy by cleaning an already immaculate room. He paused at the door and removed his hat.

"Hello, Marshal, nice to see you. Any news about Sister Sarah?" The beautiful boarding house owner asked through a wide smile. She pressed the sides of her hair flat and tightened the hair bun on the back of her head.

"No ma'am. No word yet on the Sister. I just wanted to take a moment and come down to see how you and your guests were getting along," Dodson answered.

"That's very thoughtful of you. As you can hear, they're worried something terrible has happened. I'm a bit upset myself since she's a guest and all," Mrs. Fields admitted.

"Well, just know it's not your fault and there was nothing you could have done to prevent her from wandering off when she was warned to stay close. I don't want you to be upset," Dodson said with a smile.

"Thank you. You are very kind," Mrs. Fields said, leaning back against the wash tub with her hands folded in front of her.

Dodson nodded and put his hat back on then turned to leave. He stopped and looked back at the lovely woman. "I really came by to see you, ma'am," he admitted before leaving.

"I'll be damned. Marshal Danner's here," Chance exclaimed.

"That's right, I forgot you knew him, too. Danner hand delivered your father's letter, didn't he?" Wes asked.

"Yep. Brought the letter, then stayed and shared what he knew of my father and his reputation in Fort Smith. He didn't have to do that. He's a good man. That's fer sure," Chance stated.

"Sure is. I was hope'n he'd be the one sent. We should do well," Wes announced leading Ringo across the street to the stables with Chance right behind.

After securing their horses at the stable, both men paused and watched the activity on the street for a moment. The Red Dirt Saloon looked busy and the sound of a blacksmith's hammer striking hot iron rang out nearby. Wes also noticed a small gunsmith shop tucked in between the Marshal's shed and the telegraph office.

Good. I'll need more ammunition, he thought before heading across the street to Dodson's place.

"Watch your heads. This door frame is a little low," Dodson warned as Wes and Chance entered the makeshift office. Both men ducked into the small room, then took seats in two wooden chairs Dodson had made available.

Dodson took his seat and finished writing an entry into a book he had on his desk. "I'll bring you up to date on what's happened around here in the last week or so, then I need to introduce you to Lawrence Benson. He's the mayor of this town and the reason you're here, Wes," Dodson explained.

Dodson reported the events of the past ten days including Crazy Bill's raid, and the two missing women. Upon concluding, Dodson escorted Wes and Chance over to the meeting house where they met Benson and learned the history of the town, and some of the ongoing trouble along the river between Riverbend, Range, and Eagle Springs. After finishing with the mayor, Dodson escorted Wes and Chance over to the hotel where the proprietor, Mrs. Conrad, had covered her red blouse and gray skirt with a white apron that stretched from the bottom of her neck to her knees. She supervised three other ladies moving around the kitchen like a Saturday night dance preparing for dinner in the restaurant.

Steam billowed from two large metal pots perched on top of the big, iron stove that pushed out enough heat to bake a cake on the counter. Two younger girls placed cups on trays and a boy ushered in buckets of water through a back door. Mrs. Conrad spotted the men in the doorway. Pushing dark hair, streaked with lines of gray away from her face, she donned a smile and joined the men.

"Mrs. Conrad, sorry to bother you. This is Wes Payne and Ben Chance. Lawrence said you were holding a room for Mr. Payne," Dodson stated.

"Yes. I'm sorry, but Lawrence only had us hold one room. That's all I have available right now," Mrs. Conrad advised.

"That's okay ma'am, I'll camp outside of town, I'll wait out front," Chance advised.

Mrs. Conrad hurried to the desk, removed the last key from its hook and handed it to Wes. "Do you know how long you'll be with us?" she asked.

"It'll be a few days, ma'am. Not sure how many just yet," Wes offered, taking the key.

"I hear there's a barber in town. Thought I'd head down for a shave," Chance advised.

"Come on back when you're finished. I'll buy ya dinner," Wes offered.

"Sounds good," Chance said as he disappeared into the street.

Wes headed up to his room. He didn't like Danner in the territory by himself. Technically, he had no jurisdiction in the Indian Territory, but that wasn't going to stop him from doing what had to be done. Especially now, since kidnapping women was on the list, and Danner was on the job.

The bright orange evening sun had just sunk behind the shadows of the western hills when Wes met Chance in the hotel lobby a few hours later for dinner.

"You happen to see Dodson?" Wes asked.

"Yep. I went over and checked if Marshal Danner had returned. He hasn't," Chance advised.

Wes looked out the window and shook his head. He thought about

Danner in the territory without another gun to keep watch. The territory was no place for a one man mission, even if it was Danner.

"I don't like it. It's getting dark," Chance said.

"I don't like it either," Wes answered.

"You reckon we ought to go look for him?" Chance asked.

"Don't rightly know where to look is the problem. Naw, looks like we'll just have to wait until he gets back. He won't do anything foolish. Let's get some dinner," Wes suggested.

The two men had just gotten their coffee when Wes noticed Chance staring across the dining room. Following Chance's gaze, Wes saw what had mesmerized his young partner. Seated alone on the other side of the room was a beautiful young woman sipping tea. Wes leaned back in his chair and watched Chance's intense focus on the young woman.

"May I take your orders?" Mrs. Conrad's voice broke the spell, causing Chance to spill his coffee. "I'm sorry! I didn't mean to surprise you!" Mrs. Conrad said, wiping the coffee with the corner of her apron.

"Don't mind him, ma'am. Seems he's smitten by that young lady sipping tea across the room," Wes offered, winking.

Mrs. Conrad looked over and smiled. "That's Miss Smith. She arrived this morning with Mr. Danner."

"With Mr. Danner!" Chance shouted, spilling more coffee.

"Yes, I believe it was Mr. Danner," said Mrs. Conrad. "Will you two get a hold of yourselves before I run out of coffee?" She asked, mopping up the table for a second time.

"Sorry about that, ma'am. We'll have a couple of steaks and potatoes, if you please," Wes said.

"Coming right up," Mrs. Conrad answered.

"I never thought Marshal Danner would have a girl," Chance said while exhaling in a defeated manner slumping his shoulders, then resting his chin in his hand.

"Don't look so done in, kid. If I know Danner, there's something's not right with the young lady. Danner ain't got a girl. That's for sure!" Wes laughed.

"You don't think so, huh?" Chance asked sitting straight up, his face bright again.

"Nope."

"She sure is a fine-looking gal!" Chance bellowed.

"That she is. Reminds me of a lady back in Buffalo Gap," Wes said, his smile fading. He looked over to another table where two men just sat down. "There's the Marshal and that Benson fella. I'll go check and see if they've heard from Danner," Wes announced, rising.

While Wes spoke with the others, he kept an eye on his besotted partner. He was still focused on the young woman. Glancing over his shoulder he watched as she caught Chance's gaze and returned a smile. Chance returned the smile and nodded, then quickly looked away. Wes shook his head and chuckled to himself.

Cowboys steadily made their way in and out of the restaurant during the dinner rush hour that seemed incredibly hectic. Poor Mrs. Conrad couldn't keep pace with the influx of hungry men. After several minutes, Rebecca exited the kitchen, wearing a fresh white apron, carrying food to a table near him. It appeared Rebecca had volunteered to help Mrs. Conrad through the dinner rush. He caught her green-eyed glance his way as she set the plates down in front of two hungry cowhands. Wes's return interrupted him.

"No word from Danner yet," Wes announced, draining the last of his coffee, then setting the empty cup near the edge of the table.

Chance nodded, but said nothing, still unable to focus on anything or anyone other than Rebecca.

Suddenly, Rebecca appeared with two plates and headed for the awestruck Chance. He stood and removed his hat.

"Good evening, gentlemen. Here are your suppers," she said placing the steak and potatoes in front of each man.

"Good evening, ma'am. I'm Ben Chance."

"Hello, Mr. Chance. I'm Rebecca, huh, um, Smith! Nice to meet you. Enjoy your supper." She turned and hurried away.

Chance remained standing for a moment before he realized what he was doing.

"I believe you can sit back down now, Mr. Chance," Wes said

cutting into his beef. "Whew! You got it bad, kid!" Wes added with a chuckle.

"Sorry, Wes. I've never seen a girl like her before, I guess."

"No girls in Texarkana?" Wes quipped.

"I ain't never seen one like that!" Chance answered.

"Well, it looks like you'll be stayin' in Range for bit, I reckon," Wes said with a grin. "Now, maybe you could get her back here with some hot coffee?" He added.

CHAPTER 35

LUXTON DANNER - OUTSIDE OF RANGE

Danner rested his Winchester on his shoulder and knelt next to the circle of rocks. He held his hand slightly above the charred kindling. The gray, ash-covered wood still felt warm to the touch. The fire had been extinguished less than an hour before. The tracks still indicated two horses. He saw two sets of boot tracks scattered about, but no sign of women's shoes. *Maybe these aren't the two from the river*, he thought. He looked all around, straining to see through the dusk, but could not make out any movement. Bullet snorted, then a gun cocked behind him.

"Drop the rifle, mister," a lone voice ordered.

Danner slowly laid down his rifle and stood.

"Keep yer hands away from those leg irons!"

Danner lifted his hands away from his Russians. "Can I turn around?" Danner asked.

"Just stay where you are, mister. Who are ya and what'd you want out here?"

"Name's Danner. I'm looking for someone."

"Everybody lookin' fer someone out here, mister. Who you lookin' fer?"

"A nun by the name Sarah."

"A what?"

"A nun. You know, a religious woman?" Danner heard the click of the gun's hammer as well as the gun sliding back into its leather holster. He slowly turned to see an old man with leathery, wrinkled skin behind a short tobacco-stained gray beard.

"You can put yer hands down, mister. I ain't got no nun with me."

"Who are you old timer?" Danner asked, exhaling a sigh of relief.

"Name's Silas Neely. Now who might you really be?"

"Luxton Danner. United States Deputy Marshal."

"Pounce'n coyotes! I didn't mean to draw down on no U.S. Marshal! Out here ya never can tell who yer gonna run into!"

"You the Silas Neely who used to scout for some Marshals here in the territory?" Danner asked.

"Yep. That'd be me all right! I'm on my way to Fort Sill. I was scout'n for the troops at Fort Concho, but the commander at Sill asked for me up here."

"I don't feel too bad then lettin' ya sneak up on me that way," Danner said with a chuckle before extending his hand for a shake.

"Well, I saw ya off in the distance, and it looked like you was trackin' so I thought I'd check you out. Now what's this about a nun?"

"The Marshal's office sent me out here to a town called Range. They've been having a mess of trouble with raiders along the river. Looks like they started swiping women. There's a girl missing from a week or so ago, and now a nun from this morning. I picked up a trail at the riverbank, and it's led me to this camp. You see anyone with a woman in the last couple of days?"

"Nope, can't say I have Marshal. I saw a gang ride'n west a couple days ago. They's about fifteen 'er so of 'em. Didn't see no women though. Come across a couple a camps, too. No women. Just fellas on the run, I reckon."

"Mr. Neely, when you due up at Fort Sill?"

"Oh, as soon as I can git there. Why?"

"I sure could use your tracking skills. I know the territory, but not like you. You interested in working with me for a few days. I'll pay you the going rate for a Marshal scout."

Neely looked down and ran dirty fingers through his snarly gray beard. "If we come across any wanted men, you can take the full bounty," Danner sweetened the deal.

"That's an offer I can't refuse, Marshal! You got yerself a deal!"

"Great. I was going to head back to town, but since I have you now, I figure it best to keep on the trail," Danner stated.

"Yep, ah huh. That be best. No sense trackin' in the dark though. Might as well stay here fer the night," Neely suggested.

A short time later, Danner had the earlier campfire fanning flames again. Neely shot a jack rabbit and was relieving it from its skin while Danner stripped the bark off a couple of hackberry branches for cooking.

"Mr. Neely, you ever scout for Kirby Skinner, Joel Thornton, or Ben Chance?" Danner asked.

"Oh ya, all three. Mostly Marshal Thornton. Marshal Chance was with 'em a few times though. And then Marshal Skinner. He was after Thornton and Chance. You know those fellas?"

"Yes, sir. Sure did. Marshal Thornton and Chance are dead now. Marshal Skinner stays back in Fort Smith guarding prisoners."

"Thornton and Chance dead? What happened?"

"Rustlers attacked Thornton's ranch a few months back. He was shot. Died a few days later. I met Ben Chance over in Canyon Creek. Thornton's daughter came looking for Chance, and I went along. Ben got killed in an ambush outside Six Shot. I was there with him. That was a bad day," Danner said rubbing the back of his neck.

"Killed by rustlers. Damn shame. Those were two good men. Always treated me good and fair."

"Ben had a son. Named after him. He's looks just like him," Danner added.

"I'll be! Looks just like him, huh?"

"Yep. Kind of ghostly when I saw him. He's over in Texarkana." Bullet snorted, then followed with a high nicker. Danner snatched up his Winchester and rolled away from the fire. Neely followed scurrying off into the darkness. Danner laid low in the midst of a group of tall bunch grass. He listened. Bullet snorted again, this time forcefully stomping his hooves. Danner heard the crunch of ground brush. Neely settled down under a sage, pistol in hand. He also heard the snaps of brush twigs. They watched the ring of light around the campfire. It didn't reach far but provided an area to see. *Nobody would be stupid enough to enter into the firelight out here, would they?* Danner thought.

Danner heard his own breath and felt his heartbeat inside his ears. He swallowed hard, careful not to move. Neely knelt by his side. They both kept still. Suddenly, Danner caught movement to his right. Just a shadow in the dark, but certain movement. He saw it again, moving slowly toward the horses. Danner leapt to his feet and rushed toward the shadow. He lowered his shoulder, aimed for the middle of the shadow and hit it with all his might.

Danner's broad shoulder hit the mark. The impact was met with a high-pitched shriek, then a thud. Danner realized he had bulled over a much smaller person. He looked close.

"Damn! It's a girl!" he shouted out for Neely to hear. Danner picked up his victim and carried her to the light of the fire, then laid her on his blanket. Neely looked on but said nothing. Danner couldn't be sure, but it looked like he had found the missing farm girl. Her face was scratched and soiled with red dirt, her hair matted, and her dress torn as though it had been ravaged by a puma. Danner grabbed his canteen and lifted the girl's head to wet her lips. She opened her eyes and screamed, knocking Danner's canteen into the fire. Neely pounced on the container whacking it from the flames. The girl tried to crawl away before Danner's massive hands clutched her shoulders, stopping her immediately.

"It's okay, it's okay. You're safe. I'm a U.S. Marshal, you're safe," Danner repeated.

The girl stopped and stared into Danner's face. Her eyes shone over a quivering bottom lip that had been split in two places. She looked over at Neely and pushed herself backward into Danner's saddle.

"He's not going to hurt you either. He's with me." Danner assured the young woman. "What's your name?" Danner asked gently.

The girl's eyes darted back to Danner, then to Neely. "Molly Lewis," she whispered.

"You're the girl from the farm outside Range?" Danner asked.

The girl nodded. Tears began to run down her face washing a narrow path though the prairie dirt mask she wore. Danner pulled off his blue bandana and waved at Neely to give him his canteen. Neely stepped forward causing the girl to jerk away. Danner wet his bandana and handed it to the jittery girl. She slowly wiped the grime from her face, exposing a bruised left eye.

Danner offered his canteen, which the girl shakily accepted, and gulped from as though she hadn't had a drink in days. The water splashed onto her cheeks, running down her neck, soaking the tattered collar of her once bright, flower print dress.

"I'm sorry I knocked you down, but I didn't know who or what was there. Are you hungry? We have a rabbit if you like?" Danner asked.

She continued to stare straight ahead but nodded in response to the offer of food. Neely set the meat over the fire and watched it closely. Danner untied his second extra blanket from his saddle and wrapped it around the girl before joining Neely on the opposite side of the fire.

"What'd ya reckon happened to her?" Neely asked in as low a voice as he could muster.

"Don't have to reckon, Silas. Pretty obvious she was harmed. Just don't know how bad," Danner answered, staring into the flickering flames, rubbing the slick skin on his freshly-shaven face. He ground his teeth back and forth until it hurt. Anger burned inside him. He hadn't felt this way for a long, long time.

"Marshal. You all right?" Neely asked turning the rabbit meat over.

"No, Silas. I'm not. I've never been very good at seeing abused women. We're gonna find these sons-a-bitches and they'll wish they'd hanged," Danner said his voice getting louder as he spoke.

"Yes, sir. I'm all fer that. Don't have no use fer a man that hurts a lady," Neely answered.

After finishing off the rabbit, Danner added more wood to the fire. The wind had picked up since sundown, making for a cold evening. He noticed the girl still shivering underneath his spare blanket, so he gave her Bullet's blanket, as well. The girl moved closer to the fire. She looked pale and weak. Neely set up opposite the girl and settled down with his own bedding.

"I'll take first watch," Danner informed the old tracker, who nodded before pulling his tattered calvary hat over his face.

Danner checked his Winchester and Russians to make sure they were full-up with ammunition. He knew they were, but it was his habit to double check in times like these. He took a position just outside the light of the fire, in the shadows. He didn't expect any visitors, then again, he hadn't expected Molly Lewis to stumble upon their camp, either. He was doing his best to calm his anger, but he'd welcome any fool's attempt to take Molly back.

After a few hours, Danner tapped Neely's boot. Neely woke tipping his hat back taking several moments to realize where he was, and who he was with. "It's Danner," he announced making certain the old timer knew who was standing over him.

Neely tossed his blanket back and rolled off his saddle. After taking a drink from his canteen, Neely grabbed his Winchester, then waved at Danner, and moved into the shadows. Danner added wood to the fire, then leaned against Neely's saddle and tried to sleep. As expected, sleep fought him like cornered wildcat. He kept looking out underneath the brim of his hat at Molly, making sure she was still there. The heat from the fire felt good after hours out of its warm reach.

Take it easy, Lux. Neely's got your back. Best to get some shut-eye, he thought. It was no use. He couldn't relax. He forced his eyes shut but his mind raced with thoughts of Molly, the nun, the family he met on the trail, and Rebecca Barry. He felt like this whole assignment had gotten away from him. His objective had been somewhat cloudy from the start. He dozed off, all these thoughts banging around his head. Suddenly, he heard the horse's nicker, and brush move. Tossing his hat back, he saw a big man hunched over Molly. His dirty hand pressed against her mouth preventing her screams. Danner cocked his Russian and fired a forty-five into the big man's back forcing him forward onto

Molly. She screamed. Crack! Neely fired his rifle from the shadows. Another man charged into the fire's light. Crack! Crack! A bullet hit Danner as he tried to stand. It knocked him sideways sending his pistol out of his hand. Crack! Another rifle shot from Neely sent the second man into the fire all but extinguishing the light it had provided.

"Stop! Stop!" Molly screamed.

Danner pulled his other Russian but couldn't see to shoot. Neely ran past him toward Molly's screams. Crack! Another shot rang out. The flash from the gun barrel lit up the two outlaws crouched behind Molly. Neely fell next to the fire pit. Danner raised his Russian and fired into the two shadows behind Molly. The muzzle flash both lit up the men, and blinded Danner all at the same time. He rolled away from Neely's bedroll. Bolts of pain emanating from his side shocked him. Crack! A bullet kicked up dirt next to him. Danner fired toward the muzzle flash. He heard the outlaw grunt and fall. Crack! Another bullet hit Danner in the leg. Danner fired his second Russian and emptied all six bullets at the last bandit. Molly screamed under her blanket.

Neely sat up and yelled out to Danner. "Marshal! Marshal!" Neely shouted.

Danner jerked away, reaching for his Winchester. Neely grabbed his arm.

"Marshal! It's okay! It's me, Neely!"

Shaken from another nightmare, Danner paused and looked around. Neely bent over him, wide-eyed and breathing hard. Danner glanced at the fire. The undisturbed flames flickered lazily to his left. On the other side of the fire, Molly Lewis stared at Danner, with Bullet's blanket pulled up to her chin, flames dancing in her brown eyes. Danner sweat profusely and gasped for breath. His chest heaved in and out.

"You okay, Marshal?" Neely asked.

"Yes, I'm all right now. Sorry, Neely. I should have warned you about these nightmares." Danner apologized.

"That was a bad 'un," Neely said looking over at Molly. "You okay, little lady?" He asked.

Molly nodded and released her grip on the blanket.

Neely pulled a flask out of his saddle bag, pulled the cork, and took a swig before handing it to Danner. "Take a touch, Marshal," he ordered.

Danner took a drink. The whiskey burned his throat, but he took another before handing it back to Neely. "Thanks," Danner said. "How long was I asleep?" Danner asked.

"Oh, 'bout an hour or so, I reckon," Neely answered before taking another drink. "I'll keep a look out. See if ya can get a little more shut-eye, Marshal," Neely said, then disappeared into the shadows before Danner could respond.

Danner took a deep breath and leaned back onto Neely's saddle. Molly offered a faint smile at Danner. *Sleep? Not hardly*, Danner thought.

CHAPTER 36

KYLE BRITT & TUFF JENKINS – RED RIVER & RED RIVER CITY

Kyle Britt looked through the office window to see Jared Barry sitting at his desk shuffling paper. Britt was aware of Barry's current displeasure with him for returning without Rebecca as he tapped lightly on the door. Barry opened the door, said nothing, just turned, and sat back down at this desk, leaving the door open. Britt stepped in, and waited in the shadow of an oil lamp burning brightly on Barry's desk. After what seemed like an hour to Britt, Barry paused and looked at his gunman.

"What is it, Britt?" Barry finally asked.

"It's Jenkins, sir. He wants to see you."

"He's not in town, is he?" Barry hollered.

"No, sir. He's over by the river where he usually meets with you."

"I wasn't supposed to see him for a couple more days." Barry said, sounding annoyed.

"Says it's important. It's about that Marshal in Range. Also heard about a Texas Ranger poke'n around," Britt explained.

"Damn!" Barry shouted, slamming his fat fist on his desk. "This is getting to be a real problem!" he added. "Fine. Tell him I'll be there as soon as I can. Maybe he can bring my daughter back!" Barry announced, full sarcasm in his voice.

"Yes, sir," Britt said without taking the bait, then quickly left the room.

———

Tuff Jenkins, the leader of Barry's gang, waited impatiently atop his horse with five of his best men along the north bank of the Red River. This shallow river section allowed Barry an easy crossing. Jenkins didn't like having to wait, especially since he had a two-day ride back to the ravine, he called home. A hard, two-hour ride north from Range into Indian Territory, Squaw Ravine was nothing more than a crack in the side of rocky hill that had been a regular meeting place for area creatures in search of a watering hole. For the past six months, it was home to a couple shabby shacks and tents erected by Jenkins's band of outlaws running up and down the Red River wreaking havoc on anyone who couldn't defend themselves. If it weren't for Jenkins's debt to Barry, he'd kill the little fat bastard and take over his town.

On a cold night in January 1863, Jenkins, Billy Dunham and Jared Barry crept along a narrow trail heading toward a Union Fort outside Springfield Missouri. Infantrymen in Colonel MacDonald's battalion, their unit was due to join Brigadier General John S. Marmaduke's main Confederate Army and fight for the town of Springfield. Having been told to prepare for hand to hand battle, the men had decided they'd take their chances on their own. Shortly before midnight on January seventh, the three deserters slipped through the picket lines and disappeared into the night, avoiding one of the bloodiest battles of the Civil War.

Soon after, Barry became a successful gambler up and down the Mississippi River, frequently bailing Jenkins and Dunham out of jail for their raiding and lawlessness. Growing tired of his partners' illicit activities, Barry set up Jenkins and Dunham with a fistful of cash and put them both on a train heading west. After returning to Missouri to join the border raiders there, Jenkins and Dunham, headed to the Red River along the Texas border to continue their raiding ways. That led the two varmints to Red River City, and a reunion with Barry, now the Red River City's boss, who had converted thousands of dollars in gambling pots and prosperous cattle trading into a lumber operation along the river.

Unsatisfied with the already generous income from his legitimate businesses, Barry's greedy gambling nature demanded more– a lot more than the mill could satisfy. He'd decided to take what he wanted from other settlements along the river and use the contraband to fund his interests in the growing cattle industry. The idea of owning thousands of acres of fertile grazing land with an abundance of raw timber infected his mind with delusions of power and grandeur. His greed led him to focus Jenkins on raiding border towns, supplementing his lumber revenue. He wanted control of Riverbend, Eagle Springs, and most especially, Range. That would give him power all along the river.

Jenkins snapped his silver pocket watch shut. It was after midnight. "Son of a bitch better get here quick, or I'll shoot his fat ass, anyway," Jenkins mumbled.

"Boss, rider comin' through the thicket on the other side," announced one of Jenkins's men.

"'Bout damn time," Jenkins grunted, when Barry stopped his horse opposite Jenkins.

"Look, it's dangerous for us to meet here. I told you I'd meet you over in Eagle Springs."

"No time for that. There's a U.S. Marshal in Range, and I hear a Ranger also. They still ain't built a bank. Word is that Benson fella controls the money out of their town hall. I don't know about hittin' it now with the law's hangin' around," Jenkins said.

"There's more. That damn Marshal stopped off here and left with my daughter. I figure she's still with him in Range. I'll pay you an extra five hundred dollars when you bring her back here," Barry offered.

Jenkins mulled over the offer. "Nobody said nothing about tangling with a Marshal and Ranger. Make it a thousand, and we'll get her," Jenkins stated.

"Done. Don't come back without her. One more thing: make sure your men keep their dirty hands off her. Got it?"

"Got it," Jenkins answered, then spun his horse and disappeared into the night.

Next, Barry returned to the bunkhouse to see Britt. "Get your hide over to Range. Don't do anything. Just watch and make sure Jenkins does what he's supposed to. I've already got someone to take his place if he fails. Leave tonight," Barry ordered.

"That Marshal sees me, he'll know somethings up," Britt advised.

"Then make sure he doesn't see you!" Barry kicked his horse and headed back to the mill.

B ritt waited until his boss was out of sight, then slid up onto his horse, and rode west out of town before turning to the river and crossing over to a small opening in the north side thicket where Jenkins and his men waited.

"Well?" Jenkins asked.

"He told me to leave for Range tonight. Make sure you do what yer supposed to," Britt explained.

"Hmm? Puttin' a spy on me, is he?" Jenkins chuckled. "Tell yer boys this is the last time we work for Barry. We'll take what we want from Range, including his daughter, then come back here and let this town know who and what Mr. Barry really is. That'll take care of him," Jenkins replied.

"I'll tell the boys and let out fer Range. I'll see ya'll there," Britt stated then headed back to the barracks to pass the word.

"Some of the boys ain't gonna like goin' into Range with the law there," Dunham spoke up.

"We'll take a few extra men. Nobody in that town has the guts to fight us 'cept that damn blacksmith. What's that? Two? Three guns against us? They'll be ten, twelve of us, and they won't know we're come'n."

"We kill a Marshal and Ranger, they'll come after us with an army," Dunham protested.

"Rangers ain't come'n after us at all once we get into Indian Territory, and there ain't enough Marshals to make an army. Don't worry. We own this land, not them! They don't know what they're in for!" Jenkins announced loudly with confidence.

"After this, we'll take over Barry's town and live it up!" Dunham spewed between bursts of laughter.

"Now yer talkin'," Jenkins added, snapping his reins and leading the men west.

The moon was up and in a battle with rolling clouds of fog that had crept across the plain making it difficult to see. "I can't see a damn thing. Let's camp here for the night. We'll ride on in the morning after this damn fog clears out. We have plenty of time," Jenkins advised his men.

Without a word, the six outlaws dismounted and gathered around a hastily made fire. Jenkins passed on the bottle of whiskey offered to him. He needed time to think. He had plans to make.

CHAPTER 37

REBECCA BARRY, WES PAYNE & BEN CHANCE, JR. – RANGE

Rebecca's heels clapped loudly on the solid oak steps as she hurried down the staircase. Grabbing the round oak banister post, she spun around the corner of the lobby's sitting area, then headed for the Cattlemen's restaurant in the back of the hotel. Just past daybreak in Range, Rebecca headed to the kitchen for her new job, afraid she was already late.

Mrs. Conrad worked the stove, piling fried bacon and potatoes into large pots keeping them warm on the back burners. Rebecca grabbed a freshly laundered white apron from its nail on the wall and wrapped it around her narrow waist. Several other women worked in the kitchen washing dishes and preparing for the morning's meal.

"Good morning, dear, did you sleep well?" Mrs. Conrad asked, pushing a lock of already damp hair away from her face.

"Yes ma'am. I'm afraid too well! I'm sorry I'm late!" Rebecca answered before retrieving a large basket of eggs from the back door and bringing them to the second stove which Mrs. Conrad had already heated.

"Nonsense. We worked very late last night, and I couldn't have done it without you! We have two pots of coffee ready, and I expect we'll need several more. There's a lot of people in town, so we'll be very busy this morning. It's almost seven, so Mr. Conrad will open the doors," Mrs. Conrad explained.

Right on cue, the ladies in the kitchen heard the rumbling of boots hitting the wood planked floor and voices drift in from the dining room. As if preparing for a battle of their own, the women tightened their aprons and grabbed coffee pots, then hurried out of the kitchen.

"Go ahead and make a large bowl of scrambled eggs," Mrs. Conrad directed Rebecca who began cracking the brown shells without further direction. "You can cook, can't you?" Mrs. Conrad asked.

"Yes, I can cook eggs!" Rebecca responded, manning her station at the stove as Mrs. Conrad hurried into the dining room.

Lawrence Benson, Belton Tanner, and Doc Phillips sat at the front table near the window. Benson, as usual, dominated the conversation while looking through the small framed windowpanes onto the street. One of the girls delivered plates of bacon, eggs, and biscuits to the men when Mrs. Conrad stopped to visit.

"Everything come out okay, gentlemen?" She asked.

"Wonderful as always, Mrs. Conrad," declared Benson in his usual boisterous manner. "I'm very happy to see business so good," he added looking around the near full dining room.

"Yes, sir. There's an awful lot of people in town these days. Mrs. Fields says she's just as busy over at the boarding house," Mrs. Conrad offered through a wide smile. "Enjoy your breakfast," she added hurrying off to other tables.

With the restaurant located on the back side of the hotel, Lawrence Benson only saw a small area of main street from his seat inside the restaurant. He anxiously awaited Marshal Danner's return, although the Marshal had not indicated when he would be back. Benson was an impatient man, always wanting things to be completed earlier than possible. While many of the townsfolk didn't like his oppressive manner, everyone appreciated his business sense and propensity to get things done. It was his driving persistence that had made Range grow faster than any of the surrounding towns outside the Hardeman County seat of Margaret.

The three men's conversation halted when Sheriff Zach Evans

walked into the restaurant with Marshal Dodson and paused at the door.

"Excuse me gentlemen, I see Sheriff Evans is here," Benson advised his breakfast guests.

"Good morning, Sheriff, Mr. Dodson," Benson officially greeted the lawmen with a firm handshake each. "Please, join me at my table up front," he added pointing toward Phillips and Tanner. The men maneuvered their way through the dining room with Dodson pulling up an extra chair.

"I didn't expect you this early, Sheriff," Benson stated. I believe you know everyone here," he added.

"Yes, indeed. Good morning, gentlemen. Well, Lawrence, when I received your telegram about the U.S. Marshal's arrival, I decided to leave early this morning."

"Marshal Danner hasn't returned from the territory, and we have not seen Ranger Payne yet this morning," Benson stated.

"Oh, I wasn't aware our Ranger had arrived," Evans stated.

"Yes, sir, late yesterday afternoon," Benson reported.

"Dodson tells me there's nothing new on the missing Sister?" Evans stated in between sips of coffee.

"No, sir. Nothing. This is terrible. The Deacon and Sisters just arrived and already we have what appears to be a tragedy. We're obviously hoping Marshal Danner will find her safe," Benson stated.

"Doc, has the Lewis girl been able to tell us anything about what happened out there?" Evans asked Phillips.

"No. I believe she and her brother were hidden in the storm shelter when the attack started. I don't think she saw much, and her youth hasn't helped," Phillips answered.

Evans shook his head. "My daughter's her age," he said in a low voice, shaking his head.

"Lawrence, Zach, it looks like our Texas Ranger has arrived," Doc Phillips announced seeing Wes and Chance enter the dining room through the hotel archway.

Seeing Dodson seated with Benson and several other men, Wes tapped Chance on the shoulder and nodded toward the window table.

"Good morning, Ranger Payne, Mr. Chance," Benson stated. "This is Sheriff Zach Evans, Doc Phillips, and our blacksmith, Belton Tanner." Benson completed the introductions and looked around for two more chairs. Mrs. Conrad, having seen Wes and Chance arrive, quickly made her way to the table and moved two chairs from nearby tables to what had quickly developed into an impromptu town meeting.

"Gentlemen, this is Wes Payne of the Texas Rangers, and Ben Chance," Benson announced.

Evans stood and shook both men's hands. He took a long look at Chance.

"Based on the fact that you look just like him and have the same name, I'm guessin' you're Ben Chance's son," Evans stated.

"Yes, sir, that'd be me," Chance answered.

"I'm sorry about your father. Damn good man there," Evans stated.

"Marshal, any word from Danner?" Wes asked.

"No, sir. Looks like he didn't come back last night," Dodson answered.

Benson motioned toward the two chairs Mrs. Conrad delivered. "Please join us. I believe we have a great deal to discuss what with Marshal Danner being delayed and all," Benson declared.

The men provided more details of recent events to Sheriff Evans and pontificated on the reasons for Danner's delayed return. Once their coffee cups were empty, all but Wes and Chance stood to leave.

"If you need me, or Sheriff Evans, we'll be next door at the meeting house," Benson advised Wes and Chance, who decided to remain for breakfast.

"Not many folk around who haven't heard of your father, are there?" Wes asked.

"No, I reckon not."

"Maybe that pretty girl will be here this morning?" Wes chuckled.

"Maybe," Chance answered glancing around the big dining room.

A freckle-faced young girl poured the men coffee.

"Excuse me, young lady. Is Miss Smith working this morning?" Wes asked.

"Yes, sir. She's cooking in the kitchen."

"I don't mean to be rude, but could you have her bring two plates of bacon and eggs?" Wes asked with a wide grin.

The girl caught on fast, looking over to a blushing Chance. "Yes, sir, I'll ask Mrs. Conrad," she said as she hurried off.

"That wasn't necessary," Chance said, his face flushed red with embarrassment.

Dodson pushed through the door and headed straight for Wes. "Danner's coming into town. He just crossed the river down by the freight yard. He's got a young woman and an old timer with him," Dodson reported.

Wes and Chance jumped up to leave. "Tell the kitchen we can't stay," Wes directed his young partner.

Wes and Dodson left the hotel while Chance headed for the kitchen. As he was about to step into the doorway, Rebecca appeared with two plates of hot food.

"Excuse me ma'am. Are those for the table up by the window?" Chance asked.

"Yes. I was told to bring these out," Rebecca answered, biting her bottom lip, and looking away.

"I'm sorry. Those were for me and Mr. Payne, but we have to go," Chance explained.

"Okay. I'll take them back," Rebecca responded, her voice drifting to a low tone, obviously disappointed.

"I'll come back as soon as I can." He told her.

"I'll be here most of the day," Rebecca advised, her frown growing into a bright smile.

Chance turned on a heel and hurried out the door with Rebecca watching every step.

Mrs. Conrad, watching the two young people smiled and stepped over to Rebecca. "Seems that young man is a bit smitten," she said before heading into the kitchen.

Rebecca's smile didn't wane. Her flushed cheeks felt warm as she lightly bounced back into the kitchen. She had fleeting thoughts for Danner, but not like this. The little spark she felt whenever she saw

Chance felt different. Danner had rescued her from her father, and for that he was a hero to her. He certainly was an attractive and mysterious man. Didn't all women like that? Had she misplaced those feelings for something else? Chance looked at her in a way Danner did not. The energy and excitement she felt when Chance was around was far different from how she felt about Danner. This emotion was something she'd only heard about from other girls. She took a deep breath and went about her business in the kitchen, trying to focus herself on something more concrete and comfortable.

A few minutes later, Chance caught up to Wes and Dodson, who stood in front of the meeting house with Sheriff Evans and Mr. Benson. Several people had gathered on the walkways on both sides of the street. They watched intently as Danner rode slowly down the street with a young girl's arms wrapped around his waist, and an old, gray, bearded man slumped in his saddle a short distance behind. Danner's dark drawn expression told the men the word was not going to be good.

PART II

CHAPTER 38

LUX DANNER, WES PAYNE & BEN
CHANCE, JR. – RANGE

Danner's broad shoulders shrouded his passenger. The only visible sign of Molly Lewis were her two arms wrapped around his gun belt. People began to fill the boardwalks on each side of the street watching the big Marshal's return. Danner paid no attention to the gawkers. His focus was fixed forward, stone jaw, and steel eyes set on an emotionless face. Notified of Danner's arrival, Doc Phillips and Betsy waited patiently on the front step of his office.

Seeing the doctor, Danner reined Bullet to the side of the street. Molly refused to release her death grip on Danner's holsters. He paused, then as gentle as the giant lawman could, he peeled her hands off the leather. "Everything's okay, Molly. You're safe now. You can get down," Danner quietly informed his rider.

Phillips stepped forward and waved Betsy toward Molly. Betsy offered her a hand which Molly accepted. Phillips helped her down then led the two young women to his office door. Prior to entering, Phillips hesitated and turned to Danner. "Marshal, would you ask Mrs. Jamieson or Mrs. Conrad to come to my office right away?"

"I'm right here, doctor!" Wanda Jamieson called as she crossed the street from her store. Wanda, Betsy, and Phillips then disappeared into the doctor's office. Danner looked over and saw Wes and Chance waiting with the other men in front of the meeting house. He tapped his spurs and headed to meet them. Sisters Mary and Dolores hurried past heading for the doctor's office.

"Good to see you back, Marshal," Dodson said as Danner stepped down from his stirrup. Danner nodded toward Dodson, then looked at Wes and Chance. A faint smile cracked his craggy expression. He hadn't realized how much he'd hoped Wes would be the Ranger sent here. That realization split his face into a wide grin. He marched over to Wes with easy strides.

"Damn good to see you Wes," he said, squeezing Wes's shoulder and shaking the Ranger's hand. "And, what the hell are you doing here, Ben?" he asked, repeating the warm greeting with Chance.

"Glad to see you too, Marshal Danner. I ran into Mr. Payne over in Riverbend and decided to ride along and get a closer look at what ya'll were gettin' into," Chance explained.

"He did more than run into me, Danner. Kid saved my hide in a little argument at the hotel over there," Wes added.

"Argument?" Danner asked crossing his arms and leaning back with a raised eyebrow.

"I'll tell you about it later," Wes stated.

Danner stepped aside and waved toward Neely. "This is Silas Neely. He's scouted for Marshals in the past, and I convinced him to delay his trip to Fort Sill and help us search for the missing Sister."

"Where'd ya find Molly Lewis?" Dodson asked.

"Actually she found us. Last night, just after dark, about two hours north of here, she wandered up to our campsite. Don't know if they let her go, she escaped, or was just wandering around out there. It was obvious she needed attention, so we got back here as quick as we could," Danner explained.

Several people had gathered around the men as they spoke about the events leading up to bringing Molly Lewis back to town. "Gentlemen, I'll let the folks know what happened with Molly," Benson advised, apparently never missing an opportunity to make another public speech.

"I'm heading over to the hotel and get cleaned up. I'll see you two in a bit," Danner advised Wes and Chance, patting each on the back before leading Bullet to the hotel.

"We'll be back in the restaurant. Our breakfast was disrupted by your arrival," Wes stated with a grin. Mr. Neely, care to join us?" Wes asked the old timer.

"Don't mind if I do!"

"Soldiers coming!" Someone yelled from the crowd. Everyone stopped and looked toward the cattle pens. The black and gold colors of the Tenth Calvary's flag could be seen atop the soldier's guidon. It looked like fifteen-to-twenty crisp, navy blue clad soldiers mounted in single file.

"Finally! I requested soldiers some time ago," Benson boasted loud enough for everyone to hear.

Wes shielded his eyes from the sun's glare and took a hard look. "It's the Tenth Cav out of Phantom Hill," he said.

Benson stepped into the street and moved ahead of the crowd to greet the soldiers. Evans, Dodson, Wes, Chance, and Danner all joined the mayor forming an impromptu welcoming committee. The lead soldier, a Lieutenant, raised his right hand as he stopped his horse a few feet from Benson and company.

"Company! Ready to dismount. Dismount!" the Lieutenant called.

On order, the soldiers dismounted in one motion, then stood by their horses. The Lieutenant swung down off his saddle and stepped toward Benson. "Gentlemen, I'm Lieutenant Will Blackwell, Tenth Calvary out of Fort Phantom Hill."

Will Blackwell was a tall, stocky man with the sharp movements of a West Point graduate. His youthful appearance didn't disguise the confidence he exuded. He had obviously been in the field for some time, having gained the experience necessary to lead a group of soldiers on an unconventional mission.

Benson shook the Lieutenant's hand, then introduced himself, before turning toward the men next to him. "Lieutenant, this is our Sheriff Zach Evans, our town Marshal, Lane Dodson, U.S. Deputy Marshal Luxton Danner, along with Texas Ranger Wes Payne, and Mr.

Ben Chance," Benson stated nearly out of breath. "They have come to assist us in bringing law and order to our town."

The crowd that had gathered upon Danner's arrival, pushed forward toward the soldiers. The boardwalks filled with more folks who had come out to see what all the excitement was about. The cavalry showing up wasn't exactly a common occurrence. Blackwell nodded as Benson introduced each man then removed his hat.

"We've been dispatched here to provide assistance. I hadn't expected to find a U.S. Marshal and Texas Ranger here along the river. Good to see you both. I'm aware there has been some recent outlaw activity along the river," Blackwell advised.

"Lieutenant, if you'd care to step into my office at the meeting house, we can bring you up to date on what has happened recently," Benson stated while motioning toward the front door of the meeting house.

Blackwell nodded then turned to a short burly, barrel-chested sergeant standing a few feet behind him.

"Sergeant, have the men bivouac on the eastern edge of town. Make certain our tents don't impede the road leading in," Blackwell added before returning his sergeant's salute.

Benson led the way to his office with Evans, Dodson, and Danner close behind.

"I'll just head over to the restaurant," Chance stated as Wes fell in behind Danner.

Wes and Danner stopped. "I thought you wanted a closer look. Now's the time to get it. Come on," Danner told Chance.

Dodson waved toward the group milling around in front of the meeting house, ordering them to get back to their business before he disappeared into the meeting house.

Benson directed everyone to the meeting room in the back. Danner noticed Benson was full of energy, his eyes bright, and his face flushed. He truly enjoyed being the center of attention. Danner couldn't decide if that annoyed him or not as he sat back to watch the show.

"I apologize for our delayed arrival, Mr. Benson. We had prepared to leave Phantom Hill and proceed directly here, but we were needed when a band of Indians fled the reservation at Fort Sill and were reportedly headed our way toward the Estacado. We spent a few days searching, but only found tracks that went off in multiple directions," Lieutenant Blackwell explained.

"How many?" Danner asked.

"Over a hundred, I'm told," Blackwell answered. "Both Kiowa and Comanche."

Danner shot a quick glance at Wes who frowned and shook his head.

"I understand completely, Lieutenant. We're just glad you made it. How long are you permitted to stay?" Benson asked.

"Unless otherwise ordered, I've been advised to remain for two weeks. Now with this Indian trouble, that time may be shortened."

Benson made no attempt to hide his disappointment. He rubbed his bald head and let out a loud sigh. "I understand, it's not the Army's responsibility to maintain law in every town, but I was hoping you'd be able to stay longer than two weeks," Benson said before recapping the events that had brought all the men seated at the table to Range.

Blackwell listened intently, saying nothing until Benson had finished. "Marshal Danner, how far up and down the river would you say you searched before finding the kidnapped girl?" Blackwell asked.

"Not far. Maybe an hour down river, then two more north into the territory. I tracked a group of riders until the trail went cold. I believe the track I followed was the gang responsible for taking the nun. I don't know where the girl came from," Danner explained.

"You're familiar with the territory, I assume?" Blackwell asked Danner.

"Yes, sir. I also have a former scout with me that knows it better than I do," Danner said.

"Very well. Since you and my troopers are the only ones with jurisdiction across the river, I'll assume you and your scout will be joining us?" Blackwell asked Danner.

"Excuse me, Lieutenant, but Chance and I figure on going along, too. Just as observers of course," Wes stated unable to withhold a smile, knowing he'd be far more than merely a casual observer.

Blackwell's face showed no expression for several long moments before he looked at Wes and nodded. "Of course. Glad to have you and Mr. Chance along, Mr. Payne. I'll get my men ready. We'll meet you back here in two hours," Blackwell directed.

Dodson and Evans had stepped out of the room when Blackwell brought up jurisdiction in the territory. They were leaning against the wall near the front door when Danner, Chance, and Wes passed by.

"I reckon I better stay in town, but I'd rather be going with ya'll," Dodson said.

"Anyone in town you can count on to fight if Indians show up?" Wes asked.

"There's a few. I'll ask around and have them ready," Dodson responded confidently.

"I'll stay in town for a couple of days," Evans added.

"Lieutenant Blackwell may leave a squad here with you. I'll ask," Danner said.

"That'd be a welcome decision," Dodson admitted.

Danner headed to the hotel to prepare for the latest task at hand. Wes and Chance returned to the Cattlemen's and joined Neely for their belated breakfast. An hour later, Danner joined the trio near the Marshal's office on the west end of town. The soldiers loaded their horses, and two pack mules.

"I'm going over to Doc's to check on the girl," Danner stated.

"I'll join ya," Wes announced.

The two men swung up onto their horses and slowly rode down to Doc's office. Before they could dismount, Phillips stepped out onto the boardwalk in front of this office. His face was blank, his mouth tight, and eyes dark. "How's the girl, Doc?" Danner asked quietly.

"She's dead, Marshal," Phillips said flatly. She was bleeding internally. I wasn't able to save her. I'm sorry."

Wes shifted his weight in the saddle but said nothing. Danner stared off in the distance, not able to focus on anything. He felt hollow. Bullet bobbed his head, causing Ringo to mimic the action.

After a long moment, Danner leaned back, and looked up toward the sky. A single white cloud sat next to the sun. "What kind of men kidnap and kill women?" Danner asked aloud.

Wes leaned forward pushing his boots down on the stirrups. "The same kind that nail a man to a cross and wait for him to die," Wes said.

Danner looked at Wes, whose eyes were fixed on Ringo's mane.

"Or a Ranger to the side of a barn?" Danner added.

Wes looked down at his scarred hands. "Yep," he nodded.

"I don't know how I'll be when we find 'em Wes. I'm thinkin' it won't be like a Marshal though," Danner admitted.

"Nor a Ranger," Wes added.

Both men looked at each other without another word. Nothing else needed to be said.

CHAPTER 39

The burning sun leaned across the mid-day sky, bringing with it a warm late mid-November afternoon. Danner, Wes, Chance, and Neely waited for Blackwell and the Calvary troops to fall into formation. Blackwell seemed to be preparing two different groups of six men each to conduct the search for the gang and its hostage.

"Looks like the Lieutenant's going to leave you a squad of soldiers, Marshal," Danner said to Dodson.

"That'd be good seeing Mack is headed back to the Double O, so I don't have any deputies at the moment," Dodson stated looking into the Army camp.

Blackwell led a formation of twelve soldiers in single file past to the Marshal's office. "Marshal, I left a squad behind to assist with anything you need in town. Sergeant Charles will be in charge. I'm not sure how long we'll be gone, but I don't see it being more than two or three days," Blackwell told Dodson.

"Thanks, Lieutenant. I appreciate the help," Dodson stated.

"Marshal Danner, if you and your scout will lead the way," Blackwell nodded toward Danner.

Danner reined Bullet around and headed for the ford in the river near the freight yard. The search party fell in behind. Despite the shallow ford, the river was wide in this section and moved with a quicker current than neighboring stretches. The murky red water prevented a view of the bottom causing the riders to navigate the tributary carefully. Once across the river, Danner showed Neely where they had found the nun's garment, and the direction of the trail that Danner had followed days before. Neely circled his horse around the area moving further out with each ring. Finally he stopped and waved to the group to follow. Neely didn't wait, turning his mount north riding with his head down examining the ground like a surgeon might examine a patient. After an hour or so, Neely stopped and dismounted. Danner and company had kept a short distance between them and their tracker. Danner and Blackwell joined Neely who was on a knee moving brown bunch grass aside.

"What'd you think?" Danner asked the old tracker.

"Well, sir, this trail is old and beat down, but near as I can tell, they headed off west from here. There's a bunch a horses stopped here fer a bit, then they move on again west," Neely pointed.

"Any idea how many?" Blackwell asked.

Neely shook his head from side to side. "No, sir, don't wanna be guessin' in front of no army Lieutenant," Neely said.

"Best guess," Blackwell insisted.

Neely paused and scratched his beard while examining the patterns in the earthen surface.

"I reckon ten ta fifteen or so, Lieutenant," Neely answered.

"The ground is chewed up pretty good," Danner added.

"Very well. Proceed, Mr. Neely," Blackwell ordered.

Neely jumped up into his saddle and leaned toward Danner. "I ain't never seen that many bandits all together, Marshal. I'd say their up to more'n snatch'n a lady," Neely surmised.

Danner nodded. "This has the markings of someone with money want'n more," Danner stated.

"Looks like saddle war to me Marshal," Neely offered, then tapped his spurs and started west.

Two hours later, Neely raised his hand to stop the group. He waved for Danner and Blackwell to join him. Wes and Chance joined in. As the men reached Neely's position, they noticed that the trail looked fresher, with sharp-edged hoofprints, and manure that still smelled ripe. Neely pointed north toward a rocky mesa not far off in the distance.

"Probably set up camp inside those rocks," Neely noted.

Wes looked back south toward the river. "Chance, I'd say we were right smack in between Range and Riverbend. Would you agree?" Wes asked.

"Yes, sir. I'd say we were also less than two hours from the river," Chance stated.

Blackwell sat atop his horse silent for a bit looking toward the river.

"I don't know how organized these outlaws are, but if I didn't know better, I'd say that they were preparing for a simultaneous attack on those towns. They could split their forces and cause trouble in both places," Blackwell declared.

"If that's the case, they must not know you and your troops are here. Wouldn't make sense to split forces and take on the army," Danner stated.

"Let's go see what we're dealing with then gentlemen," Blackwell suggested.

"Best thing would be to shimmy up the backside of that mesa, and get a look," Neely stated.

"We'll move slowly so as not to kick up a dust cloud," Blackwell advised.

After reaching the summit of the formation, Blackwell, Neely, Danner, and Wes began the crawl up the mesa's back to the top. The sun had begun to set, and shone square in their eyes. Danner and Neely slid forward on their bellies to the edge of the cliff. Blackwell and Wes moved up on either side. The four men looked down in silence for several minutes taking in the scene.

Down below in Squaw Ravine, they saw twenty men, all armed, milling about near a makeshift coral which had been constructed near a large watering hole. The area had been tamped down with all of the ground vegetation cleared out. A smattering of sage and three Mexican white oak trees drawing nourishment from the shallow water table near the water hole surrounded the camp. Rock formations protected the camp on two sides. Blackwell removed field glasses from his pocket and took a closer look. "Looks like bedrolls set up near the base of the cliff. Rifles all around. On the far end of the clearing, I can see a woman sitting alone on a stump," he reported to the group. "Looks like we found the missing nun," Blackwell announced before handing the glasses to Danner.

Danner peered down to see the woman sitting with her arms wrapped around herself. Her clothing didn't look like a nun's, but that didn't matter. It was obvious she wasn't accompanying the group by choice. He scanned over to a wagon, peering into the wagon's bed, identifying its contents. "This isn't just a night camp. This is a rendezvous point. This has been used for some time. They must be waiting for additional men or orders. Check the wagon's load," Danner stated, handing the glasses to Wes. "What do you think, Lieutenant?" Danner asked Blackwell.

"Per regulations, I'm to ride into the camp and learn who these people are and what they are doing here," Blackwell stated keeping his eyes down on the camp.

"With all due respect, Lieutenant, I think we know what they are doing here, and I don't much give a damn who they are," Danner stated.

"I agree with Danner, Lieutenant. You ride down there all friendly-like, you may not live to file your report," Wes added, then looked at Danner. "Arrows all right. They've been make'n it look like Indians," Wes stated.

Blackwell said nothing for a long time, then took a deep breath, and exhaled.

"I have my orders, gentlemen. Besides, what you're implying doesn't sound like the words of a U.S. Deputy Marshal, or a Texas Ranger, for that matter."

Danner looked hard at Blackwell. "Sometimes you have to do

what's right instead of what's written," Danner stated. "This is one of those times."

Blackwell said nothing, just turned, and crawled back down the rock where his troops waited. When Danner and the others descended, Blackwell huddled with his sergeant and two corporals. Danner and Wes stood by waiting for Blackwell to finish. When their conversation ended, both men mounted their horses, the sergeant turning back to speak to the troops. Danner and Wes stepped up onto their horses and waited. Blackwell and his sergeant approached the lawmen.

"We'll split our force in two. Marshal, you, and Mr. Neely will ride in my squad. Mr. Payne and Mr. Chance will ride with Sergeant Kelly. We'll split and charge in two columns. One on each flank. Sergeant Kelly's squad will move first. My squad will delay momentarily so as to not be right across from each other. I don't want a crossfire. No sense my troopers shooting each other," Blackwell explained.

Wes looked at Danner and grinned. Blackwell caught the smirk.

"You two may be gunslingers, but my troopers are not," Blackwell stated without expression. "Gentlemen, this meeting never happened, and this plan was never discussed. Understood?" Blackwell asked.

"Yes, sir," Danner and Wes responded in unison without hesitation.

Blackwell looked at Chance and Neely, who both nodded.

"You sure, Lieutenant?" Danner asked as the men took up positions.

"Like you said Marshal, sometimes you need to do what's right and not what's written. We'll come in from the west with what's left of the sun at our backs," Blackwell added.

Danner smiled. "Just don't have your bugler sound the charge, Lieutenant," he chuckled. Danner wasn't certain, but he thought he saw the glimpse of a faint smile cross Blackwell's face before he reined his horse and took the forward position in his squad.

Blackwell waved toward Kelly making a long arc with his arm, directing his sergeant to take a wide path around the rocks. He then pointed close to the base of the mound, letting his squad know they were going to stay tight to the rock wall. Both columns moved forward. Danner saw Wes with Ringo's reins looped behind his head, and Colts in each hand. When Sergeant Kelly's squad was in position, Blackwell dropped his arm, and drew his sidearm. Sergeant Kelly kicked his horse and began his charge. Blackwell waited a moment, then did the same. Danner and Neely were next to the Lieutenant, Danner with his Russians, and Neely with a double-barrel shotgun he'd had hidden in a rear scabbard.

While one of the outlaws urinated away from camp near the watering hole, he saw Kelly's men charging. Before he could close his trousers and yell, Wes put a bullet into his chest knocking him back into the water.

Crack! Crack! Crack! Gunfire erupted, sending the men in camp running in all directions like roaches in candlelight. Kelly, Wes, Chance, and the troopers sent a fusillade of bullets into the camp from the left flank. Several outlaws fired wildly at the charging men.

Boom! Neely emptied both barrels into a group of three men grabbing rifles from their bedrolls. Two outlaws went down, the third spun, and got off a shot into the dirt. Crack! Danner fired his Russian hitting the third man center chest knocking him off his feet.

Wes, Chance, and the troopers took heavy fire as bullets ripped all around them. Seeing them first, the outlaws only focused on them. One trooper was shot off his horse, another took a bullet in the leg reining his horse away from the fight. Wes emptied both Colts, holstered each and pulled his third pistol from behind his back. He continued to fire as the squad rode past the embattled camp.

Danner reached the nun and jumped from his saddle, shooting another outlaw before his boots hit the rock-hard dirt. He grabbed the woman and pulled her behind the stump. Crack! A bullet shattered the front of the stump, sending splinters into Danner's face. He fired back. Crack! Another bullet penetrated the rotted stump. This time, Danner saw the outlaw, and put a bullet through his neck, dropping him like a sack of seeds.

The gunfire stopped as quickly as it started. Both squads had charged past the camp and were turning for a second pass, if necessary. It wasn't. As the cloud of dust churned up by the thundering hooves drifted away, Danner surveyed the scene. What had been an outlaw camp was now an outlaw graveyard. None of the outlaws had survived. Danner looked at the woman, whose dirtied face held no expression. She stared into the distance.

"Sister Sarah?" Danner asked.

She looked at Danner, and weakly nodded. She then buried her face into what was left of her black tunic and began to cry. Lieutenant Blackwell rode up to Danner.

"Is she the missing nun?" Blackwell asked.

Danner nodded, and motioned for Blackwell's canteen. Blackwell handed over his.

"I need to check on my men." He then turned and rode to where the troopers had gathered around two fallen soldiers.

"Troopers Daniels and Logan, sir. Both dead. Williams and Cantly are wounded, but they'll make it," Sergeant Kelly reported.

Blackwell looked down at his soldiers and nodded. "There's a buckboard near the coral, hook up one of the horses from the coral, and let the rest loose," Blackwell ordered.

Wes and Chance sat astride their horses watching the soldiers. "Glad to see you made it, kid," Wes said to Chance, who looked pale. "You okay kid?" Wes asked.

"Yes, I'm fine." Chance said just as his eyes rolled back in his head, and he fell off his horse, hitting the ground face-first with a thud. Wes swung down off Ringo and saw the reason for his young partner's collapse. Chance bled heavily from the back of his left shoulder. He had taken a bullet.

CHAPTER 40

LANE DODSON – RANGE

Dodson scraped a match against the shed's rough-sawn wall and lit the oil lamp hanging from a rusty hook embedded in the roof of his office. The horizon swallowed up what was left of the sun, dragging dusk into Range. The activity on the street began to slow and the constant pounding of hammers at the church diminished to silence.

Dodson set a chair down on the haphazard set of boards he'd hastily fastened together in front of the office door. Not exactly a fine-planked porch, but it was better than the mud and rock that lay beneath it. He sat down and leaned back against the shed, watching the street activity. Lamps flickered in the cool, fall breeze.

Without their Lieutenant to hover over them, the squad of off-duty Tenth Calvary soldiers gave the Red Dirt Saloon plenty of business. The ladies did especially well, much to the chagrin of Mrs. Jamieson and Mrs. LeGary, who'd recently made it their business to push the saloon ladies out of town. Dodson chuckled to himself at the thought of the wives marching in front of the Red Dirt Saloon in protest of the working women inside. Dodson looked out west, past the soldier's camp, and saw two riders coming in. Dodson instinctively tipped his chair down and moved his right hand toward his gun.

As the riders closed in, Dodson noticed both had side arms and rifles. The rider closest to Dodson tipped his hat as they passed the Marshal shed.

"Good evenin', Marshal," one rider greeted Dodson the other passed with a nod.

"Good evening, fellas," Dodson answered, sizing up the strangers. He watched as the two men tied their horses in front of the Red Dirt and disappeared through the swinging doors. He decided to take a closer look at their mounts to see if there were any clues as to who they were, or where they were from. A quick walk around the horses provided no insight to who the strangers were. These days in Range, strangers came into town daily, but most were obvious farmers, families, or cowhands from neighboring ranches. These two were different. Neither looked the part of a farmer or cowhand. They looked like gunmen, which made Dodson a bit uneasy.

"Good evening, Marshal," Greg LeGary said walking up to the Red Dirt Saloon.

"How are ya, Greg?" Dodson asked.

"A little nervous this evening. We took in a wagon load of dynamite this afternoon. Tom and I got it sitting near the river inside the yard for the moment," LeGary explained.

"Dynamite? Who needs dynamite in town?" Dodson asked.

"Nobody in town. They want it out at the Meehan ranch. Not taken it out there for a few days, though. I didn't know what else to do with it. I figured if it blows, that'd be as good a place as any," LeGary added.

"It far enough away from the building?" Dodson asked, looking down toward the freight barn as if his looking would make a difference.

"Don't rightly know, Marshal. Never seen a wagon full of dynamite blow before," LeGary stated before pushing through the doors into the Red Dirt Saloon.

Great. Just what I need. Gunmen in town and a wagon full of dynamite, Dodson thought, following LeGary into the saloon to have a closer look around.

Dodson watched the stranger pour himself a shot of whiskey and push the bottle back to the bartender.

"You see a young woman, about eighteen, long dark hair come into town in the past few days? Maybe ride'n with a big, tall fella?" the stranger asked.

The bartender pushed the cork back into the whiskey bottle and took a long look at the two men. He glanced over toward Dodson near the front door, then shook his head and put the bottle back on the shelf behind him. He walked to the end of the bar where LeGary had set up camp.

"Get ya a beer, Greg?" the bartender asked the freight yard teamster.

"That'd be good, Sam," LeGary said with a wide smile.

The bartender returned with an overflowing mug, setting it in front of LeGary, then leaned over the bar to whisper. "See them two strangers drinkin' whiskey in the middle of the bar?" Sam asked LeGary who had his mug tipped all the way back guzzling his brew.

LeGary stopped for a breath, taking a quick look at the gunmen, then nodded his head.

"They're askin' about that girl came into town with Marshal Danner," Sam advised.

"What'd they want to know?" LeGary asked.

"Just askin' if I've seen her," Sam said.

What'd ya tell 'em?" LeGary asked.

"Just shook my head no. Don't like the looks of 'em, and the Marshal just walked out the door. Don't wanna get in the middle of nuthin'," the bartender added.

"Okay. Then get me another beer," LeGary ordered shrugging his shoulders, just as a group of sodbusters started hollering from across the room for more whiskey.

Dodson paused outside the door and noted the two gunmen drinking at the bar, saw the table full of farmers yelling for whiskey, and the bartender rushing over to them with a couple bottles of cheap booze. Four soldiers sat at a table in the back negotiating with the ladies. He decided to head down to the hotel and check in on the Conrad's and the Cattlemen's restaurant.

Halfway down the street, Lawrence Benson stepped out of the mercantile. "Marshal Dodson!" Benson called over to his local lawman as he proceeded to shuffle across the street.

What the hell does he want now? Dodson thought before greeting his boss. "Yes, sir, Mr. Benson," Dodson asked forcing a smile.

"They'll be a couple of ranchers coming into town tomorrow about eleven o'clock to take care of some banking with me at the meeting house. I'd appreciate it if you would be there just to make certain there's no trouble," Benson advised.

"You expectin' trouble, Mr. Benson?" Dodson asked.

"Oh my, no sir! It's the owners of the Meehan ranch. Fine men they are, no trouble at all! There'll be a substantial amount of money changing hands is all. Can't be too careful, you know!"

"Yes, sir. I understand. I'll be there just before eleven," Dodson assured the portly Mayor.

"Very well! It's good having you here, Marshal! Good having you here!" Benson said, before turning toward the meeting house, and fading into the darkness.

Dodson shook his head. *That guy always talks like he wants everybody to hear him.* Dodson walked into the hotel and found Rebecca's bright smiling face framed in black flowing hair that reached past her shoulders behind the big, oak desk. "Mrs. Conrad has you doing just about everything around here, don't she?" Dodson asked returning the friendly smile.

"I suppose so. I told Mrs. Conrad I worked a hotel desk, so she asked me to fill in for a couple of hours while she checked on the restaurant customers," Rebecca explained.

"You seem awfully young to have worked a hotel desk," Dodson said leaning against the heavy desktop.

"I'm eighteen, Mr. Dodson, and besides, my father owns a hotel in–" Rebecca's smile disappeared, and her bright expression faded. She looked at Dodson before her eyes fell to her reflection in the polished wood. She paused for a long moment.

"If you'll excuse me, I'll step into the restaurant, and have a look around," Dodson said, unsure what had happened.

"No! Please wait. I'd like to tell you something," Rebecca admitted.

Dodson removed his hat and waited.

"My real name is Rebecca Barry. I'm from Red River City. My father owns the lumber mill, store, and hotel there. He owns much of the town, and I think he's involved in some corrupt activities. He hires unsavory men with guns to intimidate people into doing what he wants. I didn't like it there. My father made me lie to people who came into the hotel to find out why they were in Red River City. When Lux, I mean, Marshal Danner came to town, I ran away and followed him. My father sent men to bring me back, but Marshal Danner wouldn't let them. When I got here, I didn't want to use my real name in case those men came looking for me again."

"Your father is Jared Barry?" Dodson asked.

"Yes. You know him?"

"I know about him and his lumber mill. I used to ride for Mr. Henry at the Double O ranch. Mr. Henry bought lumber from your father. That's where all this lumber for the church is coming from. Why did your father want to know about new people in Red River City?" Dodson asked Rebecca, who relaxed at the realization Dodson would keep her secret.

"I don't know. He didn't tell me much. Just wanted to know about everyone. When I told him Danner was a Marshal, he got nervous and went to see him right away."

"What happened then?"

"My father had his men watch Danner until he left town."

Dodson rubbed the short whiskers on his chin and thought about what Rebecca had said. He didn't know anything about Barry, having met him only once about a year ago when he and some other cowhands rode over to Red River City to escort a large load of lumber back to the Double O. He recalled Barry being a short, fat fella that made sure everyone knew he was the boss. Nothing odd about that.

He looked back at Rebecca and smiled. "It's okay, miss, your secret is safe with me. If you have any trouble, let me know right away,"

Dodson requested before starting for the restaurant. After a few steps, he stopped abruptly, and turned back to Rebecca. "Would you recognize the men who might be looking for you?"

"Yes, if they're the same men my father hired to watch Red River City," she answered.

Dodson paused and thought about the two gunmen that just rode into town, then headed for the restaurant.

CHAPTER 41

LUXTON DANNER, WES PAYNE, & BEN CHANCE, JR. – NEAR RANGE

Danner checked the dark blue sky. No clouds were in sight. The sun rolled away, allowing dusk to settle in. They would need all the moonlight possible in order to navigate their way back to Range. He wanted to start back as soon as possible to get medical care for the three wounded men. Trooper Williams's leg wasn't bad, but Trooper Cantly and Chance were seriously wounded. He felt reassured knowing Neely was as good a tracker as there was. "Mr. Neely!" Danner called over to the ole tracker.

"Yes, sir," Neely quickly responded.

"It doesn't look like we'll have a full moon tonight, but the sky is clear. Think you'll have enough light to get us back to town without straying off course?"

Neely looked at the sky, and the white sliver of moon pushing into sight. "I'll give it my best. Finding the river due south won't be a problem, then we can turn east follow it 'til we reach town," Neely advised Danner, who turned his attention to the fallen bandits as Neely joined the Lieutenant.

"Very good. We'll follow your lead then," Blackwell informed Neely.

"Marshal Danner took care of the lady, and he's lookin' at the bandits now. See'n if he recognizes any of 'em, I reckon," Neely reported.

Blackwell reined his horse around and rode over to Danner, who examined one of the dead outlaws. In the murky light, details were difficult to discern.

"Marshal, you'll be ready to head out soon?" Blackwell stated more than asked.

"Yes, sir, can't see good enough to make any more identifications anyway."

"Did you know any of them?" Blackwell asked.

"Yep, two. I have papers for both. That'll have to do," Danner answered.

"Sergeant Kelly has our wounded in the wagon. The sister is also with them. We're ready when you are," Blackwell advised.

Danner stepped into the stirrup and swung up into the saddle. "Let's go, Lieutenant," Danner said.

"Mount up! Single file! Keep a close interval. I don't want to lose anybody in the darkness!" Blackwell ordered.

"I'll stay behind the wagon," Wes stated, appearing out of the darkness next to Danner and Blackwell.

"I'll take the point with Mr. Neely," Blackwell advised.

"How's Chance look?" Danner asked Wes.

Wes shook his head. "Don't really know. Bullet's still in there. Caught 'em in the back of the shoulder. Feels broken. He's breathing okay, though. Just need to get him to Doc as quick as we can," Wes reported.

"What about the troopers?" Danner asked.

"One's okay, just took a bullet through the leg. The other's in bad shape," Wes advised.

"I'll ride in front of the wagon. Neely should get us back before midnight," Danner said, then fell into formation.

An hour into the journey, the moon didn't generate as much light as the group needed to see clearly. Scattered rock formations, mesquite trees, and ground scrub punctuated the flat terrain. Neely crept along on horseback, peering into the black abyss ahead, when his horse snorted and stopped abruptly. A nervous ripple ran through its body. At the same time, Danner caught a whiff of what alerted the column. The smell of buffalo and sweat meant one thing: Indians. Neely turned quickly and threw his hand toward Blackwell, who had already stopped, repeating the signal to the trooper behind him. The column stopped. Danner had already stopped the wagon. Everyone remained silent, straining to see around them. A horse snorted, then another.

Crack! A shot rang out up ahead. A bullet zipped past the Lieutenant's head. He swung down off his horse, the trooper behind did the same. Quickly, everyone else hit the ground clutching reins to keep their horses from bolting off into the night. Crack! Another shot, then another.

Danner and Wes saw the muzzle flashes in the scrub ahead of them. Both low and to the right. Crack! A bullet smashed into the side rail of the wagon. Splinters stung the side of Sister Sarah's face who screamed before Sergeant Kelly could stop her. An arrow whistled past the Sergeant, who rolled over onto the seat, pistol in hand.

"Hold your fire!" Danner called out to the soldiers, not wanting to take a bullet from friendly fire.

Danner and Wes ran toward the gun flashes. Crack! Crack! Two more shots. Perfect. Just what Danner and Wes needed. Both fired their pistols at the muzzle flashes. An Indian yelled. Danner and Wes saw shadows moving in the darkness. The warriors made a tactical error because their movement gave them away, even in the dark. Wes fired, his bullet hitting flesh with a loud thump! Danner emptied one Russian and fired his second. Thump! Thump! Thump! Another warrior down. Danner and Wes dove into the ground and waited. Several horses rustled in the distance. The sound of hooves pounding the dirt erupted as the remaining warriors sped away.

Danner and Wes waited until the sound disappeared into the night. Both stood, reloaded their pistols, then confirmed their suspicion. Two dead Kiowa. They hurried back to the group. Wes checked on the wagon, while Danner made his way to the front where Neely and Blackwell waited.

"I think we're okay now. Looked like Kiowa," Danner said in between catching his breath and wiping dirt from his face.

"Well done, Marshal. We're good here. Think they'll regroup and attack again?" Blackwell asked.

"I don't think so. Probably looking to steal the horses. I'm sure they heard the wagon and figured we were settlers. Didn't expect a counter attack," Danner explained.

"We'll wait a moment, then get started again," Blackwell advised.

Danner headed back to Bullet, who hadn't moved during the fight.

After another hour or so, Neely smelled the river up ahead. He took a deep breath in and held it for a moment before exhaling. *Yep, that's the Red all right,* he thought. Once they reached the bank, all they needed to do was head east until they reached town. *Shouldn't be an hour or so more,* he thought.

Neely turned to Blackwell. "Pass the word, river's straight ahead," Neely gushed, obviously happy with himself.

Wes rode rear guard behind the wagon, knowing they were close to the river. Suddenly, he felt the twinge of pain in the middle of his right hand. *No, not now,* Wes thought, panicked.

The pain spread like wildfire first through the back of his hand, then sending sharp bolts down through each finger. His hand curled at the wrist and his fingers pulled into a grotesque claw. He tried to open his hand without success. The pain radiated up his arm to the elbow. He pulled back on the reins and dropped Ringo back from the wagon, not wanting his grunts of pain to be heard. He tucked his arm across his saddle and bent forward fighting the pangs of misery. Beads of sweat erupted from his face falling onto Ringo like rain. He closed his eyes and clenched his teeth, but it was no use. The sound of pain burst from his lips as he leaned forward resting his head on Ringo's mane.

"Everything okay back there, Mr. Payne!" Sergeant Kelly called, slowing the wagon a bit.

Wes gasped for breath, trying to keep from passing out. *Just hold on, just hold on. It'll be gone soon enough,* he thought.

"Mr. Payne?" Kelly called out again.

Danner heard the commotion. He moved Bullet out of the wagon's path and stopped.

Kelly and the wagon rode slowly by. "Marshal?" Kelly began.

"I'll take care of it, keep your interval," Danner ordered the trooper as he snapped a match across his saddle horn and held it high above his head. It emitted just enough light to see Wes laying on Ringo's mane. Wes looked up. His face pale and soaked with sweat.

"You gettin' through it?" Danner asked.

Wes sucked in a deep breath. The pain had begun to subside enough for him to sit upright. "Gettin' worse each time, partner," Wes mumbled. "It's come'n around now," Wes said.

The match's tiny yellow flame flickered out, taking the dim light with it. The two lawmen sat atop their horses, side by side. Wes straightened his arm and flexed his fingers. He took another deep breath, and exhaled.

"Okay, I'm good to go," Wes declared.

"Move up behind the wagon. I'll stay back. We're almost to the river," Danner stated.

Wes chirped Ringo forward. Even in the dark of night, Ringo's white hide remained visible. Danner tapped his spurs on Bullet's haunches and moved along.

CHAPTER 42

LUXTON DANNER, WES PAYNE, & BEN CHANCE, JR. – RANGE

Neely led the group across the ford in the river near the freight yard as the wind picked up, gusting from the west. Evenly spaced ripples crept across the river's surface as hooves clapped and splashed through the shallow water. The caravan, with collars turned up and hats pulled down, had slowly made their way along the river's north bank to finally arrive back in Range. The journey had taken closer to four hours instead of the planned two. Turning west, a cool pre-dawn wind gust hit the riders square in their faces. Danner pushed Bullet up to the front where Neely had paused for a moment, uncertain what to do next.

"Hold up!" the big Marshal called out. "I told the sergeant to stop the wagon in front of the boarding house. The nuns are there. We'll get Sister Sarah inside," Danner said.

"We'll get the wounded over to Doc's place right away," Wes advised Blackwell.

Danner reached into the wagon to help the nun out. She looked at Danner's hand, then at the boarding house. "It's okay now, ma'am. You're safe." Danner whispered.

The nun extended a small, trembling hand, and allowed Danner to guide her down from the wagon and into the boarding house.

Wes stopped in front of Doc's home and office and swung down off Ringo. He rushed to the rear of the buckboard, sliding the rusted pin out that held the gate. All three men were conscious but needed help to exit the wagon. Wes clutched Chance's left arm, half carrying him to Doc's place. His fists banged urgently on the door, piercing the pre-dawn silence. After a few long moments, Doc Phillips opened the door, wearing a white night shirt that reached to the knee, and holding a big-bore derringer firmly held in his right hand.

"What is it?" Doc asked, blinking the sleep out of his eyes. Ranger Payne? Is that you?" The sleepy doctor asked.

"It's me. We have three wounded men that need attention right away," Wes announced.

"Come right in!" Doc ordered, snapping into action. He hastily lit an oil lamp on the table next to the door.

"Betsy!" Doc yelled for his niece and nurse helper. "Betsy, come quick!"

Wes dragged Chance into the front room, sliding him onto a leather chair. The small room felt cramped with so many men suddenly in the space. Wes watched Betsy and Doc anxiously waiting to bring Chance to the back. He felt bad for the troopers, but they were soldiers. They knew the risk. Wes felt responsible for Chance. The kid shouldn't have been there. He should have stayed with the girl. Doc ducked behind a curtain, then returned wearing spectacles, and carrying a huge candle, its soft light succeeding in illuminating the rest of the room.

Phillips began a methodical triage of his patients, quickly examining each man, and the malady he brought with him. After finishing, he pointed to Chance first. Wes wasted no time, he picked Chance up and headed for the examining room.

"Bring him back to my treatment room immediately," he instructed Wes, who had quickly walked past the doctor as he spoke. Barely conscious, Chance couldn't walk under his own power, so Wes carried him into the smaller treatment room.

Wes removed Chance's coat and shirt, revealing the bloody bandana that had been haphazardly applied hours earlier. Doc splashed a bit of ether on a rag and held it to Chance's face until the young gunfighter fell unconscious. Selecting a pair of bullet probes, Doc waved toward Betsy and Wes to hold Chance's shoulders still while he worked. Wes took a firm grasp and watched as the competent doctor plunged the probe into his young partner's gaping wound. Several moments later, Phillips pulled the lead invader from Chance's shoulder. Moving quickly, Phillips cleaned the wound, treated it with what smelled like alcohol, applied a fresh white bandage that Betsy had prepared.

"Okay, bring me the soldier with the neck wound. It doesn't look too deep," Phillips stated.

A short time later, Doc finished treating the two troopers when the front door swung inward, crashing against the wall. "Am I too late to provide assistance?" Sister Mary shouted, louder than necessary.

"What in the hell is all the commotion about?" Doc barked, stepping around the curtain to see Sister Mary. "Oh! Pardon me, Sister, I didn't know it was you," Doc said more demurely.

"No apologies necessary, doctor. I fear I came in like a charging bull, which was not my intent," Mary responded.

Danner stepped through the open door, ducking so as not to hit his head. "Looks like you've got a full house, Doc," Danner stated looking around the crowded room.

"Yes, Marshal, I believe I do. I also think that everyone not in my examining room can leave now and let me go about my business in peace," Doc added. "Sister Mary, Betsy, and I have everything under control," Doc ordered.

Daylight arrived without the warmth of the sun. Except for the Purple Sage Hotel and restaurant, none of the businesses had opened yet. Construction work on the church hadn't even begun yet. Danner and Wes guided their horses over to the hotel, where they both smelled cooked bacon and biscuits from the street. Although both were starved, the men passed the restaurant, instead heading up to their rooms, preferring a wash basin and clean clothes before food.

Danner disappeared into his room and shut the door just as Rebecca stepped out of hers. She smoothed her dress, and headed for the stairs, when Danner stepped back into the hallway. Rebecca jumped, startled at Danner's haggard appearance.

"I thought it might be you," Danner said, without the smile he usually greeted her with.

"You look as though you've had a rough time of it," Rebecca stated looking straight into his weary face.

"Just got in. Everything okay here?" he asked.

"Yes. I told Marshal Dodson who I am, and why I'm hiding. I thought it best. He told me he'd keep my secret," she explained.

"Any new men in town?" Danner asked, yawning.

"Not that I know of. Did you find Sister Sarah?"

"Yes. We brought her back. Chance and a couple of troopers were shot."

"Chance was shot! Is he all right?" Rebecca gasped.

Danner looked at the deep lines of anguish on the young woman's face. Her eyes filled with tears. "He'll be okay. He's over at Doc's," Danner assured her.

Rebecca didn't wait for any further talk; she spun and ran down the stairs and out the front door as quick as she could. Danner heard the front door slam shut.

Well, I didn't see that coming. Looks like I don't need to concern myself with her after all. I don't know if I should be relieved or disappointed? He thought before heading for his basin of clean water.

After cleaning up and changing into a clean set of clothes, Danner sat for a moment and looked out the window at the activity on the street. It had already been a full day and it was barely mid-morning. The street was busy, the men at the construction site were noisily working away. The town was much larger than Danner had thought, thus more potential victims when the outlaws came charging in.

Danner was energized to meet up with Wes and Chance until now. Chance wouldn't be any help for some time with that shoulder injury.

That left just three defenders. Not nearly enough. Dodson had spoken of other deputies, but Danner wasn't depending on that. *There's no way they'll raid this town if the cavalry is here*, Danner thought. That meant the targets would probably be Riverbend and Eagle Springs. Those towns weren't the prize that Range was though.

I hope Blackwell and the boys stick around for a while until we can recruit more help, Danner thought, as he locked his door and headed downstairs.

CHAPTER 43

Newws of the rescue party's return spread through town like charging buffalo. Chatter of Sister Sarah's rescue, and the gun battle with the outlaws, filled the restaurant. Ben Chance had become a local hero in the process after being shot.

Benson, Wagner, and Brad Jamieson sat at the big round table near the front window where Benson held court by boisterously praising the heroic efforts of the rescuers. Suddenly, the raucous chatter in the room faded to silence as Wes and Danner strode into the room side by side. All eyes turned to the two men as they paused to find a table. The dining room remained deathly quiet. The only sounds were the clanging of pots and pans in the kitchen. After what seem like minutes instead of seconds, several people began to stand waving for the others to follow their lead.

Benson and the other men rose to their feet with the rest of the crowd at the sight of Wes and Danner. They stood, applauding the two gunslingers. The applause spread through the dining room. Within moments, every person in the room stood and cheered for the two unassuming men. Danner and Wes nodded, each a little uncomfortable with all the attention. As the applause continued, both men smiled and waved, unsure what else to do, Benson vigorously waved the two men over to his table.

"Gentlemen, none of this would have happened had you two not been here," Benson began as the men arrived.

"The army had as much to do with it as us, Mr. Benson," Danner offered, looking around the room.

"Nonsense! Benson exclaimed. I'm certain if it were not for you, those soldiers would have handled things mighty different," Benson insisted, beckoning Mrs. Conrad with a waving hand. "Mrs. Conrad, please bring these men whatever they want. It's on me this morning," Benson added.

"No one here thought you'd find that nun alive, Marshal," Benson stated in a much more subdued tone.

"She's alive, but that's about all," Wes stated.

"Oh? She's been through a bad time. I'm sure it'll take a while before she feels better," Benson's words faded as he spoke. Wes and Danner said nothing, staring into their coffee mugs.

After breakfast, the restaurant emptied, with the occasional clack of dishes and cups being cleared from the tables the only sounds during the lull. Wes and Danner had remained, each relaxing after polishing off second helpings of everything.

"I didn't see that young lady who seemed to be taken with Chance," Wes mused after a long silence as he picked his teeth with a toothpick.

"Who?" Danner asked.

"That pretty girl you brought into town with you. She seemed rather charmed by Ben the other day."

Danner leaned back in this chair and flashed a slight grin. "That explains her reaction this morning when I told her Chance had been shot."

"What kind of reaction?" Wes asked leaning forward with a grin of his own.

"She teared up and ran out of the hotel like she was shot out of a cannon."

Wes laughed so hard his hat fell off his head.

"I can see her now, charging over to Doc's place like a wild mustang, breaking through the door kicking and screaming at Doc, firing off questions that Doc had no answer for!" Wes continued.

Danner gave him a cold glare. Wes cut off his laugh when he saw Danner's look.

"Wait a minute. You don't mean?"

"Of course not," Danner exclaimed. "I just feel responsible for the kid, that's all."

"You sure about that, Marshal?" Wes asked as he retrieved his hat and stood to leave. "That doesn't sound like fatherly concern to me."

"She's just a kid," Danner said, as if trying to convince himself of that fact, before swallowing what was left of his coffee.

"Uh, huh," Wes grunted as the two men headed for the door.

The men strolled through town. The cloud cover overhead kept the day cooler than normal and projected a gray hue over the town. As they walked, they both silently watched the hustle and bustle of town, seeing folks coming and going about their regular business. The stage rumbled down the street from the livery stable and stopped in front of the stagecoach office where Harold Baker, armed with his register and Dakota Jones with his double-barrel scattergun waited.

"Looks like a nice quiet town to settle down in, don't it?" Wes asked.

"Yep. Looks like the town Marshal want's a word with us. Here he comes now," Danner said, nodding toward Dodson, who was headed their way.

"Good morning, Marshal. How are things?" Wes asked, as Dodson arrived at the base of the steps.

"So far, so good, I reckon," Dodson answered. "I heard you two had quite an adventure out there," he added.

"Not quite the story making its way around town," Danner responded.

Dodson nodded. "People like a good story," he said.

"Anything new here? Looks like a few more wagons rolled in while we were gone," Danner said.

Dodson propped his left boot up on the first step and tucked his thumbs inside his gun belt before looking up and down the street.

"One or two coming in every day. They ain't all stayin' but the town's growin' quick," Dodson declared.

"What's the draw?" Danner asked.

"This red dirt ain't much to farm or raise cattle on, but a little south of the river is sandy loam soil. Good grass for cattle raising. Crops will grow well, also. Seems 'ole Benson got the word out, so we're getting a fair number of farmers and ranchers, not to mention the folks that start out for California, and end up stopping here," Dodson explained.

"Benson said you worked for a big rancher nearby," Wes stated.

"Yep. Butch Henry runs the Double O just southwest of town. He came right after the war. Got a big spread. Over five thousand head these days. I rode guard for him the last couple of years. He asked me to take care of the town for a while. Settle Benson down a little."

"This town's a little big for one man. Benson talked about hire'n deputies?" Wes asked.

"Didn't get around to that before ya'll showed up," Dodson admitted.

"Looks like Chance and his girl are headin' this way," Wes announced.

Danner looked to his left down on the walkway and saw Chance leaning against Rebecca, who wobbled under his weight trying to keep him on his feet. Wes and Dodson hurried over and took Chance from Rebecca's grasp.

"Thank you. Bring him up to my room!" She suggested, out of breath.

"Take him up to mine. You can look after him there, Miss Barry," Danner advised Chance's new nurse. "I don't think it's too proper for you to have him staying with you."

Rebecca frowned and slapped her hands on her hips. "Fine Marshal Danner! If that's the way you want it!" she exclaimed, before hurrying up the steps and into the hotel.

Chance tried to speak.

"You hush up, kid. Save your strength," Danner interrupted.

"Looks like you'll need it, kid," Wes added through a gaping grin.

"Just get him upstairs, Wes," Danner growled, causing Wes to laugh louder.

Danner stepped into the hotel to see Mrs. Conrad hug Rebecca behind the desk. Mrs. Conrad caught Danner's glance and smiled. She nodded her head toward the staircase, motioning Danner to move along upstairs. Danner got the message to move along and lumbered up the steps after his comrades. Danner unlocked his door, then moved out of the way so the three men could get through the narrow doorway. Dodson gave up letting Wes get Chance to the bed.

"Benson has a business deal at eleven. Wants me there. Says it's a big money transaction. Care to come along?" Dodson asked Danner.

"Sure, no sense me staying here now," Danner said. "Going over to the meeting house with Dodson," Danner called to Wes, who was removing Chance's boots. "I'm sure his nurse will be up right quick," Danner added before heading for the stairs with Dodson.

"Sorry, Wes," Chance muttered as his head sunk deep into the pillow. Damn shoulder hurts like hell," he added.

"That's okay, kid. The look on Danner's face out there was worth it," Wes said.

"Is she Danner's girl?"

"No, kid. She'll decide whose girl she is, and it looks like she's made her choice. Careful though, women are more dangerous than gunfighting."

"Is that so, Ranger Payne?" Rebecca asked, standing in the doorway, hands again pushed firmly into her curved hips.

"Uh oh, he's all yours, ma'am," Wes announced, as he rushed past Rebecca, who couldn't help from giggling as he hurried down the hallway.

Rebecca turned her attention to her patient. "Now Mr. Chance, we need to straighten out a few things," she declared before she closed the door.

CHAPTER 44

TUFF JENKINS – SQUAW RAVINE & MANITOU

Jenkins and his men had made good time. The heavy cloud cover, and the cool air, kept the horses fresh. Up ahead, Squaw Ravine plunged upward from its flat basin looking like an angry fist. The watering hole would be a welcoming embrace for horse and man, alike. Jenkins looked ahead and spotted vultures spinning above the rocks just before he saw his scout racing back to the group in full gallop.

"Tuff! Tuff! They're all dead! All of 'em! Dead!" The scout hollered.

Jenkins pulled up his horse and stopped. "What the hell are you sayin'?" Jenkins asked.

"They're all dead. Everyone in the camp is dead."

Jenkins's face dropped into a dark frown, punctuated by gritted teeth. He scratched his dirty whiskers. His thoughts raced through his head like a stampede.

"What is it?" Dunham asked as he rode up to Jenkins.

"They're all dead, all of 'em," the scout exclaimed again.

"Shut up! Let me think!" Jenkins ordered the hyper scout.

Dunham gazed up at the swarming buzzards. The rest of the riders pulled up to see the diving vultures disappear behind the ravine's rough-hewn façade.

"You see a trail?" Jenkins asked.

"Didn't stick around long enough," the scout admitted.

"Spread out, and move in slow, just in case," Jenkins instructed his men.

The outlaws cleared leather and scattered across an imaginary line before moving forward on the camp. Jenkins, certain the danger had passed, pushed ahead eager to see the damage. As he cleared the edge of the rock, the cause of the scouts' hysterics came into view. Dead bodies lay everywhere. By the looks of it, the vultures had been eating well. Most of the faces were gone. So were the hands. Coyotes had joined the birds as evidenced by the few shredded limbs scattered about.

Jenkins holstered his gun and dismounted. Thanks to the wind, the smell was tolerable as he walked through what had been his rendezvous camp. He examined the ground, looking for signs of what happened. His tracking skills had not waned since the war, and he knew a military formation when he saw one. This had cavalry marked all over it. Two columns, both flanks, and churned up ground, indicating fast-moving horses.

Why the hell would the army be out here? Damn sure not looking for an outlaw hideout. Had to be something else. But what? What did these fools do to bring the wrath of the army down on them like this? And why would the army even–Jenkins thoughts were interrupted by Dunham.

"I think this might be what you're wonderin' about," Dunham stated.

Jenkins turned to his partner, who held some sort of black skirt or dress. It was sullied and torn, but no doubt women's clothing.

"One of the boys found this over by what's left of the tent. They had a woman here," Dunham snarled.

"Damn fools snatched a woman? Sons-a-bitches should a known better! Right before we take two towns!" Jenkins shouted at the low-hanging clouds above. His voice echoed off the rock face, sending the vultures in every direction. The flapping of their wings sounded like a roll of thunder over the macabre scene.

"What do we do now, boss?" One of the men asked what all of

them were thinking.

"Barry ain't gonna like this," another man stated.

"I don't give a damn what Barry likes!" Jenkins responded. "He ain't in charge!" He added.

"Maybe, but we all got Barry's money in our pockets, and we don't need him sendin' guns out after us."

"You let me worry 'bout Barry!" Jenkins shouted.

"Dunham, you stay here with the boys. I'll ride over to Manitou and round up more men," Jenkins ordered.

"Manitou ain't much more than a whore camp," Dunham griped.

"It has a saloon and whores. That means there'll be men looking for money. I'll get as many as I can and be back before sundown. If we don't have enough, we'll ride on Range only. That's the big score anyway," Jenkins added as his boot hit its stirrup, and he hopped up in the saddle. "Clean this place up best ya can. Burn the bodies." Jenkins ordered before banging his spurs and riding off.

It was half past three o'clock in the afternoon when Jenkins trotted into what had once been a Choctaw Indian camp on the bank of Spider Creek. The Choctaw called the area "Manitou" which meant a good or evil spirit. It may have meant a good spirit when the Choctaw first settled here, but it was pure evil these days.

Much like Six Shot further to the West, Manitou had become a haven for outlaws and the rift-raff that often followed them. Fueled by the remnants of a makeshift barn built after the Choctaw had been run out, the no-name saloon kept stocked with beer, whiskey, and shine stolen from settlers, wagon trains, and supply shipments meant for the area forts. With the infiltration of the railroads, and the decline of wagon trains, keeping the old saloon supplied had become more difficult, thus Manitou found itself with fewer occupants these days. Whores scurried about like roaches on a garbage heap.

Jenkins declined a half-dozen offers by the time he slid off his horse in front of the saloon. He paused, looking around at the sparse number of horses tethered. *The pickings may be less than I thought*, Jenkins mused as he stepped through a section of missing boards that served as the entrance.

Inside, a dozen or so haggard men lounged at tables and the bar, with as many whores milling around to match. The bar was nothing more than a long timber laying on top several old whiskey barrels in various stages of decay. A short, skinny man who already looked dead but didn't have the sense to lie down, leaned against the bar. Behind him were a dozen or so bottles of whiskey, and what appeared to be a couple flagons of wine. Everyone turned and stared at Jenkins as he strolled over to the old bartender.

"What'll ya have, stranger?" The old man spewed through a toothless mouth, with breath rancid enough to singe a man's whiskers. "I got some corn whiskey and a couple bottles of wine here if'n yer willin'? Ain't got no beer or shine right now," the man advised.

"I'll take a whiskey," Jenkins stated as two whores nestled up to him on each side. "Sorry ladies, don't have the time or the energy right now. What I'm lookin' for are men who want to make good money," Jenkins announced.

The leather-faced bartender poured what he called whiskey into a dirty glass and set it down in front of Jenkins, watched as every man in the place crowded around him, thirsting for another free drink, and more information. Unimpressed, Jenkins scanned the crop of prospective recruits. Regardless, he turned to the ancient bartender.

"You got enough whiskey to set 'em up for every man here?" Jenkins asked.

"That include the bartender, mister?" The old man asked, displaying his toothless smile.

"Yes, sir! Set 'em up!" Jenkins declared stepping out of the way so the gunfighter-recruits could crowd around the bar.

A big fella with a bushy black beard and long greasy hair stepped forward toward Jenkins. "What's this about money?" he asked.

"I'm lookin' for hired guns, as many as I can find," Jenkins answered loud enough for everyone to hear.

"What's the job?" Another man asked wiping corn whiskey from his lips.

"There's a big stash of money in a town four hours south of here.

I'm gonna take that stash, and whatever else I can get in town," Jenkins said boldly.

"What town?" The big-bearded man asked, resting his hand on his gun.

"Range," Jenkins answered, now keeping a serious look and tone.

The group of men began talking at once, shaking their heads, and heading back to scattered tables.

"That's on the Texas side, mister. They got law there, and no bank," the big-bearded man said.

"How long it been since you been in Range?' Jenkins asked, covering his own Colt.

"I been there. Four or five months ago. There's no bank, had a Marshal, and some ranchers with guns," the big man offered.

"You're right about no bank. They keep their money in a meeting house. Easy pickings, and the Marshal's dead. Got himself killed a couple months ago. I figure to ride in with a dozen or so men, and take what we want," Jenkins said, omitting the report about the Ranger and U.S. Marshal.

"What's the pay?" The big man asked.

Jenkins turned toward the men who had remained bunched at the bar. "Each man gets two, fifty-dollar gold pieces, and a cut of what we take from the town," Jenkins advised.

Two more men rose from their tables and joined the five others standing with the black-bearded man. The big fella looked at the six men standing with him. "Looks like you just bought seven guns, mister," the big man stated with a grin that displayed rotted and missing teeth.

"All of you have horses?" Jenkins asked.

The men all nodded.

"Good. Bartender, set up my friends here with another drink," Jenkins said before handing the little man three silver dollars of Barry's money.

"I'll be waiting out at the end of town. We leave right away," Jenkins advised as he stepped through the hole in the wall.

CHAPTER 45

LUXTON DANNER, WES PAYNE & KYLE BRITT – RANGE

Danner stood up and stretched his six-foot six-inch frame, reaching for the meeting house ceiling. It was close to four o'clock and he and Dodson had been sitting outside Benson's office for most of the afternoon. He had recuperated and was now restless and bored. He strolled across the meeting room and looked out onto the street. Wagons, and townsfolk scurried up and down Main Street like ants on a sugar biscuit. The clouds had stubbornly refused to break, keeping the warmth of the sun from penetrating.

Danner heard the rhythmic sound of the hammer pings at the church around the corner. It was in times like these that Danner questioned the value of being a lawman. He preferred action, at least a purpose, and hanging around while Benson conducted business wasn't filling the need. He'd recently considered the prospect of settling into a town. Maybe taking a job as a Sheriff or town Marshal like Ben Chance had done those years before. Chance had seemed satisfied, if not comfortable with it. Chance had been older though. Probably got tired of hiring out his gun all over the place. Sensing the Marshal's distress, Dodson joined Danner at the front window.

"I usually make a patrol around town this time of the day. Why don't you have a look-see. I'll hang around here until Benson is finished," Dodson offered.

"Sounds like a good idea, and thanks," Danner said, not hesitating, as he headed for the front door.

Once outside, he took a long look up and down Main, then decided to head around the corner, and check on the progress of the church building. No less than a dozen men were busy cutting, nailing, and measuring boards. A pile of lumber as tall as Danner sat next to the street near a big Studebaker wagon. The nuns and Deacon cleaned debris as fast as the men dropped it. The Deacon saw Danner and stopped, taking a moment to wash his hands in a nearby barrel.

"Hello, Marshal," the Deacon greeted Danner with a handshake and a smile.

"Any word on Sister Sarah?" Danner asked choosing to omit the small talk.

The Deacon's smile faded to a frown. He removed a white handkerchief from his pocket and wiped the sweat from his face. "I'm sorry to report she's not doing very well. Doc said her physical injuries were minor, but she remains quite troubled by her experience. It doesn't help that her status in the Church is now in question," Deacon reported.

"Her status in the Church?" Danner asked.

"Yes, I'm afraid she will not be able to continue as a Sister due to the unfortunate things that happened to her," the Deacon explained, uncomfortable.

Danner shifted his weight and tugged on his gun belt. His eyes narrowed and he leaned down upon the little Deacon.

"It's not like she asked for it," Danner retorted, trying hard to curb his budding anger.

The Deacon took a nervous step back and pulled on his collar. "That's certainly understood, Marshal, but what's done is done, and the Church has its rules."

"Deacon, I've never had much use for the Church, and you're not helping change my mind," Danner stated.

"I'm sorry to hear that, Marshal, but God loves everyone," the Deacon declared.

"That include Sister Sarah, Deacon?" Danner asked as he turned and walked away before the Deacon could respond.

Benson's office door swung open and the stout mayor stepped out, vigorously shaking his guests' hands. "Your investments are in good hands gentlemen! I'm expecting our shipment any day now," Benson assured the men before escorting each to the door.

"Thanks, Marshal, for being patient. That took a little longer than I expected," Benson informed Dodson.

"This shipment you're expecting. Is it something I should know about, Mr. Benson?" Dodson asked.

Benson quickly looked around the room, then approached Dodson.

"Actually Marshal, I am expecting a bank vault to arrive any day now. I placed the order three months ago just after Marshal Taylor died. The men in town had been hesitant to build a bank due to the lack of law around here, but I believe that time has arrived. I'm going to call for a town meeting in order to propose the construction of a bank. The town has grown considerably, and there is now a need for a bank. Wouldn't you agree, Mr. Dodson?" Benson asked.

"Yes, I would. If you're going to do that, this town will need a couple of deputies and a jail. Hell, I could use a couple of deputies, and a jail right now," Dodson advised.

Danner ducked into the Red Dirt Saloon and looked around. The place seemed busier than usual for four in the afternoon. Danner recognized a few faces, but most were unknown to him, since he hadn't been in town much since his arrival. Two men behind the bar glanced his way and started down to the end of the bar nearest the door. Sensing they wanted to speak to him, Danner stepped up to the end of the bar.

"Good afternoon, Marshal, I'm Mike Donovan, the owner of this establishment, and this is Sam, my bartender."

Danner accepted both outstretched hands, keeping his eyes on a table in the back corner. Two men had their backs to the room and faced the wall.

"Glad to meet you both," Danner replied.

"Get ya a beer, Marshal?" Donovan offered.

"No thanks, Mr. Donovan."

"Please, call me Mike."

Danner nodded toward the two men in the corner. "They been here long, Mike?" Danner asked.

Donovan followed Danner's gaze to the two men. "No sir, maybe an hour or so," Sam replied.

"Ever seen 'em before?" Danner asked quietly under the humming chatter of the bar patrons.

"Came in yesterday, Marshal. The tall one in the black vest was askin' 'bout the young lady rode in with you," Sam advised.

Danner jerked his head and stared at Sam.

"I told him I didn't know of any woman come in with ya," Sam added.

Danner turned his attention back to the men at the table. He reached into his vest and removed his badge, then hooked it on the outside of his vest for all to see.

"There gonna be trouble, Marshal?" Donovan asked nervously.

Danner held his hand up to Donovan and Sam, slowly making his way through the maze of tables, men, and working ladies. As he passed each table, the chatter stopped until the Red Dirt Saloon fell silent as a church before the Sunday sermon. Danner stopped a few feet behind the men and pushed a table away from his right side. The two men ceased their conversation, both unsuccessfully attempting to catch a glance of the man behind them. Danner said nothing, just stood, and let the silence do his talking.

"Good afternoon, Marshal Danner," Kyle Britt said without turning to look. Jonny Gallup instinctively moved his hand toward his gun.

"Touch that gun, and I'll kill ya," Danner growled.

Gallup slowly moved his hand back to the tabletop. Anyone who hadn't already moved, hurried away from Danner and the seated men. Danner took two steps back and covered the Russian perched on his right hip.

"I'll say this only once. Just like last time. You're both gonna stand up and unbuckle your gun belts real slow. Let 'em fall to the floor then take one step back. Now," Danner ordered.

Gallup and Britt both stood and unfastened their gun belts, letting them fall to the floor. Each then took a step back, but Gallup spun, and pulled a gun from under his vest. Crack! Danner's draw was too fast and his Russian forty-five struck center chest sending Gallup sprawling backward onto the table, then crashing to the floor. Danner looked at Britt through the smoke rising from his barrel. Britt hadn't flinched. He just stared at Danner, grinning.

"I thought I told you what would happen if you followed me," Danner said.

"Yes, Marshal you sure did, but I don't work for you. Mr. Barry's a stubborn man and when he want's something he gets it," Britt answered.

"Well, you hightail it back to Mr. Barry, and take your boy here with you. Tell him if he wants his daughter back, he'd better send more than the likes of you two."

Britt's grin faded. "No problem, Marshal. I'll tell him, but he ain't gonna like it. He's a rich man. He'll send an army if he has to."

"He won't need to send anyone. I'll be coming to him soon enough. No get out of here, and don't come back."

"What about my gun belt?"

"It stays."

"That rig cost me a hundred dollars, Marshal."

"Like you said, Barry's a rich man. Have him buy you a new one. Don't forget your boy here," Danner stated pointing to the dead man bleeding out on the floor.

"Mike! Come get these gun belts and take 'em over to the Marshal's office!" Danner called, without taking his eyes off Britt.

"No need for that, Mike. I'll take care of it," Wes announced from the swinging front doors.

Danner stepped aside while Britt tossed Gallup over his shoulder.

"I ain't gonna forget this, Marshal," Britt said.

"Nor I," Danner answered, following Britt out of the Red Dirt to the hitching post. Britt tied Gallup to his saddle then swung up into his.

"How am I supposed to defend myself?" Britt asked.

"I figure the only gunmen between here and Red River City are on Barry's payroll, so you shouldn't need anything more than your Winchester. Now get the hell out," Danner ordered.

Danner watched Britt snap his horse and start down Main, when he was joined by Wes.

"Fella's tryin' to get a little rest, and you go and get yourself into a gunfight," Wes chuckled.

"Sorry, I didn't have time to send out an invitation," Danner cracked.

Dodson hurried across the street to Danner and Wes, catching a passing glance at Britt and his dead companion.

"Kid ran in and said there was trouble here," Dodson said.

"A little. Two of Barry's gun hands from Red River City. They were here to fetch his daughter back. One went for his gun," Danner explained.

"Damn. I saw those two ride in yesterday. Sam told me they asked about you and Rebecca. With everything else going on, I just damn forgot about it. Sorry, Danner."

"Don't be. You've enough to worry about without being concerned about me."

"Rebecca told me about her father, and her chasing after you to get away. Sounds like Barry's a real problem," Dodson stated.

"All this bandit activity up and down the river points straight at him. I figured something was wrong when I rode into Red River City and was greeted by a four-gun welcoming committee. They thought about roughing me up until they found out I was a Marshal. Next thing I know, Barry's at my door asking questions. It was obvious he ran that town, but I didn't think he had the money or power to cause trouble here, let alone Riverbend and Eagle Springs."

"Come on over to my office. I'll buy you two a drink, then I'll make a visit to our friend Lieutenant Blackwell and see how long he plans on staying around," Dodson said.

The three men stepped onto the street when Benson marched out of the meeting house making a beeline for them. "Gentlemen, I heard we had some trouble in the Red Dirt Saloon. Everything okay now?" Benson asked.

"Yes, sir. Some trigger-happy cowboy drew on the Marshal, here. They're gone now," Dodson reported.

"Very well then," Benson stated, letting out an exaggerated sigh of relief.

"Mr. Benson. You know a fella over in Red River City named Barry?" Danner asked.

"Jared Barry? Sure do. His lumber built most of this town. He's been here a time or two, but he doesn't leave Red River City much, I guess. Why do you ask?"

"Just wondering is all. See you later," Danner stated then hurried along to join Dodson and Wes.

CHAPTER 46

BEN CHANCE, JR. & REBECCA BARRY – RANGE

Rebecca knocked on the door, then let herself in, without waiting for a response. Chance sat up in bed, craning his neck toward the window, doing his best to see down to the street. He'd heard the commotion in the hallway, and saw people running near the saloon. That was enough for him to know something had happened. Frustrated, he felt like he should have been there instead of stuck in this bed healing from a gunshot wound.

"Ben Chance, you put yourself back down on that bed this instant!" Rebecca ordered the wounded cowboy.

"What happened at the saloon?" Chance demanded in a fading tone, knowing perfectly well he couldn't demand much of anything in this state.

"I guess Danner had to shoot somebody over there. That's all I heard. I don't know why or who got shot, but Danner is okay," Rebecca reported.

"Could you go find out who it was, and what happened, please," Chance asked.

"I'll find out soon enough. Ranger Payne ran into the saloon, and I saw him and Danner both come out with a man carrying another over his shoulder. Mrs. Conrad pushed me inside before I could see any more. Now, I brought you some food and coffee. You need to eat."

"Coffee? I'd rather have a beer," Chance announced, obviously feeling better than when he arrived this morning.

"Doc says no beer for a few days. He wants to make sure you don't get an infection in that shoulder."

"How the hell am I going to get an infection just lyin' here?"

"Didn't you go to school? Or did you just grow up on that farm? You can get an infection a bunch of ways, even lyin' in a bed."

"When is Doc coming back. I feel much better. I need to let him know."

"He said he'd be around later tonight. Now, are you going to eat your food, or do I have to feed it to you?"

"I'll eat, I'll eat, don't worry."

"Good." Chance watched Rebecca move the tray from the table to his lap, then take a seat in the chair next to his bed. "You gonna just sit there and watch me?" Chance asked, blushing.

"Well, yes, but I thought we could talk."

"We've been talking all day, 'cept when I was sleepin'."

"Don't you want to know more about me?" Rebecca asked dipping her head down.

"You already told me you're eighteen, and you told me all about you following Danner to get away from your rich father. You mean there's more to know?"

"Fine! I should get back to helping Mrs. Conrad, anyway. I haven't done anything for her since you arrived this morning! I'll just be on my way!" She shouted before slamming the door after herself.

Now what the hell did I say? Chance thought as he bit into a piece of fried chicken. He assumed he knew all he needed to know, but that was apparently a mistake. He'd admitted to her that he liked her, and he'd never really liked a girl before. She'd said the same. What else was there to know? He'd heard other folks talk about love and the like, but he'd never felt that way. Was this love? He didn't know for sure. He damned sure liked her and he was damn happy to see her when she rushed into doc's office to see him. *I can't think about this now! Danner and Wes need me,* Chance tried to convince himself.

Rebecca descended the staircase, announcing her arrival with loud knocks of her heels into the wooden steps. Mrs. Conrad stopped writing updates in the hotel register to peer around the corner at Rebecca, as she descended.

"I'm over here, dear!" Mrs. Conrad called.

Rebecca spun on her heel and stepped over to the big desk, plopping her elbows onto its top, resting her chin in her cupped hands.

"You're a bit feisty today. What's the matter?" Mrs. Conrad inquired.

"I don't understand men," Rebecca announced with a scrunched brow, and pouting lips.

Mrs. Conrad laughed. "My dear, no woman understands men! No matter what age you are, they're always a mystery."

"What did the young Mr. Chance do now?" Mrs. Conrad asked, quelling her laughter.

"I wanted to talk to him for a while, but he just wasn't interested. Says he already knows everything there is to know about me after one day."

"Don't rush the boy, dear. He's probably never been around a woman that wasn't his family. Plus, he's hurt pretty bad, according to Doc. Might not even know what he's saying with all the medicine runnin' through him," Mrs. Conrad assured her young assistant.

"I never thought of that. Thank you, Mrs. Conrad, you always know what to say to make me feel better. Is there anything I can do for you this evening?"

"We could use some help in the kitchen for dinner. Go see what the ladies need. I'll be along later."

Rebecca's face lit up with a smile as she headed off to the kitchen.

CHAPTER 47

LUXTON DANNER, WES PAYNE, & LANE DODSON - RANGE

Down the street, Lane Dodson opened his desk drawer to remove a half-empty bottle of bourbon, along with three glasses. After filling each glass half full, he returned the bottle to its drawer.

"Help yourselves, gentlemen," he announced, before drinking his and setting it down on the table.

Danner and Wes followed suit, finishing theirs in one quick swallow.

"Danner, if Barry sent these two after his daughter, you think he sent others to keep an eye on the town?" Dodson asked.

Danner mulled it over. "I wouldn't be surprised. Especially since there's no way of knowing, with all the new people coming in and out each day," he said.

"Have you noticed any suspicious folks?" Wes asked.

"No, not really. Those two were damn obvious yesterday, but anyone could come in on a wagon, or with a group of settlers, and I'd never suspect anything," Dodson answered.

"What about anyone who came in the past couple of weeks and been hanging around town? Most people are either passing through, or heading out to a ranch, farm, or looking to homestead outside of town, not hang around here. And, if Barry's paying, they wouldn't be looking for a job," Danner suggested.

Dodson paused, and thought about what Danner had said. He did his best to review all the faces he'd seen in his head. He finally shook his head.

"No, just too many folks coming and going," Dodson concluded.

"Well, if Barry is behind these raids, and trouble in and outside of town, it'd be best if we went to see the Lieutenant as you suggested," Danner responded.

"No time like now," Dodson declared, eager to do something useful.

The army camp was just outside the east end of town, not far from Dodson's office so the three lawmen led their horses behind. The on-duty sentry knew the three men from the rescue, so he nodded a greeting as the men passed through. A large, walled tent posted in the center of camp, a lantern already burning brightly at the tent's entrance. Obviously the commanding officer's quarters. Danner approached the guard who was unknown to him. "Excuse me sir, may we speak to Lieutenant Blackwell. Tell him Danner, Dodson, and Payne are here to see him, please," Danner requested.

"I heard, Corporal, send them in!" Blackwell called from inside.

The three men entered, finding the Lieutenant seated behind a small wooden table, scratching a fountain pen across parchment by candlelight.

"Gentlemen, good to see you again," the Lieutenant exclaimed, standing and offering a handshake to each man. "Please have a seat. Mr. Conrad over at the hotel was kind enough to provide me with a few chairs. They're not much, but all I have right now. What can I do for you?" Blackwell asked.

"Lieutenant, we have reason to believe that a wealthy fella by the name of Jared Barry over in Red River City is bankrolling the bandit activity along the river. I had a run-in with a couple of 'em this afternoon. Killed one and ordered the other out of town. There's other information that points to this Barry fella, also. If he is in fact, the money behind the problems out here, we believe we may be in for some trouble here in Range, sooner rather than later. We wondered how much longer you were planning on sticking around with your men?" Danner asked. "We know you originally said two weeks, but we're thinkin' things may have changed."

"I just finished my report and prepared to have a trooper bring it to Mr. Turner at the telegraph office. I've had a bit of a challenge conveying my actions into wording appropriate for a telegraph operator. My length of stay here will solely depend upon the response I receive from this report. If it's what I anticipate, we'll be ordered to move out in the next day or two. If your hunch is correct, and the town is attacked in the next day or two, we could be of assistance. If not, you'll be on your own, I'm afraid," Blackwell advised.

"Could you request an extension to your stay?" Dodson asked.

"Yes, Marshal, I could, and I'm willing to do that. The problem is, most of the cavalry units are being used for reservation containment, and not local outlaw problems," Blackwell explained. "Couldn't you call upon your local lawmen, such as the Sheriff, or request more Texas Rangers?" Blackwell asked.

Wes chuckled. "We have all the U.S. Marshals and Rangers were gonna get, Lieutenant."

"I could send word to Sheriff Evans. He may be able to spare a deputy. I'll also get word to Mr. Henry. I know he'll send some men," Dodson suggested.

"I suggest you do that, Marshal. If we're able to stay, that'll just mean more men to meet any attack. If we're not, at least you'll be as prepared as you can be," Blackwell concluded.

"Lieutenant, I'll be glad to take your report to Mr. Turner," Dodson offered as the men stood.

"Thank you, Marshal. I'll need to send a man with you anyway. Army rules, you know," Blackwell explained with a grin.

"Yes, sir. I understand. Don't want to bend any of those rules. We'll wait until your trooper is ready. It's a short walk," Danner added, smirking.

"We should also send that request to the Sheriff right away," Danner suggested.

"I'll get someone to ride out to the Double O and let Mr. Henry know what's happening. I hope they haven't left on the drive yet."

"Good. At least we'll know where we stand regarding help," Wes said as the trooper joined them for the walk to the telegraph office.

"Now we just need to hope that we don't get raided tonight," Dodson remarked.

"That don't make me feel any better," Wes said.

"Me neither," Danner joined in.

"Better do a weapons check when we get back," Danner said aloud.

Dodson and Wes said nothing. Nothing more needed to be said. It was just a matter of time, and they all knew it.

CHAPTER 48

TUFF JENKINS – SQUAW RAVINE

Two hours into their ride back to Squaw Ravine, darkness crept up quickly, as the temperature dropped lower. The smell of rain filled the air, and the wind had picked up, bending tree limbs and dried sage along the way from Manitou. Tuff Jenkins hadn't spoken to many of the newly hired men, mostly keeping conversation with the big fella that had since taken on the role as leader to the motley crew. Jenkins had no idea what skill level any of these men had, but he was in no position to be choosey. They'd either be good enough to do the job or die trying. Either way, he didn't much give a damn.

The black shadowy outline of the rock formation that signaled their destination came into view. Jenkins considered the number of men he had. Even with these seven, he figured he was down about ten or more. Still enough to ride on Range and take the money from the fat man's meeting house. Besides, fewer guns meant a higher take for each man who survived.

One of Jenkins's men stepped out from behind a large smooth-faced rock, and recognized Jenkins in the dim light. Jenkins caught a glimpse of the guard and reined his horse toward him.

"Anything happen while I was gone?" Jenkins asked.

"No, sir, nothing. The boys got the camp cleaned up like you said to," the guard advised.

"Good. I got seven new men with me. There ain't nobody else out here, so ride in with us," Jenkins ordered.

The guard got up onto his horse, obliging his boss. Jenkins then kicked his spurs and headed for the camp.

Jenkins rode over to the roughshod coral that held the gang's horses in check. He dismounted, removed the saddle from his horse, and let the mount go inside. The other men followed, each setting their saddle on the top rail. Dunham, Shorty, and the others circled near the watering hole, where an open fire cooked jack rabbits on makeshift spigots.

"Smells good," Jenkins announced as he and the new men from Manitou approached. "I brought seven men from Manitou," Jenkins added.

"That gives us thirteen, total," Dunham stated.

"That'll be enough," Jenkins declared before sitting down next to Shorty, and his half-empty bottle of whiskey.

Jenkins helped himself to the whiskey and took a long swig, then passed it to the big fella from Manitou.

"Pass it around," Jenkins said then took a look around and counted the men. "Okay, we're all here. This is how I figure it. It's about a two-hour ride to Range. We want to get there just after sundown. We'll gather at the river, then ride across the ford and charge through town. Dunham, you'll take three men and head for the Marshal's shack at the end of town."

"Marshal's shack?" The big fella from Manitou shouted, spewing whiskey all over himself. "Thought ya said there wasn't no Marshal?" he added.

"No, I said the Marshal there was killed a couple months back. We found out they hired a new one. Don't matter, he's one man. That too much for ya'll?" Jenkins asked.

"Hell no! Just wanna know what we're in for is all," the big fella grunted. The other men nodded.

"Like I was sayin', Dunham will take three men and take care of the Marshal. I'll take three or four and get to the meeting house. It's the big white building in the middle of town. The rest of you will ride cover and hit the store, saloon, and hotel. That's where most of the money will be. Watch for that damn blacksmith behind the saloon. He's trigger-happy, and a pretty good shot. I want two men ready with kerosene and torches. Burn the freight yard and the boarding house. With those burning, everyone will be wantin' to put those fires out, and not give a damn about what the rest of us are doin',” Jenkins explained.

"Where we gettin' the kerosene?” One of the men from Manitou asked.

"Dunham and me got two jars each. That should be enough to get things burnin' good,” Jenkins advised.

"Now. Listen up. There's a girl in town. Stayin' at the hotel. Name's Rebecca Barry. Got long black hair. Kinda young. She's the boss's daughter. Got snatched from Red River City by a passin' U.S. Marshal. She don't get shot or nothin' else. Everybody got that?” Jenkins asked.

"Nothin else?” The big fella from Manitou asked, exposing his rotted teeth.

"Anyone touches her, I'll kill 'em myself. Any other questions?” Jenkins asked.

"What about the soldiers that came here, Jenkins?” Shorty asked. "They might be stayin' near town,” he suggested.

"I thought a that. We'll find out tomorrow before we cross the river,” Jenkins answered.

"How we gonna find out?” The big fella asked.

"We got a man in town. He's been there a couple weeks. He'll meet us tomorrow this side of the river. If we don't like what he has to say, we'll hold off,” Jenkins advised.

"Man, in town? Who's that?” Dunham asked, surprised he didn't know about it.

"Name's Harry Nolen. He drove into town with a bunch of nuns a couple weeks ago. He's been hangin' around, getting the word. He'll meet us tomorrow,” Jenkins stated.

"They any horses in this town?" Another man from Manitou asked.

"Yep. Got a livery and coral at the east end of town. Why?" Jenkins asked.

"Me and boys here could sell them horses up in the territory for good money. Horses sometimes are hard to come by up there," He said.

"I got no problem with you taken horses, after we're done with the meeting house. Understand? You can take the horses as we're ridin' out of town. Got that?" Jenkins asked.

"Sounds okay," The man said looking around at the other six men from Manitou, each of whom nodded in agreement.

"How much money you reckon's in that meetin' house?" Shorty asked, before swallowing the last drop from a whiskey bottle.

Jenkins paused, and looked hard at Shorty. He didn't like fool questions, especially ones he didn't have an answer for. "Ain't no bank there. That fat mayor takes in all the money, and keeps it inside the meetin' house. Should be thousands in there," Jenkins surmised.

"Thousands, and no bunch a lawmen to guard it? This ought to be real easy," A Manitou man said.

"Yep, it ought a be," the big man echoed.

Jenkins and Dunham exchanged a quick look. Jenkins knew this wouldn't be as easy as he'd claimed. First, most of his good men were wiped out, second, there may be soldiers in the area if not the town, and finally, they had seven unknown men from a shit-hole camp in the territory he didn't know whether or not they could be trusted. "Now, I'm hungry. Them rabbits about done?" Jenkins asked.

CHAPTER 49

RANGE

Dodson slipped into his buckskin coat, and turned up its collar before stepping outside to light the lantern hanging off the roof post. He had developed a comfort-level with the town, and his role as its Marshal. Danner and Payne had made that transition easier, but as he got to know folks better, especially Benson and Mrs. Fields, he had begun to feel as though he was part of Range's family. He begged the Conrad's to allow him to pay for his meals, eventually agreeing on half-price, and Charlie Becker over at the gunsmith shop promised an endless supply of ammunition. Now, if he could only convince Benson to hire a couple of deputies, he'd get what he needed most–sleep.

The eighteen-to-twenty-hour days had caught up to him, and he feared his skills suffered as a result. He knew he'd need to be at his best with just Danner and Payne with him now that Chance was out of the mix. He felt like the town was targeted especially if the belief that Jared Barry was behind all this ruckus. Barry's daughter, Rebecca, being in town didn't help matters either. He took a seat on his ladder-back, and leaned up against the wall, mostly to keep an eye on the front door of the Red Dirt Saloon. The saloon's owner, Mike Donovan, hadn't felt the need to hire a guard, preferring to handle rowdy cowboys himself. Over six-feet tall with thick arms like a blacksmith, Donovan was more than capable of deterring most of the bad behavior.

It was pushing nine-thirty at night when Dodson heard the pounding of hooves coming down the street just before he laid eyes on a dozen or so men heading through town. *With that many riders, Mr. Henry must be with 'em,* Dodson thought, knowing the owner of the Double O's propensity to travel with at least ten riders.

Range's Marshal didn't have to speculate long, as the tall, lanky owner of the biggest ranch in a two-hundred-mile radius came into clear view. Dodson pushed his chair forward the front legs popping against the planks below.

"Good evening, Dodson," Henry greeted his former guard as he pulled his horse to a halt.

"Good evening, sir. Glad to see you and the fellas here tonight," Dodson answered in a genuine manner.

Henry and his entourage remained in their saddles, casting a myriad of shadows in the lantern's glow. "John, here, brought the word you needed a few hands, so here we are," Henry's booming voice bounced off the nearby buildings.

"Thanks, Mr. Henry. I don't know if Benson will put them on the payroll or not, but right now, there's only three of us I can count on," Dodson explained.

"This has nothing to do with Benson. I'll leave four men with you. They're all on Double O payroll. I'd stay myself, but I've got to get a big herd ready for the track up to the railhead in a few days," Henry explained.

"That'll be fine," Dodson answered.

"You have quarters for four?" Henry asked.

"Yes, sir, I'll check the hotel, but if they're full, Benson has a couple of rooms at the meeting house," Dodson assured Henry.

"Very good. You've got Mack, Bo, Cody, and Dutton. Clark wanted to come back, but he's busy with the herd," Henry announced. Turning to his men, he said, "You boys get settled here, the rest of us will see you over at the Red Dirt Saloon when you're finished," Henry reined his horse toward the saloon followed by the rest of the Double O riders.

Dodson stepped down from his perch and shook each man's hand. "Let's head to the hotel first. With people come'n and goin' like they've been, it's hard to say if there's rooms or not," Dodson explained leading the way to the Purple Sage Hotel on foot.

Dodson opened the hotel door to see Mrs. Conrad seated behind the front desk, counting money. Dodson leaned toward the hotel owner and frowned.

"Good evening, Mr. Dodson," she announced, wearing a bright grin outlined in dark red lipstick. The thin streaks of gray showing through her black hair added a warmth to her bubbly personality.

"Mrs. Conrad, what have I told you about counting money out here?" Dodson asked, trying not to sound too snarky.

"I know, I know. It was just a few dollars paid before guests left earlier," she explained, nodding her head, and leaning back in an effort to gain forgiveness.

Dodson smiled and turned toward his deputies. "Would you have a couple of rooms for my deputies?" he asked. "This is Mack McKinnon, Bo Hatten, Cody Roberts, and Tom Dutton. They'll be with us in town for a while," Dodson advised his hotel keeper.

"Hello gentlemen. I do have two rooms available, each with bunk beds and wash basins. The rooms are being cleaned at the moment. They should be ready in about a half hour," she informed her new guests.

"That'll be fine, ma'am," Mack McKinnon answered for the group, removing his hat, and offering a smile. The other men followed McKinnon's lead. "Where do we sign?"

Mrs. Conrad handed the man a pen so they could sign the hotel register.

"We need to meet Mr. Henry over at the Red Dirt Saloon. We'll be back a little later," Dodson said.

"What was all that about?" Mr. Conrad asked moments later, emerging from the back room where he had been sorting through supplies that had come in on the latest delivery, including a small Winchester safe.

"Mr. Dodson needed rooms for his new deputies," she answered.

"New deputies?"

"That's what he said."

"That's good news. With our new safe and more lawmen in town, our money should be fine," Conrad mused before returning to his duties in the back room.

The hurried steps headed down the wooden stairs announced Rebecca's arrival from her cleaning chores upstairs. With her arms full of linens, Rebecca made her way around the front desk to the back room, where Mr. Conrad was learning how to operate his safe. Rebecca dropped the linens into a large basket in the corner of the room and hurried back to Mrs. Conrad.

"The rooms are finished," she declared, plopping her arms down on the desk next to Mrs. Conrad.

"Thank you, dear. We have new guests coming in tonight. Were you able to put clean water in the wash bowls?"

"Yes, ma'am. Everything is done," Rebecca quickly answered.

Debra Conrad smiled at Rebecca and took a deep breath. "I honestly don't know how I managed before you arrived here. Go ahead, go check on your patient. I'm sure he's wondering where you've been all evening!" Mrs. Conrad laughed.

"Thank you!" Rebecca gushed, then quickly headed back upstairs.

Rebecca's quick, single knock preceded her bursting through the door.

"Take it easy, kid," Chance said leaning back onto his pillows.

"What do you mean, kid?" Rebecca retorted. "You're only a year older than me!" she reminded him.

"Oh? And how do you know how old I am?" Chance asked, attempting to fold his arms across his chest, then being reminded of his wound with a sharp piercing pain in his shoulder. "Ahh!" Chance winced, returning his arms back to his sides.

"Oh, are you okay?" Rebecca's voice went from stern to soft.

"I'm fine. Doc said it was looking very good earlier this evening when he stopped by with Betsy to check on me," Chance assured his nurse.

"Don't you be making eyes at Betsy, Ben Chance!" Rebecca said firmly.

"Why?" Chance curtly asked, smiling.

"If you don't know by now, you won't ever know!" she said, exasperated. "Besides, I heard she's waitin' for that fella, Ross Mabry, to come back from Wichita Falls!" She added, then turned for the door.

Rebecca opened the door and stopped. She closed the door and walked over to Chance, firmly grabbing each side of his face with her hands. Chance instinctively pulled his head back and banged it on the wall.

"Ouch," he muttered before Rebecca planted a robust kiss on his unsuspecting lips. "What'd ya do that for?" Chance slurred his words in shock.

Rebecca said nothing. She just smiled, and skipped out of the room, quietly closing the door behind her.

Chance gathered his thoughts, then grinned. *I've never been kissed like that before,* he thought, before closing his eyes unable to wipe the lipstick-smeared grin off his face.

Dodson and his deputies pushed through the Red Dirt Saloon's swinging doors to find Butch Henry sitting at a corner table with Danner and Payne. The five men proceeded to Henry's table. Dodson waved his deputies over toward the bar, where the rest of the Double O riders enjoyed whiskey, and the company of the saloon girls.

"Evenin', gentlemen," Dodson said, pulling a chair from the next table over.

"Mr. Henry, here, was telling us about four new men," Wes said.

"Mighty glad to hear about that," Danner chimed in.

"We should do well if the need arises," Dodson added.

"We'll need 'em. I'm certain Blackwell and his men will leave tomorrow or the next day," Danner advised.

"What makes you say that?" Henry asked.

"The Army ain't going to like one of their units raiding a bandit camp, even if it was to save a nun," Danner said flatly.

"Figured the Lieutenant could explain it in an acceptable way," Henry suggested.

"Them West Pointers ain't much on altering the truth," Danner added, shaking his head.

The chatter in the saloon suddenly faded, causing the lawmen to turn toward the swinging doors at the entrance. Deacon David, followed closely by two Sisters, had entered, and made their way to the lawmen's table. Dodson stood, meeting the trio halfway across the big room to have a private conversation. As the Deacon spoke, Dodson nodded. After a brief conversation, the Deacon and nuns departed the Saloon and Dodson returned to the table.

"What is it" Danner asked.

"Sister Sarah has disappeared again. This time, she crawled out the window in her room," Dodson reported.

"When?" Wes asked.

"Sometime after sundown. The other Sisters have been taking turns watching her. When one of 'em checked after dark, she was gone, with the window left open. The Deacon said they looked around the boarding house but couldn't find her. Poor thing ain't been right since those outlaws took her and did God only knows what to the girl." Dodson reported.

"Well, finding her in the dark will be a challenge," Wes offered.

"I guess it'd be best to head out at sunup," Danner agreed.

All four men stood realizing their night was over.

"I'll get my men and head back to the ranch. I'll check back before we take the herd out," Henry said.

"Why you reckon that nun ran away?" Wes asked Danner.

Danner recalled the conversation he'd had earlier with the Deacon. He narrowed his eyes and grit his teeth. "Not for any good reason. Deacon said the Church wouldn't allow her to continue because she'd been violated by a man. I guess she wasn't pure anymore, though no fault of her own.

"Apparently, a woman can't get raped and still be a nun," Danner growled, bouncing money on the table and heading for the door.

Wes watched Danner leave. He sensed a tension in Danner that he'd not felt before. He'd not heard Danner talk that way. Not even when Chance's father was killed. Wes realized he'd been holding his breath listening to Danner. He'd felt that way right before a herd of mustangs broke into a wild stampede. Wes stood and picked up Danner's money from the table, then walked over to the bar where he added his own and handed it to Donovan. *I wouldn't want to be the one to cross Marshal Luxton Danner right now*, he thought.

CHAPTER 50

Wes pushed through the swinging doors and paused to take a look up and down Main street. It was close to midnight, and everything looked closed up tight. The sound of the piano from the Red Dirt Saloon flooded out into the street. Wes started toward the Purple Sage Hotel, and saw Danner talking to Doc in front of Doc's place.

"Hello, Doc," Wes said as he joined the men under the glow of Doc's porch lantern.

"Ranger Payne," Doc answered with the nod of his head. "I was just telling Marshal Danner that Mr. Chance is progressing just fine, thanks to the added attention of that young lady, Rebecca," Doc said, smiling.

"Doc, what about the nun we brought back. How was she when you last saw her?" Danner asked.

Doc ran his hand over his hair and took a deep breath. "Truth is, Marshal, physically, she seemed pretty good overall. There's trauma around her legs and such, but at least those bastards didn't beat her, but–" he paused.

"But what?" Danner pushed.

"Her mind isn't right. She had a pretty bad experience. She

wouldn't say, but I'm certain she was raped by more than one of them, probably several, and she's having trouble getting it right in her mind. I'm no mind doctor, but I've heard of people having a bad time and losing their ability to get past it," Phillips explained.

"You mean psychologically?" Danner asked.

Doc tipped his head back with raised eyebrows and a thin grin on his lips. "Don't know I've ever heard a lawman use a word like that, Marshal, but yes. It's new to medicine. I've read some on the subject, but it's well beyond my capabilities, I'm afraid," Phillips admitted.

"Danner here is a college man, Doc," Wes offered.

"Oh?" Doc asked, putting his hands on his hips, looking square at Danner.

"Long time ago, Doc," Danner said quickly.

"Where?" Phillips prodded.

"Lancaster Pennsylvania. Franklin and Marshall College a couple years after the war," Danner admitted.

"Well I'll be," Doc muttered.

"It doesn't mean much now, Doc," Danner replied.

"The hell it doesn't! We need educated men out here. This could be good country, probably will be someday, but it's going to take educated men to make it," Doc responded with emphasis.

"Maybe, Doc, but right now, it takes gunfighters on the right side of the law," Danner suggested.

"I suppose your right, Marshal. Let's just make sure those righteous gunfighters don't get themselves killed. Goodnight gentlemen," Doc added before heading inside for the night.

"What ya thinkin'?" Wes asked Danner, who was staring down the street toward the boarding house.

"Wondering how Sister Sarah is holding up tonight. Thought I'd take a look around the boarding house before I turned in," Danner answered without looking back at Wes.

"Sounds like a good plan, let's go have a look," Wes answered, as the two men began walking.

As the lawmen reached the barber shop, Wes ducked into the opening next to the stage office to check behind the buildings while

Danner stayed along the street, checking the front of the freight yard and boarding house. Wes searched the myriad of houses and tents behind the boarding house, then made his way toward the holding pens on the west side of town.

After checking the feed store next to the freight yard, Danner made his way toward the pens as well. The light from the lanterns on the edge of town faded to black darkness the closer the men got to the pens. There were no cattle in town, so the pens were empty, except for a few horses owned by lodgers. The men were met with a couple of snorts from alert horses, but nothing more. After making the circle around the pens, Wes met Danner in front of the freight yard.

Crack! Crack! Crack! Gunfire erupted out in front of the Red Dirt Saloon. Wes and Danner could only see a commotion in the street. Several more shots rang out. The lawmen started running down the middle of Main Street, their guns drawn. Front doors opened as people stepped out in their nightclothes to see what all the commotion was about.

Crack! Crack! Wes ran to the right boardwalk, Danner to the left. Both yelled at a couple of bystanders to get back inside as they passed. Danner heard Dodson yelling for someone to drop his gun. Crack! More shots exploded into the night. Dodson and his men scattered across the fronts of the meeting house, telegraph office, and gunsmith shop, firing across the street toward the Red Dirt Saloon and the livery stable. Wes ducked behind the water trough in front of the meeting house where Dodson was already face down in the dirt.

"What the hell happened?" Wes asked peeking over the edge of the wet boards.

"A couple of drunks didn't pay their women, and Donovan stepped in to collect. One of 'em pistol-whipped him and shot another who tried to help. One of the girls came running down to my office, and by the time we got over here, they were out front shootin' the place up," Dodson reported. "One's behind the tack shack next to Wilhelm's place and the other's buried behind those empty whiskey barrels on the side of the saloon," Dodson added.

Crack! Crack! Two shots came from the tack shack. Boom! The

sound of a double-barrel shot gun blew up the night. Wood splintered, buckshot rang metal inside the shack, and a man yelled out before falling to the ground with a thud.

"Marshal! You out there?" Belton Tanner, the burly blacksmith shouted from behind the saloon.

"We're out here, Tanner!" Dodson answered, knowing what had happened.

"That one won't be any more trouble. Any others?" Tanner asked, breaking open his shotgun and plunging two fresh shells into the smoking barrels before snapping it closed.

"That's it! I've had enough!" A voice called out from behind the whiskey barrels.

"Throw your gun out and put yer hands up!" Dodson yelled.

The man didn't respond, didn't toss his gun. A gust of wind blew past permeating the silence.

"I said, toss out your gun, and come out with your hands up!" Dodson repeated.

Dodson glanced down toward his deputies, then waved his hand, telling them to stay down. He and Wes peered over the trough. They saw Danner look around the corner of the saloon, trying to get a glimpse of the drunk gunman.

Danner slowly stepped up onto the saloon's boardwalk, moving slowly along the face of the building, his forty-five Russian cocked, and leading the way in his right hand. He passed the open doors, and held up a big left hand, motioning for everyone to keep where they were. Danner carefully moved quietly along the wall, toward the barrels.

Suddenly, the gunman leaped forward. Crack! Danner's forty-five hit like a sledgehammer, knocking the drunken gunman over a barrel onto the dirt street. A sliver of smoke curled up from the Russian's barrel. Danner paused, then immediately loaded a fresh cartridge into the empty cylinder before sliding it into his holster.

Dodson, Wes, and the deputies emerged from their positions, making their way across the street to the fallen drunkard. Dodson knelt, and confirmed the man was dead. Tanner stepped around the corner, shotgun resting on his right shoulder. Dodson looked at Tanner and nodded toward the other man behind the tack shack. Tanner said nothing, answering with a nod of his own. People inside the saloon, and around town, rushed out into the street, gathering around the dead gunfighters, even at such a late hour. Dodson stepped up onto the saloon's boardwalk.

"Thanks Danner. I appreciate it," Dodson said.

"Let me through! Let me through!" Benson, cloaked in a dark gray sleeping gown that reached to the top of his thick ankles, pushed his way to the front of the saloon. He looked down and saw the dead man.

"What happened here, Mr. Dodson?" The sleepy mayor asked.

"Two men got drunk, pistol-whipped Donovan, and shot a fella in the saloon. They came out shootin'," Dodson answered.

"Two men?" Benson asked.

"There's another over next to the livery stable," Dodson informed the mayor.

"Who are they?" Benson asked.

"I don't know 'em. Anybody know who these two are?" Dodson asked aloud.

Everyone turned and looked at each other. A rumble of talk ensued without anyone answering.

"How's Mr. Donovan?" Benson asked pushing past the last couple of men between him and the Red Dirt's swinging doors.

Benson entered the Saloon to see Mike Donovan's head already bandaged, with Doc tending to Roy Halliburton, a farmer that lived west of town.

"You all right Roy?" Benson asked resting a hand on the farmer's shoulder.

"He'll be okay, Doc assured. "He was lucky that fella was drunk and a bad shot. The bullet just caught the outside of his ribs," Phillips added.

"Yeah, but it hit one of my whiskey barrels in the back. A whole barrel wasted," Donovan exclaimed from his seat at the next table.

"Sorry for your loss!" Halliburton shouted before both men broke into laughter.

"Thanks for your help there, Tanner," Dodson said, extending his hand to the blacksmith.

"Man's tryin' ta get some sleep. Don't need no fools shootin' up the town at this hour," Tanner said flatly.

A short thin man with a pale complexion, and long, stringy hair hanging from beneath a narrow brim black hat, stepped forward from the crowd. "Excuse me, Marshal. My name is Elmer Brantley. I'm a mortician by trade. May I be of assistance here?"

Dodson stared at the man who looked like a ghost in a black suit. Wes, Danner, and the rest of the crowd loitering around joined Dodson in examining the embalmer. Brantley removed his hat and smiled, displaying a crooked set of yellow teeth.

"I'm sorry to announce myself in this fashion, but I just arrived earlier today, and I was attempting to determine if this town could use my services. It appears it may," Brantley explained.

Dodson stepped forward and shook the man's hand. "Yes, sir, I believe we could use your services at the moment. I'll bring these two over to my shed and you can meet me there in about a half hour, if that's acceptable," Dodson offered.

"That will be fine, sir, and thank you," Brantley answered.

"Bo, show this man where our office is. Mack, Cody, Tom, ya'll bring these two over to the office. We'll check in the morning to see if they have horses over at Otto's," Dodson ordered.

"You need me for anything?" Danner asked Dodson.

"Not tonight. Can you two stop by in the morning?" Dodson asked both Danner and Wes.

Both men nodded then headed for the hotel. As the two men approached the hotel, they saw Mr. and Mrs. Conrad, along with Rebecca, standing in the doorway. Wes climbed the steps first.

Mr. Conrad opened the door and stepped aside with the two women. "Get you two a cup of coffee, or a drink?" Mr. Conrad asked.

"I'll take a drink if you don't mind," Wes, answered looking back at Danner.

"Sounds good," Danner agreed, removing his hat, and following Mrs. Conrad and Rebecca into the dimly lit dining room.

Mr. Conrad took a bottle of whiskey from a shelf next to the kitchen door and brought it over to a table that Wes and Danner had claimed. Mrs. Conrad brought two glasses to the table and joined the men. Rebecca sat down next to Mrs. Conrad and folded her hands on her lap, looking hard at Danner.

Mr. Conrad poured the whiskey and broke the silence. "What happened out there?" he asked, setting the bottle down in front of the men.

Wes gave them a summary of what occurred as he drank his whiskey.

"Is Donovan okay?" Mrs. Conrad asked.

"I think so. I just looked into the saloon after the shootin' stopped, and saw Doc working on him and the other fella. They both looked like they would be all right," Wes added.

"What happened to the two drunk men?" Rebecca asked.

"They're dead," Danner said matter-of-factly, setting down an empty glass. "Thank you for the drink. I'll be turning in now," he added before leaving the room without further explanation.

"He's an interesting fella," Mr. Conrad said.

"I'd say so. That's it for me, put the drinks on my tab, Mr. Conrad," Wes said, standing up.

"On the house, Mr. Payne. Damn good to have you here," the hotel owner said warmly.

Rebecca reached out, grabbing Wes's arm as he passed. "Did Danner kill those men, Ranger Payne?" she asked.

"Just one. The blacksmith got the other," Wes recounted.

"Is he, Danner, I mean. Is he a violent man?" Rebecca asked holding her grip.

"I reckon he's whatever he needs to be, Miss Barry," Wes stated before disappearing around the corner.

CHAPTER 51

R ain tapped on the shed roof like a bored woodpecker beating against bark. Dodson opened his eyes, and started to move, but a sharp pain in his back told him otherwise. His cot more closely resembled a plank, not a bed. He forced himself into a sitting position letting the ripples of pain pass through him. A knock at the door broke Dodson's focus on his aching back.

"Come in!" Dodson shouted.

Mack McKinnon entered, water streaming off his hat and slicker. He shook his arms in a hopeless attempt to limit the mess he was making.

"You look like hell," McKinnon said.

"I feel worse than I look," Dodson answered.

"What's the problem?" McKinnon asked, hanging his waterlogged Stetson on a rusty hook just inside the door.

"I'm not as young as I used to be. This cot is slowly killing me. Back's hurtin' worse every day," Dodson reported. "What time is it anyway?" he added.

"About six. Danner and Payne are already out searching for that nun. Me and Bo found their horses over at the livery. Still don't know who they were. Otto says one of 'em said his name was Riley, but that's it," McKinnon advised.

"Damn, I forgot about the nun. Trying to track her in this rain won't be easy," Dodson accurately surmised, turning up the flame on his oil lamp.

"That new undertaker already built one casket and is working on the other," McKinnon advised.

"That's one ghoulish fellow," Dodson said, trying to light a fire in the wood stove to take the chill out of the room and make some coffee.

"You ain't whistling Dixie. He looks worse in the daylight," McKinnon said. "But at least that fella is in the right line of work."

Both men laughed.

"I'll file a report with Sheriff Evans. Maybe he, or his deputies, will know who those two were. We should have a deputy here today. Evans sent a telegram late last night," Dodson said.

"One more thing. Looks like the army is packin' up. Getting ready to leave, I reckon," McKinnon reported.

"I'm not surprised. The Lieutenant as much as said they'd be pullin' out. That's okay. With Evans's man, us, Danner, and Payne, that makes eight. We'll do well if anyone tries something. I'll get cleaned up and meet you over at the hotel. No sense us trudging out after Danner right now," Dodson said.

McKinnon retrieved his soggy hat, and put it back on his wet head before plunging out into the steady rain.

The rain intensified, hitting Danner and Payne in the face like bee stings. They weren't finding any track to follow, and everywhere they looked seemed shielded by a thick gray mist. Worse, they had no idea which way the nun might go. They'd made their best guess, heading west out of town, staying near the trail. After talking to everyone at the boarding house, Danner was certain she hadn't been taken again. This time, running out had been her decision. That made Danner uneasy. Two men had already lost their lives, and three more were wounded rescuing her the first time. He hoped it wasn't for nothing.

Needing a respite from the tenacious rain, Danner moved Bullet under a big willow, and dismounted. Payne, seeing enough of Danner to figure out what he had done, quickly joined him under the protection of the big tree's canopy.

"Any ideas?" Payne asked, tipping his head enough to let the water pour off the brim of his hat.

"None." Danner responded.

"We might just go back to town to wait out this downpour," Payne suggested.

"Agreed. We're not doing any good out here."

"What do you really think happened to her?" Wes asked in a voice that said don't beat around the bush.

"I think she felt ashamed and decided life wasn't worth living anymore. I think when we do find her, she won't be in any condition to tell us much of anything," Danner said in a low, grim voice.

"All the more reason to get back to town then," Wes said slipping up onto his drenched saddle.

Danner didn't move. He just stared into the driving rain. Thoughts of her being told she was no longer welcome by the church infuriated him. He felt his hands curl into fists and his shoulders push back. Images of her running away and staggering around in the rain flashed through his mind. The realization that he'd become attached to the young woman hit him like a gut punch. He was ready to fight, but his nemesis was unseen. He wanted to tear apart the bastards that did this to her. He didn't even know the girl, but it didn't matter. He wanted to make the wrong right but knew he couldn't. He didn't want to find her, he had to find her.

Wes reined Ringo to the left, and headed for Range, leaving his partner alone with his thoughts. A short time later, after he'd secured Ringo in his stall at Wilhelm's, draping his thick, brightly-colored Indian blanket onto his chilled horse, Wes took his time walking over to the hotel. He couldn't get any wetter than he already was. He stopped in the middle of the street, and looked west for Danner but did not see him. He continued on into the hotel, where he hung his slicker and hat next to the front door, then made his way to the restaurant where the smell of bacon, eggs, and coffee changed his soggy disposition.

"Good morning, Ranger Payne, would you like coffee?" Rebecca greeted the dejected Ranger.

"Yes, ma'am, the hotter the better."

Rebecca tightened her powder-blue apron, rushing off to the kitchen. Wes had chosen the small table near the kitchen, not interested in conversation, especially with that blowhard, Benson. Rebecca returned quickly with hot coffee, three steaming biscuits, and a small dish of honey.

"I thought you might like these," she said, setting everything on the table, then turning to leave.

"Ma'am," Wes said, stopping Rebecca abruptly. "How's our boy doing this morning?" he asked.

"I haven't seen Ben yet this morning. We've been busier than usual with the rain and all, so I haven't taken his breakfast up yet," Rebecca advised in a low voice delivered without the usual smile.

Wes wrapped his hands around the steaming coffee cup, hoping to gain much-needed movement that the cold and rain had stripped from him. He looked closely at this hands. They looked like the hands of a dead man, maybe worse. The scars formed a grotesque sphere, elevated, and purple. His palms weren't nearly as hideous. The dark red marks were smaller in the center of his hand, and not nearly as gruesome. Just like a bullet's entry wound wasn't as bad as where it came out. Wes clenched his fists, then opened his hands repeating the movement several times. With each motion, the flexibility improved, allowing him to pick up a biscuit. *Morning's getting better already*, he thought wryly.

"Well! Good morning, Mr. Payne!" boomed Lawrence Benson's voice behind Wes's back.

So much for the morning getting better, Wes thought, before turning around to greet the mayor "Mr. Benson," Wes kept his greeting abrupt, hoping Benson would take the hint and move along.

"Please join me at my table up front, Mr. Payne. I'll be happy to buy you breakfast," Benson offered.

"Not this morning, thanks. I'm going to finish eating these biscuits then change into some dry clothes," Wes explained.

"I understand. No luck finding our missing Sister, I assume," Benson said.

"No, sir, Danner's still out, but I expect he'll be along soon. The rain made it impossible to track her," Wes advised.

"Of course, of course. Thank you for your efforts." Benson said, shuffling over to his customary table where a few of the town's businessmen awaited.

Danner tapped his spurs, encouraging Bullet down a narrow path off the main trail. The cloud cover had thinned just enough for him to see the path that had been well-camouflaged earlier when he and Wes had passed. Danner noticed the buffalo grass in the middle had been tamped down in places. Unsure if it was the rain or footsteps, he decided to have a closer look. The narrow path had been made more so by the waterlogged scrub branches pushed down to the ground by the unrelenting weight of the rain.

Danner's eyes darted from the ground to the path opening, then back again. No question, the tracks in the buffalo grass were not caused by the rain. The tracks had been caused by human or animal. Bullet was hesitant, snorting every few yards. The big bay protested each tap of the spurs. Whatever was down here made his horse uneasy.

Danner kept his eyes forward. His senses heightened. Up ahead, he noticed the path turned sharply to the left. Bullet stopped, bobbing his head, and snorted again. This was as far as he would go.

Danner slipped off his wet saddle, rubbing his partner's nose before drawing a Russian and proceeding on foot. The soft, wet ground and the falling rain muffled any sounds his movement made. He stepped around the bend of a sycamore and froze. Any hope he had of finding the nun alive flowed out of him like blood from a wound.

Danner slowly holstered his gun and sighed into the pouring rain. He saw the nun about twenty paces ahead of him. Clothed only in a white sleeping gown that reached to her ankles, she hung a few inches off the ground from the branch of a mesquite tree with a rope tightly knotted around her neck. Her slender body swung back and forth in the wind. He tried not to look at her face.

Oblivious to the rain, Danner stepped forward, withdrawing a knife from its sheath inside his slicker. He gently wrapped his left arm around the nun's limp body and cut the rope above her head. Her dead body slumped over his shoulder, arms falling to each side. He carried her body back to Bullet, who stepped back and snorted again, sensing death. Danner rubbed Bullet's mane to calm him, then untied his bedroll from the saddle. Its cover hadn't prevented his blanket from being totally soaked, but it would have to do.

Danner pushed the wet, matted hair away from Sarah's pallid face, then wrapped her in the blanket. Clutching the young woman tightly, he stepped into the stirrup and swung into the saddle. He held her across the front of his body and maneuvered Bullet around the narrow confines of the path Danner knew he would never forget.

As he rode along, his vision narrowed to the path directly in front of him. His mind exploded with thoughts of failure. Failure to rescue her in time. Failure to find her before she ended a short, twenty-year life that only wanted to serve her faith and help others find it. Her life had been wasted because he didn't help her in time. What little faith Danner had managed to keep until now evaporated into the air, replaced by a budding rage that no lawman should possess.

CHAPTER 52

L ike tears from heaven, the deluge continued to pummel
Range as though God had decided punishment was due.
Danner slowly passed the cattle pens west of town. Several
people sat under the covered porch of the boarding house as Danner
slowly rode past, not bothering to acknowledge their presence. One of
the women leapt to her feet, and ran inside, no doubt to announce
what she had seen. Danner kept his eyes forward, trying to balance
the hollow feeling in the pit of his stomach.

He continued down Main Street, drawing the attention of anyone
who caught a glimpse. A young boy ran into Doc's office, bringing the
physician and Betsy onto his front step. Danner stoically continued
past Doc's office, because his healing services would not be required.

News of Danner's return moved swiftly through town, reaching
the hotel before he did. Danner stopped at the Marshal's shed, placing
Sarah's body in Dodson's ladder-back chair, out of the rain.

Danner continued inside the office, placing his badge atop the old
wooden bureau. Dodson watched him without saying a word. Dodson
quietly took his seat opposite Danner, and removed the bottle of
bourbon from its drawer along with two smudged glasses.

"I know it's a little early," Dodson said, before pushing the half-filled glass toward Danner.

Danner accepted the drink and finished it in one gulp.

"I'm finished," Danner said. "And I don't mean the drink," he turned his eyes toward his badge. The silence pushed down on Danner as if he carried a chuck wagon on his massive shoulders. He stared at the badge but didn't see it. The image of Sarah's limp body hanging in the middle of nowhere, being further assaulted by the pummeling rain clouded his vision.

He'd seen more than his share of dead men, but seeing this young, innocent woman hanging from a tree was too much for him. If there was more of this coming, he wanted no part of it. *First Elizabeth Thornton shot, then Molly Lewis killed. Now Sarah.* He didn't even know her last name. Where she came from, why she had chosen to become a nun. None of that mattered now. She was dead. A wasted life.

"Care to tell me what happened?" Dodson asked quietly.

Wes came through the door, stomping the mud off his boots, then took in the view. Danner didn't flinch at the noisy intrusion. Wes stopped and said nothing.

"I backtracked and found a path we hadn't seen on the way out. Followed it to a mesquite. Found her hanging. She'd dragged a rotted log under a branch. Just enough to get the job done," Danner relayed the scene imprinted on his memory.

Wes lowered his head. Dodson looked out the water-blurred window, rubbing the whiskers on his chin. "Why would she do a thing like that?" Dodson whispered, almost rhetorically.

"Your Deacon friend can answer that," Danner growled.

"Wes, would you get someone to fetch the undertaker?" Dodson asked. "He's taken up shop over at the new church building," he added.

"I'll get 'em," Wes said, then ducked out the door.

Dodson stood, walked around his desk and picked up Danner's badge. He looked at it, then held it toward Danner. "I know you're tired Danner, but do us all a favor and hang onto this for now. We're gonna need you. I don't know when, but I reckon we won't have to wait long," Dodson said.

Danner paused and sighed. He wearily accepted the badge, sliding it back inside his vest pocket.

Just as Danner was about to leave, Wes returned with the new undertaker, along with a crowd, led by the Deacon and the other nuns. Within moments, people crowded inside the small shed, filling it with the smell of wet wool and leather.

Danner towered over everyone, staring down at the Deacon. "Your church murdered one of its own," Danner growled, then pushed through the group, and walked out.

"What does he mean, murdered?" Someone asked.

"Marshal Danner found Sister Sarah hanging from a tree. Probably not a good time to ask him," Dodson said. "Mr. Brantley, would you see that the Sister gets a proper casket. I'll see to it that you get paid," Dodson advised the town's suddenly busy newcomer.

Brantley nodded and left the shed.

Just then, Mack walked in from the rain with Bo and Tom.

"Keep a close eye on any newcomers in town today. I expect this Jenkins to send in a spy or two before he makes any kind of move," Dodson added, turning his attention back to the impending threat.

***

Danner put Bullet up at the stable before heading to the hotel. A bell rang when he opened the front door, surprising him. Must've been a new addition that arrived with the other supplies. As he closed the door, Rebecca emerged from the back room behind the desk.

"Hello," Rebecca gushed, then stopped well behind the desk, quickly taking in Danner's blank look, fallen shoulders, and generally menacing demeanor.

Danner removed his hat and looked hard at Rebecca. A stone face and drawn brow held back the flood of emotions sweeping through his mind. Anger swirled in his head like a tornado. Sarah hadn't been much older than Rebecca. Maybe they were the same age. He said nothing, trying to tamp down the rage that pervaded his body.

"Are you okay? You're scaring me," Rebecca's words jolted Danner from his daze.

"Ya, kid, I'm fine. Sorry, I was just thinking too hard, I guess," Danner said meekly.

"Maybe some dry clothes and coffee might help?" Rebecca asked hesitantly.

"Sure, that'll help," Danner trying hard to be as pleasant as possible.

"I'll bring some up to your room. No need to come back down," Rebecca offered, then disappeared into the back room.

Danner slowly climbed the stairs, leaving a trail of water on each step. He realized he still wore his soaking wet slicker. He turned, slightly ashamed of his watery trail when Mrs. Conrad appeared at the bottom, holding a mop. "I'm sorry for the mess, Mrs. Conrad. I didn't realize what bad shape I was in," Danner apologized.

"No need to apologize, Marshal. I'll take care it. Rebecca told me you had just arrived and were soaked to the skin," Mrs. Conrad explained.

"Thank you," Danner responded, then disappeared into his room.

Rebecca joined Mrs. Conrad on the staircase, carrying a tray of coffee, biscuits, and honey.

"You better wait a while before you take that up to Mr. Danner," Mrs. Conrad suggested.

"Yes, ma'am. This is for Ben. I'll take the Marshal's up in a little while," Rebecca said as she climbed the stairs, trying to avoid the puddles left by Danner.

Rebecca tapped the door with her toe then barged into Chance's room, nearly losing her grip on the tray. Chance sat on the edge of the bed fully dressed, watching the rain pelt the window. An awkward silence hung between them. After all, the last time they saw one another, Rebecca had kissed him. They heard a door close out in the hallway. Rebecca turned just in time to see Danner heading out of his room down the stairs. Why wouldn't that man ever sit still? She turned back to Chance, boasting a wide smile to break up the awkwardness between them. Chance smiled, back. As much as their budding feelings toward each other were evident, Chance's primary focus was on getting up and out of the room so that he could be useful.

"Doc said you could get out of this room for a while," Rebecca announced.

"Don't look like a good day for a walk in town," Chance answered with a chuckle. "Do you mind taking that back downstairs?" Chance asked. "I'd like to eat in the restaurant," he added.

"Of course! Do you need help?" she asked.

"No. No help. I can do it. The shoulder's more sore now than painful," Chance assured her as he stood and gingerly walked toward the door.

Due to the foul weather, the restaurant was uncharacteristically busy for this late in the morning. No one seemed to be in a hurry to leave after finishing their breakfast. Rebecca directed Chance to the small table near the kitchen, then ducked inside.

Mr. Conrad stepped out of the kitchen, slipping his arms into his coat, and caught a glimpse of Chance, "Hello! Good to see you down here," Conrad said cheerfully to Chance.

"Thanks Mr. Conrad. It feels good to be up and about. You headin' out in this weather?" Chance asked.

"Got to go over to the Jamieson's store and get more coffee. We're about to run out."

Rebecca hurried out of the kitchen with a tray of food, pausing to smile at Chance, who returned the gesture. The side door suddenly opened, pushing wind, rain, and three malicious-looking men into the dining room. All were armed, and mud covered each man's boots and legs. They looked like they'd spent several hard days on the trail. Chance reached down for his gun, but felt only trousers. He'd forgotten his gun belt.

PART III

CHAPTER 53

HARRY NOLEN & TUFF JENKINS – SQUAW RAVINE

The bright orange flames from Harry Nolen's fire flickered against the stone walls of his shallow cave, keeping him warm and dry while he impatiently waited for Jenkins and his gang. Tucked into the talus of a small cliff along Jagged Rock Creek, the grotto provided the infiltrator with just enough protection from the torrential rain.

Although certain he hadn't been followed, or anyone knowing what he was, the old man kept watch, trying to calm his right leg which shook nonstop with nervous energy. He really didn't like Jenkins or his sidekick Dunham, but he'd been intoxicated with the promise of a big payday after all this was over. He'd take his cut and head to New Mexico, where there was plenty of land to ranch.

Despite his agreement, he'd grown to like the Deacon and the nuns and didn't want to see anything bad happen to them. He'd also grown friendly with Sam at the Red Dirt Saloon and Otto over at the stables. The conflict inside him fought like wildcats, making him uneasy, keeping his leg humming like a timber saw. He peered out into the storm. His attempt to see through the deluge for approaching riders failed.

He pictured Jenkins with his head down, getting hammered by the rain, cursing with every step. He knew from his own ride to the cave that the outlaw and his gang would make poor time against the wind and rain. His own horse had nearly slipped and fell a couple of times in the muddy terrain.

Nolen took a deep breath and exhaled slowly. At least the bad weather would probably stop Jenkins from riding into town tonight.

After an hour or so, Nolen caught a glimpse of several riders in the distance. *Almost here*, he thought looking around the small enclave.

Not enough room in here for a gang of men. There should be a few openings along the bottom of the crag. They'll be here in less than thirty minutes. Nolen leaned back out of his hole, looking into the teeth of the storm. He strained his eyes to make sure it was Jenkins he saw coming. Yep, it was him all right. He searched his coat pockets, locating his tin of chew tobacco. After shoving a wad into his mouth, he replaced the lid, and returned the tin to its pocket. He didn't smoke, but he liked his chaw. This would ease his thoughts of Jenkins until he arrived.

He didn't have to wait long, as the sound of horses snorting cut through the beat of the rain. Nolen peered out, making out the outline of horse and rider from the mist. As more riders appeared, Nolen looked around the cave again. Room for maybe five men, not the bunch dismounting outside. Jenkins ducked into the opening, looked around, then turned to the men.

"Check down the line. See if there are any other openings. Only room for four here," Jenkins called out. Three men stepped past Jenkins not waiting for an invitation. The rest of the gang started down the rock base, looking for anything that resembled shelter.

Jenkins threw his hat and slicker into a corner, and got right to business. "Well, what do you have to say, old man?" Jenkins asked the nervous informant.

"It's not good, Mr. Jenkins, not good at all."

"What the hell ya mean not good!" Jenkins asked.

"There's lawmen all over town. The Marshal, name's Dodson, he has four deputies and there's a Ranger and U.S. Marshal in town along with a squad of cavalry soldiers," Nolen reported.

"Damn!" Dunham exclaimed.

"Who's the Ranger and U.S. Marshal?" Jenkins asked.

"Nobody said nothing 'bout goin' up against the army," the big man with the black beard growled, stepping through the cave's opening, looking more like a grizzly bear than a man.

Nolen gulped, and tried to step back, only to hit the rock wall behind him.

"Now take it easy, mister. Let's think this through," Jenkins returned the growl.

"There's nothing to think through. All we've been told till now is this was gonna be an easy job. Now I find out the army's involved. I ain't speakin' fer everyone else, but I'm not fightin' the damn army for money I've only heard about," the man exclaimed.

Jenkins paused, and watched a scorpion cautiously crawl along the base of the wall. He slowly nodded. "Look, we're not ridin' on the town in this weather anyway. Won't rain like this much longer. Nolen, you go back to town and find out what you can about the soldiers. See how long they plan on stayin'. We'll wait here a day or two. If it looks like the soldiers ain't leave'n, we'll ride down river, and see what we can get in Eagle Springs. That sound more to your like'n?" Jenkins asked the big man.

The man let out a groan, then stepped on the scorpion, its shell crunching under his mammoth boot. "Come this far. I reckon we'll stick around a day or two," he answered, then disappeared into a wall of water.

"Not sure I'd want to make that fella angry," Dunham said aloud.

"Ain't nobody gettin' angry," Jenkins said. "You know what you need to do, Nolen?" Jenkins asked.

"Yes, sir. There was a rumor the soldiers were pullin' out soon. The bartender at the saloon will know. I'll see what I can find out," Nolen assured his boss.

"Good. Get back here before sundown if you can. Wait a spell, and see if the damned rain lets up. Can't rain like this much longer," Jenkins said.

"You keep sayin' that, but it don't look like it's stoppin' anytime soon," Shorty cackled, sticking his hand out the cave into the rain.

312 | JOHN LAYNE

The big man left Jenkins and pushed his way into a small cove under a broken overhang, where the rest of the outlaws from Manitou huddled around a small fire not even strong enough to make coffee. Bates looked at the feeble fire and frowned.

"Ain't no dry wood around to burn," one of the men spit through a mouth, void of ample teeth.

"At least its dry under here," the big man grunted, pulling off his soaked coat.

He sat down and slipped a package of jerky from under his vest, biting off a large piece of dried bison. The tired and wet men stared into the small flames. "We're gonna wait here for a bit. Jenkins's spy is going back to town to check on a few things, then come back with a report," he announced.

None of the men bothered to look up from the flickering flames so he decided not to share his knowledge of the cavalry squad or the law in town. He leaned back against the frigid rock wall and closed his eyes. If that squirrel came back with bad news, he'd know what to do. It wouldn't be the first time he'd killed the boss and took over a gang.

CHAPTER 54

RANGE

Three rough-looking saddle tramps came into the restaurant sizing up the place before sitting down at a table near the side door.

Chance scanned the restaurant looking for Dodson but did not see him. He considered his options. Stay, watch what happens, or head up to his room for his gun. He decided to stay, at least for the moment. The men found a table, looked around the room, no doubt sizing up anyone who would challenge them.

Rebecca slowly walked over to the men wiping her hands on her apron, obviously intimidated by their ragged appearance. "What can I do for you, gentlemen?" She asked.

All three men leaned back and took a long look at Rebecca, two of them laughing out loud. Rebecca took a step back, clutching her apron.

"No reason to be afraid, little lady," one of the men said. "We're just lookin' for some food and whiskey!" he added.

"We don't serve whiskey," Rebecca advised.

"You don't understand, little lady, we want whiskey with our food. You just bring a bottle right along!" The man, wearing a tall black hat shouted.

Mrs. Conrad had seen the men and made her way to the table next to Rebecca. "Gentlemen, if you're wanting to drink, maybe you should go across the street to the saloon," Mrs. Conrad suggested.

"We want steaks and whiskey. Can we get steaks at the saloon?" The man asked while the other two laughed.

"We'll have good fried chicken in a while, gentlemen. We'll have steaks later at dinner," Mrs. Conrad advised with a firm voice.

"We'll take steaks now!" The man shouted, his tall hat nearly falling off his head. He stood up from his chair, pulling up on his gun belt.

The two women retreated to the wall at the front of the room. Chance stood up, as did Belton Tanner, who had just finished a late breakfast with his family. The three men looked at Chance and Tanner.

"Well, looks like we got us a couple heroes here. A cripple and a unarmed horseshoer," one of the men shouted, pulling his coat away from his gun.

The other two gunmen did the same.

"Please, please, gentlemen, no need to get angry," Mr. Conrad announced as he hurried out of the kitchen door toward the men. Rebecca and Mrs. Conrad scurried back toward the kitchen, Rebecca rushing to Chance's table.

"Please sit down, Ben. You're in no condition to fight these men," she whispered.

"Go up to my room and bring down my gun. Hurry. Go through the kitchen around the other side so they don't see you leave," Chance ordered.

"But Ben," Rebecca said, worried.

"Now," Chance said as forcefully as he could without raising his voice.

Rebecca ran into the kitchen and disappeared. Chance sat back down, keeping an eye on the threesome. Tanner also returned to his seat with the help of his wife, pulling on his suspenders with both hands.

"That's what I thought!" The grizzly looking man shouted, his eyes wide, and black as coal.

"I believe you men should leave immediately, or I'll have to call the Marshal," Mr. Conrad advised.

"You go right ahead and call your Marshal, mister!" the man shouted.

Mr. Conrad started to walk past the man when he drew his gun, and bashed it into Conrad's head, sending the hotel keeper to the floor in a loud thud.

"No!" Mrs. Conrad dropped to her knees tending to her unconscious husband. Several people who initially feared moving, jumped from their seats and hurried out of the restaurant like rats fleeing a sinking ship. Chance and Tanner remained seated, but said nothing. Chance heard Rebecca's heels drumming down the stairs. He stood, and slowly walked to the high archway leading to the hotel lobby where he could meet Rebecca.

"Where you think yer goin', cripple?" The man shouted.

Chance ignored the question, and kept his head down. As he reached the archway – Crack! The man fired a shot into the ceiling above Chance. Splinters of wood and paint rained down onto his head and shoulders. Undeterred, he stepped around the corner as Rebecca hit the last step with his Colt in hand. Chance grabbed his gun and paused. *Don't walk back in the way you walked out,* he thought.

He hurried around the big lobby desk into the backroom, which led to the kitchen, pulling his left arm out of its sling. He stopped just inside the kitchen door. He could hear the men laughing and shouting. Crack! Crack! Two more shots. Chance stepped through the kitchen door and found the three men all looking at the front archway. Chance cocked his gun. The men turned. Crack! Crack! Chance fired his forty-five knocking the boisterous gunman back into a table.

The two others cleared leather – Crack! Crack! Crack! Three shots sounded before Chance pulled on target. The two others went down, guns flying into the air, then clanging to the floor.

Dodson stood at the side door of the restaurant, his Colt Peacemaker barrel billowing smoke. Dodson scanned the room. "That all of 'em, Chance?" He shouted.

"Yes, sir, just three," Chance answered as Rebecca rushed to Chance, hugging him tightly.

"Glad to see you, Marshal!" Chance added, with a wave of his gun, and a grin to match.

"Glad I got here in time. I saw everyone running out, and heard the shots. Figured I'd come around the side. Took me a little extra time," Dodson explained holstering his Colt. He knelt, and looked at the men's faces. He opened one of the men's mouth, met with a gaping void of teeth. The one that had been doing all the shouting had a scar on the left side of his neck under a dirty, red bandana. "That's what I thought," Dodson mumbled.

"What is it?" Chance asked.

"I heard about three men robbin' a group of settlers north of Riverbend. Sheriff Evans sent a telegram sayin' one had no teeth and another a bad scar on his neck. Said to keep a look out. Don't need to look no more, I reckon," Dodson said.

Mr. Conrad woke with a loud coughing fit, bleeding from a nasty gash on his face. Mrs. Conrad had already sent Rebecca to fetch Doc.

"You gonna make it, Mr. Conrad?" Dodson asked with a grin.

"He'll be fine, Marshal," Mrs. Conrad answered, returning a faint smile. "Thank you both," she added looking back at Chance.

CHAPTER 55

Nolen dismounted, and tied his horse outside the Red Dirt Saloon. Piano music filled the saloon, along with an over-crowded group of cowhands who had arrived earlier in the afternoon with a cattle drive from further south. Nolen paused, and took a long look up and down Main Street. The rain had cleared out earlier, and the air felt crisp and clean.

Teamsters battled with heavy weighted freight wagons, their wheels pushed four to five inches into the soupy mud the rain caused on Main Street. Even lightweight buckboards struggled to make their way. Men on horseback rode cautiously as their horses' hooves delicately navigated the slippery thoroughfare.

The doors of the saloon swung open, both top hinges snapped, dropping the louvered doors to the floor. Three men simultaneously flew through the doorway, crashing down the steps into the red mud. Donovan stood on the top step, glaring at the men.

"You sons a bitches stay out! You hear me? You come back inside and the undertaker will have more business!" he shouted.

The three cowboys peeled themselves out of the mud and staggered off down the street.

318 | JOHN LAYNE

"Hello, Nolen! How the hell are ya?" Donovan asked, exchanging his scowl with a wide grin as soon as he saw the old man standing near the hitching post.

"Better than those fellas, I reckon," Nolen answered, then climbed the steps, following Donovan into the saloon.

Due to the inclement weather, the Red Dirt Saloon was crowded with several card games going, and a parade of activity up and down the stairs to the girls' quarters. Nolen squeezed into a spot at the bar, and ordered a beer. Nolen could barely hear Donovan talking behind the bar.

Not going to find out anything from him now, Nolen thought as he gulped half his beer without taking a breath. He hadn't figured on a drive coming through, since he hadn't heard any rumors about it. He finished his beer, put down his money, nodded at Donovan, then squeezed through another group of cowhands coming through the broken front doors.

Once outside, he checked east of town. The soldiers' camp looked to be cleaned out. That answered that question. He checked his pocket watch which showed four o'clock. He decided to visit the general store and investigate. The store owners always seemed to know what was happening around town. He purposefully got to know Mr. and Mrs. Jamieson for that very reason. He made his way across the street to the store, where a bell sounded as he opened the front door. He stomped his boots on a small rug just inside the door turning it from brown to red with mud.

"Good evening Mr. Nolen," Wanda Jamieson greeted the former chauffeur.

"Hello, Mrs. Jamieson. Just thought I'd step in off the street and sit for a bit. You have any of that buffalo jerky around?" Nolen asked.

"Yes, sir. Mighty popular, but we still have some. How much would you like?"

"Oh, I'll take three sticks."

Mrs. Jamieson hurried to the back where she kept the jerky inside an old whisky barrel. She removed three, foot-long strips of the dried meat, rolled them in thick brown paper and returned to the counter. "That'll be fifty cents."

Nolen paid for the meat then got down to business. "I see the soldiers camp is gone. They decide to leave town?" He asked.

"I believe so. My husband was down at the meeting house when Mr. Benson talked to the commanding officer. We heard there was some Indian trouble, so they left," Mrs. Jamieson offered.

"Oh, that's too bad. It was kind a nice have'n them around," Nolen lied.

"Yes, it was. But now that Mr. Dodson has some deputies, things seem to be okay," she added.

"For sure, for sure. How many deputies he have now?" Nolen probed, nervously fumbling with the wrapped jerky.

"I don't know. A few, I hear," she said.

Afraid he'd raise suspicion, Nolen decided that was enough information to take back to Jenkins. "Well, I'll be getting along, you have a nice evenin', ma'am," he said, his voice wavering a bit as he turned to the front door.

"Thank you, Mr. Nolen. Always nice to see you," she said as Nolen rang the front doorbell. He paused briefly without turning around, then stepped out onto the porch, and slowly closed the door behind him. He looked down at the wrapped meat in his hand. The sharp neat creases in the folded paper. He knew Mrs. Jamieson could have asked for more than fifty cents for buffalo jerky. Buffalo meat was becoming harder and harder to get, and he knew it. He took a deep breath.

"Mr. Nolen, everything all right?" Brad Jamieson asked as he climbed the steps.

Nolen had been so deep in thought, he'd not seen the store owner walk up and extend his hand to shake. Nolen's muscles twitched, and his head jerked up at the sudden sound of the greeting. "Sorry Mr. Jamieson, didn't see you there!" Nolen uttered excitedly, accepting the hand shake. "Your wife, err, uh, was kind enough to sell me some buffalo, much obliged," Nolen stuttered.

"Very good. We're almost out. Hard to find nowadays," Mr. Jamieson responded, then stepped past his startled customer and entered the store. Brad Jamieson stopped and looked out the front window, watching Nolen for a moment. Nolen finally stepped into the muddy street and headed across toward the Red Dirt Saloon.

"That Harry Nolen seem okay to you?" Brad asked his wife.

"Yes. Why?" she asked.

Mr. Jamieson looked back out the window, watching Nolen mount his horse across the street, and carefully ride toward the cattle pens west of town. "I frightened him out on the porch. I said hello to him several times before he jumped, and knew I was there. He seemed troubled about something."

"He was fine in here. He asked for buffalo jerky, talked for a few minutes then left," Mrs. Jamieson reported.

"What'd he want to talk about?" Brad asked.

"Oh, about the soldiers leaving, and Mr. Dodson's deputies, was all," his wife answered.

"I don't know why he'd be so interested in the soldiers and deputies. He's only been in town a short time. He doesn't really seem to do much but drink in the saloon, and come around here from time to time," Jamieson surmised.

"Well, we've got stock to take care of in the back, and there's no time to worry about Mr. Nolen," his wife announced. The bell rang again, bringing Mr. Jamieson's attention back to the store front.

Mack McKinnon closed the door, doing his best to wipe the mud off his boots before entering the store.

"Don't bother, it's a losing cause," Jamieson laughed, catching a glimpse of the silver badge on his guest's buckskin. "What can I do for you, deputy?" he asked.

"Well, sir, I don't believe we've met. I'm Mack McKinnon, one of Marshal Dodson's new deputies."

Mr. Jamieson walked around the counter and shook McKinnon's hand. "I'm Brad Jamieson. My wife, Wanda, and I own the store," he advised.

"Yes, sir. Good to know ya. Marshal Dodson wanted all of us to make the rounds around town and meet as many people as we could.

Been pretty busy with the cowhands around, and all. Everything okay here?" McKinnon asked,

"Yes, Mr. McKinnon. We've had no problems," Jamieson advised.

McKinnon offered up the best tobacco-stained smile he could muster. "Yes, sir. Very well, I'll be gettin' along then," McKinnon said before putting his hat on, and leaving the store.

CHAPTER 56

Doc removed the sling over Chance's left arm. Danner and Payne sat at a table nearby inside the restaurant, their feet propped up on chairs, drinking coffee that Rebecca kept well-supplied. Danner watched Rebecca as she moved around the dining room floor more like a dancer than a waitress. Her steps were light and her dark brown dress swayed back and forth with each step. He noticed she looked over at Chance and smiled every opportunity she could. Chance responded about half the time with a thin grin of his own, seemingly embarrassed by the attention in front of Danner and Wes.

"You ever been in love, Marshal Danner?" Mrs. Conrad asked the big lawman.

Danner slowly looked up at the hotel matriarch and narrowed his blue eyes saying nothing.

"How about you, Ranger Payne?" she asked.

Payne tipped his hat back on his head, and looked at Mrs. Conrad with an expression that showed neither approval nor reproach. His expression softened, and he looked down at the remaining coffee in his cup. "Not sure what that feels like, ma'am," Payne answered.

"Oh hogwash! I've been watching both of you for a while now.

That's fine if you're both incapable of answering a simple question," Mrs. Conrad quipped, before moving across the room to several tables occupied by cowhands waiting for an early dinner.

Payne looked at Danner, who managed a brief shoulder shrug before taking a sip of tepid black coffee. Payne pulled his hat back down on his forehead. Rebecca hurried by the silent lawmen with glasses of beer perched on a tray for the cowhands.

"How's it look, Doc?" Chance asked the doctor has he finished applying a fresh bandage.

"Well, considering you've insisted on getting in gunfights and hugging your girl there, it's looking mighty fine, son," Doc said with a chuckle.

"She ain't my girl, Doc," Chance declared loud enough for Rebecca to hear as she returned to the kitchen. Rebecca stopped, tossed the empty tray onto the table, and jammed fists into each of her hips.

"Benjamin Franklin Chance, if I ever hear you say that again, I'll break your other arm!" Rebecca shouted. Rebecca retrieved the tray, spun on her heels, and stomped off into the kitchen.

"Young man, you've a lot to learn about women, I'm afraid," Doc sighed.

Danner and Payne laughed, Payne so hard that he spewed a mouth full of coffee all over the table. Chance stood, his face flushed with a red hue reminiscent of the mud on the street. He started to speak, decided better of it, then turned and marched off to the stairs, where he climbed up to his room, boot heels slamming into each wooden step, sounding like the echo of a gunshot.

"I've had enough coffee. Buy you a beer?" Payne asked Danner.

"Naw, thanks. I'll head over to the telegraph office and see if anything has come in, then go down to Dodson's office and check in," Danner stated.

"You waitin' on a message?" Payne asked.

"Sort of. I figure our rescue tactics will get back to Fort Smith eventually. When it does, there'll be a response," Danner said.

Payne said nothing. Just nodded. Danner strolled out of the dining room, ducking under the door frame as he left.

Doc watched Danner leave.

"What do you know about him?" Doc asked.

"Not much, really. He's always been a mystery. You know, we rode together in Six Shot. He was a kid in the war. His father forced him to join the Union army even though his older brother was a Johnny Reb. Don't know for certain, but I think his brother got killed in battle. After the war, he finished school, went to college for bit, then something happened. I don't know what, and he joined the Marshal's office. Ended up in Fort Smith where Parker took a liking to him. Been there since," Payne explained.

"I see," Doc mumbled, scratching his head. "Had to be tough on him. I'm guessin' he's no Yank," Phillips added.

"From Charleston. Folks up and left right before the war. Moved north. I don't remember where," Payne admitted.

"You two going to sit here all evening gossiping like old ladies, or are you going to order dinner?" Mrs. Conrad asked flashing a bright smile.

"Oops! I've got a few more calls to make, I'll be seein' ya," Doc said, rushing out of the dining room.

"Mr. Payne, you have any calls to make?" Debra asked, a hint of good-natured sarcasm in her voice.

"No ma'am. Got nowhere to go. I'll have whatever you think I should," Payne said, removing his hat, and placing it on the chair next to him.

"We have some good fried chicken. I'll bring that right out," she suggested.

"Yes ma'am. I'll wait right here," Payne answered.

———

Danner waited outside the little wooden box that passed as the telegraph office. A cowboy of some importance sat inside reciting a message to Jacob Turner. *Probably the foreman or trail boss of the drive that's in town*, Danner thought. If the owner wasn't with them, he'd want updates along the trail.

After a few minutes, the cowboy finished and left. Danner leaned in, not bothering to try and enter. He knew his six-foot-six, 245-pound frame wouldn't fit.

"Anything from the Marshal's office in Fort Smith?" he asked Turner.

"No sir, nothing yet," Turner informed him. "If something comes in, I'll bring it over to the hotel right away, if that's okay with you, sir?" Turner asked.

"That'll be fine, Jake. I'll be in Dodson's office for a bit," Danner advised the young operator.

Dodson sat, perched on his old ladder-back leaning against the wall of his shed, when Danner strolled up. "Pull up a stool and take a load off," Dodson offered with a wave of his hand.

Danner accepted the seat, using the shed as a chair back. "How are things, Marshal?" Danner asked, taking in the sights and sounds of the livery stable and saloon across the street.

"Fine. I've got the boys out all over town checking on things. I told Cody to stay inside the Red Dirt Saloon and keep the card games honest," Dodson reported.

After twenty minutes of silence, Dodson spoke up. "They buried Sister Sarah today. Mr. Brantley has a graveyard started east of town. I didn't see you there," Dodson said.

"She wasn't a Sister any more. Didn't the Deacon tell you? She'd been soiled. Then she killed herself. Apparently, the church doesn't tolerate those things. Didn't see any need to be there," Danner calmly answered, keeping his eyes fixed on the stable doors.

Dodson nodded and changed the subject. "Benson took in several thousand dollars from that cattle drive today. Seems the foreman sold a herd of horses to a group of settlers down in Medicine Mound. He didn't want to carry the cash all the way to Kansas, so Benson convinced him to keep it here, and pick it up on the way back," Dodson reported.

"Of course, he did," Danner replied.

"I don't like Benson keeping money at the meeting house, Damn town could use a bank," Dodson added.

"Give it time. It'll build one eventually," Danner said.

"How much longer you figure on stayin'?"

"Don't know. I've been waiting for the telegram for a couple of days now. Seems like you and the deputies have things under control, especially if the Rangers let Wes stay for a bit longer," Danner said.

"You have any other Marshal business to tend to before you turn in your badge?" Dodson asked.

"I told you, after this I'm done. I need to make a stop in Riverbend and Eagle Springs on the way back. I've got a few warrants with me, but no one I expect to ride into town here," Danner offered.

"I don't know. Look at those three jackasses came in this morning. They rob a wagon train, then waltz in here like its nothing," Dodson pointed out.

"They're all not that stupid," Danner said as he watched Belton Tanner walk past the stable carrying a wooden door with iron bars over a small window. "Looks like you got company, Marshal," Danner announced.

"My new jail door," Dodson said with a chuckle.

"Evenin', Marshal. Got that door barred up just like you asked," Tanner announced swinging the door to the porch planks bars first.

"Looks perfect. Can I help you hang it back up?" Dodson asked the barrel-chested blacksmith.

"Naw, only take a minute," Tanner announced picking up his work, heading for the shed door which Dodson quickly opened.

"Jail door?" Danner asked.

I reinforced the back-storage room, and had Tanner cut a window in the door so I could check in on prisoners. I figure I could hold two or three back there without much trouble," Dodson advised.

Danner nodded, and returned his attention to the activity in the street. The muddy surface had begun to dry so the wagons navigated the ruts with greater ease. The horses still seemed tentative, keeping the riders at a slower pace. A large group of cowboys flooded out of the Red Dirt Saloon, a few stumbling and falling into the street. Shouts of vulgarity intermingled with laughter as the cowhands made their way toward the holding pens, where the drive's camp had been set up just beyond.

"Well, barring any tin horn gamblers in the saloon, this should be a quiet night," Dodson said, taking his hat off, and rubbing his fingers through his hair before returning the Stetson back to its roost.

Danner said nothing, just sat quietly with his massive arms crossed over his equally formidable chest.

A n hour's ride away, Harry Nolen closed in on Jagged Rock Creek to give his report to Tuff Jenkins. The more he thought about the Deacon, Sisters and the Jamiesons, the more he hated what he was doing. The lust for money had gotten him into this, and now it wasn't worth it. It was bad enough that one Sister had already died. He didn't want any more bloodshed on his hands. He had to figure out a way to get out of this. But how?

CHAPTER 57

HARRY NOLEN & TUFF JENKINS – SQUAW RAVINE

The murky, orange setting sun sent long dark shadows across the east side of Jagged Rock, cloaking Billy Dunham, who kept watch atop his horse near the southern edge of the canyon wall. He'd seen Nolen approach in the far distance and had watched as the old man grew from a speck on the vista to a recognizable single rider with each gallop. Dunham, like the other men, had had enough of sitting under a rock, waiting. They all had money in their pockets and the craving for whiskey and women. He'd listened to the men from Manitou bitch about not getting what was promised, and the big fella found it more and more difficult keeping them in order. Jenkins wasn't much better. His anger with Barry had manifested into questionable decisions, making things worse. Dunham wondered what Nolen would have to say. It had better be the truth, if he knew what was good for him.

"Evening Mr. Dunham," Nolen greeted the outlaw as he pulled up his horse.

"Nolen. Jenkins is waitin' for ya," Dunham answered with a nod toward the large break in the rock wall.

Nolen stepped down from his horse as a shock of nervousness shot through his body. Images of Mrs. Jamieson, the Sisters, and Donovan flew around his head like a flock of quail. His head began to spin. He didn't like spying on good people. He didn't know what to do or what to say.

"Nolen!" Jenkins's voice crushed his thoughts like a rambling longhorn. "Well? What the hell's happening in town?" Jenkins barked.

"I don't think you should go into Range, Mr. Jenkins. The army hasn't left and there's plenty of deputies all around," Nolen lied.

The men gathered around Jenkins and Nolen. "The army's still there huh?" Jenkins asked.

"Yes, sir. The U.S. Marshal and Texas Ranger are still there, too," Nolen advised.

"Hear that, Elmer? Seems like the army's stickin' around," Jenkins called out.

Elmer Pierce pushed his way through the men to Jenkins's side, looking hard at Nolen. Nolen's eyes widened, and he began to sweat profusely, despite the cool November air. Nolen had seen Pierce around Range, but hadn't given him any thought. Nolen looked at Jenkins whose dark eyes narrowed into snake-eyed slits.

"Strange. Elmer here says that the army pulled out, and the Marshal's deputies are nothing more than ranch hands from the Double O. I understand Marshal Dodson is also a ranch hand. As for Deputy Marshal Luxton Danner, and Texas Ranger Wes Payne, I reckon even they're not good enough for a surprise attack by a dozen men. They'll be more worried about townsfolk getting killed than anything else," Jenkins stated. "I had a bad feelin' about you, so I had Elmer go check on things. Sure enough, you failed me, Nolen. Why?"

Nolen stood silent, knowing anything he said wouldn't matter. "You're wrong, Jenkins. Danner and Payne are good enough for this bunch of crap you've assembled," Nolen responded defiantly before reaching for his gun.

Crack! A single shot from Jenkins's forty-five knocked Nolen onto his back. Nolan fired a shot straight into the air before his gun fell to the ground. The big man bent down and grabbed Nolen by the hair. "He's dead," he confirmed, letting Nolen's head bang against the rocky ground.

Jenkins holstered his gun.

"Get ready. We'll leave just after dark. They won't expect us tonight," Jenkins said, before turning to retrieve his gear from the cave.

A short time later, Jenkins tied his gear to his horse and called for Pierce, Dunham, Shorty, Miller, Sooner, and Bates to meet him near the fire. Jenkins drew a diagram of Range into the dirt floor of the cave. Using his buffalo knife, he began to etch locations of buildings as best he could remember.

"Pierce, let me know if this is right. We'll cross the river at the ford near the freight yard. Dunham, you take Sooner and break open the gates. They'll be locked by the time we get there. See what's in the yard. Take anything we can use. Here across from the freight yard is the restaurant and hotel. Shorty, you take a couple men with you, and get the money from the hotel. It's probably in a cash box in the kitchen somewhere. Bates, you and a couple of your men take the store. It's right here," Jenkins pointed, looking at Pierce who nodded in agreement. "Dunham, start a fire in the freight yard, and any other buildings you can reach quick. Me and Miller will ride to the meeting house, and get the stash there. Miller, you stay with me. We'll take one of your Manitoba men, big man. He'll watch the front door, kill anyone who tries to get in. We'll burn the place as we're leave'n. The rest of you will ride the street covering us. They'll be shootin' by then. If we git time, we'll hit the gunsmith shop and livery as we're ridin' out of town on the east side. Everybody got it?" Jenkins asked.

"What about Barry's daughter?" Dunham asked.

"Leave her. I don't give a damn about her. Barry wants her so bad he can come get her himself. Understand?" Jenkins asked.

Everyone nodded. Jenkins looked toward the sky. The sun had set, and the sky was clear and black.

"Good, almost a full moon. No trouble seein' our way to the river," Jenkins announced as he kicked dirt into the fire, and joined the men who were already mounted and ready. The horses shuffled and snorted. The big man looped Nolen's gun belt over his head and shoulder so that his gun was against his chest. Shorty looked at him.

"He don't need it anymore!" The big man shouted before snapping his reins and charging into the darkness behind the rest of the marauders. Shorty smiled and took a quick look around camp. Nothing left but Nolen's body laying right where it fell. He spurred his horse and disappeared into the night.

CHAPTER 58

RANGE

Mary Fields lit the oil lamp hanging from the front porch of her boarding house and sat down in one of the hefty weathered rocking chairs that adorned the long front entryway of the house. The cool night air engulfed her like a brisk hug. She looked down at her once-white apron, now marked with an array of different colored stains, and brushed off bits of food each falling onto the wooden floor at her feet. *I'll need to sweep those up before the ants come*, she thought.

The sound of pots and dishes clanking inside brought a smile to her face. The Sisters had been an enormous help since their arrival, insisting on helping with meal preparation, and cleanup.

A young, shapely woman of thirty, Mary Fields had been widowed two years earlier when her husband, ten years her senior, died while chopping wood for the winter. He had managed to build the boarding house, only the fifth building in Range at the time, but had grown ill in the process. Without the money to go back to Tennessee, she remained, and made the best of her fate. A few passing cowhands had shown interest in her, but she had declined their advances. While becoming a strong business woman, she'd begun to miss the comfort and security that a husband provided.

The hinges on the door squeaked like a mouse caught in a corner. Deacon David stepped out. "May I join you, Mrs. Fields?" the clergyman asked.

"Certainly," she replied.

"It feels like a beautiful night is in store," the Deacon added.

"Yes, it does. I'm awfully grateful to the Sisters for allowing me to enjoy a few minutes of this," she said.

"Now that there's less to do at the church, they enjoy helping around the boarding house," Deacon advised.

"The town looks forward to the time when we can have service there," she stated.

"As do we," the Deacon replied, lighting a pipe.

"I'm so sorry about Sister Sarah," Mary Fields belatedly stated.

"Yes. It was a tragic end to a promising young life," the Deacon answered, sucking pipe smoke deep into his lungs before sending a blue cloud of smoke up above his head. "Will that nice, handsome Marshal be visiting this evening?" David asked, with a smile of approval.

"Oh, I hope not! The way I look tonight, he'd be mighty disappointed!" she exclaimed.

"Nonsense! I can tell he sees beyond simple appearances. At least when it comes to you, Mrs. Fields," he offered.

Mary Fields blushed in the glow of the oil lamp. She felt her face turn warm against the brisk air. She hoped the Deacon wouldn't notice. She looked forward to Lane Dodson's visits, few as they were. They began as routine checks on her and her guests, after she witnessed the Lewis boy's wagon come into town but had become more personal over the last few visits. He begun to stay longer and wanted to learn more about her. She'd shared the story of her husband's death and her choice to stay and run the boarding house herself. Subsequent visits had him first shaking, then kissing her hand. He'd not let it go farther than that. She admitted she found him charming, in a roughneck sort of way.

Sister Dolores stopped Mary's reveries in their tracks. "Excuse me,

Mrs. Fields. The dining room and kitchen are clean. Is there anything else we can do for you?" the Sister asked.

Mrs. Fields stood, and removed her apron. "Would you be a dear and hang this in the kitchen next to the cupboard?" she asked.

"Yes ma'am. If you need anything further, we'll be in Sister Mary's room for evening Bible," Sister Dolores advised, before disappearing into the house.

Mary Fields had a charm about her most folks couldn't elucidate. A tall woman with a shapely figure and large brown eyes, she possessed an unpretentious beauty not lost on the people she encountered. She ran her hands over her long skirt attempting to smooth out the day's wrinkles as best she could, then unpinned her dark brown hair letting it fall below her shoulders. She looked at Deacon David. The two paused without expression, then broke into simultaneous laughter.

"I think I'll retire to my room. Just in case," the Deacon said with a wink.

Mary leaned back and closed her eyes. She listened to the sounds of the cattle penned up not far away, and the drifting piano music in the distance at the Red Dirt Saloon. A coyote howled beyond the pens its long-drawn cry sounding lonely and lost. Clank! The sound of a heavy boot heel reverberating across the long wooden floor planks swept her back to reality. She let out a frail cry and her body jolted.

"Pardon me, ma'am! I didn't mean to startle you," Dodson said, standing at the end of the porch, hat in hand.

"That's quite all right, Mr. Dodson. I was just resting."

"If everything's all right, I'll just leave you with your thoughts then," Dodson said.

"No, no, please sit down," she insisted, unconsciously pulling on her dark blue prairie skirt in an attempt to be as presentable as possible.

Dodson stepped forward, pulling the rocking chair Deacon David had vacated closer to the house's proprietor. He peered at Mary, who seemed to radiate in the soft light of the oil lamp.

"Everything okay at the Marshal's office?" Mary asked, noticing he was gazing at her like a boy would at a candy jar.

"I'm sorry, I guess I don't know what to say this evening," the embarrassed Marshal admitted.

Mary smiled. "Is this a personal visit, Mr. Dodson? If it is, I'm glad it is," she assured the uncomfortable cowboy as the wrinkles on Dodson's brow vanished with a smile.

"It's as much of a personal visit as it can be, me being Marshal and all," he chuckled.

"Well, I want you to know that I enjoy your company and you're welcome at any time," she offered.

"Thank you. If I weren't in the middle of this bandit mess, if I had more time, I'd—"

"I understand. You have much more to worry about than me and this boarding house," Mary said through a wide smile.

Dodson stood and put his hat on keeping eye contact with Mary.

"No ma'am, there isn't," he assured her before leaving.

Cody Roberts had just settled an argument between two cowboys over a poker hand misunderstanding, making his way to the bar where another cowhand had just endured a stiff slap in the face by one of the girls. It was almost ten o'clock, and the Red Dirt Saloon had cleared out some but was still full-up with boisterous patrons much to the delight of Donovan, who intercepted the determined deputy.

"It's okay, Cody, she knows how to handle the cowhands," Donovan said, not wanting to lose a paying customer.

Cody stopped, nodded, then returned to his post in the corner of the saloon. Having caught a glimpse of the deputy's actions, the girl gathered up the bottom of her red, satin dress, and swiftly moved through the crowd to her would-be champion, where she placed a soft kiss on his forehead before continuing on in one motion to a nearby poker table.

Cody Roberts, all of twenty years old, had become a top ranch hand and good gun, but other than his mother, he'd never been that close to a woman before. He slowly rubbed his forehead smearing lipstick into a bright crimson streak.

Deputy Bo Hatten pushed through the hastily repaired swinging doors of the saloon and took a quick look around. He spotted Roberts sitting on a tall bar stool in the opposite corner of the room, and slowly made his way through the labyrinth of tables, chairs, and humanity, pausing at each table hosting a game. Poker and dominos were the games of choice on this night, which appeared to be all in order.

"Evenin' Cody, I'll take over here. Go get ya some dinner," Hatten instructed his junior partner.

Cody, stood, donning his hat and coat when Hatten stopped him. "What ya got on yer face, kid?" Hatten asked, failing to hold back a grin.

"What? I don't know?" Cody replied sheepishly.

"A little bonus from the ladies?" Hatten asked, laughing hard.

Cody pulled on his hat and hurried over to a mirror hanging on the back wall. A quick glance confirmed the kiss, which he quickly wiped off with a dirty shirt sleeve. He looked back at Hatten who was still laughing. He grinned at the noticeable conquest. Hatten saluted shaking his head. Cody stood straight and marched out of the tavern like a soldier who'd just been awarded a medal.

Rebecca and Chance sat on the front porch swing at the Purple Sage Hotel watching the night's activities pass by. Mrs. Conrad had given Rebecca a break from her duties after she'd noticed Chance alone on the porch, even though they were busy with a full house in both the restaurant and the hotel. The Conrads hadn't seen this kind of money since they had built the hotel. After some lean times, they were finally beginning to see a reward for their efforts.

Mr. Conrad counted another two hundred dollars, placing the bundle inside his new safe in the storage room. He spun the combination dial and checked his pocket where he had written down the combination numbers, fearing he'd forget them. He unfolded the small paper. Eleven, nine, fifteen. He ran through the numbers out loud a few times, then returned the paper to his pocket, before returning to the kitchen.

Danner and Payne had informed Dodson that they'd stand watch until midnight. Payne took a position up on the balcony of the hotel while Danner remained at the Marshal's office at the other end of town. This way, they had eyes on the entire street from the pens to the west of the freight yard, to the black abyss of the valley to the east.

Danner figured any raid on the town would come from the valley, or the ford on the river near the docks. From his elevated position, Payne saw most of the town, although he'd have to lean far over the railing on the west side of the hotel in order to see the docks along the riverbank.

"Marshal Danner, that you?" Benson asked the shadowy figure sitting in the darkness on the porch of the Marshal's shed.

"It is, Mr. Benson. Come on over," Danner said.

"I wasn't certain in the dark," Benson explained taking a seat on the round stool opposite Danner.

"I thought it better to keep the light out. I'd be a sitting duck propped under an oil lamp," Danner stated.

"You're always thinking Marshal, always thinking. That's why I'd never make a good lawman. I don't think about those things," Benson admitted.

"I'm sure Mr. Dodson told you about the money we have over at the meeting house?" Benson inquired.

"Yes, sir, he did. You have it locked in a safe I don't know about?" Danner asked.

"Well, it's locked up, all right. The safe I ordered hasn't arrived yet, but it's secure in a big oak bureau equipped with two good locks. The room is also locked. Deputy Dutton is over there now, keeping watch," Benson advised.

"Good. Sounds like this town could use a bank," Danner suggested.

"You're absolutely correct, Marshal, but banks are very expensive to build, and Range is just now beginning to bring in that kind of money. I've asked the county for assistance, but Hardeman is a young county, still growing. The surrounding ranches are doing well from what I understand. Hopefully, we'll be able to build a bank very soon. Until then, I do the best I can," Benson explained.

Danner shifted in his chair, the wooden legs creaking under his weight, but said nothing.

Benson stepped into the street. "I'll be down at the hotel for a late dinner. Thank you again Marshal. It's good to have you here," Benson said, walking away without waiting for a response.

I hope you don't have anything to thank me for, Danner thought shifting in his chair again.

CHAPTER 59

The moon lit up the prairie floor, which had dried quickly from the drenching rains, thanks to the steady brisk wind. The firm ground and lighted path allowed Jenkins and his bunch to move near gallop speed. The rumble of the horse's hooves spooked an occasional jack rabbit or javelina, but nothing stood in the way of the raiders.

In less than an hour, the town of Range wouldn't know what hit them. Most wouldn't even see what happened, choosing to keep hidden inside their homes, tents, and shacks. Only the brave and foolish would try to bring Jenkins and his raiders down. Thoughts of triumph ran through Jenkins's mind, bringing a smile to his whisker-framed lips. Up ahead, Elmer Pierce slowed his horse. Jenkins raised his right hand and waved back toward his men. The line of riders all took the heed and slowed their mounts. Jenkins caught up to Pierce.

"Gettin' close to the river. They may have a lookout at the ford. Should keep quiet from here on in," Pierce advised.

Jenkins nodded, then turned to the rest of the men passing the word to stay quiet. The riders fell back into single file. Thirty minutes later, they gathered on the north side of the river stroking their horses' necks and manes in order to keep them quiet.

"Okay, everyone know their job?" Jenkins asked.

The men mumbled and nodded in agreement.

"All right, Billy, you and Jake go first. The freight yard is just across the river on the right. The hotel is on the left after the freight yard. Move!" Jenkins ordered.

Billy Dunham and Jake Sooner waded across the shallow water with Shorty and two Manitou men close behind. Jenkins led the rest of the raiders through the lazy river. Dunham and Sooner calmly rode up to the wide freight yard gates, and quietly dismounted. Dunham removed a small pry bar from his saddle, and tucked the end into the large lock. He and Sooner grabbed the opposite end, and heaved downward with all their strength. Pop! The lock broke from its bolts.

Wes heard the popping sound around the corner. He leaned around the edge of the hotel's second floor to see two men pulling on the gates. A quick look below onto the side street brought his Winchester to his shoulder. He saw a line of riders move down the middle of the street right in front of the hotel's restaurant. Unsure who they were, Wes held his fire. Three men turned onto Main toward the front of the hotel. Wes looked back at the lead rider, who pulled his gun and fired into the air.

Crack! Crack! Crack! Crack! Gunfire erupted. The men charged forward onto Main Street yelling and firing their guns. Crack! Wes fired, blasting a hole in the second rider's chest, knocking him off the saddle. One of the Manitou men's raid ended before it began. He'd not make it to guard the front door of the meeting house.

Wes fired again, and again, Crack! Crack! The raiders returned fire, sending a fusillade of bullets into the second floor wall and railing of the hotel. Splinters of wood exploded into the air all around Wes. He rolled to his left onto the balcony floor. Bullets smashed into the underside of the balcony. Wes jumped to his feet and ran to the opposite side of the ledge. He leaned over and fired at raiders in the street. Thump! Another raider hit the ground.

That's two! Wes thought as he dove though the open window into his room as bullets blasted through the balcony's floorboards.

———————

Dodson grabbed Mary from her chair, then shielded her with his body as he tried to open the door to the boarding house. Thump! Thump! Dodson opened the door and pushed Mary inside before falling into the threshold with two bullets in his back.

"No! Please no!" Mary screamed, clutching Dodson's hands. She pulled as hard as she could. Bullets hit all around the door and on the floorboards of the porch. Jenkins jumped from his horse, landing on his feet at the boarding houses steps. He stepped up, and stood over Dodson's body, looking down at Mary, who'd stopped pulling, and was on her knees fighting back tears. Deacon David came running down the hallway and froze. Crack! A single shot from Jenkins's pistol sent the Deacon sprawling. The nuns screamed in fear further down the hall.

Jenkins looked at Mary. "Get up! Get up now!" Jenkins ordered.

Mary rose, staring down the barrel of the outlaw's gun.

"Get me the cash box now!" Jenkins ordered cocking his pistol.

Mary's vision blurred. Her hearing dulled. She saw the huge circle of the gun barrel and a voice yelling something she couldn't understand. Everything moved in slow motion. She could hear herself breathing.

"I said get me the cash box now!" Jenkins ordered again.

This time, Mary heard the order, and staggered to the counter, where she tried to open the cabinet door. She pulled on the handle but it wouldn't budge. She'd forgotten it was locked.

Jenkins pushed her out of the way, sending Mary headfirst into the wall behind the counter. Crack! Jenkins shot through the feeble cabinet lock and removed the steel box. He then ran out the front door into the yelling, and endless gunfire.

Dunham and Sooner rushed through the freight yard, grabbing oil lamps from the front of the building. Sooner lit his lamp, and threw it into a mound of hay piled neatly in the corner of the yard opposite the loaded wagons. Fire erupted, sending flames high into the cool night air. The freight yard owner, Tom Wagner, heard the front door glass break. He grabbed his shotgun and pushed open his backroom door. Boom! Wagner pulled both triggers sending two barrels of buckshot into the big room. Boxes and cans blew off shelves.

Billy Dunham jumped up from behind the counter and fired. Crack! Crack! A bullet ripped through Wagner's right arm, sending his shotgun to the floor. Wagner slammed his door and locked it, then dove for his Colt on the night table. Dunham kicked opened the bedroom door. Wagner fired toward the opening, still blinded by the flash of his shotgun blast. Wagner's forty-five hit flesh in Dunham's right leg. Dunham fired wildly into the room then turned, emptied the cash register, before hobbling out of the building, where Sooner filled saddle bags with boxes of ammunition.

"I'm hit! Let's get the hell out of here!" Dunham yelled as he reached his horse.

The fire had spread to the north side of the freight building to an empty wagon near the hay.

Deputy McKinnon ran out of the Marshal's office as Danner charged toward the gunfire at the other end of town. Otto Wilhelm ran out of the stable, shotgun in hand.

"Get back inside! Get back inside!" Danner yelled toward the old stable keeper.

Another deputy, Bo Hatten, stepped through the doors of the Red Dirt Saloon frantically looking up and down the street.

"Raiders come'n down the street!" Danner hollered to the deputy. A bullet hit the trough in front of the telegraph office at Danner's feet. He dove behind the trough, and fired at the stampede of raiders heading right down Main. Bullets hit all around as McKinnon took refuge behind the corner of the telegraph office.

"What the hell's happening? How many of 'em are there?" McKinnon yelled out.

Crack! Crack! Crack! Crack! Bullets flew in every direction. Glass windows shattered; women screamed. Men ran for cover. Danner looked across the street and saw blacksmith Belton Tanner armed with a shotgun and pistol tucked inside the front of his suspender.

"Stay there!" Danner yelled over to the giant blacksmith, who waved acknowledgement.

Two raiders charged down the street randomly firing into buildings. Danner rolled back onto a knee and fired. Crack! Crack! Two shots, two hits. Both raiders flipped off their horses.

"Get to the meeting house! That's where they're headin'!" Danner called to McKinnon, who didn't hesitate. He bolted for Benson's barracks. As McKinnon cleared the corner of the telegraph office, a bullet ripped through his left hip spinning him to the ground. Another bullet kicked up dirt next to him. Crack! Crack! Crack! Danner fired both Russians dropping another raider in the middle of the street.

"Find cover! I'll be back for you!" Danner yelled to the fallen deputy.

McKinnon pulled himself under the porch of the telegraph office and checked his wound.

———

Wes reached the top of the hotel stairway, immediately met by gunfire. Bullets crashed all around the top step, shattering the once gleaming oak into a mash of kindling. Crack! Crack! Wes fired down the stairwell to no avail. Another round of bullets hit wood and ricocheted off the walls.

Damn it! I'm trapped! Wes thought, the anger about to explode inside him. He looked around, then ran to a back room door, kicked it open and made his way to the back window. As he thought. The

344 | JOHN LAYNE

window looked out over the roof of the restaurant, which was several feet lower than the hotel. This offered him an escape route.

Wes climbed out the window, and jumped to the roof below. A jolt of piercing pain shot through his right ankle. Wes rolled onto his side. He looked down and saw his right foot folded inward. He'd just broken his foot. He took a deep breath and paused. He heard the ruckus down below. He rolled his leg over and pulled down on his foot. Sweat billowed from his body. Then he gritted his teeth, and slammed his pistol down on the opposite side of his ankle. He snapped it back into place as best he could. The pain shot from his foot all the way to the top of his head.

That'll have to do, he thought.

Wes crawled to the edge of the roof and rolled off. He hit the ground, then jumped to his feet. The pain from his ankle caused him to drop to a knee. "Damn it! Get back in the fight!" he yelled aloud to himself, pulling both pistols.

———

The big raider from Manitoba kicked in what was left of the Jamieson General Store's front door, stepping inside, gun ready. He didn't see anyone. Two Manitou men followed, grabbing the cash box, and as much tobacco as each could carry.

"Get yer saddlebags!" He yelled to his men, slowly stepping into the back room. He lit a match and looked around. The pickings were great, but it was all too much to take with them. *Too bad*, he thought, before climbing the steps to what he figured would be the owners' room.

He reached the door at the top of the steps and tried to turn it but it was locked. He grunted, then kicked the door off its hinges. The door flew into the room crashing into a dressing mirror, sending shards of glass in every direction. He stepped into the dimly lit room.

"I know you're in here. Might as well come out now," the big man growled. He stepped forward next to the broken mirror.

"Over here, mister," Brad Jamieson announced, stepping out of the shadows in the corner of the room hands held high above his head. "I'm sure you've taken everything you wanted downstairs. Leave us be," Jamieson said, his voice shaking.

"Not everything. Where's your woman?" Bates snarled, before letting out a guttural laugh.

Squeezing a skinning knife with a two-handed death grip, Wanda Jamieson jumped from atop her dressing table and plunged the blade deep into the raider's neck just above his right shoulder before tumbling to the floor and scrambling to her husband's side.

The big man screamed, dropping his gun. He tried to grab the knife but couldn't reach the handle. The blade was buried to the bolster. He turned and stumbled down the stairs, falling at the landing. The other two raiders filled their saddlebags and headed for their horses when their boss hit the floor. He pushed himself up, and staggered through the store, leaving a bloody trail to the doorway where he caught himself. Blood filled his mouth, matting his black beard as he spit. Seeing the knife, both thieves ran to their horses and rode off. The injured outlaw tried to reach for the knife again, but his once powerful strength drained like the blood from his wound. He gulped a mouthful of blood, and collapsed on the planks spewing a red pool around his head.

———

Jenkins and Miller roared up to the meeting house, and jumped onto the porch. Bullets struck Jenkins's saddle and the support post to his left. He turned and fired back at Danner, who took cover on the corner of the telegraph office. Bo Hatten fired from across the street. Miller spun and fired, hitting Hatten in the head ending the deputy's fight.

Seeing Hatten fall, Danner charged toward Jenkins and Miller, both Russians firing. Crack! Crack! Crack! Crack! Two bullets hit Tad Miller, one in the chest, the other in the neck flipping the dead raider over a railing. Jenkins crashed through the front door of the meeting house. Danner ducked behind Miller's horse and paused.

Jenkins pulled an oil lamp from the entry table and smashed it in the doorway. Fire quickly spread across the entryway. Jenkins ran to the office and kicked in the door. The big bureau was locked. Frantic, Jenkins fired two rounds into the lock, then rushed out of the office, and saw a door near the back of the meeting hall. He ran toward it, crashing through the door into Lawrence Benson's room where the mayor hid next to his bed.

"Get up you fat bastard!" Jenkins yelled. Crack! Jenkins fired a shot into the wall just above Benson's head. "Unlock that damn cabinet! Now!" Jenkins demanded.

"I've forgotten where I put the key!" Benson screamed in a childish wail.

Crack!

"Don't shoot! Don't shoot! Oh God, my leg!" Benson moaned looking at his bloodied left leg where Jenkins bullet had blown a gaping hole. "The key is in the top drawer of my night table," Benson groaned.

Jenkins snatched the key and ran out past the fire, which crept toward the middle of the hall. He reached the door and froze.

Danner stepped from inside Benson's office, both Russians cocked and pointed at the outlaw. Jenkins took a step back and raised his hands belt high. He smiled.

"You must be that U.S. Marshal I heard about," Jenkins said calmly. "Or are you the Texas Ranger?" Jenkins asked.

Danner said nothing, just glared at the outlaw taking a step forward. The fire's flames sent dark shadows across the giant lawman's stone-cold face. Jenkins countered with another step back toward the flames that now burned black rings in the high ceiling behind him.

"I reckon it don't matter none, Marshal or Ranger. Ain't gonna shoot me now that I'm givin' myself up," Jenkins said through a thick grin.

"You're Milton Hicks, deserter, bank robber, and murderer," Danner broke his silence.

"Your mistaken, mister, name's Tuff Jenkins," he answered his grin fading fast.

"You're Hicks all right. Wanted dead or alive," Danner said. "Changing your name doesn't change who you are."

"Well, I guess you got me alive."

Crack! "Nope," Danner muttered. Danner's forty-five punched a hole in Jenkins's chest, knocking him back into the rim of the fire. Jenkins gasped and reached for his gun. Danner stepped on his hand before he could pull it. Jenkins looked up at the tall gunslinger.

"Just who the hell are you anyway?" Jenkins blurted.

"United States Deputy Marshal Luxton Danner."

Jenkins eyes narrowed, then grew wide. "You any kin to Landon Danner?" Jenkins's question faded.

Danner knelt and grabbed the dying outlaw's vest. "What do you know about Landon Danner?"

The outlaw's eyes rolled, and he spewed a bloody laugh. Then died.

Danner pulled the body away from the fire, and went to Benson's room where he found the town's leader unconscious and bleeding badly. After tying a belt around Benson's leg, Danner carried the wounded man out the back door. After removing Benson from the burning building, Danner returned into the meeting house to grab Jenkins's body before it burned with the rest of the building.

Just as Danner dropped the body on the street, two raiders charged past, trying to escape further gunfire. Boom! Both raiders crashed to the ground. Belton Tanner popped open his shotgun and loaded two fresh shells, then waved at Danner. Sporadic gunfire still sounded on the west end of town. Danner made his way toward the Jamieson's store.

Wes looked through a small back window into the restaurant's dining room. Several townsfolk lay on the floor, hands over their heads in an attempt to shield themselves from gunfire. Two men, guns drawn, stood in the middle of the room. He couldn't see if there were any other gunmen, but he figured there were. The two in the dining room were only guards. The others would be in the back getting the cash box. Wes heard footsteps. He turned, guns ready.

"It's me, McKinnon." McKinnon limped over to Wes and leaned against the wall holding his side. Wes saw blood soaked through McKinnon's trousers.

"Get down. You're no good like that," Wes whispered.

"Yes, I am. I saw four go in. How many you see?" McKinnon asked.

"Two guards in the dining room," Wes answered.

"Wait until I get around front. I'll go in and head to the back room. You get the two in the dining room then come double-quick," McKinnon ordered moving around to the front of the hotel before Wes could argue or tell him about his broken foot.

Wes waited, then heard McKinnon fall on the front steps. The thump drew the guard's attention to the front door. Wes crashed through the side door, rolling over onto his knees and fired. Crack! Crack! Crack! Both raiders fell to the floor, dead.

The two remaining outlaws turned toward the dining room. "Jake, you stay here. Any more shootin', kill 'em," Shorty ordered.

Sooner turned his pistol on Mrs. Conrad, Rebecca, and Chance, who were all lined up against the wall.

Mr. Conrad, on his knees fumbled with the safe combination, having forgotten the sequence of the numbers in his panic. "No! Don't shoot! I remember the combination!" Mr. Conrad shouted at Sooner.

"Elmer, you out there?" Shorty called into the dining room. "Jake, you go around the other way. See who's out there. I'll watch from here," Shorty ordered.

Sooner hurried through the back room out the door – Crack! McKinnon fired point blank, killing Sooner instantly. McKinnon rushed into the back room, where Shorty turned and opened fire on his hostages. Crack! Crack! Crack! Mac McKinnon used the rest of his strength to throw himself in front of a screaming Mrs. Conrad and Rebecca. Bullets punctured McKinnon's back. Chance grabbed the deputy's gun and pulled the trigger.

Shorty collapsed onto Mr. Conrad. Wes rushed in looking for more.

"That's all! Just us!" Chance informed the Ranger.

The pounding sound of boots hitting the porch reached to the bloodied back room. Danner and Cody Roberts appeared in the doorway.

"One of the deputies has another holed up in the barber shop," Danner advised.

"Let's go," Wes said trying to hide his limp.

"You hit?" Danner asked Wes.

"No, busted ankle, I'm all right," Wes assured his fellow lawman.

"I'm goin', too," Chance announced.

CHAPTER 60

Danner, Wes, Chance, and Roberts stepped into a chaotic scene on Main Street. The fire brigade arrived at the meeting house to salvage what was left of the building. Doc Phillips and Betsy set up a make-shift hospital in the Red Dirt Saloon with most of the town's women lending a hand.

"Spread out, this ain't over yet," Danner instructed his men. They made their way across the street to the front of Charlie Wilson's barber shop, where Tom Dutton stood over a crippled and bleeding Dunham in the doorway.

"Hello Marshal. Near as I can figure, this-here is the last of 'em," Dutton explained.

Danner stepped up onto the boardwalk and looked down at the outlaw. "Jasper Wilson," Danner said flatly to the man who'd been going by the name Billy Dunham.

"Howdy, Marshal," the outlaw answered. "You remember me, huh?" he added.

"I remember you," Danner said.

"How many of you were there?" Danner asked.

"I need a doctor. Been shot in both legs," the outlaw said.

"How many?" Danner asked again, this time more forcefully.

"I don't know what yer talkin' 'bout, Marshal," the outlaw defiantly declared.

Danner took a stride forward and stepped on the outlaw's bullet-riddled left leg causing the man to writhe and scream in pain. Danner leaned with all his two hundred forty-five pounds, sending a stream of blood onto his boot.

"Okay! Okay! Stop!" The outlaw shouted.

Danner eased off.

"Thirteen, no fourteen! Fourteen with that Pierce fella," the man groaned.

"Elmer Pierce?" Dutton asked.

"That might have been his name, I don't know. Jenkins had him join us tonight," Dunham admitted through clenched teeth.

"Excuse me, gentlemen," Sister Mary interrupted the interrogation.

"Yes, ma'am," the lawmen answered in unison.

"Marshal Dodson has been shot and Deacon David killed at the boarding house," Mary calmly announced.

"Is Dodson alive?" Danner asked.

"Yes, the Marshal was still alive when they took him over to the doctor." Sister Mary advised.

"Anyone else hurt at the boarding house?" Wes asked.

"Mrs. Fields was badly beaten. She injured her head, but I believe she's okay," Sister Mary stated. "Me and the other Sisters will assist the doctor," Mary said.

"I need a doctor!" the outlaw shouted.

Danner looked at the bleeding raider, then cocked his Russian.

"Danner," Wes called to his partner.

"Okay, Wes, we'll do it your way," Danner answered in a low voice.

Danner looked at Dutton. "Deputy, you stay here with him. We'll go see what else happened," he ordered.

Dutton nodded. The rest turned their attention to Main Street. The flames at the meeting house turned the dark sky a bright orange.

"Wes, that ankle good enough to allow you and Ben to take the other side of the street?" Danner asked.

"Sure enough," Wes replied, then he and Chance started for the feed store and freight yard. Danner and Cody took a look into the stage office, which by some miracle, hadn't been disturbed, then continued on to Mrs. Fields's boarding house where they found the front door shot to hell, and a fair amount of blood on the threshold and in the hallway.

"All right, let's get over to the store. It didn't look good when we passed by," Danner stated.

Danner stepped up onto the boardwalk in front of the store, and took a close look at the big, bearded man lying dead in the doorway. Danner grabbed a huge handful of hair and pulled the man's head up in order to take a good look at his face. "You recognize him, Cody?" Danner asked his young partner.

"No, sir," Cody answered, then pointed into the store at Mr. and Mrs. Jamieson, who were descending the stairs. They looked pretty beat up, but alive.

Danner placed his hand on Mrs. Jamieson's shoulder and patted her back with his fingertips.

"She'll be okay after a while," her husband confidently said.

"I have no doubt. We'll clear out your doorway," Danner advised, before nodding toward Cody. Danner then grabbed the dead Manitou leader by the gun belt, and in one smooth motion, he tossed the big man over his shoulder like a sack of flour. Without a word, he walked to the meeting house, which was now a smoldering ruin over at least half the building. Danner threw the dead man's body down next to the others.

"Looks like we saved the right side of the building," Belton Tanner announced.

"The office, papers, and money were spared," Jacob Turner added.

"I took Benson over to the saloon so Doc could fix up his leg," Tanner advised as the men crossed the street, headed towards the saloon. Otto Wilhelm waved the all okay before returning into the livery stable.

The Red Dirt Saloon had been transformed into an infirmary, with tables pushed against the walls, and chairs piled in the middle looking like kindling for a bonfire. Doc moved from table to table checking on the injured, blood stains covering is vest, with Betsy and a couple of Sisters at his heels.

Danner scanned the room to see Wes sitting in a chair with his foot propped up on a table in the far corner. Mrs. Fields, donning a white bandage around her head, stood next to Lane Dodson, who was face down on two tables with two large, blood-soaked bandages on his back. Benson sat nearby, his leg wrapped tight. Danner recognized several other men from town. Men ushered in others who'd fallen victim to the fires. Some were burned, while others appeared to have various cuts and wounds from falling debris.

"Is it over, Marshal?" Mike Donovan asked, handing shots of whiskey to Danner and Cody.

Danner nodded. "I believe it is, Mr. Donovan," he added, as he looked behind the bar, where he saw Rebecca and Mrs. Conrad sitting on tall stools. Rebecca stared off into nothing.

Mrs. Conrad looked at Danner, put her arm around Rebecca, and squeezed. "We're okay," she said, Danner reading her lips, unable to hear above the clamor in the room.

Danner walked over to Dodson and Mary Fields. "What the hell happened?" Dodson asked, turning his face from the tabletop.

"Jenkins and his men," Danner answered.

"How many were there?" Dodson asked wincing at the question.

"We counted fourteen," Danner replied.

"Any get away?" Dodson asked.

"Nope," Danner answered simply.

"I heard we lost McKinnon and Hatton," Dodson said.

Danner nodded. "The Deacon, too," Danner advised.

"Sorry I let you down, they got me quick," Dodson said, his voice gravelly. He laid his face back on the table and closed his eyes.

"Don't you dare apologize!" Mary Fields shouted. "It was me, Marshal! He saved me and got himself shot!" she said, her voice thick with emotion. She grabbed her bandaged head, starting to tip over to one side.

Danner caught Mary just as she lost her balance. "Get her a chair," Danner told Cody, who'd not left his side.

Cody retrieved a chair from the kindling pile and set it next to Mary. Danner guided her into the chair then nodded at Dodson's back.

"How bad is it?" he asked.

"Doc said I was lucky. The bullets hit on an angle, so they didn't get anything important," Dodson said with a faint smile. "Hurts like hell though," he added.

Danner managed a brief smile, then moved on to Benson, who for the first time Danner could remember, sat quietly, arms crossed at his chest.

"You gonna walk again?" Danner asked the Mayor.

"Thanks to you, Marshal," Benson said, reaching out to shake Danner's hand in thanks. "You also, young man," Benson added shaking Cody's hand, as well. "This is exactly what we were afraid of, Marshal. But, because of you, Ranger Payne, and the deputies, I believe Range has served notice to outlaws that we won't bow to their lawless ways," Benson exclaimed with as much vehemence as he could muster.

"This town might have bowed, but it damn sure didn't break, Mr. Benson. There were good people here before this. Now, they'll be better people after it," Danner declared before making his way to Wes.

"Marshal!" A voice called out to Danner as he passed. Danner paused, noting the familiar face, but unable to put a name with it.

"Tom Wagner, freight yard operator," he reminded Danner as he shook the Marshal's hand. "They got me in the arm, but I put one back in his leg. I hope you got the son of a bitch," Wagner stated.

"What'd he look like?" Danner asked.

"Average sort, short, brown hair, shaven, with tan pants, and dark brown or black shirt, as I recall," Wager recounted.

Danner thought a moment, then he tipped back his head, and looked at Wagner with raised eyebrows. "We have a deputy watching him over at the barber shop. Seems that bullet you put in his leg kept him from doing much after. I reckon the deputy shot him in the other leg, and put him down," Danner stated. "Well done," he added, as he continued over to Wes, who sat leg-up in a receiving line of well-wishers.

"How's the ankle,?" Danner asked.

"Now that I'm just sittin' here, it hurts like a bitch," Wes laughed.

"It also looks twice the size of your other one," Danner observed.

"Yep. Doc says it'll be like that for a week or so. Says it was dislocated, but I popped it back into place. He says he could use me as an assistant," Wes said wryly.

"Where's Chance?" Danner asked.

"Where'd ya think?" Wes asked, nodding toward the bar.

Danner followed Wes's nod to see that Chance had joined Rebecca and Mrs. Conrad behind the bar.

"Well, he'll have to take a break from that, for a bit," Danner said.

"Oh, I don't know about that. Don't think she'll let 'em," Wes said through a wide grin.

"I'll see about that," Danner responded, strolling over to the trio.

"Chance, got a moment?" Danner asked.

"Sure," Chance answered, then followed the big Marshal to the front door.

"You good enough to lend a hand for a couple of days?" Danner asked.

"Yep. Shoulder's fine. What'd ya need?" Chance asked eagerly.

"Follow me," Danner said then walked straight to Dodson. "Marshal, I need you to swear in Ben Chance here as a deputy. You up to that?" Danner asked Dodson, who still lay face-first on the tabletop.

"Sure am. Raise your right hand. Huh. Hmm, do you give your word to uphold the law and keep the peace in the town of Range, County of Hardeman, State of Texas?" Dodson asked, turning his head to the side.

"Yes, sir, I do," Chance responded.

"Okay. I don't know if those were all the right words, but you're now a Range deputy Marshal," Dodson announced. "Oh, and that means taking orders from Marshal Danner here, for now," he added.

"Thanks. We'll see you later," Danner said to Dodson, tapping him gently on the top of his head.

Danner, Chance, and Cody headed for the door when they heard Wes's voice call out. "Where the hell you three goin'?" Wes said, quickly standing and trying to get his swollen foot inside his boot.

"You sit on that chair, and don't move, until Doc says you can!" Danner yelled at the Ranger. "I got enough problems with two green kids here. I don't need a one-legged Ranger limping around," Danner shouted to the delight of the folks in the saloon.

CHAPTER 61

D anner stepped out into the street. Dawn had broken on the eastern horizon. The far edge of the valley floor began to brighten as the sky shifted from ebony to auburn. A touch of the morning breeze sped through Range, twirling up a whiff of charred-timber aroma, the kind a campfire delivers at the break of dawn out on the trail. With the help of Belton Tanner, Danner and Cody Roberts brought the dead outlaws to the front of the meeting house where Mr. Brantley, the undertaker, began to arrange for burial.

The sun had peeped over the valley ridge, bringing a new day to Range. With the arrival of daylight, everyone who wasn't injured gathered around the dead outlaws lined up neatly in a row at the foot of the meeting house.

Some people yelled "Burn 'em!" As folks became angrier and more restless after the long night. "Let's hang 'em from trees along the river and show everyone what happens to outlaws in these parts!" A man called from the back of the crowd. People roared in approval at the gruesome recommendation.

Not a bad plan, Danner thought, then realized it was up to him to quell the group before they became a mob the lawmen couldn't handle. Danner stepped up onto what was left of the meeting house porch and raised his hands. The chatter subsided enough for him to speak. "Folks! Folks! Settle down. I know you're angry and you want revenge. I can tell you with confidence that all fourteen of the outlaws who came in last night were killed," Danner began.

A roar of approval flooded the street. Danner waved his hands gesturing for the crowd to quiet down. He continued, "I believe Range already showed what happens to outlaws who come here. At times like these, it's best to put your efforts into rebuilding the town as quickly as possible," Danner suggested.

A low rumble of chatter swept across the crowd. Then folks in the back began to separate, making way for Mayor Benson to limp through. After a few moments, and with the help of a makeshift cane, the portly Mayor took a position at Danner's side. Many of Range's residents applauded their wounded leader.

"Marshal Danner speaks righteous words! We repelled evil thanks to the brave lawmen we are so fortunate to have here in Range, and to the men and women who dowsed the fires and tended to the wounded," Benson's said, his boisterous voice carried up and down Main Street.

Loud applause erupted from the crowd, which had grown in size with the arrival of wagons and carriages from the outskirts of town.

"We will send word over to the towns of Margaret and Red River City, informing them of what occurred, as well as our urgent need for lumber and assistance to repair our town. Let's return to our businesses and get to work," Benson gasped, expending all of his remaining energy. He leaned heavily on his cane. The crowd began to break into groups, and disperse.

"Thank you, Mr. Benson. We certainly didn't want a ruckus on our hands," Danner said.

"Help Mr. Brantley, our undertaker, get these bodies out of here as quickly as possible," Danner instructed his deputies, who all nodded in approval.

Danner and Benson entered the meeting house, and made their way to Benson's office, which had miraculously been spared fire damage. Benson took a seat in his office chair and breathed a sigh of relief. "I see the town's money is safe, Marshal. Thank you," Benson said.

"I'm not sure what you have inside that cabinet, but it would be a whole lot safer in a bank," Danner said flatly.

"I quite agree. If you'll recall, I have a large safe ordered, but we'll need to construct a bank as soon as possible. There'll be no opposition after this," Benson mused.

Danner stood on the charred steps of the meeting house and saw a group of riders charging hard into town. He wasn't certain, but they had the look of Butch Henry's men from the Double O. He looked out toward the valley, and saw three more wagons approaching from the east. More settlers he figured. *Wait'll they get a look at the town. Might just keep on going*, he thought.

CHAPTER 62

Danner glanced out his window to see three heavily-loaded Studebaker wagons making their way down Main Street, no doubt on their way to the meeting house, where the sound of hammers and saws cut through the morning quiet. A week had passed since the raid on the town, and things had slowly returned to normal. It had been an extraordinarily peaceful week with no bar fights or drunken cowhands. Everyone had seemed to be dedicating themselves to repairing the town in their own ways. A couple of drifters had made a ruckus one night at the Red Dirt Saloon, but were shouted out of town before Danner or the deputies could even respond.

Danner splashed water on his face, grabbed his hat, then headed for the door. Stepping into the hall, he found Chance doing the same.

"Good morning," Chance said brightly.

"How's the shoulder?" Danner asked.

"Feeling better every day," Chance answered, allowing Danner to pass, then following the big Marshal down the scared oak staircase.

Rebecca stood behind the big desk, renting a room to a couple of well-dressed ladies. The men stopped to take in the sight, when Rebecca glanced over to see Chance ogling the women. "Can I help you, gentlemen?" Rebecca asked, glaring passed Danner toward Chance. Chance blinked, then tipped his hat. "I thought so," Rebecca said, smiling.

The two men quickly headed for the dining room, which appeared filled with the breakfast crowd. As usual, Benson waved to Danner and Chance, beckoning them to join him at his customary table. Danner tapped Chance on the shoulder, and nodded toward Benson.

"Good morning, gentlemen, please join us," Benson stated keeping his seat.

Danner and Chance joined Brad Jamieson, Charlie Wilson, and Jacob Turner. "How's Mrs. Jamieson?" Danner asked, as he took his seat next to Benson.

"Much better. She's become somewhat of a hero to the other ladies in town. That has helped her greatly," her husband advised.

"She's a brave woman," Benson chimed in.

"And the leg, Mr. Benson?" Chance asked getting into the conversation.

"Oh, fine, young man! Fortunately, Mr. Jamieson had a couple of hansom canes in his store. They were quick sales for me and Ranger Payne," Benson answered with a chuckle.

"How is Ranger Payne getting along, Marshal?" Charlie Wilson asked. "He was in for a haircut the day before yesterday. He seemed to be moving better," Wilson added.

"With the all the attention Mrs. Conrad has been showering on him, he ought to be doing quite well!" Danner said, allowing himself a rare smile.

"It's true! Mr. Conrad had better be careful of that Ranger!" Benson laughed aloud.

"What should Mr. Conrad be careful about?" Mrs. Conrad asked, smacking the burly mayor's shoulder from behind.

"Oh my! I'm in trouble now!" Benson exclaimed, laughing.

Mrs. Conrad poured coffee into cups in front of Danner and Chance. The events of a week ago had solidified relationships amongst the people of Range. Danner had seen this grow over the past week. He was grateful, since he was preparing to announce his departure.

While his job here had ended, the next leg of his task remained ahead with a two-day's ride east to Red River City. "Gentlemen," Danner began just as Wes limped into the restaurant, capturing everyone's attention.

"Mr. Payne! Please join us!" Benson said jovially to the Ranger, who gimped over to the table and took a seat. "Good morning sir, good morning," Benson said as Mrs. Conrad appeared out of nowhere to pour coffee for Wes and bring him two warm biscuits and honey.

The men around the table laughed. None of them received warm biscuits and honey with their coffees.

"I apologize, Marshal, I believe I interrupted you," Benson said, returning his attention to Danner.

"Gentlemen, I'll be leaving Range tomorrow morning, heading back to Fort Smith," Danner advised.

The mood at the table turned suddenly somber. "I suppose we all knew this day was coming, but it doesn't make the news any more palatable," Benson said, speaking for the others, who nodded in agreement.

"I'll be joining him," Wes announced.

Chance had wanted to go with Danner and Wes, but the decision had been made the night before, during a meeting with Dodson, Chance, and Cody Roberts. Torn between joining the two men he most admired, and his growing feelings for Rebecca, Danner had made Chance's decision for him. Danner and Wes would head to Red River City while Chance would remain in Range as a deputy Marshal until Dodson was back on his feet.

"Marshal, this town owes you and Mr. Payne a great deal," Benson stated looking around the table at his guests, who nodded in assent. "I'm sure you both know that you'll be welcome here any time you're passing by, and especially when you decide to settle down, we'd all be mighty grateful if you chose Range as your home," Benson said, his voice filled with emotion.

Danner stood, and placed a hand on Chance's shoulder preventing him from doing the same. "Chance will stay on as a deputy until

Dodson can take over again," Danner said, as if reminding Chance of their agreement.

The men exhaled a collective sigh of relief. Benson reached past Danner, and shook Chance's hand. "Glad to keep you, young man!" Benson said.

"We'll see you all later," Danner spoke for he and Wes as the two lawmen slowly made their way out of the restaurant.

"Where's that cane of yours, Ranger Payne?" Danner asked fighting back a grin.

Wes stopped in the middle of the street. "Look, Mr. U.S. Deputy Marshal, don't you start on me about no damned walkin' stick!" Wes said, his voice low.

Danner looked back at his partner. "I just never heard of a Texas Ranger needin' a cane, is all," Danner joked.

"I did use that damned thing a time or two the first couple of days!" Wes admitted, slapping Danner on the back as the two made their way down a sun-drenched Main Street. "It did help."

A short time later, Danner and Wes occupied their usual chairs propped against the front of the Marshal's shed watching the activity on the street as late afternoon turned to evening. Daylight faded fast, as cloudy November evenings do. Danner looked down Main to see a buggy heading their way. "Looks like Mrs. Fields is bringing a visitor," Danner announced.

Chance rode his horse alongside the one-horse lorry that Mrs. Fields allowed her guests to use during their stay. As the buggy drew closer, Danner and Wes recognized Dodson sitting next to Mary.

"Good evening, Marshal," Danner said as Mary brought the buggy to a halt in front of the shed.

"Danner, Wes, good to see you both," Dodson answered as he gingerly stepped out of the carriage.

"I tried my best to convince him to stay in bed, but he's as stubborn as an old mule," Mary began.

"I've never spent so much time in a bed in my life!" Dodson exclaimed, to rounding laughter.

Mary kept her seat in the buggy, watching Dodson navigate the low single step up onto the planked porch with a concerned expression on her face. Danner vacated his ladder-back and stepped aside, allowing Dodson to sit.

"I told him he could take fifteen minutes, then it's back to the house," Mary informed the men, as if ordering them to follow the instructions, too.

"She's worse than a trail boss!" Dodson said through a smile.

"Well, the good news is that the town has been pretty quiet this past week. Seems everyone is too busy to cause trouble," Wes chimed in.

"Yep, and the bad is that I hear you two are let'n out in the morning," Dodson answered.

"I reckon we will," Danner said flatly and without expression.

"When you'd plan on tellin' me?" Dodson asked, failing in an attempt to cross his arms over his chest.

"Oh, I figured I'd make my way down to see ya sometime this evening. Now I don't have to," Danner advised.

"It won't be the same around here without you two desperados," Dodson chuckled.

"We're leave'n ya in good hands," Wes said, nodding toward Chance, who rolled his eyes and shook his head.

"I'll see ya in the morning before ya go," Dodson said. Mary snapped the reins, turned the buggy around and headed back to the boarding house.

CHAPTER 63

Danner closed the hotel's big front door behind he and Wes, noticing Rebecca standing behind the desk.

"Evenin', ma'am," Wes said, removing his hat, before limping into the dining room.

"Could I speak to you, Danner?" Rebecca asked, before he could pass by.

"Certainly," Danner replied, letting Wes go ahead of him.

Rebecca wrapped a bright yellow shawl around her shoulders, and walked past Danner to the front door, where she disappeared onto the porch. Danner followed, finding her standing against the railing, under the soft glow of an oil lamp.

"What is it?" Danner asked.

"The talk around town is that my father was involved with those men who raided us. Is that true?" She asked, turning to look up at the big Marshal's face, a pained expression on her face.

Danner paused, peering into her concerned green eyes that held the flicker of the burning lamp. He said nothing for a few moments, turning his attention to a lone horse tethered to the hitching post across the street at the Red Dirt Saloon. He watched while the big paint dipped its nose in the trough, deciding whether it was worthwhile to take a drink.

"Tell me the truth," she pleaded. "I need to know."

"Yes, I believe he hired Jenkins to raid along the river to steal, and create fear among the townsfolk," Danner said plainly without looking away from the horse.

"Are you and Mr. Payne going to Red River City to get him?" she asked.

"It's our job," Danner answered, shrugging his shoulders.

"I understand. Can't say I'm really surprised. I knew something was wrong. Ever since my mother died, my father wasn't the same. We were never close. The most he talked to me was when he had me spy on people at the hotel. He rarely came home, and when he did, it was very late. He always had those men watching everyone and everything," she explained.

"I'm sorry it's come to this, Rebecca," Danner offered.

"It's okay. I'm never going back there again," she said. "There's your real family, then your chosen family," she said quietly.

Danner broke his gaze from the horse, and looked at Rebecca. She stepped close and wrapped her arms around him.

"Thank you for rescuing me from that awful place," she whispered.

It's surprising how a woman's touch can penetrate the most hardened of men. Danner returned the hug, such as he was capable of doing. "Ben Chance is a fine young man. Don't let him get away," Danner said in as fatherly a tone as he could muster.

Rebecca released her grip, and looked up into those steel blue eyes, and that stone face. "I won't," she smiled. "And, you promise me you'll come home safe," she said, making her allegiances perfectly clear.

"Home?" Danner said, surprised at the word, and how it meant so many things to him, but more to him now than ever before. A gust of wind swept across the two, flickering the oil candle as if breaking a spell. "Reckon we can go in now?" Danner asked.

Rebecca smiled, took Danner's hand, as they walked through the door of the hotel together.

CHAPTER 64

The next morning, Wes descended the oak stairway as quietly as he could, stumbling in the pre-dawn darkness. He saw a dim light casting a hazy shadow on the wall at the foot of the staircase. Working with one good foot, he clumsily made it to the bottom, dropping his saddle bags. Mrs. Conrad and Rebecca, still clad in their night gowns, stepped around the corner of the big hotel desk. Once more, Rebecca wrapped her arms around Wes, and said nothing, squeezing tightly. Wes returned the gesture.

"My turn," Mrs. Conrad whispered to Rebecca, who released her grip and turned away, so as not to let the Ranger see here tears. Mrs. Conrad hugged Wes briefly, then clutching his hands, she leaned back, and looked into the lawman's weathered face. "You take care of these hands, Ranger Payne. And, everything else attached to 'em. You hear me?" she asked.

"Yes, ma'am," Wes replied.

"That damn, stubborn Marshal snuck out before we could say goodbye, so tell him for us," she ordered.

"I'll tell him," Wes assured the women.

"You come back," Mrs. Conrad added.

Wes nodded, and tossed his saddlebags over his shoulder, then

368 | JOHN LAYNE

walked out of the hotel without turning back.

Although the wind had died down, the morning air felt frigid. As Wes passed Doc's place, the physician stepped outside. "Take care of yourself," Phillips quietly directed.

"See ya around, Doc," Wes said without breaking stride. He crossed First Street and passed the dark, silent Red Dirt Saloon. The smell of stale beer and whiskey clung to the open doorway guarded only by the crooked swinging doors that stirred ever so slightly.

Wes saw Danner walk both their horses toward him.

"For a minute, I thought I might actually get out here before you this morning, Marshal," Danner said, handing Ringo's reigns to Wes.

The two men saw an oil lamp ignite across the street at the meeting house. Lawrence Benson stood in the newly constructed meeting house doorway, lamp in one hand, cane in the other. Apparently by now, everyone knew the lawmen's penchant for starting out early. They slowly walked over to Benson, who remained on the porch, cane in one hand.

"Gentlemen, I'll make this short. Neither I, nor this building, and possibly this town, would still be standing if it weren't for the two of you. I know you had assistance, but no one will ever convince me that this town would have survived without the two of you. If there ever comes a time that either of you decide to settle down, I certainly hope you'll return to Range."

Benson leaned his cane against the rail and offered his hand to each lawman. "Be careful gentlemen. Jared Barry is no fool. He'll be waiting for you, surrounded by as many gunmen as he can hire. Your task there won't be easy, but I'd never bet against the two of you, no matter the odds," Benson said.

With that, the town official gathered his cane, turned, and disappeared inside the meeting house without a further word. Danner and Payne swung up on their horses. Darkness had begun to turn from black to gray, allowing a halo of golden light onto Range. The men paused briefly to take a final look around, then tapped their spurs, and headed east out of Range, and into the valley on their way to bring Jared Barry to justice, once and for all.

CHAPTER 65

Danner and Payne rode in silence through the valley floor, in no particular hurry. Faint rays of sunshine brought a hint of warmth to the valley. Danner took a quick look over his shoulder, then reined Bullet to the left, pushing the big bay stallion up the side of an incline. Wes silently followed Danner's lead. They stopped at the top of an overlook so they could take a final look at Range from a distance.

Just then, as if on cue, two riders stopped in front of the hotel and slid off their horses, taking their time tying them to the hitching post. One leaned forward, squinting down Main Street, watching two additional riders doing the same in front of the boarding house. Another two stopped across the street in front of the meeting house. All six men paused, shielding their faces with soiled bandanas, then loomed at the entrances of the respective buildings, opening the doors.

The doors at the hotel and boarding house were already unlocked, ready for business, but the newly hung door at the meeting house remained locked. The first lout drew his gun, reared back and kicked the meeting house door in, knocking it off its hinges. The other two duos dashed into their targets with their guns drawn.

Two bandits rushed into the meeting house, heading directly for the office. Crack! Crack! Crack! Bullets drilled both thieves before they got halfway to the office, dropping each to the floor. Ben Chance stepped out of the office doorway, the barrel of his Colt smoking.

The boarding house bandits crashed through the front door, the first rushing around the long desk, the second covering the hallway. Crack! Crack! Crack! Both would-be thieves tumbled backward, dropping in dead heaps. Lane Dodson slowly stood up behind the desk, immediately loading fresh cartridges into his Colt.

The final two outlaws busted past the big oak desk in the lobby of the hotel. Crack! Crack! Crack! Crack! The first outlaw squeezed off a wild shot that splinted the molding above Cody Roberts' head near the backroom. Remembering Ranger Payne's instructions, he quickly loaded four new cartridges into his pistol, and waited. He counted to ten, then slowly moved to the front door of the hotel and peered out. Chance stood on the boardwalk in front of the meeting house. Dodson stood in front of the boarding house, as well.

The gunfire woke most of the folks in town, and they began to flood the street, looking around in fear. Lawrence Benson joined Chance in front of the meeting house, patting the young deputy on the back. Cody strolled over to Chance and Benson, as did Dodson and Doc. Together, the men looked to the top of the north ridge of the valley, where they could just make out the figures of Danner and Wes, seated tall in their saddles, watching. Chance stepped forward, drew his gun, fired one shot into the air, then waved his Colt high over his head.

"Looks like they handled it," Wes broke the hilltop silence.

"They did," Danner answered.

The two gunslingers then turned their mounts and headed east down the hill toward Eagle Springs.

"I reckon we'll be in Eagle Springs about supper time. You gonna eat today?" Wes asked.

"Haven't decided yet," Danner said. "When the hell did you start worrying about whether I eat or not, anyway?" Danner asked, mildly irritated.

Wes mumbled an imperceptible response.

"What you mumbling about?" Danner demanded.

"Nothing, nothing at all," Wes answered with a grunt, before tapping his spurs on Ringo's haunches, picking up the pace.

"Look here, Ranger Payne, don't you start on me," Danner began, before busting out in laughter as the two rode on.

Back in town, the ruckus died down as everyone learned no threat remained.

"What happened, Marshal?" Belton Tanner asked Dodson on behalf of the crowd that had gathered around.

"Everything's all right now! There's no more trouble!" Dodson announced. "Yesterday, Marshal Danner recognized one of Jared Barry's men go into the Red Dirt Saloon along with five other men. Deputy Roberts kept an eye on them. Late last night, Marshal Danner and Ranger Payne met with several of us. They figured the men would wait until they left town, then the bandits would rob the meeting house, hotel, and boarding house. We were ready and waiting. Sure enough, the bandits did exactly what we thought they'd do. Marshal Danner and Ranger Payne are on their way to Red River City to arrest Jared Barry for sending these men here," Dodson explained.

"Excuse me Marshal–" Mr. Brantley, the undertaker, interrupted.

"Yes, Mr. Brantley, we have more business for you," Dodson informed the undertaker.

CHAPTER 66

LUX DANNER & WES PAYNE – RED RIVER CITY

D anner pulled up on the reins. He and Wes looked over the terrain on either side of the road into Red River City. Figuring Barry would have gunmen watching the roads leading into town, they had decided to find another way.

"We're about an hour, maybe less," Danner indicated.

"So, what's the plan," Wes asked.

"This road leads directly into town. The first building on the left is a bunkhouse where Barry's hired guns are. The mill, where Barry spends most of his time, is on the opposite end. There's a hotel, saloon, and store near the center of town. The livery is right across from the bunkhouse. There's a corral behind it."

Danner continued, "If we make our way through the brush behind the livery, we could leave the horses in the corral and move in on the bunkhouse on foot. That'd give us a chance to get the drop on whoever is in there. There's no jail that I recall, but there is a shed next to the bunkhouse I figure they use to lock up any troublemakers they don't kill. If we could take 'em without a fight, we can lock 'em up in the shed, and walk right through town to the mill and Barry," Danner explained.

"Sounds good. We'd need to go in from the south end then," Wes clarified.

"Yep," Danner nodded.

"Well, no time like now, I reckon," Wes said tapping his spurs.

Despite it being mid-November in North Texas, most of the ground scrub was alive and green. Because of this, their final approach behind the livery stable was met by a mass thicket of thatch, thorns, and sage with a fair number of prickly pear cactus catching occasional horse flesh. Danner and Wes dismounted and walked ahead of the horses, who did their best to stubbornly resist the forced march through the pickers.

After what seemed like an hour, the lawmen reached the edge of the thicket, to a cleared area adjacent to the corral. Three horses and a burrow occupied the four-rail pen, with a barbed-wire loop securing the gate. The far side of the street had plenty of activity, but the men didn't see anyone behind the stable or the blacksmith shop next door. Wes looked up at the sun, which had already passed its peak. "I'm thinkin' it's about three o'clock, or so," Wes surmised.

"This time of day, he'd have men all over town, unless he sent the rest to Range," Danner continued.

"No way of tellin' from here. Might as well do what we said we'd do, and see what happens," Wes said.

After they secured the horses in the corral, Danner and Wes walked out into the street to survey the scene. Wagons, buggies, horse, and foot traffic dotted the town. Danner pointed to a lone guard on the boardwalk in front of the bunkhouse. They had already drawn the guard's attention. He stood from his chair and adjusted his gun belt. They had to move now. Danner walked briskly straight to him, pulled his gun, and pushed the barrel into the guard's stomach.

"Unhook your gun belt and let it drop," Danner whispered into the guard's surprised face.

The guard dropped the belt, which Wes quickly snatched up.

"Now, how many men are inside, and I strongly advise you not to lie," Danner continued.

"One," the man answered quickly.

"We're going in, you first. I'll be right behind. If you do anything I don't like, I'll kill you. Got it?" Danner asked.

The guard nodded, then turned toward the door. He opened the latch and walked in, Danner's gun pressed against his back. Wes stepped around Danner, and drew down on the surprised guard, who was seated on a bench without his gun belt.

"Stand up slow. Any move I don't like and I'll kill ya," Wes warned.

The guard stood slowly, his hands raised. "Who the hell are you?" the guard asked.

"We'll ask the questions," Danner informed the guards in a low growl.

"How many guns does Barry have in town?" Danner asked.

"A dozen. You'll have no chance," the guard pressed against Danner's gun barrel replied.

"Try again. We already killed the twenty he sent to Range. He don't have a dozen more," Danner stated without emotion.

Neither guard spoke.

"Doesn't matter how many, you two won't be of any use," Wes said looking around the room, spotting a ring of keys hanging from a nail next to the front door. "Here's what's gonna happen. You're both gonna walk out of here, real easy like, and say nothing to anyone. You'll walk directly to that shed next to us, and go straight in. If either of you don't do what we say, neither of you'll live to know it. Understand?" Wes explained.

The two guards looked at each other.

"Now you see. I don't like that look in your eyes, mister," Danner said. "Get this, I don't care whose fault it is. If either of you flinch to our disliking, we'll kill both of you, and Barry isn't payin' you enough for that. Got it?"

Both men nodded. Danner grabbed the guard in front of him, and swung him around like a rag doll. Wes stepped aside, grabbed the keys off the nail, and motioned to the other with his gun. The second guard stepped behind his partner. Danner opened the door and stepped out, taking a quick look around. Nothing looked suspicious.

"Move," Danner ordered the men.

They walked out, and turned toward the shed. Danner kept his gun shielded by his arms. Wes kept his buried in the second guard's back. They walked to the shed, where the first guard opened the door and stepped inside, the second right behind, followed by Wes. Danner paused at the door, keeping watch up and down the street. He noticed two men, both armed, walking down the street heading toward them.

"Hurry up, Wes, we got company come'n," Danner announced.

Wes stepped out of the door and cycled through three keys before he found the right one that locked the door. Wes looked past Danner and saw the gunmen. "So much for sneakin' down to the mill, partner," Wes said.

"Yep," Danner answered.

"How do ya want to do this, Marshal?" Wes asked. "We don't have much time to make a decision."

"You're a Texas Ranger. Let's walk right up to 'em and tell 'em who you are. We'll tell 'em were looking for someone, and see what happens," Danner suggested.

"Good a plan as any, I reckon. Let's go," Wes said, pinning his Ranger badge on the outside of his coat, then heading toward the gunmen down the middle of the street.

The two gunmen slowed their approach and separated.

"You need a bigger badge," Danner said sarcastically.

"Good afternoon gentlemen! Wes Payne, Texas Ranger!" Wes announced loudly touching his badge.

The men paused, and took a quick look at each other, keeping their distance. Wes and Danner kept walking.

"They ain't goin' for it," Wes said.

"Nope, you got the one on the right," Danner advised.

Both gunmen stepped back and reached for iron. Wes and Danner cleared leather. Crack! Crack! Crack! Crack! Crack! Gunfire erupted from all four gunslingers. Danner's fell first, followed by Wes's on the right. Both lawmen quickly reloaded, as they approached the fallen gunfighters. Both were dead. People stopped, staring at Danner and Wes.

"I got a problem," Wes stated between gritted teeth.

Danner looked over to see Wes clutching his side.

"You hit?" Danner asked.

"Yep, caught one in the ribs," Wes grimaced.

"Son of a bitch!" Danner shouted. He pulled Wes's coat back revealing a blood-soaked bib shirt.

"Looks like you've ruined a good shirt, Ranger," Danner said attempting to lessen the severity of the wound.

People gathered around the duo, creating chaos.

"Look, he's a Ranger!" someone yelled.

"I'm a U.S. Marshal, there a doctor in town?" Danner asked.

"Yes, sir! Follow me!" a man shouted before turning to run up the street.

Danner started to help Wes, who shrugged and shook his head, indicating he didn't need assistance. They made their way to a small building next to the store where the doctor waited at an open door. Danner scanned the street looking for more of Barry's men. None came.

"Get him inside, mister," the man, ordered stepping aside. Danner ushered Wes to a table at the back of the room.

"You a doctor?" Wes asked, as he pulled his coat off, and slid up onto the table.

The man rolled up his sleeves and looked at the Ranger badge on Wes's coat. "Yes, sir, at least, I'm the best the town's got. Name's Alexander Boone," the doctor offered.

"Doc, I'm Luxton Danner and this is Wes Payne. He's a Texas Ranger, and I'm a U.S. Deputy Marshal," Danner stated.

"Well gentlemen, it didn't take you long to meet our so-called protectors," Boone stated.

"Is that what you call them?" Wes winced, as Boone tore his shirt open, exposing an ugly gash in his flesh.

"No, but that's what Mr. Barry calls them, so the rest of us just try and ignore them as much as we can," Boone explained.

"How many more of them are there?" Danner asked, pulling a curtain aside and looking out the front window.

"Far as I know, there's one or two out watching the roads, and one called Crazy Bill with Barry over at the mill office. I can't say I'm an authority on them, Marshal. There could be more," Boone said as he worked.

"Aahhh!" Wes groaned.

"You're as lucky as a man who's been shot can get, sir. Bullet passed clean through, although it looks like it broke a rib in the process. I'll clean it out and get you stitched up easy enough," Boone assured his patient.

"I'm headin' over to the mill before those two on the road come running. I'm sure they heard the shots," Danner told Wes.

"Wait for me!" Wes said forcefully. "Doc, patch this up quick. I'll come back after we're done," he added.

"You're not going anywhere for about an hour," Boone advised.

Danner hurried out, and headed for the mill at the far end of town. He looked around, checking every rider, man on foot, and in a wagon. The two dead gunmen remained in the middle of the street. People passed, only briefly slowing to look, making it clear the townsfolk didn't care much for Barry's men.

Crack! A bullet kicked up dirt to Danner's left. He darted to the right. Crack! Crack! Two more shots came from Barry's office door, kicking up dirt at Danner's heels. Danner dove behind a half-dozen barrels stacked across the street from Barry's building. He checked the building behind him but saw no one. It looked like a warehouse. Crack! A bullet splinted a barrel knocking off its lid.

"Name's Luxton Danner! I'm a Deputy U.S. Marshal! I'm here for Jared Barry! No one else. Stop shootin'!" Danner called toward the mill's office.

Crack! Another bullet ricocheted off another oak barrel.

"Nobody's take'n Mr. Barry today! Not even a U.S. Marshal," a deep voice boomed from the doorway.

Danner looked around but couldn't see any cover between him and Barry's office. Charging across the street would be suicide. He crouched behind the barrels, and looked over his left shoulder to the corner of the warehouse building. He thought a moment, then rushed for the side of the building. Crack! A bullet blew wood off the corner of the building as Danner hip-slid past. *Son of a bitch is a damn good shot*, Danner thought, as he got back to his feet, and ran toward the back of the enormous building.

Danner ran around the rear of the building, then into the thicket on the south side of the road, leading into town from the east. He figured if he could get far enough away from Barry's office, but before the mill, he could cross the road, and come up behind the shooter.

He pushed his way through the brush thorns, ripping at his face and neck as he went. He circled around, then rushed across the wide road. The sound of the mill saws slicing through timber muted any noise he made pushing through the scrub.

Danner dashed into the wooded area next to Barry's building, making his way well past the front door. He then found himself behind a small wood shed near the office. There were several windows in the building, but nothing that allowed him to see inside. A bead of blood trickled down his cheek, settling into the whiskers on his chin. He wiped it away with his sleeve, and watched intently for a long minute. He pulled both Russians and cocked the hammers. *No time like now*, he thought, then rushed the building.

Danner reached the back of the building, catching a glimpse of Barry scurrying through an interior door, which he slammed shut behind him. A wall blocked his view of the front door. Danner waited, breathing heavy. Running around the building to the front door wouldn't work. He looked around. He saw a large window, low to the ground, about ten feet to his right. It looked as though it led to the main office room in the front. Danner crouched, and crawled to the window. His six foot six inch frame didn't hide well beneath the window.

Crack! A bullet shattered a glass pane above Danner's head. He leaned back then dove headfirst through the broken window, crashing to the floor in a cloud of glass fragments. Crack! He rolled over and came up firing both Russians. Crack! Crack! Crack! Crack! The forty-fives pummeled the guard, as he charged toward Danner. Crack! A final shot from the guard's pistol punched a harmless hole in the pine ceiling, before the gunman collapsed on the floor amid glass and a haze of gun smoke.

Danner sprang to his feet, and burst through the door he saw Barry hide behind. Blood flowed down Danner's face, courtesy of a glass shard gash in his forehead. Danner stood still, Russians pointed at Barry, who calmly sat behind his desk, a Remington double-barreled Derringer pointed upward under his own chin, hammer cocked.

"I knew this day would come the moment Rebecca told me you were at the hotel," Barry said calmly. "I thought Jenkins might be able to take care of you, but when I heard what happened in Range, I knew it was no use. Those six fools I sent to Range afterwards wouldn't be able to do what Jenkins and Dunham couldn't," Barry added matter-of-factly.

Danner said nothing. He just stood, towering over the defeated outlaw boss. He didn't give a damn if Barry killed himself or not. He'd hang anyway.

"Is my daughter all right?" Barry asked, closing his eyes.

"Yes, despite having a good-for-nothing father," Danner answered.

Barry's face remained expressionless. "I'm not going with you, Marshal," Barry said. "I'll do the judge's business here, if you'll allow," he added.

Danner released the hammers on his Russians and slid them into his holsters. He knew perfectly well Barry was too much of a coward to make a stand against him. After all, he always hired someone else to do the killing. As Danner reached the threshold, he paused. Crack! A single shot rang out, followed by the sound of a gun hitting the floor.

Danner didn't bother to turn around. He stepped out onto the street, checking for any riders coming down the road. He casually walked over to Doc Boone's, where he found Wes grousing about Boone taking too long to stitch him up. Boone looked at Danner's bloodied face.

"Take a seat, Marshal, I'll be with you in a moment," Boone exhaled shaking his head.

"I heard the shots. What happened?" Wes asked impatiently.

"I took care of the guard he had with him. Barry did the rest," Danner said, wiping blood from his eyes with what had been a clean, blue bandana.

"Doc. You'll find the guard shot to hell. That was me. You'll find Barry seated at his desk with one bullet in his head. That was him," Danner explained.

Boone nodded as he wrapped Wes's midsection with a wide, white cloth bandage.

"I'll get with a few of the businessmen in town, and we'll tend to it, Marshal," Boone assured the men. "And you sir, keep this on until you reach another town with a doctor, and have him put a fresh one on. Understand?" Boone ordered.

"Yes, sir. I'll get right on that," Wes said.

Just then, the door flew open, and a small man wearing a bowler hat, white shirt, and red vest stepped into the barrels of two Russian pistols.

"Aahhh!" the man shouted, covering his face with both shivering hands.

"It's okay, Marshal. This is Roger Nexall, our store owner," Boone said with a chuckle.

Danner returned his guns to their holsters, blood flowing down the middle of his face. He retrieved his bloodied bandana from his vest pocket, and held it against the wound on his forehead.

"Would it be all right if we got some men to remove the dead men from the street?" Nexall asked.

"That would be fine, Mr. Nexall. There's two more over in Barry's office," Danner advised the skittish store keeper.

"There's also two of Barry's men locked up in the shed next to the bunkhouse," Wes announced, while gingerly putting his bloody tattered bib shirt back on.

"You may want to leave them there until they can be told Barry is dead," Danner suggested. "I figure they won't be in town long after they find out there's no pay coming," Danner added.

"Mr. Barry's dead?" Nexall asked. "What'll we do now?" Nexall added.

"I'll ride down to Wichita Falls, and notify the District Judge. I reckon we'll need to notify his daughter," Wes said looking at Danner.

Danner nodded as he replaced Wes on Boone's treatment table.

"We can send a message through the telegraph office. I understand Miss Rebecca is in Range?" Boone asked.

"Yes," Danner answered as Boone began to clean his wound.

"I'll get you fixed up, Marshal, but I'll warn ya, this is gonna leave a nasty scar," Boone advised.

"Probably make him look better," Wes quipped. "How long until this rib heals, Doc?" Wes asked.

"A couple of months, or so," Boone replied with a grin.

"Two riders coming," Wes said, cautiously watching out the window.

Mr. Nexall looked out past Wes. "It's Mr. Barry's men," he confirmed.

"What are they doing?" Danner asked, unable to move his head while Boone sewed him up like a patchwork quilt.

"Stopped in front of Barry's place. Looks like they found your handy work. They're headin' down the street to the bunkhouse," Wes reported.

"If I'm right, they'll let those other two out of the shed and ride out of town," Danner said. "Mr. Nexall, would you mind stepping out and watching from the street here?" Danner asked.

Nexall left the office, and stood out in front of Boone's place to watch for several minutes before returning. "Just like you said, Marshal. They let the others out, and talked to Archie Smith at the stable, then they all rode out of town," Nexall confirmed.

"That didn't take long," Boone said.

"It usually doesn't when the boss is dead, and nobody in town likes you. Mr. Nexall, did you recognize any of Barry's men who rode out?" Danner asked.

"Just one named Kyle Britt. Didn't really see the other three too good," Nexall answered.

Boone finished closing the wound then washed the remaining

blood off Danner's face. "Probably should have a bandage on that, Marshal," Boone suggested.

"It's fine. Thanks," Danner assured the physician.

After both men got patched up, Danner and Wes made their way back to the stable, where they stopped briefly to talk to Archie Smith. He confirmed that Britt was the gunman Barry had sent after his daughter with Johnny Gallup. With no lawman in town, there was no report to file, so they left the business at hand with Boone, Nexall, and a couple other men before getting back on the trail.

CHAPTER 67

LUXTON DANNER & WES PAYNE –
OUTSIDE RED RIVER CITY

As daylight faded into night, Danner and Wes traveled slower than usual, thanks to their respective thundering headache and a painful ribcage. Each step Ringo took sent a bolt of lightning through Wes's side, matched by the clap of thunder knocking around inside Danner's head. They had put Red River City an hour behind them when Danner broke the silence. "Figure we're far enough?" Danner asked.

"Hope so, I'm about done in," Wes replied, bringing Ringo to a stop.

"Let's move up to that hilltop where we can see all around us, and call it a day," Danner suggested, looking toward a nearby bump in the terrain.

Settling into their camp for the night, they took care of the horses, then started a small fire for coffee. Their four-day trip from Range had left them with some stale flat bread and jerky they'd picked up in Eagle Springs. Both men leaned against their saddles, and stretched out toward the fire to keep warm. After a half hour of watching the flickering embers send up burning ash like lazy fireflies on a hot summer night, Danner filled his tin cup with coffee and looked over at

Wes. "After your stop in Wichita Falls, what do you plan on doing?" Danner asked.

"Been thinkin' about that. I figure I'll head south toward Fort Worth. Company B has a post just west of there. I'll let the captain know what we ran into in Red River City. They may send a Ranger up there. Then I'll head back to my post," Wes answered.

"That's not what I mean," Danner said.

"Yeah, I know. After that, I'm not sure what I'll do. I won't get another assignment until this ankle and rib heal. I'll probably check in with the Sheriff in Buffalo Gap. Stay there for a bit, then decide if I'm gonna go back to the Rangers. What about you?"

"I figure Upham and Parker will decide for me. Neither's gonna be happy with the way things turned out."

"Ain't yer fault things went sideways."

"Maybe, but they like it when we bring a few back alive. I haven't done that much lately. And, that rescue up in the territory didn't sit well with 'em either," Danner explained.

"When the captain finds out about that, he may just tell me I ain't no Ranger anymore," Wes admitted.

"Tell him you were assisting a U.S. Marshal," Danner quipped.

"Sure, and he'll say, 'What about bein' a Texas Ranger don't you understand, Payne!'"

Both laughed, Wes clutching his side in pain. "Damn it! Keep forgettin' not to laugh!" Wes exclaimed, shutting his eyes tight.

"What'll ya do if ya stop Marshaling?" Wes asked.

"Well, I'm no farmer or cattleman," Danner said flatly.

"Nope. Me neither," Wes replied, squeezing the stiffness out of his hands.

"I'll take first watch. Get some sleep," Danner said.

Wes didn't wait to be told twice. He crawled under the Indian blanket Chet Unger gave him back in Throckmorton, and quickly fell asleep.

Danner thought back to his first meeting with Rebecca, their journey to Range, and the like. He'd started to have feelings for her, but just as well she met Chance, he thought. *I'm too damned old, and nothing more than a gunfighter with a badge. Chance had a farm and a future thanks to his father. She's far better off,* he thought as he drifted off to sleep.

Brush snapped out in the darkness. Danner perked up and listened intently. He picked up his Winchester, just in case. He couldn't see anything, but he sensed something near. Suddenly, he saw two red eyes perched above. A wolf lunged, hitting him high on the shoulders, knocking him back against his saddle. White teeth sunk into his shoulder, turning his shirt blood red. He swung his Winchester, its barrel smashing into the skull of the beast. The wolf lunged again, this time, its fangs finding Danner's neck. It growled as Danner wedged his huge hands into each side of the hound's open jaws. He gasped for a breath, then ripped at the beast's mouth with all his might. The razor-sharp teeth sliced gashes into his fingers as he threw the wolf into the fire.

"Danner! Danner! Stop! It's okay!" Wes yelled.

Danner grasped the grip of his pistol, swinging his left arm wildly. He rolled over onto his back to see Wes in a two-handed death grip, on the hand and pistol. He breathed heavily and sweat so badly that he could barely focus.

"It's okay, Danner. It's just a dream," Wes said in as calm a voice as he could muster.

Danner fell backwards and tried to take a breath. After several ragged attempts, he succeeded. The stitches in his forehead had torn, causing the gash to rip open, sending a river of fresh blood down his face. "Sorry, Wes. I'm all right now," he exhaled.

Wes released his grip and leaned back. "I'll get one of those bandages the doctor gave us," Wes said, reaching for his saddle bags.

Danner sat up and wiped the blood from his face. He quickly felt his shoulder and neck for puncture wounds, but felt nothing. He pulled another bandana from his pocket, and wiped the blood and sweat from his face. Wes returned with a thick white bandage and a clean bandana. Danner adjusted the bandana and nodded. "Thanks," he said shakily.

"This calls for a whiskey," Wes announced, returning a second time to his saddle bags.

"Whiskey? You didn't say you had whiskey," Danner lamented.

"Donovan set me up a few days back. Been waitin' until it was needed. I reckon now's the time," Wes said with a chuckle. Wes handed the bottle to Danner, who took a long swig before returning it. Wes followed with a similar action, then pushed the cork back in, and slid it into his bag. "Well?" Wes asked, adding a log to the fire.

"A damn wolf," Danner answered leaning back into his saddle, closing his eyes.

Wes levered a round into the chamber of his Winchester and took a seat on a nearby log. He'd finish out the night's watch.

The next day, the two lawmen found themselves at a fork in the trail. To the left was Wichita Falls. To the right was Fort Smith. Danner pulled Bullet to a stop. Wes reined Ringo over to his partner.

"It's been an honor," Wes said offering his scared right hand.

"It's been more than that, my friend," Danner answered, shaking Wes's hand.

"If you ever want to look me up, send word to Buffalo Gap. The Sheriff there is a good friend. If I'm not there, he'll know where to find me," Wes offered.

"Buffalo Gap. I'll do that," Danner answered with a nod.

Wes swung Ringo's head around and tapped his spurs, sending the big white stallion down the trail heading first to Wichita Falls, then on to Fort Worth.

"Take care!" Wes called not bothering to turn around as he rode away.

Danner sat atop Bullet and watched Wes disappear around a bend before he nudged his partner toward the road to Fort Smith.

CHAPTER 68

WES PAYNE – FORT GRIFFIN

Thunder boomed, and lightning cracked the sky, ushering in another wet fall day. Boom! The old barn wood rattled as if the rusty nails that held it together would fail any moment.

Wes slowly sat up, peering at Ringo through blurred eyes. He looked around, catching a flash of lightning through the lone grimy window near the barn door. The pain in his ankle and side returned. He reached down and felt the dressing on his ribs. He'd need a fresh one soon. Wes rubbed his head, then realized he could barely move his right hand. His hand looked like a crimped claw, with the fingers curled and stiff. He took a couple deep breaths, then winced at the pain in his side.

He hadn't given much thought to what he'd do if he stopped being a Ranger, but if Captain Tobias saw this hand, he'd have trouble arguing to stay. He heard the barn door open.

The proprietor of the 'ole rickety barn that doubled as the Ranger's livery stable, shuffled in, pausing over Wes.

"Captain Tobias said to have ya go over to the Fort, and check in at the infirmary before you see him," the old stable keeper advised.

Wes sat silent for a long time. He figured he might as well get it over with so he went directly to the Ranger's office to see Tobias.

Wes stepped into the room, and glanced around. Captain Tobias sat behind a dilapidated desk reading, while Captain Franklin sifted through wanted posters at a table nearby. Both men stood when Wes entered.

"Hello Wes," Tobias greeted Wes with a firm handshake, crushing his stiff fingers. Franklin repeated the gesture. "Grab a chair," Tobias waved toward a vacant ladder-back waiting in front of the desk.

Wes sat down, and leaned forward slightly. Tobias and Franklin remained silent for a moment before Tobias spoke. "I heard about last night, Wes. Also heard about your ankle and side. What'd the doctor say?" Tobias asked.

"Didn't go over to the Fort, Captain. I wanted to see you first. I'm a little banged up at the moment, I reckon," Wes admitted.

"Charlie gave me your report from Range. It included you crossin' the river into Indian territory, but it didn't say anything about you being shot, though," Tobias said.

"No, sir. Me and the Marshal headed over to Red River City to get the fella that was behind the raids along the river. He had a couple a guns waitin' for us. I took a bullet there," Wes advised.

"You report that to Company B in Fort Worth?" Tobias asked.

"No, sir, the district judge in Wichita said he'd send a couple of men over to Red River City, so I passed on Company B and didn't go on to Fort Worth," Wes admitted.

"How are those hands?" Tobias asked.

"Just fine, Captain. They get a little stiff now and then, but they're okay," Wes answered.

"I know it was a long time ago, but that was some bad business down there in Presidio. Never should've sent you down to the Mexican border alone. That was my fault," Tobias said shaking his head. "Wes, there's no reason to beat around the bush. I need to relieve you of duty. I don't like it, but I've got no choice. You need to rest and heal up. If after a while, you feel good enough to come back, you come see me directly. Understand?" Tobias asked.

Wes stood and removed his badge from his coat pocket. He placed it on the desk in front of Tobias. "Yes, sir. I understand," he said.

"Wes, you've given an awful lot to the Rangers and Texas. If there's anything the Rangers can ever do for you," Tobias started.

Wes interrupted him. "Yes, sir." He had no interest in hearing the rest. He stepped forward holding his side, shook hands with Tobias and Franklin, then turned to leave.

"Stop by later, and get the pay you have coming," Tobias ordered.

Wes didn't answer as he walked out of the office into the cold gray day. *I should be in Buffalo Gap by suppertime*, he thought.

CHAPTER 69

LUXTON DANNER – FORT SMITH

anner's rain-soaked boots sloshed through the muddy road leading into Fort Smith as he walked Bullet into the public square adjoining the brown brick structure that housed the United States District Court for the Western District of Arkansas. Even the thick, dreary mist covering Fort Smith like a wet blanket couldn't diminish the lambency of Judge Parker's chamber of justice.

The wet, muddy roads created problems for the carriages and wagons, horses, and pedestrians, alike. The bell tower sounded eight times, marking the hour and official start of the judicial day. Danner made his way to the massive barn north of the courthouse and jail, where the deputies kept their horses and prisoner wagons. Having traveled the last half-day of his journey in a steady rain, Danner was soaked to the bone.

The trusted caretaker for the Marshals swung the big storehouse door open for Danner as he approached. "Good morning, Marshal Danner, good to have you back," the caretaker pleasantly greeted the weary lawman.

"Good to be back," Danner answered, pausing to shake his hand, leading Bullet to the double-wide stall where all the Marshals' horses received top-hand treatment. After removing his bedroll and saddle bags, Danner looked down the middle of the massive structure, and caught glimpses of several Marshals and their guards preparing to depart. Marshals heading into Indian Territory usually brought two guards and a cook with them. Looked like plenty of each this morning. Deputy Eugene Bracken checked his supplies a couple of stalls down, and saw Danner.

"Hey Danner, we was wondering when you'd be back," Bracken shouted.

"Where you headin', Brack?" Danner asked, while peeling off his wet slicker.

"Up in the territory. Got eight warrants," Bracken said, stepping up to Danner. "We heard you had some trouble up there," Bracken whispered.

"Some," Danner answered quickly.

"Heard the army was with ya," Bracken added, probing for information.

"You hear too much, Brack," Danner said with a grin that told his fellow Marshal not to ask any more questions.

Bracken got the hint and nodded. "See ya when I get back then," Bracken said, before returning to his pre-departure duties.

"Danner, Marshal Upham said for you to get cleaned up then go see him right after," the caretaker advised Danner as he passed Bullet's stall.

Danner walked over to the Marshals' bunkhouse and followed his orders about getting cleaned up. A half hour later, he looked in the mirror and thought what a difference hot water and clean clothes do for a man. The rain had stopped, and rays of sunshine had begun to peak through the clouds as Danner made his way across the courtyard to Western District Marshal Daniel Upham's office.

He'd thought about this meeting for the last few days, taking a couple days longer than necessary, allowing an extended period to think about his future. In the end, he figured it would come down to how Upham and Judge Parker felt about his assignment.

Danner stepped into the building that housed Upham's office, as well as the runners and bailiffs for the court. The small, well-built building had high ceilings, and dark paneled walls. Despite the rain and mud outside, the floor remained bright and clean.

Upham's secretary sat at a desk outside the closed door leading to the Marshal's office.

"Good morning, deputy Danner. I'll see if Marshal Upham is ready for you," the young secretary advised.

A moment later, the man opened the door, and waved Danner inside. Despite being a man of average size with short dark hair, and a long dark goatee, Daniel Phillips Upham was a formidable presence, having been personally chosen by President Grant to lead the Marshal's office of the Western District. A former plantation owner and militia commander, he had a reputation of being strict, but fair with his deputies, and held good standing with Judge Parker. Upon Danner's entrance, he stood, and offered his hand in greeting.

"Good to see you back Danner. Please take a seat," Upham said pointing to a chair in front of his dark oak desk. Upham opened a folder containing numerous documents, and briefly scanned the first two on top of the pile. "First, let me commend you on the thoroughness of your reports, particularly since some were sent by telegraph. I also appreciate your candidness in describing your actions and the events that transpired," Upham stated.

Danner remained still and said nothing. Upham continued.

"I thought your handling of the events in Range were appropriate, and represented the U.S. Marshal's office well. The decision made to leave Texas and travel into the territory was also acceptable, considering your position and assignment. I will say that I was uncomfortable with the decision to have the army accompany you, but under the circumstances, it probably was the best option. The result of your actions, including rescuing the kidnapped nun, warrants a citation of merit in my mind. Unfortunately, the subsequent elimination of the group responsible for taking the girl wasn't looked upon quite as positively. I've been told the Lieutenant that joined you on that mission has been reprimanded. It has been recommended that I do the same with you, which I am not in favor of," Upham explained.

Danner remained silent. Upham's circuitous words were whirling around in his head like a tornado on the plains. He'd told himself not to make any irrational decisions when confronted with his actions in Range.

"I've discussed this with Judge Parker, and while he'd like to see you bring a prisoner or two back alive now and then, he's a staunch supporter of you, as am I. Do you have anything to add to these reports?" Upham asked.

"No, sir. I did what I believed was right at the time," Danner answered simply.

"Very well. What I'm proposing is this: You can use some time off anyhow, so I'm going to relieve you of your duties for one month. After that, you'll be reinstated and eligible for an assignment. Is that acceptable?" Upham asked.

Danner let the words sink in. After a moment's pause, he stood and removed his badge from his vest pocket, where it had safely spent most of the last five years. He rubbed his thumb over its smooth worn surface. "That's unnecessary sir. I've decided to leave the Marshal's office for good," Danner announced as he placed his badge on Upham's polished desk.

"Now wait a moment Danner, I–"

Danner interrupted. "Save your words, sir. My decision was made the day I cut that young nun down from that mesquite tree. I knew it then, and I know it now. It's time for me to move on," Danner declared.

Upham sat quietly looking at Danner's badge. The silence in the room hung heavy on both men. Upham reached across his desk and picked up the badge. He then placed it in his desk drawer, before standing to look hard at Danner, who'd already stood to leave.

"No one else will ever wear that badge. As long as I'm Marshal here, it will be right where it is now, waiting for your return. Understood?"

"Understood, sir," Danner answered with a nod, before turning toward the door.

"What'll you do now?" Upham asked the now-former Deputy Marshal.

Danner paused momentarily, then smiled. "I think I'll go back to Texas. I believe there's people out there that could use the services of a man like me," he offered before closing the big oak door behind him with a thud.

Danner walked out towards the sunshine; his head held high. It felt good to move on.

THE END.

EPILOGUE

A frigid February winter day had settled into Range, bringing a trace of snow, filling the air like the shedding of a cottonwood tree. A sturdy wind from the western Rocky Mountains pushed the freezing temperature into late afternoon. Most townsfolk kept warm inside, except a few ducking in and out of the hotel and saloon. Main street appeared empty, except for a single buckboard wagon slowly navigating its way into town. The driver and passenger huddled close, both bundled in heavy coats. The driver had his wide brim hat pulled down over his face to keep the cutting wind from lashing it mercilessly. His passenger donned a blanket over her head and a scarf covered the lower half of her face. The driver snapped the reins, encouraging the two horses to pick up the pace.

"Yah! Yah!" Chance shouted, snapping the reins again, urging the horses along.

Rebecca peeked out from under her blanket. Between the bright yellow scarf covering the lower half, and the blanket shielding the upper, all Chance could see were those gorgeous green eyes.

"I'll take you up to the hotel, then turn back around and drop-off the horses and wagon at the stable, okay?" Chance asked his bone-chilled bride.

Rebecca vigorously nodded in approval squeezing his arm tight. The newlywed couple were returning from Red River City, where Rebecca had sold the lumber mill, store, and hotel to one of the local wealthy cattle ranchers. Knowing of her dislike for the town, Chance had suggested she sell the businesses and return to Range before deciding her future.

Chance leaned toward Rebecca, pressing himself against her as best he could. He smiled to himself when he thought back to their conversation of her future. "Your future is my future, Ben Chance, and you better understand that," she had declared back then. When he tried to think of a good reason to leave her and Range behind, he couldn't find one.

"Whoa" Chance called out, pulling back on the reins, bringing the wagon to a halt in front of the Purple Sage Hotel.

Chance jumped down to help Rebecca. After escorting her into the lobby, he retrieved their bags, then headed for the livery stable to care for the horses, and stow the wagon, which were now the proud property of the newlyweds.

"Good evening," Otto Wilhelm greeted Chance.

"Good evening, Mr. Wilhelm. I've got two new horses and this buckboard. Can you take care of them for me?" Chance asked the stable owner.

"Yes, yes, no trouble. I will put your wagon in the back and brush and feed your horses right away. Anything else?" Wilhelm asked.

"No sir. See you later," Chance answered, hurrying back toward the hotel.

A few moments later, Chance stepped through hotel's wide door into warmth he'd not felt in the five hours since leaving Red River City. He and Rebecca had taken the stagecoach to Red River City but didn't have that option to return, thus the purchase of the buckboard and horses.

"Welcome back, Chance," Mr. Conrad announced, stepping around the big oak desk to shake the young man's frozen hand. "Rebecca is already upstairs in your room with your bags," Mr. Conrad advised.

"Thank you," Chance answered, then quickly looked around the room to ensure the two men were alone. "Mr. Conrad, Rebecca and I are carrying a large amount of money from the sale of her father's businesses. I'd like to keep it in your safe, if you wouldn't mind?" Chance asked in a low voice.

"Certainly. When you are ready, just let me or Mrs. Conrad know, and we'll take care of that for you," Mr. Conrad affirmed.

Chance nodded, then started up the stairs and abruptly stopped when he saw Mrs. Conrad making her way down. Chance stepped back and smiled as she stepped down.

Mrs. Conrad immediately drew him into a big hug. "Welcome back. Your lovely bride is thawing out up in a tub of hot water. You might want to give her a few minutes to herself," Mrs. Conrad suggested through a wide grin.

"Yes ma'am," Chance answered through a wide smile of his own before heading up stairs two steps at a time.

Chance washed and changed into fresh clothes for supper before checking the bundles of money Rebecca had hidden under her clothing in her travel bag. The click of the door handle caused him to reach for the gun belt hanging on the bedpost.

"It's me!" Rebecca shouted, closing her eyes, half-hiding behind the door.

"Sorry. I'm a little nervous having this money in here," Chance admitted, exhaling and wiping his forehead.

"Did you ask Mr. Conrad about the safe?" Rebecca asked, closing the door behind her.

"Yes. He said when we're ready we can put it there," Chance said standing and hugging his wife.

"I'm so happy to be back," Rebecca whispered inside her husband's arms.

"So am I," Chance admitted.

A soft knock at the door interrupted the young couple. Chance stepped to the door and cracked it open slightly to see Mrs. Conrad. He opened the door to greet her.

"Sorry to bother you two, but Lane Dodson and Mrs. Fields are downstairs, and when I told them you had returned, they asked if you two would join them for dinner," Mrs. Conrad said.

"Yes, Mrs. Conrad, tell them we'll be right down," Rebecca said, looking around Chance in the doorway.

"Very well, I'll let them know," Mrs. Conrad said as she hurried down the hallway to the staircase.

A few minutes later, Chance and Rebecca entered the dining room to see Dodson and Mrs. Fields seated at a table near the kitchen. At five-thirty, the restaurant had begun to fill up. The aroma of fresh, baked bread coupled with the sound of sizzling frying pans made for a welcome atmosphere.

As Chance and Rebecca reached the table, Dodson stood to shake Chance's hand while Mrs. Fields and Rebecca shared a warm hug. "Good to have you two back in town. Everything go all right in Red River City?" Dodson asked, sitting down with his back against the wall in order to watch both doors to the restaurant.

"Everything was fine. My father was very organized, so the sales were easy to complete," Rebecca explained. "We decided to buy two horses and a wagon to ride back in," she added.

"Well, you two have only been married a month and you already own livestock!" Dodson chuckled.

Rebecca glanced over to see Chance smiling and shaking his head. "Still not used to being married, Mr. Chance?" Rebecca asked, laughing.

"Nope," Chance responded.

"I'm only engaged, and I can't get used to that either!" Dodson said joining in the laughter.

"Oh really, Mr. Dodson? Well, I can take care of that pretty easy if you'd like," Mary Fields chimed in.

"No, no, I'll come around, dear, just give me a little time," Dodson assured his betrothed with a hug.

Mrs. Conrad came over to the jubilant table with cups of coffee for the men and tea for the ladies.

"Mrs. Conrad, I feel awful not helping you with supper tonight," Rebecca said.

"Nonsense. I didn't expect you back today. We're fine. It won't hurt Mr. Conrad to do a little cooking in the kitchen!" She snickered. Fried chicken for everyone?" Mrs. Conrad asked.

"That'll be fine, Mrs. Conrad, and put it on my tab," Chance instructed the woman who'd become a mother-figure to both him and Rebecca.

"Well, sounds like Mr. Benson needs to reconsider your pay, Deputy Chance!" Dodson chuckled.

"Oh no, sir! If needed, I'll ask Mrs. Chance for a loan," Chance said, winking and putting his arm around Rebecca, giving her a tight squeeze.

Chance saw the jovial expression on Dodson's face fade to a serious look of concern. He quickly looked around and saw Mike Donovan walk into the dining room, scanning the restaurant. It was odd for the saloon owner to be away from his bar at this hour. Dodson stood and waved at Donavon, who spotted the Marshal and quickly walked to their table.

"I'm sorry to bother you Marshal, oh, hello Chance, but a dozen or so men just came into the saloon. They ain't done nothing, but they're pounding whiskey and look like gunmen. Since we ain't had no trouble since the bad raid, I figured I'd let you know," Donavon reported.

"No trouble Donovan," Dodson began, standing up.

"They say what they're doing here?" Chance asked, standing up as well.

"Nope. Didn't seem right to ask," Donovan explained.

"Wait a moment, I'll get my gun in my room and join you," Chance said, leaving without waiting for a response.

Chance hurried to his room, strapped on his gun belt, then quickly returned to the lobby where Dodson, Rebecca, and Mary Fields waited.

"You ladies go back to the table. We'll just go over and make sure there's no trouble, then we'll come back and join you," Dodson said.

Rebecca looked at Chance with a worried expression on her face as she hugged him hard. Chance nodded in approval of Dodson's suggestion. "I told you when you agreed to marry me that I wasn't giving up my badge," Chance reminded his wife.

"I know, but–"

Chance pulled away and headed for the door a step behind Dodson.

"They'll probably be at the bar. Separate when we get inside, and let's just watch for a bit and see what happens," Dodson instructed his deputy as each man pinned their badges to the outside of their coats.

As the two lawmen walked toward the saloon, they heard piano music and laughter, always a good sign. They pushed through the swinging doors to find the place busy with townsfolk, cowboys, card players, and the group of strangers, all armed, gathered around a big round table in the back of the room. Two empty whiskey bottles sat in the middle of the table. One of the men called for another bottle of whiskey as Dodson and Chance walked through the crowd stopping to briefly chat with men at the card tables and the ladies looking for customers.

Dodson walked up to the bar and spoke to Donovan while Chance watched the men in the back. The man who called for the whiskey saw Dodson and Chance then stood up. The other nine men also stood stepping back from the table. Dodson turned and walked up to the men. Chance stayed back a few steps to Dodson right.

"Good evening gentlemen," Dodson began.

"We done something wrong, Marshal?" one of the men asked.

"Not at all. Just wondering what business you fellas have in town. You part of a cattle drive we ain't heard about?" Dodson asked.

"Now, Marshal, do we look like a bunch of cowpokes?" the man asked, resting his hand on top of his gun.

"Don't nobody reach for a gun!" Chance ordered the men.

The men looked over at Chance. A couple of them grunted. The piano music stopped and several of the patrons began to file out of the saloon and gather outside at the window to watch.

"Now there's no reason to get mad fellas. Where ya'll heading?" Dodson asked trying to ease the tension.

"We're on our way up to Canyon Creek. Been hired by a big

rancher named Gilford Knox. Seems he's expecting trouble up there. Hired us and a few others. Thought we'd get out of the cold for a few hours, have a few drinks then be on our way. That okay with you, Marshal? We ain't interested in no trouble." The man looked at Dodson and Chance then continued. "We heard all about you boys up here. Killed a bunch of raiders a few months back. We're just passin' through is all, Marshal," the man said.

"Let's just get out of here, the whiskey ain't no good anyway," another gunman spouted. The other gunmen grumbled amongst themselves, then they started to walk toward the door.

"Don't forget to pay for those two bottles on the table," Dodson reminded the men.

The men tossed money on the table then headed to the door in single file. The gunman that had done most of the talking stopped in front of Dodson and Chance. "You think two of you could have taken all of us, Marshal?" he asked with a grin.

"Just two of us?" Dodson asked raising his eyebrows.

The gunman looked around the saloon and saw Belton Tanner holding a double-barreled shotgun in one corner, and Donovan clutching another behind the bar. The gunman smiled.

"Like I said, Marshal, we heard all about you boys up here in Range," he said, then pushed through the swinging doors out into the frozen darkness.

ABOUT THE AUTHOR

John is a veteran of law enforcement whose career began with the Houston Texas Police Department in 1981. After bringing his badge to a couple of additional agencies, he retired in 2012 but never left the profession. He is currently a Senior Detective for a state-wide law enforcement agency in North Texas.

His writing career began in the sports industry as a freelance writer and sports editor for national magazines and online publications.

He grew up watching western movies and reading stories of the old west. His theatrical influences included actors John Wayne, James Stewart, Clint Eastwood, and Sam Elliott as well as directors John

Ford, Henry Hathaway, and Howard Hawks. He drew literary inspiration from Louis L'Amour, Robert B. Parker, C. J. Box, and Lee Child. His passion for history and the classic western genre inspired him to write his first novel, *Gunslingers* (Newman Springs 2019), and its sequel, *Red River Reunion* (Labrador Publishing 2020), both classic westerns set in 1877 Texas.

John is an avid sports fan and horse enthusiast. He is a member of Western Writers of America, Western Fictioneers, The Authors Guild, American Paint Horse Association and the American Quarter Horse Association.

Visit John's Official Website at www.johnlaynefiction.com.

[f] facebook.com/johnlaynefictionbooks
[o] instagram.com/labradorpublishing

A MESSAGE TO READERS

Dear Reader:

Thank you so much for reading my book. I'd love to know what you thought of the book, and would like to invite you to write a short review on Amazon.com. It will only take two clicks and will be invaluable to me.

Thanks so much,

John Layne

John Layne

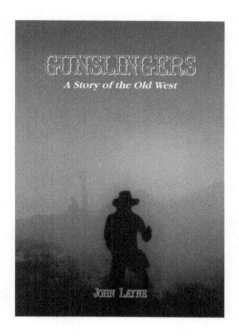

Joel Thornton is a retired U.S. Deputy Marshal now living a quiet rancher's life outside the Texas town named in his honor. Days after welcoming his daughter, Elizabeth, home after seven years back east in Philadelphia, an old fugitive attacks the Tilted T Ranch, seeking revenge and Thornton's cattle. Wounded in the ensuing gunfight, Thornton calls upon his daughter to find his old partner, former U.S. Deputy Marshal Ben Chance, informing her, "Chance will know what to do."

The young woman's journey leads her on an adventure that exposes her to the dangers of the Old West, where she meets two gunslingers, who together hunt for the outlaws who shot Elizabeth's father and stole his herd.

CPSIA information can be obtained
at www.ICGtesting.com
Printed in the USA
FSHW021550020221
78110FS

9 780999 879672